Ronnie

Ronnie

BETWEEN THE CRACKS
BOOK FIVE

P.D. WORKMAN

PD WORKMAN

ISBN: 9781988390987 (IS Hardcover)

ISBN: 9781988390970 (IS Paperback)

ISBN: 9781774688328 (KDP Paperback 2 ed)

ISBN: 9781774688335 (KDP Hardcover)

ISBN: 9781988390956 (Kindle)

ISBN: 9781988390963 (ePub)

ISBN: 9781774688342 (Lulu Paperback 2 ed)

ISBN: 9781774685433 (accessible audiobook)

Also by P.D. Workman

YOUNG ADULT FICTION:

Medical Kidnap Files:

YA Suspense

Mito

EDS

Proxy

Toxo

Pain

Fail

Pulse

Between the Cracks:

Gritty Contemporary YA Family Saga

Ruby

June and Justin

Michelle

Chloe

Ronnie

June, Into the Light

Tamara's Teardrops:

Gritty Contemporary YA

Tattooed Teardrops

Two Teardrops

Tortured Teardrops

Vanishing Teardrops

For those searching for themselves and their families

~

CHAPTER
One

AGE 32

(I)

Dusty Coleman came home from work to an empty house. It was odd for Ronnie and the children to be gone when he got home, but there might have been something on the family calendar that he had failed to notice. A piano recital or Little League game. Maybe a birthday party. He showered and changed. When the house was still empty when he finished, he went down to the kitchen and looked at the dry-erase calendar on the wall. There was nothing indicating a scheduled activity.

He tried Ronnie's cell-phone, but she was notorious for not answering it, so he didn't panic when there was no answer. She was having a conversation and it was buzzing away in her purse, or she was driving and the hands-free wasn't kicking in, or one of the kids was crying and she just wasn't available.

Dusty popped a couple of frozen waffles in the toaster and got himself a beer. Maybe he should put some macaroni on to boil so that there would be something for the kids to eat when they got home, heading off the hungry-grumpies at the end of what had probably been a stressful day for Ronnie.

But if they had gone to a birthday party or stopped at the food court in the mall, they wouldn't be hungry and it would be a waste of his time.

At six o'clock, he was starting to worry. He called and messaged Ronnie several times. He tried Margret, a friend from work, to see if Ronnie had talked to her.

"I haven't heard from Ronnie in a few days," Margret said, a frown in her voice. "You don't think something has happened to her...?"

"No... no, nothing has happened. I'm sure it's nothing. She probably told me where she was going and I just forgot."

"Have you called the hospital? Maybe one of the kids had an accident. You're not allowed to keep your phone on, so she wouldn't be able to answer you."

"It's nothing," Dusty said. "She's fine."

But he made a call to the hospital just to be sure. None of their names was on the admissions list. He started calling the names from the list Ronnie kept on the fridge. A quick reference of numbers of her friends and the children's little friends. She didn't trust the cell-phone directories and complained that they always ended up losing numbers.

He looked out the window for the car, hoping to see her pulling up. He paced, regretting the waffles now sitting like a lead weight in his stomach.

Finally, he called the police.

"I feel a little silly," he explained, "but I think my wife and my kids are missing... I can't reach her, I've called all of her friends. They're always home by now..."

"What's your name, sir?" the police dispatcher asked calmly.

"Dusty Coleman."

"What is your address?"

He gave it. He knew his tone was terse. He was worried and he wanted to tell his story, not to have to give them all of the routine details.

"What is your wife's name, and how old are the children?"

"Ronnie Coleman. The kids are Mandi, she's four, and Dane, just about six."

"Has anything happened to indicate that they might be in danger?"

"No. Just that they're not home. I called the hospital, but they haven't been admitted."

There was a long pause as the dispatcher typed information into her computer. Dusty had an uneasy feeling that she knew something, but he brushed it off. What could the dispatcher possibly know that he didn't, when he had just called the information in?

"I am dispatching a police unit to come and talk to you," she told him, giving nothing away. "ETA is about... ten minutes. When is the last time you saw or talked to your wife, sir?"

"Not since this morning. She often calls me over lunch, but not today..."

"Have you had an argument recently? Any domestic problems?"

"No, nothing like that."

Dusty paced, answering more routine questions, until he finally saw the police car pull up in front of the house.

"They're here," he told the dispatcher.

"Thank you, sir. I hope everything turns out all right."

Dusty Coleman looked pretty much like Omar had imagined him while listening to a replay of his phone call. A thirty-something blue collar worker. Medium height, muscular build, hair that was close-cropped but not shaved. He had five o'clock shadow, but was clean and smelled of soap.

"Mr. Coleman? I'm Omar Bluff. I'll be heading up this investigation." Omar held out his hand and Dusty shook it. Good firm grip. Fleeting eye contact. Dusty turned and looked out the window as if expecting his wife to roll up any minute.

"Dusty. Just call me Dusty."

"Fine. Can we sit down, Mr. Coleman?"

3

Dusty was too restless to sit down. He circled the living room, looking for a place to settle, but couldn't select a seat. Omar sat down anyway, powering on his tablet and flipping through the files that Jane Withers had sent to him, arranging them so that he could put his fingers on whichever one he wanted in an instant.

"Please walk me through your day today," he told Dusty, touching the record button on the tablet app. "From the time you woke up this morning, anything that you can remember, whether it seems significant or not."

"I was worried that you were going to tell me I had to wait twenty-four or forty-eight hours before I could report them missing," Dusty confessed. "I don't know how I could have gotten through the night, let alone a whole day or two."

"Where children are involved, we don't wait," Omar said. "The two of you haven't had any custody issues? You are both custodial parents? No separation, the kids are both of yours?"

"Yes, nothing like that. Everything has been fine."

"Right. If you could tell me about your day, then...?"

Dusty did his best, attempting a chronological narrative. But he kept jumping forward to coming home and discovering that they were gone. Omar had to keep directing him backward, making him go through his day a step at a time, listening for anything that sounded off, considering Dusty's alibis, and analyzing his emotion and the words that he used.

"You haven't had a fight recently?"

"No, nothing. I mean, nothing serious. Worries about finances, chores getting done, normal stuff like that. Nothing... we don't have any big issues. We're a happy family."

"Neither of you were seeing someone else?"

Dusty looked floored. "Seeing someone else? Like, dating? An affair? No, certainly not. Ronnie had the kids all day, she couldn't exactly carry on an affair. And me... I'd never... I love Ronnie. I'd never cheat on her."

In Omar's experience, everyone who cheated said at some point that they never would. Everyone lied.

"Has anything unusual happened? Strange phone calls? Hang ups? People you don't know who recognize her?"

"No."

"How did the two of you meet?"

"Uh... at work, actually. Ronnie was hired on as a temp receptionist. I saw her every day... thought she was kind of cute... we went out a few times and it all just fell into place."

"Does Ronnie have any family? What do you know about her past?"

"No, she's on her own. I gather her parents were killed in some kind of car accident. She didn't have any siblings. We're her only family."

"You don't know the details of how her parents were killed?"

"It upsets her to talk about them, even casually. So, I don't know much. Just that they're dead."

"How about her childhood and her life before the two of you met? What can you tell me about that?"

Dusty shook his head, frowning. "I... don't know. She didn't talk about herself. It was just... we didn't really talk about it."

Omar paged restlessly through the reports on his tablet. "Mr. Coleman... your children were picked up at the park today. By themselves, no supervision."

He gaped. "They're safe? Why didn't you tell me you found them? Where's Ronnie?"

"Ronnie was not with them. They were alone."

"Well, what did they say? Where did she go?"

"She told them she would be right back and then never returned."

"That doesn't make any sense. She wouldn't leave them alone there, and she'd never leave and not come back again!"

Omar didn't give Dusty any of the other information available to him. As the spouse, Dusty was the most likely suspect in Ronnie Coleman's disappearance. They would give him no more information than necessary and then would wait for him to slip up.

"Where did she go?" Dusty demanded. "Someone else must

have seen her. There are always people at that park. The other mothers must have seen her if she left the kids there."

"What park?" Omar said.

"The park over by the school. Isn't that where they were? You said the park, and that's the one that they go to…"

"No, that's not where they were."

Coleman looked baffled. "Why would she take them to a different park?"

"You don't have a guess?"

Dusty didn't come up with one. Omar watched the doubts fly across his face. Omar could think of plenty of reasons. The kids wanted to go somewhere new. It was near an errand that she wanted to run. She was meeting someone else and needed to do it away from people that she knew, who might slip up and say something to her husband. It was unusual behavior. When people who follow a routine suddenly break the routine and do something out of character, that was worth looking at.

"I want to see the kids. Where are they? I have to see them. They should be home, I'll need to put them to bed."

"The kids are being taken care of right now. You'll see them in time. Right now, we need to be concerned about your wife and what might have happened to her."

Dusty nodded. "You're right," he agreed. He looked out the window. Still, Ronnie didn't drive up to the house, full of explanations as to what had happened that made her abandon their children at the park and disappear for hours.

"What kind of car does Ronnie drive?"

Omar already knew this. They were way ahead of Dusty on the investigation. Let him flounder behind, trying to figure out what they knew and what was still a secret.

"A white Mazda, about ten years old." Coleman gave him the plate number.

"Any car trouble lately? Something that might have left her stranded?"

"No… not really… but finances have been tight. We haven't had it in for a while and there's a few things that needed to be checked out. We were just waiting, you know, until we had a bit more cash to get it fixed up…"

"Sure," Omar agreed. He tapped the tablet for a few minutes, letting Dusty sweat it out.

"You haven't found her car?" Dusty asked. "No sign of her anywhere?"

"I didn't say that," Omar said.

"What's that supposed to mean? Have you found her or not?"

"We have not found your wife, Mr. Coleman. Maybe you could help us with that."

"Help you?" Dusty's voice rose. He stared at Omar. "What do you think I'm trying to do? Why do you think I called you? I'm scared for her. I don't know where she is or what I can do. Don't you understand that?"

"You called the hospital. Why?"

"To see if something had happened to Ronnie or one of the kids. If one of them had gotten hurt, Ronnie would have to turn off her phone and wouldn't have been able to answer when I called. I just called there to… to be sure."

"What made you think that one of them might have been hurt?"

"I was just checking. Nothing made me think they might be, but they were missing. It was unusual. I was just checking."

"Right. How late was your wife getting home at that point? What time does she usually get home? She hasn't ever been that late before?"

"Sometimes she's later getting home, but I always know where she is and what she's doing. So, I don't worry. But today… there wasn't anything on the calendar. I couldn't remember her telling me she was going to be anywhere special. She's never that late without telling me why."

"What time is she usually home by?"

"Well, if Dane has Little League, or piano, then maybe five-thirty…"

"She wasn't even an hour late and you were calling the hospital."

"She's usually home before me. Other than when they have

7

something scheduled. There wasn't anything scheduled, so she should have been home at four-thirty. She was almost two hours late getting home and I'd called everyone on the list. Everyone who might know where she was. I was getting scared. It was just to reassure myself that nothing had happened to them."

Omar said nothing.

"Did you find her car?" Dusty asked. "I don't understand what you're telling me."

"Yes. We found her car."

"But... Ronnie wasn't in it? So, where's Ronnie? Was it stolen? Carjacked?"

"No, it doesn't appear so."

"She just parked it and went shopping or something, and never came back?"

Ronnie Coleman hadn't gone shopping. Her wallet and purse were still in the car. There was no sign of any violence, but the lab boys would be checking for any minute drops of blood or other evidence of what had happened to her.

"Does that sound like your wife?" Omar asked.

"No... no, she would never leave the kids at the park, or leave her car and never come back. None of this makes any sense."

Dusty appealed to Omar.

"Do you know what happened? Can you explain it to me?"

"I'm afraid not, Mr. Coleman. Your wife is missing. It would appear she might have been the victim of a crime. At this point... we are just as confused as you are."

Dusty rubbed his eyes, suddenly looking exhausted. "Where are my kids? Mandi and Dane will need to go to bed, and someone will have to explain to them..."

"They are taken care of tonight," Omar said. "You don't need to worry about that right now."

"Taken care of?"

"They were turned over to Social Services when they were abandoned at the park. Once they have a chance to evaluate the situation they will be returned to you. But being abandoned like that triggers an investigation."

"But that was Ronnie, not me. I should be able to go and get them back."

"Not the way it works. They have to satisfy themselves that this is a safe environment. I'm sure they'll be talking to you tomorrow."

Jane Withers was ready for Omar when he returned. She sat expectantly with her fingers hovering over the keyboard, waiting for instructions.

"Background on Dusty Coleman is already started," she said. "So far, no red flags, but we've only just begun. *Ronnie* Coleman, however…"

"She has a record?" Omar guessed.

"No. She doesn't exist."

Omar lowered himself into the chair beside her so that he could see the reports that she brought up on the screen.

"She's a ghost?"

"Never existed until she started working at Starcan, the company that Dusty works at now. At that point, she applied for a social and started working."

"Birth certificate?"

"A Veronica Stern, born June first, twenty-three years old. Only problem is, Veronica Stern died at age two."

"She created a paper trail for herself. Professional?"

"Doesn't appear to be. Professionals usually develop an identity very thoroughly. Library card, gym, social, driver's, everything you can think of. Ronnie's trail is very low-key. Minimal. A social and a fake driver's. Nothing else. No credit cards, her name is not on the house or on the car registration. Her marriage license and children's birth certificates. Everything else kept below the radar. No store loyalty cards, library, gym."

"Phone, email, social networks?"

"Her cell is in Dusty's name. I can't find any email or social networks. We'll have to get her computer and take a look."

Omar studied the screen. "What was she running from? Criminal past? Abuser? Someone who just wanted to start fresh?"

"What did her husband say about her past and her family?"

"It upset her to discuss them, so he didn't. He thought that her parents were killed in a car accident."

"I'll check for car accidents six or seven years ago, just to be sure. Also any missing persons reports around the time that she assumed her new identity. She came from somewhere."

"But where? She could be from out of our jurisdiction."

She shrugged. "I'll keep it narrow to start with. We'll widen the net if nothing shows up."

Omar had watched the videos of the children's interviews with Mrs. Vital, the social worker. Mandi, age four, hadn't had much to say, other than that she wanted to go home to her mother. Dane was almost six and was more articulate in his interview.

"Where did Mommy go?" Mrs. Vital asked him.

"She went to the car."

"Why did she go to the car?"

Dane considered the question seriously. "Maybe she forgot something," he suggested.

"What do you think she forgot?"

"Snacks?"

"Were you guys hungry?" Vital asked.

"We were hungry when the police came."

"Yes, you were. But you'd been at the park for a long time, then. Were you hungry when your mom left you there and went back to the car?"

"No."

"What did Mommy say when she went back to the car? Did she say she was going to go get some snacks?"

He shook his head and looked around the room restlessly. Omar got the idea that he was normally a pretty active little boy and not used to having to sit still for long. But the interview room, although made to look cozy and furnished with toys and teddies, was an unfamiliar place and he stayed in his seat.

"She just said… 'I'll be right back,'" he reported.

"And did she come right back?"

He shook his head vigorously. "We played for a looong time. Usually we can't stay for a long time. But we got hungry, and Mandi got dirt in her eye, and my hands were cold."

"She just let you play there for the whole time? And then you got sad because she hadn't come back from the car?"

"Uh-huh," Dane agreed. "Where is she? Can we go home now?"

"I still need you to talk to me. Did you see your mom go back to the car?"

He nodded.

"I want you to think about it, Dane. Did she get into the car?"

He was hesitant. "Nooo…"

"Did she get anything out of the car?"

"I don't know."

"Did she have a bag or a suitcase in the car, like she was going to go on a trip?"

"No."

"Did she talk to anyone else at the park? Any of the grown-ups?"

Dane thought about it. "No."

"Did she usually talk to others?"

"My friends' moms. But they weren't there. It was a different park."

"Yes, it was, wasn't it? Did your mom say why you were going to a different park today?"

"No."

"She didn't say that there was something special about it?"

"No."

"Or that she wanted to meet someone there?"

Dane played with his sandy curls. He looked around the room, getting up on his chair to look around. Then he sat back down again.

"I want my mom. Is she coming here?"

11

"Where did she say she was going, Dane? She must have told you."

"No. She said, 'I'll be right back.'"

"Did your dad go to the park?"

"No," he shook his head, brows drawn down, at such an idea. "Daddy doesn't go to the park. Daddy goes to work."

"He never goes to the park?"

"No."

"You didn't see him at all today? He didn't go to the park to surprise your mom?"

"No."

"Did anybody go to the park to surprise your mom?"

"Uh-uh."

"A special friend? Did your mom have any special friends?"

Dane chewed on the end of his finger, this question apparently not prompting any memories. "No."

"When she went to the car, was there anyone else around watching her? Standing nearby? Did anyone talk to her?"

He gave a frustrated sigh, scowling. "No," he huffed.

"Where did she go after she went to the car?"

Dane shrugged. "I don't know."

"Did you see her walk away from the car?"

"No."

"Or get into someone else's car?"

"No."

"Was there anyone at the park who made you feel scared or icky?"

He arched his eyebrows and shook his head, scornful at the idea. "There were no *strangers* there."

"Did you know the other kids playing at the park?" Vital questioned in surprise.

"No."

"Or their parents?"

"No."

"Then they *were* strangers."

"No," Dane asserted. "They weren't strangers. You're not supposed to talk to strangers. But they were nice."

Vital nodded, understanding. Omar rolled his eyes at this, but was used to this common misconception among children. Strangers were scary monsters. People who tried to steal you or rip your clothes off. People who were nice to you were obviously not strangers. A stranger could be recognized by his scowling face or scary music that accompanied his entrance. Vital had obviously run into this situation before as well. She didn't try to force understanding, just continued to question him.

"And when you started to feel tired and cold and hungry, you talked to the adults and told them that you wanted your mom."

Dane agreed. "They helped us and gave us snacks and mittens. Then the police came to help and gave us a ride in their car."

"That was nice, wasn't it?"

"But they left Mommy's car there. Where is Mommy?"

"We're still looking for your mommy. Did she say she was going to visit a friend today?"

"No."

"Or to run errands? Maybe she had some shopping to do?"

"No. She went shopping *yesterday*."

"Maybe she forgot something."

Dane shook his head with all of the assurance a five-year-old could muster. He yawned widely, making no attempt to cover his mouth.

"Where is my mom? When can I go home?"

"We're going to let you sleep over at someone else's house tonight. Then we'll work on getting you back home once we know it is safe."

"It's safe. I want to go home."

"I know, sweetie," she agreed. But she didn't tell him that he could.

They had slept at a respite home, and went back to Dusty Coleman the next day. Omar met up with them and Mrs. Vital at the respite home to observe the reunion and to see what he could divine from it.

Mandi and Dane were reticent with the social worker. No smiles. No childish chatter. Each clung to one of Mrs. Vital's hands, looking at Omar and then Mrs. Vital's unfamiliar car with nervousness. Omar followed the social worker's car in his own vehicle and stayed to the side, unobtrusive, when they got out at the house.

Dusty was watching for them and hurried out the door as soon as the social worker got out of the car to unbuckle the kids from their booster seats.

"Mandi! Dane!" He called to them and hurried down the sidewalk in stocking feet. "Oh, I'm so glad to see you!"

He didn't look like he had slept a wink the previous night. There were dark circles under his eyes and he hadn't bothered to shave that morning. He crouched down and gathered the kids into his arms, hugging them tightly, eyes brimming with tears.

"I'm so glad to see you. Are you guys okay? Are you all right?" He looked at their faces, and then hugged them again.

Mandi, who had been mostly silent during her interview and the intervening time, was noisy.

"Daddy, Daddy, Daddy!"

"What is it, Mandi?"

"Daddy!"

"Yes, Daddy's here. What do you want? Are you okay?"

"Daddy!"

He hugged her to him tightly, grinning at Dane over Mandi's shoulder.

"I missed you kids so much last night! Are you okay? Did you sleep okay last night?"

"We had to sleep at a lady's house," Dane announced. "A lady we didn't even know!"

"I know, Dane. But you are back home now. You can sleep back in your own bed tonight."

"I missed it!" Dane said with a dramatically weary sigh.

Dusty laughed. "How about you, princess? How did you sleep?"

Mandi was still pasted to Dusty, lying limply against him. Her eyes were glazed and far away, like she had just woken up.

"I want Mommy."

"I know, princess," Dusty agreed. "I do too."

Dane addressed his father in a stern tone. "Where is Mommy?"

Omar was interested to note that Dane assumed that his father knew exactly where Ronnie would be.

"Mommy didn't come home yesterday. We… we don't know where she is. I'm sure the police will find her, and they'll bring her home safe and sound. Okay?"

Dane scowled at this. He looked over his shoulder at Omar.

"That policeman came with us. Does *he* know where Mommy is?"

Dusty followed his gaze to Omar and stood back up, straightening from his crouch at the children's eye-level. He picked up Mandi with him, not shifting her from the spot where she had landed, her arms still around his neck.

"Do you know anything?" Dusty asked, as if nervous what the answer might be. He acted as if he believed that Omar knew more than he did about where Ronnie was. Whether that was true, or whether he knew exactly where Ronnie or her body now resided, Omar wasn't at all sure.

"We haven't found your wife yet," Omar said. "Have you heard anything from her? Had any phone calls? Any friends who have called you up to talk about it?"

"No," Dusty said flatly. "No one knows anything about where she could be."

"Unless you can give us something, we have very little to go on."

"There must be some clue of what happened to her… isn't there anything in her car? Something to suggest…" he trailed off, looking frightened by his own words.

"Mr. Coleman… I don't believe that your wife just walked off the face of the earth. Somebody did something. Somebody knows something. The most likely person is… you."

"You think I did something to my wife?" Dusty demanded, his voice rising in anger. "I was at work all day! You know that, didn't you check with the others? I was at work all day, I couldn't have done anything to her."

"You'd be surprised how many times we hear that line. Maybe you snuck off at some point. Or maybe you hired someone, or talked someone else into helping. There are ways around alibis. Nothing is ever ironclad."

"I didn't do anything to hurt my wife. You need to be out looking for her."

"Where?"

"I don't know. The hospital. Put out news announcements asking for help. Hand out flyers. Go door to door. Surely you have a protocol!"

"The protocol is to wait twenty-four hours. You really want me to do that?"

"I want you to do something!"

"I am. Right now I'm seeing that you get your kids back, which is the thing that you were most concerned about last night."

"I was concerned about getting the kids back and about my wife."

"You keep saying 'my wife' instead of Ronnie. Is there a reason you are having problems saying her name?"

"Ronnie. I don't have any problem saying Ronnie's name. I'm just trying to impress on you how important it is to me that you find her. She's not just a random woman. She is the woman I love. The mother of my children. Please find her."

"We're doing our best, Mr. Coleman. We will continue to work on it."

Dusty rubbed Mandi's back, his eyes misting over. He closed them for a moment. "Okay," he agreed. "Thank you."

"Anything?" Jane asked, coming upon Omar while he was rubbing his eyes, stinging and dry from staring at the computer screen for too long. "Looks like you need to take a break."

Omar sat back in his chair and looked up at the statuesque blond.

"It's got to be the husband," Omar said. "There's no indication of foul play. If it was a kidnapping, carjacking, or murder, her purse wouldn't still be sitting in the car with her wallet in it. It's like she just walked away."

"Wouldn't the husband know to take her purse and wallet if he wanted to make it look like a carjacking? Maybe whoever it was got interrupted."

"If he got interrupted, then where the hell is Ronnie Coleman?"

"Well… true."

"Have you had any luck tracking down her previous identity?"

"No, 'fraid not. I've checked back ten years, but generally, anything older than that has been archived and warehoused. Active cases should still be on the computer network, but that's going back to before everything was standardized and integrated into a single database. Not much we can do if it never made it onto the integrated database. Some jurisdictions are still working their way backward, adding old information onto the system. Others just have an arbitrary cut-off and only cases that were opened after that date are required to be entered into the system."

"Or there's the possibility that she was never reported missing. If her family thought they knew where she had gone, or she had no family, she may never have made it to the missing persons database at all."

Jane nodded, conceding this point.

"You're right, of course." Jane leaned on Omar's chair. "You know, though… if she's done this before, maybe it's not the husband. Maybe she just takes on a new identity every so often."

"You think she walked away from a four-year-old and a six-year-old? That's pretty cold for a mother."

"It's been known to happen. Mothers have been known to kill their children too. At least she didn't do that."

"She could have just walked away," Omar admitted. "But without even the cash in her wallet? If you were leaving your life behind, wouldn't you at least take the cash with you?"

"Yes… of course I would."

CHAPTER
Two

AGE 33

(1)

I t was a full year later, almost on the anniversary of Ronnie Coleman's disappearance, that the news story broke. Omar had stopped at a diner for a quick meal between interviews, and the television was set to a news channel with a running ticker at the bottom of the screen. Omar's eyes caught the words on the banner.

Woman who disappeared eleven years ago reunited with family.

That was an unusual story, but what happened next grabbed Omar by the throat and shook him. The picture of the woman tentatively approaching her teenage children for the first time in eleven years. It was Ronnie Coleman. He was sure of it. He'd studied her photo, he'd spread it across all the networks. He'd made sure it was posted in any forums where people might happen to see her.

"Can you turn this up?" Omar waved at a waitress. She looked grumpy, like she would argue about it, but a couple of the other patrons eating dinner made noises of agreement. It was a feel-good story. People wanted to see and hear the reunion. To hear how such a miraculous thing had happened.

The waitress turned it up.

The woman, who had to be either Ronnie Coleman or her twin, tentatively hugged each of the two teenage children, a boy and a girl, and greeted her ex-husband with a handshake and a kiss on the cheek, looking very awkward.

The television reporter pressed in close to Ronnie with the microphone.

"How does it feel to be reunited with your family?"

"Uh... good," Ronnie said in a low voice that was almost a whisper. "It's... really... nice."

"Can you explain to us what happened to you? You disappeared without a trace eleven years ago. Your family gave you up for dead. But here you are. You weren't murdered, you weren't kidnapped, so what happened?"

"I don't know," Ronnie said. "I don't remember."

"You don't remember? Do you have some kind of amnesia? Did you have a head injury?"

"I don't know. I'm trying to figure out what happened. I'm sorry, I just don't know."

"Do you remember your husband and children?"

There was a long moment of silence and then Ronnie shook her head. "No... this is all news to me. I didn't even know that I had been married, let alone that I had a family."

"What is the first thing that you can remember?" the reporter's tone was bullying. "Didn't you try to find out what had happened to you?"

"I... I'm sorry, I can't answer any more questions."

She turned away from the reporter, and walked away from the crowds toward a car that then whisked her and her family off to an undisclosed location.

"Didn't even know that she had a family!" Omar growled. "What about two families?"

The other patrons looked at him with confused, questioning looks. Omar dialed Jane Withers. It took him a while to get through. She was probably having supper at a similar diner on the other side of the state.

"Withers," she announced.

"Jane. Omar. Listen, there's a story on—"

"You talking about the mysterious reappearance eleven years later?" Jane demanded. "I'm on it. Did you catch her name?"

"No. I'm at a diner. Turned it on too late."

"Ronnie Plum."

Omar caught his breath. "No way."

"She kept the same first name. I'm seeing what information I can get."

"What about informing the Coleman family?"

"We're behind the eight ball on that one. He's the one who called the hotline number and put me onto it."

"Oh. Well, we can't be expected to know things before they happen, can we? How is he?"

"Pretty upset. She's claiming to be an amnesiac, so he has some solace in the possibility that she doesn't remember anything that happened in the past. The fact that she has abandoned not just one but two families... I've never heard of such a thing before, have you?"

"No. It's a first for me. Even doing it once... most people who claim that they left their families in some kind of fugue or amnesiac episode are later proven to be lying. So, I'm not expecting any different from her. I think it's a story."

Floyd Plum faced off against Adah Cruz, the police investigator who had not only had the gall to challenge his alibi and accuse him of having something to do with his wife's disappearance eleven years before, but had actually had him arrested for her murder a year into the investigation.

Floyd, once a reasonably handsome man, had been imprisoned for two years, had lost custody of the children for another two years beyond that, and his name had been blackened in the public eye forever. The prosecution had eventually been abandoned when they decided they didn't have enough to go to trial. He could no longer get employment as a CPA and ended up working a string of short-term contractor jobs. Not something that supported his family very well. The instability of the employment always left him on the brink of homelessness and having to give the children up again. He hadn't aged well. He had lost much of his blond hair, become a little paunchy, and gained a stoop, losing an inch or two off of his height.

"Mr. Plum," Adah started awkwardly. "Floyd... this has taken us all completely by surprise."

"I should think so," Floyd growled. "Since you accused me of murdering my wife. It is somewhat surprising to have her suddenly show up alive ten years later."

"You have to admit, things looked bad. Ronnie just disappearing without a trace like that. You claiming that you had come home to find your children abandoned, wife missing. It's a very unusual case."

"I told you all along that something had happened to her. I told you that she wouldn't just have abandoned me and the children. And that I didn't have anything to do with her disappearance. I told you over and over again."

"You did," Adah acknowledged. "But it was a very unusual case. Women don't usually just disappear like that. There is usually a reason. Someone has abducted or murdered them. And the prime suspect is always the husband or boyfriend."

"That's profiling."

"That's investigating. Going by the numbers and identifying the most likely suspect. And in ninety-nine percent of the cases, I would have been right."

He stared at her, waiting. Adah cleared her throat and fidgeted with her computer, running a finger along the smooth edge.

"I want to apologize, Mr. Plum. We were wrong, and I acknowledge that. Your life has been changed by our investigation as much as by your wife's disappearance. Maybe more so. And... for that I apologize. But we were not wrong in pursuing you as a suspect, given the circumstances."

Floyd folded his arms across his chest. "So, here we all are. Has Ronnie been able to give you any details, to explain what happened?"

"Unfortunately, not much. She claims not to remember her life here. Not her own childhood, you, or the children. Not her parents or any of her friends. Of course, we're having a psychiatrist interview her, trying to determine whether she is telling the truth. She's scheduled to go to the hospital for x-rays and a scan of her brain. See whether there is any sign that she was the victim of violence eleven years ago, or if there's any organic explanation for why she can't remember her former life. You do hear of these things happening sometimes... a head injury or extreme stress... the person wakes up with no memory and starts a new life..."

"Where has she been for eleven years?"

"For the last year, she has been here. As you know, Kent and a few old friends saw her and recognized her. When we started getting reports, we investigated. But the ten years before that... I'm afraid they're still a blank. Ronnie hasn't been able to tell us anything that happened during that time. We can only assume that she left town, or people would have seen her."

"She has no idea where she was for ten years."

"No. So she says."

"But she's going by the name Ronnie Kepler. So, she knows her name is Ronnie. She must remember something."

Adah nodded. "That's one of the inconsistencies that we are trying to reconcile."

"How long is the investigation going to take? When can she come home?"

"Floyd... she can go home whenever she wants to. We're not keeping her. She's cooperating with our investigation. She's not being detained."

"When I asked her to come home, she said she couldn't."

"We're not stopping her. If she can't, she's the one who is blocking it, not us. I assume that after all this time... she doesn't feel comfortable moving in with people that—she claims—she does not know."

"We're her family. Whether she remembers or not, that's where she belongs. She should be with us. Everything else... we'll sort it out. I'm sure if she was with us, she'd start to remember. She'd fall in love with the kids all over again, at least. They've been without a mother for most of their formative years. She has to come back."

"You'll need to address that with her."

He shook his head, scowling. "Can you give me her phone number? Her address? I have no idea how to reach her."

"We can't release private information."

"I'm her husband!"

"The same rules apply as would if you were an abusive husband trying to track his wife down at a shelter. We can't give you any personal information without Ronnie's permission."

"The children want her home."

"I understand that. But that is up to Ronnie, not up to me."

Adah watched Floyd Plum's departure. She felt bad for him. For all that he had suffered since his wife's disappearance, including his incarceration based on her own recommendation. She had been right to suspect him. All of the indicators were that he had killed and disposed of his wife, right down to the freshly muddy shovel in his car trunk. But she had been wrong.

Looking down at the transcribed messages on her phone screen, though, she realized that even more pain was in store for him. If the report from the neighboring town of Anchor was correct, then at least part of Ronnie's ten-year blank had been spent with another husband and another family.

She went back to her desk to put in a call to Omar Bluff.

Ronnie double-checked the house number and climbed reluctantly out of the car. She studied the house as she shut the car door, still hesitant to step off the road onto the property. She felt like Alice Though the Looking Glass, entering into another world. One where nothing made any sense.

Had she lived in this house? She hadn't thought to ask. Nothing about it was familiar to her. If she had lived there with this new family who claimed that she was a member of, she couldn't remember it. She had hoped that something would stir in her memory and she'd recognize the mailbox or the siding. That something about it would whisper 'home' to her. Then these people would start to emerge like ghosts from her memory, gradually gaining substance until she remembered everything about them. It would all come back, and she would remember her life with them and all that had happened since.

Floyd opened the front door and stood there, waiting for her to come up the walk. The children weren't with him. They weren't waiting excitedly for her return, clamoring to tell her everything that had happened since her departure. They had been reserved at the media event. As awkward as Ronnie was herself.

Ronnie pulled her hands back from the car, feeling like it would disappear as soon as she let it go. Or that *she* would. But nothing happened. The car and the house and her supposed ex-husband could all coexist in the same bubble of reality.

She walked up the cracked, uneven sidewalk to the front door.

"Hi," Floyd greeted, with a nod and a forced smile.

"Hi."

"Thanks for coming. I know it has to be pretty weird for you..."

"You too," Ronnie pointed out. For him to have his ex-wife return from the dead, that had to be a really weird feeling.

Ronnie stepped into the house. She didn't cease to exist. She didn't remember anything there. She looked around.

"This is very nice."

"It's a rental," Floyd said. "I can't afford to buy a house. All of the stuff that has happened since you disappeared... I don't have the same earning power as I did before that."

"Oh." Ronnie nodded politely. "What is it you do?"

Floyd studied her a moment. He motioned her into the living room and Ronnie selected a chair rather than the couch, so that he wouldn't sit down next to her. She perched on the edge of the seat, uncomfortable, not wanting to sink into it. She would feel trapped if she got too comfortable.

"I used to be a CPA," Floyd said. "Accounting. But I can't get work in that anymore. So, I'm working odd jobs... short term... contracting in home building. It's a little rocky in this market."

"Oh. Right."

The house was quiet. She wished that there were a stereo or TV on. The kids playing with their friends. Some kind of background noise that would cover up the awkwardness between them.

"Where are the children?" she asked.

"Kent went out to a friend's. Carrie is here. Reading or on her computer. But I figured... it might be too overwhelming if we were all here. The kids... don't quite know what to make of this whole thing."

Ronnie sighed. "Me too. I can't believe it's even possible for me to have kids that old. Teenagers. I don't feel like... what? Thirty-three?"

"By my calculation."

She shook her head. "That just doesn't seem possible."

"You were just eighteen when Kent was born. You were seventeen when we got married."

"Seventeen..." Ronnie shook her head. "That's really young to get married. Were we... was I already pregnant?"

"No. It wasn't like that. We just... we loved each other and we knew what we wanted. There was no point in waiting for years to formalize what we already knew and felt."

"What did your parents think? How old were you?"

He looked older than Ronnie. Older than thirty-three.

"I was twenty-five," he said. "So, I'm forty-one now."

Eight years older. His face was old for a forty-year-old. She supposed that the stress of losing her and being a single father had aged him prematurely.

"My parents were a little concerned," Floyd admitted. "Me getting married to such a young girl. Afraid that you were too immature. That you'd get older and realize that you'd made a big mistake."

He stopped, looking like he regretted what he had said. Maybe they had been right. Maybe at twenty-two, finding herself married and with two young children, Ronnie had just decided that it wasn't what she wanted, and left.

"Your parents were the ones that should have been worried," Floyd plowed on. "A seventeen-year-old marrying a twenty-five-year-old. You were just barely finished high school. You were so young."

"My parents?" Ronnie echoed. She hadn't reunited with them yet. The media had wanted Ronnie and her husband and children, and her parents hadn't pushed to see her on camera, so she had put it off. She couldn't remember anything about her parents. Meeting them was just one more chore the she would rather put off.

"They were over the moon about it," Floyd exclaimed. "Delighted. They said…" he flushed a little, and his eyes slid away from her. "They said I was a great catch and they were happy with your choice. I would give you stability and be a good breadwinner for you." He shrugged. "It wasn't an arranged marriage, but they were certainly happy with your choice."

Ronnie's stomach squeezed into a tight knot. She wasn't sure why his words made her so uncomfortable. She should be happy that she had made choices that made her family happy. Except, of course, she had later undone those choices in the worst possible way.

"I'm sorry," she said.

Floyd looked surprised. He didn't say anything at first.

"I know… you don't remember what happened," he said. "Probably, it wasn't anything that you made a conscious choice about. I think it was probably… an accident, or some kind of psychotic break or something. A psychiatrist that I talked to said that sometimes, when someone is having a stressful time… they can have a psychotic break, as a way of the brain just stopping all the stress…"

Ronnie stared down at the worn brown carpet.

"I don't think you have anything to apologize for," Floyd said. "Not if it wasn't a conscious choice."

It was an 'out' and a challenge. She could accept his olive branch, or she could repeat the apology, affirming that she couldn't remember what had happened and that it hadn't been a conscious choice to leave them. Ronnie didn't want to do either one. She didn't want to be forced into telling him any of her story. Her life was her own. Or it had been up until a couple of days ago when the police had landed on her doorstep. Every time she had to meet with Floyd, or a policeman, or a psychiatrist, she felt them pulling her life out of her hands. It was a tug-of-war, everyone else pulling on what she held in her hands, wanting a part of it, wanting to control a part of it.

So Ronnie just stared down, saying nothing. Floyd looked at her, wanting to ask her all of his questions. Wanting to know why she had left him and her two young children eleven years ago. Expecting her to be the same person as she had been before they left.

"Was there a lot of stress?" Ronnie asked.

"What?"

"If I had a psychotic break, then I must have been under stress… a lot of stress."

Floyd raised his eyebrows.

"I've talked to a psychiatrist too," Ronnie went on. "It would have to be more than normal stress, or people all over would be having psychotic breaks… running away from their lives… and they don't."

"I guess."

Ronnie didn't speak the question. What stress had they been under?

"We had the usual issues," Floyd said uncomfortably. "Arguments about finances. The stress of having two young kids. Intimacy." At Ronnie's change in expression, he hurried on.

"Neither of us was having an affair, or anything like that. Just... recently married, two kids really close together... You were tired a lot. Not really... interested."

Ronnie felt her face flush. She looked away from him.

"It must have been hard after I disappeared," she observed. "Taking care of two little kids by yourself. You'd have to... get help."

"People were really good, that first year, volunteering to look after them without charging babysitting fees, taking them off my hands when I needed to talk to the police or take care of other issues. Then... your parents took custody when I..."

Ronnie looked at him, waiting for him to finish his sentence. Her parents took custody of the children. Why? He couldn't handle them anymore? He had remarried? He had been accused of being abusive and they were taken away?

Floyd sighed and stared off into space.

"It's been tough, Ronnie."

"Yeah, I know."

"No, you really don't. It's not just tough because my wife left me. I was arrested for your murder."

Ronnie's jaw dropped. "What? But I wasn't murdered!"

"Well, that's obvious to the police now," he said wryly, "but it wasn't then. In fact, they were pretty sure that I had murdered you, buried your body out in the woods somewhere, and then reported you missing. I was arrested and I was in prison pending trial. Your parents took custody of the kids."

"But... how long were you in prison? Not until now...?"

"No. Eventually, they decided that they didn't have enough evidence to prosecute it, so they had to let me go. After a couple of years. But your parents still had the kids. And I guess they still thought that I had killed you, so they didn't want me getting the kids back. We fought for two years, before Social Services finally returned custody to me. Your parents had been in the process of trying to adopt them. Even though I hadn't been convicted. They figured since I was out of the picture for an indefinite period, they'd be able to get the kids permanently."

28

"Oh." The thought made Ronnie anxious. Even though this man was a stranger to her, the thought of him having his children ripped from him and given to someone else, through no fault of his own, upset her. That shouldn't happen. Bubbling under the anxiety was something else. Something darker. Anger. Fury that her parents, who she couldn't even remember, would do such a thing. "I'm... I'm really sorry they did that."

He must have seen something in her expression, because he didn't argue with her this time. He just nodded, accepting it.

"It's good that you got them back. That was a really long time not to have them, though."

"Four years. Yeah. But they didn't have you for eleven."

Ronnie shook her head. "I really messed up your family."

"*Your* family," Floyd said.

Ronnie traced the pattern on the upholstered arm of the chair. There was a sound, and she looked up.

Carrie stood in the other doorway to the living room. Ronnie supposed that Carrie looked a little like she did. Shoulder length brown hair. Brown eyes. She didn't have much of Floyd in her face. It was a little like looking in the mirror. It wasn't just her features, there was something inside Carrie's eyes that Ronnie identified with. A sort of a sad, haunted look. Ronnie hadn't seen her smile yet, except for the plastic smile she had pasted on for the television reconciliation.

"Oh, hi," Ronnie said.

"Hi."

Carrie stood there. Waiting. Expecting more. Ronnie swallowed.

"You like to read?" she asked.

"What?"

"Your dad said you were probably reading. So, I thought... you must like to read."

"Yeah, I do."

Ronnie nodded.

"Do you like to read?" Carrie countered.

"Uh... not really. I'm usually doing other things. I can read okay, I just... I'm not big on books, I guess."

Carried shifted, leaning against the doorway as she looked in on Ronnie. "What *do* you like to do?"

"I don't know... watch TV. Go out."

"Go out where? To bars?" Carrie's tone rose accusingly.

"I don't know... sometimes, bars or clubs. Sometimes I want to be around other people. Where else would I go?"

"Is that why you left us? So you could go party?"

"Carrie," Floyd said in a warning voice.

"I want to know," Carrie insisted.

"I don't know," Ronnie said, hating to see them fighting with each other. "I don't remember what happened, why I left. I'm sorry. I don't know why I would ever have done such a thing. It's wrong. I just... I don't remember. I don't remember what happened."

"How could you forget your own children?"

Ronnie shook her head, tears welling up in her eyes. "I don't know. I keep feeling like... it's all a big mistake. That it must have happened to someone else, and you just think that I'm your mom. It doesn't make any sense to me. It's like it happened to someone else."

"Well, unless you have a clone, you're my mom."

Ronnie stared at the girl, trying to force her brain to recognize the child in front of her. Surely if she were Carrie's mother, she couldn't forget?

"Maybe I have a twin," Ronnie said, rubbing her aching temples. "Couldn't I have an identical twin?"

She had floated this theory with both the police and the psychiatrist, but neither one bought it.

"Then why wouldn't you remember?" Carrie demanded. "Wouldn't you remember your twin? And what happened to you in the last eleven years?"

Ronnie covered her eyes, resting her elbows on her knees.

"Carrie, let her alone," Floyd said. "You're upsetting her."

Ronnie swallowed, wiped her eyes, and forced herself to face the teen. "You were only two when I left? Do you remember me?"

"Kent does."

Ronnie nodded. She couldn't very well forget that Kent had recognized her. "Do you?"

"No. I don't remember anything from that far back. I remember living with Nana. That was after you were gone, when Daddy was in prison. I don't remember anything about you."

Ronnie must have nursed her, rocked her to sleep, taken care of her when she was sick. Watched her crawl and take her first steps. She probably recorded all of those things in a baby book. Played with the children, took them to parks, made their meals every day. She tried to remember what their favorite meals were. Hot dogs? Macaroni and cheese? Chicken fingers? Why couldn't she remember any of those things that must have mattered so much when they were little?

"Do you still see them? Your Nana and...?"

"Nana and Papa. Yes, we go see them lots. We're really close."

Ronnie's skin crawled when she really comprehended that Carrie was talking about Ronnie's parents. Whom she hadn't met yet.

"Did they ever talk about me?"

"Yeah, all the time."

Ronnie scratched the back of her head. "That's weird. That kind of... creeps me out."

Floyd laughed, and they both looked at him.

"It creeps you out that your parents talk about you? That's ridiculous."

"It creeps me out that people I don't know talk about things that happened when I was a kid, that I can't remember happened. That *really* creeps me out!"

Floyd shook his head again over that. "We thought you were dead," he said. "How were we supposed to keep your memory alive, unless by talking about you?"

He had talked about her too, Ronnie realized. Told the children stories about when she had been alive. How he had met her. About their wedding, and the children's births, and dozens of other things that Ronnie had no memory of.

Everybody that she knew had talked about her.

And if she stayed in the community, there would always be talk going on around her, out of her hearing, about how she had disappeared and reappeared. About the person that she had been eleven years ago, and the person she was now.

They would always be talking about her.

She didn't see Kent again before she left Floyd's house. She couldn't think of it as her house, even though he had repeated the invitation that she was welcome to move in with them at any time. She could take the spare room while they rebuilt their family. He wouldn't insist on her taking up her place as his wife again, but she could at least reintegrate with the family.

Ronnie wondered what would happen if she tried, and then one day her brain just turned off again, and she walked away.

She wouldn't plan it that way, but she couldn't guarantee that it wouldn't happen. She couldn't imagine how devastating that would be to the children. Disappearing from their lives again a second time... They would never get over that.

They hadn't gotten over her leaving the first time. She couldn't get Kent's face out of her mind, the first time that she had seen him.

Ronnie had been walking home from the grocery store. He was riding his bike down the road and suddenly skidded to a stop, the bike nearly flying out from under him as he stopped and stared at her. Ronnie turned and looked behind her, thinking that he was looking at something beyond her, not at Ronnie herself. But there was nothing going on behind her, and when she looked at him, his eyes were riveted on her, wide with shock. Ronnie stood stock still, with a grocery bag in each hand, looking back at him.

"Mom?" he asked in astonishment. He had dark blond, spiky hair and a face that was just gaining definition as he changed from boy to man.

Ronnie was confused. She again looked around for someone else he might be talking to.

"Mom!" he repeated. He threw his bike down on the road and approached her. "Mom, it's me! It's Kent!"

She shook her head. "I don't know who you are. You've mixed me up with someone else. I don't have any kids."

"Yes, you do!" he insisted. "I'm Kent. Kent Plum. You're my mom. You're Ronnie Plum!"

It astonished her that he knew her first name. It was the one thing that kept her from just shaking her head and walking away from him.

"No... I'm Ronnie Kepler," she said. "I don't know anyone named Plum."

"You're my mom! You're Ronnie Plum! What are you trying to pull?"

"I'm sorry... you're mixed up. I don't know who you're talking about."

His mouth opened and closed like a fish. He stood there, his eyes so wide she wondered if he would ever blink again.

"I'm sorry," she repeated again. "I don't know who you are."

It was difficult to turn her back on the boy. He was somebody's son, and she knew he was hurt, but she couldn't help him. She couldn't pretend to be his mother. That wouldn't help him. It wouldn't fill the hole in his life. Pretending to be his mother when she wasn't would just be cruel.

"Mom!" he called after her, his voice breaking.

Ronnie blinked back tears, ignoring him. It would be cruelled to stop again and to build up his hopes. She had to just walk away and let him be.

She was relieved when she turned the corner and knew that she would be out of his sight. He could go and pick his bike back up and go back home. She felt bad for him, and for his confusion. Maybe he was mentally ill. She wondered if he often accosted women in the street, mistaking them for his mother.

When she got back to her apartment, she was shaking. She put her groceries in the fridge as calmly as she could. She didn't make anything to eat. Normally one of her favorite things was making something special to eat right after she got done a grocery shopping trip and had lots of good food in the fridge. Instead, she went to the couch, and turned on the TV, and just sat and tried to forget about Kent, the boy on the street.

It didn't last for long. Before she knew it, there was someone knocking on her door, and when she opened it, there were two uniformed police officers standing there.

"Ronnie Plum?" one of them asked.

"No. No, it's Ronnie Kepler."

He held up a picture of a young woman. "Is this you?"

Ronnie couldn't deny that it looked like her. The hair and clothing style were different. The makeup a little heavier. But it was her face looking back out of the picture at her. Ronnie frowned, studying her. She couldn't remember ever seeing a picture of herself before. It was a weird feeling, seeing herself looking out of her picture just like she looked at herself in the mirror every day. It would be like turning on the TV and seeing herself talking.

"That... looks like me. But it isn't."

"Do you have a twin?"

"Uh... no..."

"Then I would say this is you."

"No."

"We'd like you to come in with us. Someone will need to talk to you, verify your identity."

"My name is Ronnie Kepler. I can show you my driver's license." Ronnie went into the kitchen and picked up her purse from where she had left it on the counter beside the empty grocery bags. She pulled out her wallet and removed the driver's license. She handed it to one of the officers. He examined it with interest, looking at her face and then back down at the license again.

"Where did you get this?"

"From... the DMV. Where else would I get a driver's license?"

"How did you get it?"

"I... took the driving test."

"What information did you give them? Birth certificate? Social?"

"Yes."

"Let's see them."

Ronnie retrieved the other pieces of identification. He looked over everything carefully.

"It's all issued in the last year."

Ronnie thought about that. "Well, yes..."

"What happened before that?"

"I... lost my wallet. I lost everything, and had to get everything reissued."

"Where was your previous driver's license issued?"

"I don't remember."

"What was your address before this one?"

She gave it to him, stumbling over the zip code but eventually remembering everything.

"And before that?"

"I don't remember the address..."

"You don't remember the address you lived at just a year ago? What city was it in? What neighborhood?"

"A lot has happened," Ronnie said anxiously "I don't remember everything."

"You don't remember what city you lived in?"

She swallowed and didn't answer.

"We'll need you to come in to the police station."

"I haven't done anything wrong."

"I think your identification is forged. That's enough to start with. You can come with us willingly, or I can put you in cuffs. Which is it going to be?"

Ronnie stared at him in disbelief. She knew that she hadn't done anything wrong. There was nothing wrong with her ID. There was no reason that she had to give him all of her previous residences. She had the right to privacy.

"I don't want to come in with you," she objected.

"Please put your hands behind your back, ma'am."

He moved around her, and his partner stood there in front of Ronnie, his hand on the butt of his gun.

"What...?"

He grabbed her hands roughly and pulled them behind her, where he clipped handcuffs over them.

"Do you have any weapons on you?"

"No."

"Anything sharp in your pockets?"

"No."

He patted her pockets. Turned them inside out.

"This is your purse?"

"Yes."

"Let's go, then."

He picked up her purse and they escorted her out of her apartment. The cop locked her door and put her keys back into her purse. In the car, he put the purse in the front seat, and Ronnie in the back seat, graciously helping her to sit down and warning her not to bump her head. Ronnie slid into the car, objecting.

"I didn't do anything. You can't arrest me for nothing. I don't have to go with you."

But she was already in the car, and she was going with them, whether she liked it or not.

The questions at the police station went by in a blur. She was shown pictures of a man and two children. More pictures of the young woman who looked like Ronnie. They fingerprinted her, and told her that her fingerprints matched those of Ronnie Plum.

"I'm not Ronnie Plum," Ronnie insisted. "I don't know who that is. I'm Ronnie Kepler."

"Well, you have Ronnie Plum's fingerprints," the cop told her. And he told her about her family. About the family that she had apparently walked away from eleven years ago. Part of a past that she couldn't remember anything about.

When Ronnie got back to her apartment after the visit with Floyd at his house, she was met by Adah Cruz.

Ronnie rolled her eyes and shook her head.

"I'm exhausted," she said. "I just met with Floyd and Carrie, and I can't take anymore. I can't answer your questions any more today than I could yesterday, or the day before that. I just don't remember any of it. Nothing is familiar."

"I know you were hoping that visiting the house would trigger something," Adah said with no sympathy in her voice. "As it happens... I have more information to show you. Maybe this will trigger something more."

Ronnie unlocked the door to her apartment. "I can't take it right now."

"You're going to have to."

Adah followed Ronnie into the apartment without an invitation. Ronnie looked at the couch in front of the TV. She would give anything to just be able to lie down and veg out in front of one of her favorite shows. She didn't want to have to think. Didn't want to have to go over anything else from her supposed past. She didn't want to be Ronnie Plum. She just wanted to be herself. Ronnie Kepler, the nobody.

"Maybe we could sit at the table," Adah suggested.

Ronnie looked longingly at the TV, then at the kitchen table, stacked with flyers and unopened mail. She sighed and went to the table. She tossed out the flyers and put the mail on the counter. She brushed toast crumbs into her hand and then emptied them into the garbage.

Sitting down on one of the thrift-store chairs, she put her elbows on the table and her head in her hands.

"Do we really have to do this?"

"Yes."

Adah sat in the other chair, directly across from Ronnie. She didn't make small talk about the weather or ask Ronnie how she was doing. It should have been pretty obvious how Ronnie was doing.

Adah put a picture of Ronnie on the table. Another missing poster.

Ronnie didn't know why that should be news. Adah looked at her face for some change in expression. Then she put down a series of family pictures. Ronnie posing and smiling with Floyd, Kent, and Carrie. As Ronnie studied them, her heart sank. Her chest got tight and sore. It wasn't Floyd. It was another man, built much more solidly, his hair short and sandy colored. And the children seemed older than Kent and Carrie had been when their mother had disappeared. Ronnie studied their faces, not even sure that it was Kent and Carrie.

"I… don't understand," Ronnie said. "What's this?"

"This is Ronnie Coleman and the family that she abandoned a year ago."

Ronnie swallowed. "That's not me."

"It was a year ago. You don't look any different now."

"A year ago."

Ronnie stared down at the happy-looking family. She had a feeling of unreality whenever she looked at the pictures Adah showed her. It felt like some kind of prank. Some huge, elaborate prank to make her think that she had done the horrible things that they said. But she hadn't; she knew it in her heart. She couldn't just abandon a family like that. Those sweet-faced, innocent children.

"That's not me," she insisted. "Does that make any sense to you? Someone is playing a trick. Or I have a twin. It's not me!"

"We can check your fingerprints against Ronnie Coleman's. Just like we checked them against Ronnie Plum's."

"But if I have an identical twin…"

"Identical twins do not have identical fingerprints. No two people have the same fingerprints. If you have the same fingerprints as Ronnie Coleman, then you *are* Ronnie Coleman."

Ronnie shook her head. She felt light-headed and nauseated and the tight band around her chest was really hurting.

"How many more families like this are were going to find?" Adah demanded. "How many times have you done this?"

"I don't know what happened. I didn't do anything wrong."

"Ronnie, even if you are claiming amnesia, you still know something. You know that you set up a new identity for yourself, even if you pretend not to know who you were before that. You know that you stole the identity of the infant Ronnie Kepler. You know that's not who you are."

"I didn't *steal* it," Ronnie protested. But that argument had already failed with Adah. Adah Cruz refused to acknowledge that it was the only course of action for Ronnie to take. She couldn't work or drive with no identity. Couldn't own a credit card and pay for an apartment. She couldn't live without an identity, and that meant that she had to find one. She spent hours looking through public records to find an identity that felt right. She clearly remembered the feeling of relief that came to her when she found the name Ronalda Kepler. Ronnie. That was who she was. She had proceeded to follow the procedure she had researched on the internet to order her birth certificate and apply for a social, credit card, and driver's license.

"Why don't you explain it to me?" Adah said. Not for the first time. "Why don't you explain to me why you left your family? Two families? Normally people don't just walk away from their whole lives, Ronnie. Tell me what happened. The two of you had a fight. You were having marital problems. Did he hit you, and you decided you'd had enough? Did he threaten to do something to the children if you didn't just go quietly? Explain to me how someone decides to just walk away from everything." She tapped the table. "Not just once, but twice! Maybe more."

"Who are they?" Ronnie asked, looking at the pictures of the family.

"Dusty," Adah said, pointing to the father, "Dane, and Mandi. Now, I've answered your question, you answer mine. Explain why you left them."

"I don't remember anything about them. I don't remember ever seeing them before."

"Just like with the Plums."

"Yes," Ronnie said. "I don't know what happened. I don't remember."

"What is the earliest thing that you do remember?"

"I don't know. I don't remember, exactly... I just know... I lived here... I got a job... got this apartment... lived here..."

"You don't remember your parents or your childhood."

Ronnie remembered Carrie talking about Nana and Papa, and the anxiety she had felt over the thought of their raising the kids and talking about Ronnie grew in her chest again. It hurt to breathe. She was going to be forced to meet the people who claimed to be her parents. She might be able to put it off for a few days, but not forever.

"No. Not really."

"What does that mean?" Adah pounced. "Not really?"

"I don't remember anything clearly... like yesterday... but I know some things... like riding a bike... eating peanut butter sandwiches for lunch..."

"You remember doing those things?"

"No... I just... remember about them. Like... I watch a TV show, and I think, 'I used to wear my hair in braids.' But I don't remember braiding them... or what they felt like or looked like... I just think... I had them."

"Uh-huh." Adah's disbelief was not veiled.

Ronnie sighed. "Can you go now?" she asked. "I can't tell you anything, and you don't believe me if I do. I just want to go to bed."

Adah gathered up her pictures and stood.

"I'm sure we'll have more questions."

"I'm still not going to know the answers."

"We'll see. I'll be back."

"I don't have to meet those people, do I?" Ronnie asked, nodding at the bundled in Adah's hands.

"So far, no. It doesn't look like Dusty wants to put himself or his children through that. They've had a year to get used to the idea that you were gone, and what good would it do the children to be traumatized again? It's not like you're going to go back to Anchor to live with him, are you?"

"No."

Adah nodded and let herself out.

~

At first, they had seen Ronnie as a victim. In spite of having to put her in handcuffs to bring her in for questioning, they had believed that she was the victim of foul play or some form of traumatic amnesia. They were gentle with her and assumed that she wanted to remember.

But while Ronnie put on a facade of cooperating and wanting to help them, Adah gradually came to realize that there was something more going on. While she didn't seem to recognize her family, Ronnie wasn't telling them everything she knew or suspected. She wasn't telling them everything she remembered. Behind those dark eyes, there was some recognition of a past. She knew more than she let on.

And Adah was going to sort it out, if it took another eleven years to do so.

[III]

Ronnie could see that she was going to have to quit her job and find something else. Which was too bad, because she had enjoyed her job and the economy was not good. Finding a new job would not be easy. Everybody at work had seen her on TV, or at least heard about it. They all looked at her and whispered behind her back and asked her awkward questions. She would have to find something else.

She avoided meeting her parents, Chris and Cynthia Dare, for as long as she could. But the phone kept ringing and the police and the TV station kept insisting that she should meet them. Maybe it would trigger a memory. Maybe if she could look at pictures of when she was young, talk about things that she had done when she was young, then she'd be able to remember something. It would all start coming back, and then she would want to move back in with her ex-husband and children and they could all live happily ever after.

Except that Ronnie knew that even if she did remember anything about her childhood or her marriage, she still wasn't going to want to go back to them again. The children were very nice and she felt sorry for them. She even felt a little sorry for Floyd. But she didn't have any desire to live with them and have a relationship with them. She did want to know who they were, but that was all.

She forced herself to ring the doorbell of the big brick house. There was no media, and her parents were not standing at the door to meet her. It was a few minutes before they opened the door.

The man was heavyset. On the tall side. He was balding. The sides where he had hair, it was gray. He wore a checkered blue and gray shirt. The woman was smaller than Ronnie. Short, dark hair. Her face looked kind, but tired.

"Hi... I'm Ronnie."

The woman laughed. "We know who you are, Ronnie! Come in!"

Ronnie's face flushed. She was the one who needed introductions. Was she supposed to call them Mom and Dad? Had she had special names for them? Was she supposed to call them Nana and Papa, or was that just the grandkids? Ronnie followed them into the living room. Nothing looked familiar, but there was a TV playing, which Ronnie found soothing.

She aimed for the easy chair but her mother caught her by the arm and guided her over to the couch, where they sat uncomfortably close together. Her father sat in the easy chair with a grunt.

"So, you finally came back to us," he said.

Ronnie looked from one to the other, her stomach twisting with anxiety.

"I'm sorry... I didn't mean to..."

"What happened?" Mom asked. "Where have you been all these years?"

"I... I don't really know. I guess... I was somewhere else... That police detective, Adah Cruz, she thought I had another family, somewhere else."

Mom's jaw dropped. "You had another family? *Ronnie!*"

"Well... I didn't know! I didn't plan it that way."

"We raised you better than that," Dad said. "This whole

thing…" He shook his head. "It's hard to believe a daughter of ours would behave that way."

"But I didn't know. I didn't plan to leave. I didn't remember that I had another family. It was just… a psychotic break… it wasn't something I could control."

Her parents exchanged looks that Ronnie couldn't interpret. Did they not believe her? They thought that she had rebelled? Intentionally walked away from them and her children and just started over again somewhere else?

"Show her the pictures," Dad said.

Ronnie expected Mom to get out a big photo album stuffed with memories, but she had just a small selection of pictures. A picture of a baby. A girl with braids. A group shot, with parents and some other children. A picture of Ronnie's wedding, standing beside Floyd. Ronnie holding a baby that looked very similar to the one in the first picture.

Ronnie studied them closely, waiting for a rush of recognition. They should trigger something. A memory. An emotion. Love or hate. But all she felt when she looked at them was anxiety. People she was expected to know. People that knew things about her. It just made her want to run away.

"Who is in this picture?" Ronnie pointed to the family shot.

"Those are brothers and sisters. We had foster children, so not all of them stayed with us. But we adopted Alex," Mom pointed to a red-headed boy grinning at the camera, "and Janessa." A thin, awkward-looking girl with glasses.

"The others aren't part of the family anymore?" Ronnie looked at the three other children of varying ages and races.

"No. They were just temporary. You can't keep them all, even if you wanted to."

Even if you wanted to. It was obvious from her voice that they hadn't wanted to adopt all of them. Ronnie thought about what the foster kids would have been like. Troubled homes, rough backgrounds; there had probably been a lot of behavioral problems to deal with. Ronnie was lucky to have been born into a well-off middle-class family who had been so giving.

"Do you remember anything?" Dad asked. "Anything at all?"

"No."

Mom and Dad exchanged another look.

"Something must have happened to you," Mom said. "You got hit on the head or something. You hear about that kind of thing happening."

Ronnie nodded. "That's what the psychiatrist said. He thinks I either got hit or had... a psychotic break."

Mom shook her head, frowning. "Why does he think that?"

"He thought maybe... I was under stress. Something made me... disassociate..."

"What stress could you have been under? You had a perfect life. Good stable marriage to a man who provided well for you. Two lovely children. You didn't have any stress in your life."

Ronnie stared down at the floor, pondering over this. No stress? There wasn't anybody who had no stress in their life, was there? Floyd had admitted that they had been dealing with marital issues. The police had arrested him for murder; *they* certainly hadn't thought that everything had been perfect.

"When are you going to be moving back in with your family?" Dad asked.

"I'm... I'm not. I don't know them. It's been eleven years. They don't know me either."

"Then you can move back here. Your mother has gotten the room ready for you."

Ronnie looked at him, then looked at her mother.

"I'm not... I'm not looking for somewhere else to live. I have my own apartment."

It was Mom who answered. "You need someone to look after you; you're not... well. You should come and stay with us until you're better. Who better to look after you than your own parents?"

"No. No, I'm fine. There's nothing wrong with me. I don't need anyone to take care of me."

"Your old room is ready for you."

"That's really nice of you. But I don't need it."

~

Ronnie looked around her apartment. Everything seemed foreign to her. She was looking for the soothing familiarity of her own place and her own stuff, anxious after dealing with her parents, but it all seemed like it belonged to someone else.

Was this what it had been like before she had left Floyd? And that other man? Had she just gotten home one day and nothing seemed right anymore? Had it happened gradually, or had she just snapped unexpectedly, herself one moment and gone the next?

She moved around her apartment like a sleepwalker, gathering together a few necessities and putting them into a suitcase. The suitcase was new. If she really had run away before, she hadn't taken it with her. She hadn't packed a bag before. Hadn't had the foresight. Before, she had just disappeared without a trace. At least, according to Adah Cruz.

It only took a few minutes to pack. She hadn't acquired much in the year that she had lived there and she didn't have space to take much with her. A couple changes of clothing. Toiletries. There was nothing of sentimental value. She was like a robot. Not a human.

In the bathroom, she saw herself in the mirror. She didn't even recognize herself. She gathered her shoulder-length hair and held it away from her face. She remembered the pictures of herself with her family before her disappearance, and those dreadful school pictures of a girl in braids and felt unaccountably furious. She bounced through the apartment, opening and closing drawers, until she found a pair of scissors. Not even bothering to look in the mirror, she grabbed hanks of hair and chopped them off at ear level. She didn't want to be that person. She couldn't ever be that person again.

When she got down to her car, she hesitated. The police could trace a car. They could put out an APB on it and track it down by its license plate. There were far too many surveillance cameras in the city to avoid detection forever. If she wanted to be untraceable, she needed to walk away without it. But if she were going to get far enough away to start a new life, she needed a car to get there.

Ronnie got into the car and sat in the driver's seat for a long time before turning the key in the ignition. Was she really going to do it intentionally? After all that they had told her about how she had hurt everyone, abandoning them as she had, was she really going to do it cold-heartedly this time? With forethought?

She wasn't leaving a family this time. There were no husband and children to abandon. It was just her, all alone. Her parents had lived without her for eleven years. She was already dead to them. They would forget all about her brief reappearance, like a ghost from the past. Their lives would go on just as they had.

She got to the highway. Red and blue lights flashed in her rear-view mirror. Ronnie pulled over a lane, slowing and waiting for the police car to pass her. It didn't; it stayed behind her, lights still flashing. Ronnie pulled over to the shoulder. Had she been speeding without realizing it? Forgotten to signal?

Ronnie watched in her mirror as she put the car into park. It was an unmarked police car. The policeman who approached the car was in a suit, not a uniform. Ronnie reluctantly rolled down the window. He held up a police badge to identify himself.

"Police, Miss Kepler," his lip curled when he said her name, like it tasted bad to him. "Get out of the car, please."

Ronnie forced her body to obey. She was shaking. They didn't have anything to arrest her on. There was nothing illegal about leaving town. It wasn't a police state where people were required to have visas in order to leave their own city. The policeman turned her around and pushed her against the car. He patted her down and pulled her hands behind her back to handcuff her.

"Wait—" Ronnie resisted.

"You're under arrest for breach of bail conditions," he said briskly. "Do you understand?"

"Bail...?" Ronnie vaguely recalled Gordon, her boss, offering to put up bail for her, tut-tutting the police accusing her of identity theft when, with no past and no identification, Ronnie had had no other option than to create a new identity for herself.

"You're outside the city limits," the officer told her. He looked in at the suitcase on the back seat. "You're obviously attempting to flee custody. So, guess what? It's back to the pokey for you."

He reeled off her rights as he strong-armed her into the back seat of his car and slammed the door. Ronnie just sat there while he talked on his phone, used his on-board computer, wrote up citations, and performed a cursory search of her car. Eventually, a tow truck arrived. The cop talked to the driver and waited until the tow truck took Ronnie's car away. Then they were on their way back to the police station.

"I knew she was going to run again," Adah Cruz said with satisfaction. "Once a runner, always a runner."

Eddie Paine nodded slowly. "But… this doesn't match her usual MO. There was no indication of planning when she left the Plums. She walked away without a vehicle. Left behind her purse with her cash and her ID."

Adah didn't look at him as she tapped a few notes into her phone.

"We didn't *find* any indication of planning," she corrected. "That doesn't mean that she didn't plan it. Just that we didn't find any evidence. She could have been planning it for months. What if she arranged her new ID, squirreled away some cash, and bought a new car before leaving? How would we know that?"

"We couldn't then, but maybe we could now," Eddie said. "We can see when her ID was issued. When her car was registered."

"It's relevant as part of the identity theft investigation." She nodded and looked up at him with a hard smile. "Good thinking."

"I'm not sure it contributes anything to the missing persons case… that file is resolved, now that she's back. There was no foul play."

"Maybe so, but I still think that Floyd Plum deserves some answers. To know whether his wife was a victim of circumstances, or whether she ran away." She cocked her head at Eddie. "I'm leaning towards running away, in case you were wondering."

He grinned. "No, really?"

Booking finished with Ronnie and an officer escorted her into the interrogation room. They watched her on the closed-circuit camera. Ronnie was obviously agitated. She initially sat down and looked expectantly at the door. But as time passed and no one came in to talk to her, she got up again and paced around the bare room. She sat back down again, jiggling her legs. Rubbing her arms. Folding her hands together in front of her and then wringing them as she was forced to sit.

"Did she ask for a lawyer?" Adah asked.

"Nope."

"Say anything in the car on the way in?"

"Just that she hadn't done anything wrong."

She studied Ronnie's slim figure, her chopped-off hair, and her pale, pinched face. Eventually, Adah decided there was nothing left to learn by observing Ronnie alone, and she went into the room and sat down across from her.

"So nice of you to come and see us again."

Ronnie scowled. "It's not like I had any choice."

"Well, you had a choice about running away or not. As usual, you took it."

"I don't have to stay here. I'm allowed to leave if I want."

"Your bail requires you to stay here. Because you haven't gone to trial yet."

"I didn't do anything wrong. So I shouldn't have to stay here."

"You're welcome to your own opinion. But you're still required to abide by the terms of your bail."

"Okay. I'll stay."

"You're going back to jail now," Adah pointed out. "This isn't a three-strikes thing. You don't get a second chance. You left the city, your bail is revoked, and you get to await your trial in jail."

"That's not fair."

"That's the law. You break it at your own risk."

Ronnie sat there looking at her, face pale and petulant. Adah wasn't sure that Ronnie really comprehended what was going on. She acted like a kid that had been grounded, rather than someone who could be incarcerated for the next several months or years. There were no tears. No indication that she realized how much she had just screwed up her life.

Ronnie was escorted to a cell. Not an open-barred jail cell like she had seen on TV. It was a small room with two bunks, one steel toilet, a writing desk and bookshelf. It was probably less than half the size of the bedroom in her apartment, and two people were expected to live there. Ronnie knew she had roomed with others before. Her foster sisters. But it would be close quarters.

The woman who was already there sitting at the desk was older than Ronnie, or looked it, anyway. Deeper lines on her face. Dry, wispy blond hair, cut short. From the tattoos all over her arms and the holes in her ears, Ronnie suspected that she was used to having a lot of product in her hair. Gel, mousse, colors, maybe she spiked it. The limp does it was in didn't do anything for her. She had glasses, but probably used contacts when she was on the outside.

The guard locked the door behind Ronnie. She looked at the other woman and looked at the beds.

"This one?" she guessed, pointing to one of the bunks. It was stripped, the sheet and blankets folded in a pile on top, waiting to be used.

"Brilliant, yeah," the blond said.

"Thanks." Ronnie sat down. "I'm Ronnie."

"Anna Stegner. Ronnie what?"

Ronnie sighed. "Kepler. Dare. Plum. Take your pick."

Anna lowered her eyebrows at this. "Which one do you go by?"

"Kepler."

Anna nodded. "Ronnie Kepler, then. That's good enough for me."

Ronnie looked at the folded blankets. She knew that she should make the bed, in case she was too tired to do it before going to sleep. Making the bed would mean that she was going to stay there, and she wasn't ready to admit that. She kept thinking that she would get out. Go home. They wouldn't hold her in jail just because she had tried to leave town. That would be cruel.

"What are you in for?" she asked Anna.

"None of your business."

"Oh."

"You?"

Ronnie should just answer back that it wasn't any of Anna's business, but she wanted to visit, wanted to make a connection. Just one person that hadn't known her before. One person who would just take her at face value, without trying to dig down below the surface.

"Broke bail conditions."

Anna snorted. "Bail for what?"

"Uh... identity theft. But I didn't mean to do anything wrong. I just needed..." She trailed off. Anna didn't need to know that. She didn't care what Ronnie's reasons were for assuming a new identity. Ronnie didn't want to explain the whole amnesia situation.

Anna's eyes drifted away from her, back to the letter or journal she had been writing before Ronnie got there.

"Well, just stay out of my way, Kepler, and we'll be just fine."

"Sure... okay."

Ronnie stared at the blankets on the bed, still refusing to acknowledge that she was going to need them.

Ronnie slumped in her seat, looking down at the table instead of at the psychiatrist. She didn't want to talk to him again. He really hadn't done anything to help her out, and she didn't like the idea of someone digging around in her psyche. She pictured him bent over her brain with a fork in his hand, delicately dissecting her. How much could he really figure out without messing things up? She might not be able to remember what had happened in the past, but she was still sane. She could only imagine the damage he could do poking around in her brain.

"Your family said that you used to draw," Dr. Able said, laying down a sheaf of paper on the table, and supplying her with a box of pencil crayons of various lengths. Some of them had long scars or bite marks on them. "I think today, we'll try a little art therapy."

Ronnie looked down at the pencils. "I don't draw. What do you expect me to do?"

"It doesn't matter whether you can draw well or if all you can do is stick figures. Let's just see what you come up with. I'd like you to draw what comes to mind when I say... family."

There was a shocker. Ronnie rolled her eyes. "Can't I do something else? I already met my family and I don't want to draw them."

"You don't have to draw the people you met. You can just draw something that represents family to you. It could be someone you know, or just a picture like you might see on a cereal commercial on TV. It could be something other than people. A Christmas tree or a puppy. A warm plate of spaghetti. Really. Just draw me... family."

Ronnie frowned, staring down at the blank white paper. It was open, pristine, waiting for her to make her mark. Even though she didn't draw, she had a sudden impulse to fill it with something.

She started with some tentative lines. Her fingers seemed to know what they were doing, and the picture began to come together, even though she wasn't sure what she had in mind. She switched pencil crayons a few times, adding some color, filling in the forms. After a while, she pushed the paper away, frustrated.

"I can't do it. I can't... I can't get the details right. I can't see their faces."

Dr. Able picked up the paper and studied it. "Well, they were right about you being able to draw. This is very good."

"But it's no good if I can't get the faces. They're just... bodies. They're not right."

"Close your eyes and tell me what you see that you weren't able to get in the picture."

Ronnie closed her eyes, searching for the images. She shook her head. "I can't. That's the problem. I can't see them. Just this!" She gestured at the paper. "It's not right."

"What isn't right about it?"

"You can see it's not my family," Ronnie pointed out.

He lowered it so that they could both see it at the same time.

"It isn't Floyd and the children," Ronnie said.

"No. But it doesn't have to be."

"And it's not my mom and dad. He's tall and gray and going bald. And she's a little woman. Petite. Smaller than me. Not like these people. I saw pictures of my brothers and sisters, or foster brothers and sisters." Ronnie looked over the other shadowy forms in the picture. "These just... they aren't right. I don't get it."

"I told you that you didn't have to draw your own family. Maybe this was a picture that you saw. Or a movie. Sometimes my patients remember things from movies and think that they happened to them in real life. It's very hard to differentiate sometimes, especially if you've had a traumatic incident. Your brain tries to fill in the holes and sometimes it fills them in with things that don't actually belong."

"You think I saw this family on TV? I drew them because I don't have a family of my own?"

"It could be a family you saw on TV," he repeated.

Ronnie didn't mind that idea. She had had so many new people claiming to be family forced on her lately that she was happier with having picked a family of her own. Safe, with no real claim on her. Not anyone that she would have to meet in real life to explain why she had abandoned them. She looked at them with new eyes, thinking through the programs she liked to watch on TV. Were they from one of her sitcoms? A soap? Maybe even a reality show or one of the talk shows where they did lie detector and paternity tests. Those always fascinated her. Or maybe they were from a movie. Something that she had gotten a happy feeling from. A classic, nuclear family.

The mother figure was large and fat. She scowled out of the picture, even if her face was only an outline. Something about her just exuded disapproval. Probably not a sitcom or family movie, then. The man was less distinct. Not the big, tall, balding man that Ronnie had met. He was smaller than the woman. His hair darks. He hugged a couple of the children close to him.

"Is this a family from TV?" she asked Dr. Able. "Do you know them from anything?"

There were five children. The two biggest blond, and the smaller ones all dark-haired. Ronnie felt a kinship with the middle child. Stuck between two older siblings and two younger siblings. Alienated. She wasn't one of the children that the father was cuddling.

"I don't recognize them," Dr. Able said. "But I don't watch a lot of TV. They could be very well-known, and I still wouldn't recognize them. Why don't you tell me something about them?"

"There are four girls and just one boy," Ronnie observed. "I wonder how he feels, being the only boy after all of those girls."

"Is he the youngest?" Able asked, his eyes intent on the picture.

"I don't know. I think so."

"What else can you tell me?"

"They're all together," Ronnie observed. "One big, happy family."

"Are they happy?"

Their faces were blank, so what made him ask that? Ronnie looked at their body language. Tried to imagine what it would be like to meet them in real life.

"The mother is angry," Ronnie said. "She screams at the kids when they act up. But this is a happy picture. Everybody's happy in this picture."

"I see. That's good. What other feelings do you get when you look at them?"

"I want to go home…" Ronnie was startled by putting the thought into words. She wanted to go home? Where was home? Back to her own apartment? With Floyd? With her parents? None of them evoked the feeling of *home*.

Able was nodding. He rubbed the stubbly growth on his chin. "What else? What do you feel about family and home?"

"I don't know. I feel like it's been a long time… and that I'll never go home. I feel… abandoned… isolated."

"Yes, yes…?"

Ronnie shook her head at him. "None of *those* people are my

53

family. I don't feel connected to any of them. They just *say* they're my family. Why would they do that?"

"Why would you feel that way?" he countered. "That's what we're here to find out. We want to dig down into those feelings. See what's behind them."

Ronnie rubbed her eyes, feeling distant and dreamy. "What good is it to look at my feelings when I don't remember anything?"

"Because even if the memories aren't there, the feelings still are. We can learn something from them. I think this," he tapped the picture, "tells us that the memories are still there, locked up somewhere."

"You said it was from TV."

"I said that it could be. But you attach very strong emotions to it for it to be from TV or another outside source. I think that there is meaning in it, even if it came from TV."

"That's stupid," Ronnie scoffed.

Able shrugged, seeming unoffended.

"Do you want to try another one?"

Ronnie was interested in what her brain might reveal to her, but she didn't want to let him see that. So she shrugged like it made no difference to her. "If you want."

"Okay, let's try another one. How about… yourself."

"Myself?"

He nodded.

"I can look in the mirror and draw myself. What's that going to prove?"

"Why don't you just try?"

Ronnie considered, picking out a fresh sheet of paper and hovering over it with a pencil. She started to sketch her own face. At least she didn't have to concentrate to remember what that looked like. It wasn't like the blanks in the family picture. She stalled and restarted several times before pushing the picture across toward Able without a word. He picked it up.

"You're very small," he observed. "You had the whole page to use, and you are small and alone in the middle of it."

"What does that mean?"

"I guess it means you feel small and alone."

Ronnie nodded. That wasn't news to her. She couldn't see the picture the way that he was holding it, but she knew what it looked like. Not a picture of her as an adult. Not a mother and wife. Not the adult that she was now, single and apart from anyone else. But her as a child, similar to one of the pictures that her mom had shown her. Long, dark braids. A pinafore dress that came down to her knees, neat and clean. Hands joined in front of her, like she was posed for a photograph.

"Tell me about yourself here," Able suggested.

"I don't know. I don't remember."

"You drew it. What made you draw yourself that way?"

"I guess just one of the pictures that I saw. Of me when I was a little girl. I kind of thought I had braids before I saw it, so it was… like I remembered, but not really."

"Are the braids important?"

"No. They're just braids."

"Did it make you feel happy when you saw the picture? Familiar?"

"No."

"Tell me how you felt."

"I felt… anxious. Like I did when I had to meet Floyd and the kids. But… more so. I didn't want to be there."

"How do you feel toward your parents?" Able put down the picture, and his eyes drifted back to the family picture again, studying out the figures with their blank faces.

"Unreal. I feel like someone is just setting this all up, like a hoax. I don't feel like they're my parents, like I love them. I feel like they're actors in some bizarre movie. Gaslight."

"Gaslight?"

"It was a movie where this guy tried to make the girl think she was crazy—"

"I'm familiar with it. I'm just interested about the connection. This feeling of disconnection could be Depersonalization or Derealization Disorder. You feel like you're watching yourself in a movie?"

"No…" Ronnie was frustrated. "Like everybody else is an actor, and I'm the only one who knows who I really am. Or they know, but they're trying to keep me from believing it."

He nodded slowly, mulling that over.

"If you could get out of here, what would you do? Where would you go?"

"I'd get away… go somewhere else. Where there aren't all of these people who know me, or pretend to know me. I'd go somewhere I could be myself again."

"And who are you? Who is Ronnie?"

"I don't know. Just an ordinary person. I just… I just go to work, curl up to watch TV… go to the grocery store… I'm just ordinary, maybe a little boring."

"Don't you get lonely?"

Ronnie hesitated. She teetered between wanting to have someone in her life, someone who just appreciated her for who she really was, and never wanting to get close to anyone. Never wanting to have to face another family who claimed to know who she was and where she had come from.

"A little, maybe. But I don't want a family."

Able scratched his ear and looked down at the picture. "You don't want *this* family? Or any family?"

"Well… maybe I want that family. But not any others. And… I don't know who they are."

(IV)

Ronnie tossed and turned on the hard bunk, unable to settle in and find sleep. She groaned and pressed her face into the pillow.

"Be quiet, Kepler," her cellmate growled. "Some of us are sleeping."

"I'm trying," Ronnie protested. "I can't get comfortable…"

"You ain't gonna get comfortable here. It's not possible. Just be still and shut up."

"I didn't say anything."

"You're moaning and groaning and driving me crazy. Zip it, or I'll shut you up myself."

Ronnie sighed and squeezed her eyes tightly shut. She didn't think that Anna Stegner was going to do anything about it, but it was prison—Stegner might be capable of violence. It was medium security. Not somewhere that Ronnie could walk away from, but she wasn't being housed with murderers or violent offenders. Stegner was probably guilty of theft or hacking. She was a thin blond, with short messy hair and studious-looking glasses. Ronnie wasn't particularly afraid of her.

Ronnie turned her pillow over and curled her toes and tried to find the sweet spot in the uncomfortable cot that would allow her to find sleep.

She found sleep, but her night was filled with restless dreams. Her mind roved from one problem to another, trying to sort through the questions that Able had asked her, her feelings of not belonging to the families who claimed her, how she could persuade Adah to let her out of prison.

Her head hurt, and it was dark. Ronnie became aware of a repetitive noise near her head. A *clunk-scrape*, *clunk-scrape*, over and over again. Broken by the occasional swearing or period of silence, and then it started over again. What was it? Ronnie's eyes were too heavy to open. The headache grew until it was overwhelming. She wanted to throw up, but she didn't want to wake up and move. Her body was too ponderous to even raise her head. She curled more tightly into a ball. The noise stopped.

"Ronnie? Are you awake...?" the question was soft, furtive. Whose voice was it? Floyd's? Ronnie was afraid to answer. She couldn't anyway, not with her head pounding and her body so heavy. She didn't seem to have any control over her body.

There was a hand on her. Fingers searching for a pulse on her wrist, then flinging her arm away again with a grunt.

The man was muttering something to himself, unintelligible to Ronnie. Then Ronnie felt arms under her, lifting her behind the back and the knees, and then dumping her back to the ground with a crash that sent Ronnie's head spinning so badly that she must have blacked out for a time. She awoke again later, unsure how much time had passed. The clunk-scrape continued, but at the end of each *clunk-scrape*, a patter of rain hit Ronnie's body. *Clunk-scrape-spray, clunk-scrape-spray.*

There was an increasing weight on her body, and it seemed a very long time before full awareness reached Ronnie's consciousness. It wasn't a spray of rain. It was dirt. It was piling up on her body, getting heavier and heavier. Suffocating.

Ronnie tried to escape, but the dirt was too heavy. Her body was too heavy. She couldn't use her voice, screaming in her head without a sound. He was burying her! Burying her alive!

All at once, Ronnie was screaming aloud, her limbs were her own again, and she was clawing, trying to escape, crying and gulping and taking great gasps of air before he could cover her face. His hand was on her arm, shaking her, trying to get her to stop screaming.

"Wake up!" Stegner shouted, shaking harder. "What the hell is your problem? Wake up!"

Ronnie opened her eyes. It was dark, but there was enough light from the security lights outside and in the corridor that she could see around her. See Stegner standing over her. The shapes of the cell's furniture around her. She was in prison. Not being buried alive. That was a dream.

Stegner dropped Ronnie's arm, just like Floyd had in the dream after checking for a pulse, letting it fall back to the bunk.

"Just when I get to sleep, you wake me up screaming bloody murder!" Stegner complained. "What's that all about? You keep that up and I'm going to get you moved to solitary! I need my sleep."

"Sorry," Ronnie gasped. "I'm sorry. I just had a nightmare."

"No kidding!"

"I'm sorry."

She lay there, her whole body tense, waiting to see if Stegner were going to hit her. Eventually, the other woman backed off.

"You'd better not wake me up again."

Ronnie sat up, propping herself against the concrete blocks of the wall. She cuddled her blanket close.

"I'll stay awake," she promised. "I don't want to dream anymore."

"Make sure you don't. I don't like being woken up. I need my sleep!"

"Okay, I'm sorry. It was... really scary."

Stegner climbed back into her bunk. "What was it about?" she asked, in a more conciliatory tone.

"I was..." Ronnie swallowed. "I was being buried alive."

"Yeesh. That's freaky."

"Yeah."

Stegner was quiet, going back to sleep. Ronnie lay there, thinking about the dream. Was it true? Had it really happened? Adah Cruz had told her that Floyd had been suspected of her murder. They thought that he had killed her and buried her. There was a shovel in his trunk that had recently been used, and his explanation hadn't rung true.

Was it possible that he really had buried her? He knocked her out and thought that he had killed her, but Ronnie had awakened while he was burying her? Or maybe she had woken up afterward and clawed her way up to the surface to escape? The nearly-fatal injury and the trauma of being buried could have caused her amnesia.

Wouldn't someone have reported a woman wandering around disoriented, covered with mud and blood? That wasn't normal. As soon as Ronnie reached civilization, someone would have said something. It would be reported to the police, she'd be taken to the hospital. She would need clothing and a shower, at the very least. Probably medical treatment.

Ronnie sighed. More likely, it was just something that her brain had made up, inspired by Adah's words. She was restless and entombed in prison, and her brain had just taken the idea and made a dream out of it.

It had felt so real.

"Visitor, Plum," a guard said curtly, motioning for Ronnie to come forward.

Ronnie approached the cell door and put her hands through the access hole for him to handcuff. "Can you not call me that?" she said. "It's not my name. Not what I go by."

"According to your booking records, that's your name."

He opened the door and Ronnie joined him in the corridor. She waited while he closed the cell door again, and then he took her by the elbow and escorted her down the hall. They worked their way through a maze of hallways that Ronnie hadn't been able to get accustomed to yet, to the open visitor room. It was mostly filled with small tables and chairs, but there were a few couches and more homey pieces of furniture around the outer perimeter. Good for families with kids.

Ronnie looked around to see who was there to visit her, expecting another cop or lawyer. Or maybe a social worker or some other kind of case worker. She couldn't keep track of all of the professionals who came to see her, claiming that they had some task or another to complete on her behalf. Mostly, they seemed to be people who were curious and just wanted to get a look at her. To say that they had talked to the woman who had disappeared for eleven years with amnesia, not even knowing that she had a family and starting another one.

But it wasn't another professional. It was Kent. Ronnie swallowed and didn't walk up to talk to him. When the guard pulled her hands toward him to uncuff her again, Ronnie resisted.

"No, just…"

"I'm taking them off, Plum. Hold still."

"No, I want to go back. I don't want to talk to him."

He stared at her. "You don't want to visit? You want to go back to your cell?"

Ronnie nodded quickly. "Yes. Please. I don't want to have to talk to him."

The guard stood there, unsure of what to do. Ronnie didn't know whether protocol was that she had to visit even if she didn't want to. Surely, they wouldn't force to meet with someone that she didn't want to. She still had some rights, didn't she?

"Mom," Kent said, when he saw that she was trying to go back to her cell without talking to him. "Mom, please. I came all the way here. Had to get special permission to come see you. Please talk to me."

"We don't have anything to talk about." Ronnie still resisted the guard removing the cuffs. But he persisted and turned the key in the locks, removing them, and gestured toward a table.

"Go sit down with your son," he said gruffly.

Ronnie gazed at him unhappily.

"Please," Kent pleaded again. "I just want to talk. Why won't you let me talk to you?"

Ronnie dragged herself over to the table that the guard had pointed to and sat down, breathing out a long sigh. Kent sat down across from her. His eyes were sharp, watching her intently, taking note of every detail. It was humiliating, having to face him like that with her orange hospital jumper. Like a murderer or rapist. She had done nothing wrong. All she had done was try to make a life for herself.

"I'm sorry," she told Kent.

"It's my turn to talk."

She stared down at the top of the table. People had scratched words and crude drawings into it. With what? Ronnie hadn't been allowed so much as a pen. They wouldn't let anyone have a knife or anything that could hold a point.

Ronnie looked at the graffiti and not at her son. The stranger that they said was her son.

"I just want you to know," Kent went on, his adolescent voice cracking. "I want you to know what you did to our family, leaving like you did."

Ronnie didn't answer. He didn't want her to say anything. He came with his own speech prepared.

"I was four when you left," he went on. "I don't remember you much. I know your face from all of the pictures. Dad and Nana always talked about you. Talked about how great you were and how they missed you. No one ever thought you would come back. We all thought you were dead."

"I didn't... I didn't abandon you on purpose." Ronnie thought about the dream. The dream of being buried. She felt that way again, short of breath, like she was suffocating. Like she wanted to scream, but couldn't get enough breath, the weight on her stomach and chest too heavy. "I don't know what happened. I didn't do it to be mean. I... don't know what happened."

"You should have come back. Or maybe you shouldn't have, I don't know. Maybe it's worse, you coming back, instead of letting us think that you were dead. I could handle having a dead mother. People understood that. Teachers at school were nice about it. They didn't whisper behind their hands about it. Having you come back... having all of the kids say that you left because of me, because I was so horrible and you didn't want to be my mom... that *hurts*."

Ronnie nodded. "I know... but I didn't. I didn't leave because of you. I didn't mean to come back. I didn't mean to mess everything up. Twice. I just... I didn't know you were here. Didn't know what had happened. That I used to live here. I would have stayed away. I would have gone on to another town. But I didn't. I liked the sound of it here... it felt... like home."

"It's not. Not anymore. You shouldn't have stopped here."

"I didn't mean to. I didn't know all of this. I just... I thought I was settling down somewhere new. Somewhere I'd never been before. I didn't know I was going to cause any problems."

"Why did you leave us?" he demanded plaintively. "Why?"

Ronnie stared down at the table. She felt so bad for him. But there was nothing that she could do to change all that had happened to him. Or to her.

What was done was done.

Adah looked down at the stack of messages on her desk, sighing.

"What's up with the flood of pink slips?" she asked Eddie, not bothering to pick them up.

He scratched the back of his neck, pursing his lips. "Ronnie Plum."

"Plum? What about her? How can she be causing me this much trouble from inside a prison cell?"

"There have been a number of objections raised about her being incarcerated awaiting her trial. Public sympathy is on her side."

"What do I care about public sympathy?" Adah gathered up the message slips and tapped them into a neat stack, then set them to the side without reviewing them. "The woman was running. We can't keep a tail on her twenty-four hours a day to make sure she gets to trial."

Eddie could have just gone back to his desk and left her to stew about it, but instead he slipped into the visitor chair on the other side of her desk and made himself comfortable.

"People think that what she did, while it might be a technical theft of identity, shouldn't be counted as identity theft because of the extenuating circumstances."

"Because they think that she did have amnesia and that breaking the law was the only way for her to survive."

He inclined his head.

"If we allow that, we'll get a whole avalanche of people claiming to have amnesia as an excuse for ripping people off and bilking them out of their life savings."

"Except that's not what Plum did. She never took money from anyone, as far as we can tell. She lived her quiet life and used her identity just to work and survive."

"I thought you were on my side on this." Adah looked away from Eddie and tapped her login into the computer. When her email box popped up onto the screen, she saw that, as she had dreaded, it was also full of messages regarding the pain in the neck, Ronnie Plum.

"I'm not on anyone's side. I agree that what Plum did was breaking the law. She doesn't get to just walk away from it without facing justice. On the other hand... it appears that it was a victimless crime. If she does have amnesia, there is at least a defense."

"But we don't know if she really does have amnesia."

"Right."

"Are they going to release her? I can't control it if they do. But I'm not going to tie up our resources surveilling her if they do."

Eddie looked at the pile of pink messages slips. "From the volume of messages and some of the names on them, I think the scale is tipping."

(V)

Ronnie had been invited several times to the family's Sunday dinner. She had avoided it for a couple of weeks, giving excuses about having to get settled back in after getting home from jail. Getting caught up at work. Eventually, she ran out of excuses and agreed that she would go.

"We'll have the whole family together again," Mom gushed happily over the phone. "All of my babies in one place."

"Okay," Ronnie told her. "I'll see you then. What do you want me to bring?"

"Nothing. Just bring yourself. I'm cooking."

"I could bring a bottle of wine or something."

There was a sharp intake of breath. "You don't drink wine," Mom said sternly, "and neither do we."

"Oh... yeah. I forgot." Ronnie bit her lip, pondering this new piece of information. Was it a religious thing? Moral? Personal preference? The family might have lost a loved one to a DUI. She had no clue what the basis for the wine prohibition was. "Well then, dessert? Brownies?"

"I suppose, if you want to go to all of that work," Mom said, her voice doubtful.

"Okay. Great. See you then."

Ronnie wasn't going to go to any work on the brownies. She would buy a just-add-water mix. Or maybe buy them frozen or from a bakery. She wasn't a baker, but she did enjoy sweets. A family Sunday dinner wouldn't be complete without some kind of dessert. Maybe Mom had been planning on another dessert and Ronnie was insulting her by insisting on bringing something. Ronnie sighed after hanging up the phone. Navigating the waters around this family she couldn't remember was dangerous work. She had no idea what sharks lurked beneath the surface.

When Sunday rolled around, Ronnie was at the brick house at four o'clock on the dot. There was an unfamiliar car there ahead of her. A red Beetle. As Ronnie got reluctantly out of her car, a man pulled up on a noisy, exhaust-belching motorbike. He turned in behind Ronnie and cut the engine. He unstrapped his helmet and Ronnie looked at his short-cropped red hair.

"You must be Alex," she guessed.

"And you're Ronnie." He looked her over thoughtfully. "You haven't changed that much. Cut your hair, though. It was longer when you were on TV."

Ronnie nodded. She had gone to a hairdresser to get her self-inflicted bob tidied up and made to look presentable. It actually ended up looking pretty cute.

"Come on in, they'll all be waiting."

Ronnie looked at her watch. "She said four. It's just four now."

"Well, Mom expects us to be here early. If you don't get here until four, you're late. Then she starts to worry that..." He cut himself off and pursed his lips. "Well, that something has happened to you."

"Oh."

Mom started to worry that she had disappeared and was never coming back. That she'd been kidnapped or murdered or disappeared into thin air again. Ronnie hadn't meant to worry her. She thought that four meant four.

"Don't worry about it," Alex said. "If you don't give in to her paranoia, maybe she'll learn to relax about it."

"Is that why you're here at four?"

"Once I was even five minutes late," he teased. "Of course, by the time I got here, she'd already called the police."

Ronnie narrowed her eyes at him, trying to decide whether he was serious or kidding about that part.

He just raised his rusty eyebrows and grinned and Ronnie couldn't figure it out.

The woman who came to the door when Alex knocked and let himself in was gorgeous. Ronnie divested her coat and studied her surreptitiously. Surely this wasn't Janessa, the awkward girl with the glasses in the family photos? She was a willowy blond with perfect teeth and makeup. No glasses; maybe she had contacts.

"Ronnie!" she greeted in a low, rich voice. "Oh, it's so good to finally see you!" She gave Ronnie a brief hug, hands on shoulders, leaning in close and landing a kiss in the air somewhere near Ronnie's ear. She smelled of a flowery perfume. "Wow, I can't believe you're back." As she pulled back from the stiff embrace, her eyes flicked around. "I honestly assumed that you were dead. I never thought I would see you again."

"Sh," Alex hushed her.

Then Mom was there. "You finally made it! I was starting to worry. Was traffic a problem?"

"No, Mom, we're right on time," Alex said. He greeted her with a quick hug and kiss, and Ronnie followed suit.

"We'll just be visiting with Dad until suppertime anyway, won't we?" Alex said. "It's not ready yet, is it?"

"Of course not. I'm still slaving in the kitchen. You go see what your dad's doing."

"I already know what he's doing," Alex laughed, looking at Ronnie. "He's watching TV."

"Do you need help in the kitchen?" Ronnie offered. She'd rather watch TV, but knew she should be polite and help out if she could.

"No, no, I've got it under control. You guys go visit. Get caught up. You've got eleven years of gossip to catch up on!"

Ronnie had a lot more than that to catch up on. She had thirty years of lost memories. She looked uncertainly at Alex and Janessa. Janessa nodded and linked her arm through Ronnie's.

"Come on. We'll go see what Dad's up to and get caught up."

Ronnie let herself be pulled along to the living room, where she had visited with Mom and Dad before. Again, the TV was on and Ronnie felt soothed by its presence. Just a normal family, doing normal things, living normal lives. She could fit in there. She could be a part of that family and not mess up or feel out of place.

They all greeted their father and sat down. Ronnie turned her attention to the program on the TV, but that didn't last long.

"So... tell us all about it," Alex said. "You disappear for eleven years, then show up again. Big hoopla. You must have a pretty good story."

Ronnie glanced over at him. "Well, no. Not really. I don't remember what happened."

"Not at all?"

She shook her head. "Nothing. I just... I just remember being in town, for the last few months... a year... I don't remember anything about living here." She gestured to indicate the house around them. "Or with Floyd. I don't remember him or the kids... or anyone..."

"Not Mom or Dad?" Janessa asked in surprise. "Not us?"

"No. Sorry."

"Oh, wow!" Janessa's eyes were wide. "That's incredible. I thought... you'd remember your childhood and everything. I thought that when you met Floyd and the kids... well, you'd start to remember. That's the way it always works on TV." She gave a little shrug. "I know you can't judge real life by TV, but I thought that was the way that it worked."

"They said that familiar things might help to trigger memories, to bring it back. But so far... no, nothing has really made a difference. I don't remember any of this. Not here, not... anyone."

Janessa swore. She and Alex exchanged looks.

"You must have all kinds of questions, then," Janessa said. "Don't you? What do you want to know?"

"I'm watching TV," Dad pointed out, gesturing at the program he had on.

Janessa flapped a hand in his direction, brushing it off. "You're supposed to be visiting. This is Ronnie! Your long-lost daughter! Don't you want to talk to her? To help her?"

"She came and visited before. She can't tell us anything about what happened. Or won't. So, what's the use of asking her about it?"

Janessa rolled her eyes. She looked back at Ronnie. "Just ignore him," she said. "He's not really mad. When he's mad, you'll know it."

"Oh... okay."

"So? You must have all kinds of questions."

"I don't know. I don't know what to ask. You guys..." she considered, "are you married? Do you have families?"

"No. Yours are the only grandkids. Mom and Dad spoil them rotten. Let them do all kinds of things that we were never allowed to do," Janessa raised her voice, pointing this comment at their father. "Feed them all kinds of sweets and let them get away with murder."

"Grandparents are allowed to spoil kids," Dad said. "That's our job. It's the parents' job to raise them. Teach them how to behave. It was different when they were here... while... you know."

"While Floyd was in jail," Alex contributed. He raised an eyebrow at Ronnie. "Did you know that part? That he was in jail and Mom and Dad took the kids?"

"Yeah, I know."

"I'll bet you do," Janessa agreed with a little laugh. "Floyd's been pretty bitter about it all along. I don't suppose all is forgiven now that you're back."

"No," Ronnie shook her head slowly. "He said that I could go back there to live. In the spare room. But... it's kind of weird. I wouldn't want to. He did tell me about being in prison. I know it's no fun. But... I didn't want that to happen. I didn't leave... because I wanted him to suffer."

"Of course not," Janessa said quickly. "I don't mean that. I just know the way he is. He's been pretty miserable about it. Never let it go, all these years. Still complains about how he can't get a good job, and being in prison ruined everything for him. The injustice. He still talks about it."

If Janessa were trying to make Ronnie feel better, she wasn't doing a very good job of it. Ronnie looked at her father, who didn't appear to be listening anymore, and then back at Janessa.

"What about before I left?" she asked. "What was Floyd like then? Did we... get along?"

Janessa bit her lip and stared at the TV, but Ronnie didn't think that she was watching the show.

"You and Floyd..." Janessa sighed. "Well, you never were lovey-dovey. Over the moon. I mean, you liked each other well enough, but you were never... mushy... starry-eyed. With having kids so fast, and financial stuff... you were so young! I can't believe that we all just acted like it was normal for a seventeen-year-old to marry a twenty-five-year old right out of high school. You never had any time to find yourself, mature, or even get to know Floyd."

"What happened?" Ronnie tried to build a picture in her mind. That young bride in the pictures. Floyd, who she had met. The children were only four and two when she left. "Did we fight?"

"Sure you fought. I don't mean you didn't love each other anymore, or were threatening divorce, or anything like that. Just... it was stressful. You fought. You argued over money, over parenting, the housework, chores, how late Floyd worked... all the usual. I mean, it's perfectly normal for couples to go through tough times, especially that early in the marriage. Perfectly normal."

"I guess."

"I didn't think you'd stay together," Alex confided, his eyes on the TV. "I thought... Mom and Dad rushed you into it too fast, and once you got tired of the fighting, you would separate. Share custody or give him visitation, and he'd give you child support, and you'd be better off living in different houses."

"Really?" Janessa looked at Alex. "I never knew that."

Alex shrugged. "I just figured. What do I know? I was just a kid myself. But I didn't think it was going to last."

"You thought I got married too fast?"

Both siblings nodded immediately. Dad looked away from the TV. "You needed someone to look after you," he said. "Someone more mature, who could help you through... your issues."

"My issues?"

They were all silent, looking at each other. Dad looked back at the show. "Well, maybe issues is the wrong word... but you always had some... difficulties."

"What kind of difficulties?"

He didn't answer right away. Ronnie looked at Alex and Janessa, but they didn't jump in with any suggestions.

"You were just... immature. You needed a good, stable provider. Like Floyd. You weren't ever going to go to university or be some big executive. But you liked kids. You were good with them. Being a stay-at-home mom was a good choice for you."

"Until it got to be too much," Alex offered, brows raised.

"She didn't leave because of the kids," Dad said. "Those are good kids. It wasn't because of them. It was just..." He scowled. "I don't know. She was never good with stress."

Ronnie breathed out. *Never good with stress.* Well, that at least sounded like her. She wanted to just run away. She had already tried once to just run away. Or drive away. She wanted to veg in front of the TV, not to discuss the past or her psyche. She didn't want to have to deal with the stress. Just to leave it behind and think of more pleasant things.

"What happened when I got stressed?" she asked.

Dad rubbed a hand over his bald head. He looked toward the kitchen.

"Cynthia? Did you need any help out there?"

They all looked at him. Mom popped out of the kitchen and looked into the living room.

"I already said I don't need anything. What's wrong? Is something wrong?"

Janessa giggled. "I think Dad wants to be rescued. He's got himself into a corner."

Mom looked at her husband, puzzled. "What does she mean?"

"Nothing is wrong. I just wanted to know if you needed any help. Get you something from the storeroom or open a jar or something."

She smiled, still looking uncertain, and shook her head. "No. I'll call you if I need anything... *manly* done."

Mom retreated back to the kitchen. Dad looked back at the TV and ignored his children. Ronnie looked at him, and then at the other two.

"Was I depressed? Schizophrenic? What? I should know what my history is, shouldn't I?"

"That was a long time ago," Janessa said. "A lot has changed since then. You seem like you're really together now. Matured."

"I am thirty-three, not seventeen anymore," Ronnie pointed out, "and I've had four kids."

Janessa's jaw dropped. "Four?"

"Well, that I know of. The police investigator seems to think that I've started dozens of families everywhere I've gone. But a person can only have kids at certain intervals, right? At one per year, so I couldn't have had more than... eleven since I left."

Dad looked over, his face red and thunderous.

"You will not talk that way here! It's not a joking matter!"

Ronnie pressed her mouth closed and swallowed. She felt horrible. Her stomach clenched tightly and she watched him, worried that he was going to get out of his chair and come after her. He looked so angry. Of course, he was right. It was serious, what she had done. A horrific thing she had done to the two families that she knew about, the four children. In addition to her own parents and siblings. It wasn't funny to joke about having eleven more children after she had left Floyd. Even having just two more was devastating to her. Those poor children were now motherless and Ronnie hadn't even been legally married to their father. She wondered if he could come after her for child support, now that he was raising them alone. Garnish her wages to help to care for them. Even if he didn't, she should probably try to do something. Kids had school fees. Orthodontia. Psychiatric bills.

"I'm sorry," she said, barely able to voice the apology. "You're right. That was… inappropriate." Ronnie looked down at her hands. "I feel bad for those kids. Kent and Carrie, and the other children that I left. I never meant to hurt anybody. I don't think. I just… I don't remember what happened. I guess it was just too much."

"You *should* feel bad for what you did," Dad said. "That's not the way that you were raised. If you needed help, you should have asked for it. Running away is never the answer."

They were all silent for a while, the mood of the room subdued.

"Because this family never runs away," Janessa said suddenly, "or hides anything."

Alex looked at her. Dad scowled and stared at the TV screen, starting to flip restlessly through the channels.

"What does that mean?" Ronnie asked.

Janessa considered for a minute before answering, her eyes flicking over to Alex for support.

"It's just… the way that we've grown up in this family. We all come from different backgrounds, and the way that we deal with it is just… to forget about it. Pretend that it doesn't even exist. Live in the present. Think about what's best for the family."

"Because you're adopted," Ronnie said slowly. "You're just supposed to forget about what happened before you came to this family?"

"Yeah," Janessa nodded. "Forget everything. Cut all ties."

Alex scratched at an invisible spot on his pants. "When you become part of the Dare family, that's all you know. No contact with old family or friends. No talking about them, even. You have a new life and you live without a past."

Ronnie pondered over this. She rubbed at the frown lines in the middle of her eyebrows where a knot was forming. "But isn't that… doesn't that sound like what I've been doing?"

"Well... we're not talking *literally* forgetting," Janessa contributed.

"But that's right, isn't it? That's what I've been doing. Forgetting about the past. Starting a new family with a fresh slate, completely new. That's what I've been doing the past eleven years."

"We never told you to do that," Dad growled. "Don't you act like this is all our fault. We raised you to be better. You were married and the mother of two children. You were supposed to stay there and raise them up, not run off somewhere. You can't lay this at our feet. We tried to give you the best upbringing we could."

"No. I didn't mean that. I'm sorry. I just mean... there's sort of a parallel. Maybe... something broke in my brain and my subconscious decided to take it literally..."

"This isn't because of us," he repeated.

"No. Of course not. I was an adult. Whatever happened was all on me, not you."

He nodded.

Ronnie watched the TV for a few minutes, trying to distract herself and to let the room calm down a little. She didn't want to get her father upset. Every time that he raised his voice or expressed disapproval, she felt like a little child, waiting for the belt. Sick and frightened and guilty. Had he whipped her when she was young? Was she unconsciously afraid, reliving whatever he had done even though she couldn't remember it?

When he seemed to be fully engaged in a TV show again, Ronnie looked at Janessa.

"So... what kind of a background did you come from? You weren't a baby when they got you?"

"No. Not a baby! I was... I guess I was six, almost seven." She looked at their father. "Been here ever since."

"But you don't live here." Ronnie gestured to their surroundings.

"No!" Janessa laughed. "Little birds get kicked out of the nest. Gotta learn how to fly."

"Do you remember your family? From before? What were they like?"

Janessa cleared her throat and looked at Alex.

"Didn't you get the part about forgetting your previous family and never talking about them again?" Alex asked Ronnie. "We don't talk about it. Not at all. I don't even remember them anymore. My birth family. I've been able to completely block them out." He looked pleased with himself over this. "I was eleven when I came here. Almost a teenager!"

"You don't remember your real family at all?"

"*This* is our real family," Alex said. "This is our forever family. The families that we were with before, they were just... surrogates. That's just how we came into this family."

"That must be really weird."

He cocked an eyebrow at her. "Weirder than your situation?"

Ronnie had almost managed to forget about her own situation. Maybe that was what they all shared. The ability to forget.

"Well... of course that's weird... but I prefer to think about other people's situations."

The three of them all laughed.

"What's it like for you?" Janessa asked after a while. "I mean... we're talking about intentionally moving on. Forgetting your troubles from the past so that you can make a future for yourself. But what's it like to unintentionally forget? To come back here and meet your family again, like it was the first time? To realize what you've missed?"

Ronnie had been avoiding thinking about it as much as possible. She studied the room around her. It was completely foreign to her —other than the fact that she had been there once before—it was like she had never lived there. When she looked at the pictures over the mantel, she could pick out herself, her children, Janessa and Alex. But she didn't feel like a part of it. The books on the shelf might have been ones that she had read when she was younger. Maybe for school. But she had no memory of them. There were clay vases and crafts made by children's hands. Had she made one of them? Had Kent or Carrie?

Had any of the furniture or decorations in the living room

changed since she had lived there? Or was everything still precisely the same?

"It seems like someone else's life," Ronnie confessed. "I feel like it's one big prank, and at some point everyone is going to say 'surprise' and laugh, and admit that it was all just made up. I feel like I'm an actor in a play, only I don't know my part."

"Did you just melt when you met Kent and Carrie? They're such sweet children. I bet that you loved them, even though you couldn't remember them."

Ronnie started to chew on her thumbnail. "Well, no. They're pretty mad at me. And they should be," she hurried on, "that's not saying anything against them. But it's hard to feel love toward an angry teenager you don't even know. I just feel… attacked. It's unfair. I'm not the mom that they lost. Even if I am."

[VI]

Ronnie wanted to quit her job. She wanted to find something else. Somewhere they didn't know who she was and that she'd been arrested. But she found it impossible whenever she clocked in. Everyone was so nice to her. They'd even covered her bail, which ended up being a really bad investment. Gordon hadn't even censured her when she had broken the terms of her bail and been sent back to jail. He should have. He barely knew her and certainly should never have invested money in her.

So Ronnie found herself unable to give notice. But it was getting harder and harder each day to get to the office and to check in and do her work. Harder to wake up in the morning. Harder to drag herself out of bed and to drive herself to work. She had to have the job to survive, but she could barely function. She wasn't doing well, and it would probably be better for the company if she just quit and they didn't have to carry her anymore.

Then came the morning that she couldn't get out of bed again. Ronnie turned off her alarm and went back to sleep. The phone rang and she ignored it. She managed to drag herself out of bed to make a trip to the bathroom, and made a cup of coffee that she didn't drink, just climbing back into bed again and finding it later in the evening, cold, still on the counter.

Ronnie told herself that she was just sick. She'd feel better the next morning and she'd get up and go to work. But she didn't get out of the apartment the next day, either. When her body got too sore from lying in bed all day, she got up and sat in front of the TV, eventually falling asleep there.

Day and night became a blur. The TV played constantly in the background, giving her restless dreams when she fell asleep. She unplugged the phone and let the battery run down so that it would stop ringing. There were even some knocks on her door, but Ronnie ignored them, afraid of facing the police again, having to look at more pictures of forlorn families or face more questions that she simply couldn't answer.

Adah Cruz would not normally have been part of a simple welfare check. Certainly, she wouldn't have gone on it herself, but would have simply have sent a subordinate if it were in her circle of responsibilities. But the subject of the check was Ronnie Plum. No one had seen her and they had received more than one concerned call.

Since Ronnie was no longer on bail or under charges, there had been no reason to keep her under surveillance. They couldn't just surveil random people on the chance that they might commit some crime. The crimes that Ronnie had been guilty of were not violent murders or thefts, not drugs, not anything that they could watch for to go down again. She had taken years to start a family, head to a breakdown, and to run off again. That in itself was not a crime, except maybe for failing to provide for her children. It was only taking on a false identity that they could prosecute her for, and for the time being, she had her own identity back. She had her own identification numbers and cards. They didn't have anything to charge her with, let alone any reason to keep a watch on her, which was incredibly expensive for the department.

When the welfare check came in, Adah snatched up the chance to look in on Ronnie again and see what was going on. Ronnie had probably run again, though if she had, there was nothing that Adah could do about it.

They knocked on the door. Eddie rapped it sharply. When Ronnie didn't respond, he called out her name. Still no answer. No sound from within. The sounds of a TV that was coming from a neighboring apartment. No footsteps or call for help. Eddie rapped again. Still no answer. He stepped back, nodding at Adah.

She slid the landlord's key into the lock and swung the door open, pushing it quickly and standing back out of the way. There was no movement from within. They entered cautiously, but without drawn weapons. There was no indication that Ronnie was a danger or that there was anyone else there who might be. It was just a welfare check. Look in and make sure she was okay and hadn't fallen in the tub or taken a bottle of pills.

The TV was not the neighbor's, but Ronnie's, which was the first indication that she had not run away this time. There was a litter of unwashed dishes in the kitchenette. Ronnie was not sitting in the easy chair in the living room, but there was evidence that she had spent plenty of time there lately. At least, a lot of garbage had accumulated there since the last time Adah had been in the apartment.

They moved on to the bedroom and that was where they found her. Ronnie's slim form was stretched out on the bed in the ratty t-shirt and yoga pants that served as her pajamas. She was thin, pale, and unmoving. The room stank of sweat and rank, unwashed body. Eddie moved into the room first, shaking the girl and then feeling for a pulse on her thin neck.

"She's alive," he confirmed.

Adah had dared to hope, not being able to smell any decomp.

"I'll call an ambulance." Adah glanced around the bare room. "Any sign of overdose? Illness? Injury?"

Eddie gingerly checked her wrists and pulled back the covers she clutched to her chest to get a better look at her body.

"Nothing obvious. I'll check the bathroom."

He left Adah there and ducked into the small bathroom.

"I don't see anything. No drugs or prescriptions. Tylenol is almost full."

Adah nodded at him, waiting for the emergency dispatched to pick up. As they waited for the ambulance, they took a look around the apartment. The welfare check call enabled Adah to check things like fridge and cupboards for sufficient food, and they found nothing. The place was bare. There had obviously been food there to start with, as evidence by the dirty dishes, but at some point Ronnie had run out and had not bothered to go out to buy more.

"Either she's been sick or she's a psych case," Adah said.

"We already know she's a psych case," Eddie pointed out.

"Yes, well... at this point it looks like she can't take care of herself; we'll ask them to put a hold on her."

Eddie nodded agreement. "Looks that way."

Ronnie awoke in a hospital bed, with an IV in her arm. She looked around listlessly at first, barely even taking in her surroundings. Eventually, it all started to seep back. She sighed deeply.

"You awake and alive over there?" a girlish voice asked.

Ronnie turned her head toward the sound. There was a curtain pulled between them, but somewhere beside her was another bed, with another patient in it.

"Yeah, looks like it," Ronnie admitted.

"You attempt suicide? They don't usually put suicides in this section. Not to start out with."

"No. No, I just..." Ronnie grunted as she moved her body and tried to find a comfortable position. "I guess I just... wasn't feeling well, or something. I don't really know what happened."

"Huh. I'm Faith. You?"

"Ronnie." Ronnie didn't say anything for a while, not sure how to continue the conversation, or if she wanted to. But it turned out that she was lonely and she did want to continue the conversation. "So... what are you here for?"

"Cutting."

"Cutting... your wrists? I thought you said they didn't put suicides in this section."

"No. Not attempting suicide. Just... cutting... you know, to make me feel better."

"How would cutting make you feel better?"

"Endorphins. It really does work. Makes you all calm and relaxed. But... it's self-destructive and addictive, so you get caught and they send you here."

"Right."

"You never cut?"

"No."

"Take pills? Anything?"

"No. I just..." Ronnie trailed off, not wanting to discuss her coping mechanisms.

"What?" Faith prodded.

Ronnie didn't answer. She punched at the pillow, trying to get more comfortable. She was too restless to go back to sleep, but she didn't want to be awake. There were noises from Faith's direction and in a few minutes, the sound of the curtain being pulled in the track, and Faith was peeking around at her.

"Hey, roomie," she greeted. She sat back down on her own bed, looking Ronnie over.

Ronnie also studied her. Faith wasn't at all what she had expected. With the soft voice and a name like Faith, she had expected an angelic face. Slim, willowy body. Even knowing about the cutting, Ronnie had expected someone who looked frail and vulnerable.

But Faith looked like none of that. Dyed black hair. Lots of tattoos down her arms. A hefty girl. Solidly built, like someone who would be comfortable on the back of a Harley. She didn't have on any makeup or piercings, but Ronnie was sure that when she was out in public, there were plenty of piercings and stark, dramatic makeup.

Faith had been evaluating Ronnie at the same time.

"Anorexia?" she guessed. "You look like you've lost a lot of weight recently."

Ronnie had, having given up food for the past little while. "No... I've just been sick."

"Sick with what? This is psych. Not stomach viruses."

"I don't really feel like talking about it."

"Well, they're all about the talk here. If you don't talk to me, you'll be talking to someone else. You're going to have therapists poking into every private corner. Get used to it. There's no keeping quiet around here."

"I'll walk to a psychiatrist if I have to," Ronnie said, "but I don't want to tell everybody my problems."

"Yeah. Good luck with that, all right?"

Ronnie shrugged.

Dr. Wanger looked at Ronnie over the tops of his glasses, and back down at the paper file in front of him. Ronnie could tell that he had at least the records from Dr. Able. Maybe there was more too, it seemed to be pretty thick for the file of someone who had just been admitted.

"Why don't you tell me about your history," Dr. Wanger suggested.

"Looks like you already have it all there." Ronnie folded her arms protectively in front of her, covering up the vulnerability she felt sitting there in a hospital gown having to talk about her history or innermost thoughts. "That's more than I know about myself."

He chuckled at that. "Tell me anyway," he cajoled. "I'll tell you if you get anything wrong."

Even in her melancholy mood, Ronnie found herself smiling at that.

"I mean it. I don't really know anything about myself. I have amnesia." The word always made her feel odd. She didn't like to use it. A clinical word, thrown around in budget TV movies and treated like a plot twist or a joke. Ronnie didn't feel like it really described her. She wasn't crazy or crippled. She wasn't mentally ill. She just happened not to be able to remember most of her life.

"How far back does your memory go?"

"About a year."

"Good. You've at least had a year to learn about yourself. How about before that? Your childhood?"

"No. Nothing else."

"Nothing from your childhood."

"No."

"Have you visited any old haunts to see if they would trigger memories?"

"Yeah. Nothing happened."

"Fine, fine," he assured her. "Not to worry. Your parents are here?" he asked, flipping through pages of the file.

"Yes."

"You've met them? What did you learn about your childhood?"

"Well… there's Mom and Dad and me and two adopted kids, Alex and Janessa. They were foster kids that stayed with them."

"Uh-huh. Did you meet them too?"

"Yeah."

"Wonderful! Were you adopted from foster care as well?"

"No. I was their natural daughter."

"Interesting. Were they not able to have more children after you?"

"I don't know." Ronnie thought about it. "I think they just liked having foster kids."

"Some people find it very fulfilling. Helping less fortunate children out."

"I think it's really nice. They took care of my kids when I was gone and… my ex-husband was in jail."

"That's nice of them," Dr. Wanger agreed. He didn't ask her why she had been gone and why Floyd had been in jail, and Ronnie didn't offer it.

"The kids really like them. They call them Nana and Papa. So, I guess they did a good job. They're still really close."

"What did you think of them when you met them?"

Ronnie considered. "I don't know. They seemed a little... weird. But I guess you can't judge real families by what you see on TV."

"We'd have a pretty skewed view of the world if we did. Weird in what way? Were you comfortable around them?"

"No. Not really. I felt like... they treated me like a lost dog. Something that they owned. Instead of... another person. I haven't had anyone treat me like that before." She hesitated. "That I can remember," she tacked on.

"I imagine they did feel pretty possessive about having you back again. Maybe afraid that they would lose you again. Or that you would not want to be with them."

"They acted like I did something wrong. Leaving my families behind. When I had an episode. It wasn't like it was something that I wanted to do. It wasn't like I planned it. But they acted like... that wasn't the way they raised me. Like I had done it out of anger. I don't know."

Dr. Wanger nodded. "That would feel awkward. Anything else? Something that seemed out of place?"

Ronnie shrugged. She stared at the shiny clock on Dr. Wanger's desk. It was brass and glass and she could see the inner workings spinning away. "None of it seems right," she said. "I drew pictures for Dr. Able, and the picture that I drew for family didn't look anything like my real family. It feels like they are all impostors. Just trying to trick me into thinking that they are really my family."

"Have you talked to them about these feelings?"

"No!" Ronnie was horrified. "Why would I do that?"

"It's important to have open and honest communication. Especially in a situation as difficult as this one."

"They don't seem very open to hearing what I have to say... It's like... they want to wipe out what happened in the past. We're not allowed to talk about it. We're just supposed to focus on the present."

"Focusing on the present is one thing. But I think there's a whole lot of the past that you're going to need to be reminded of. I think that you should have them come visit you here. Maybe we can have a session together. Maybe a facilitator would help."

Ronnie had already been through x-ray, which she had found frustrating enough, having had to wait for several hours, then been constantly repositioned for the x-ray, as if they were looking for the most uncomfortable position possible. Then she had to wait for the brain imaging that they wanted to do, and then the procedure itself, which involved lying in a coffin-like chamber until she felt like she really was going to die. She was supposed to be as still as possible, and she tried, worried that if she moved they would have to start all over again. But her breathing started to feel labored, her legs were itching like crazy, and she really had to pee.

"Are you almost done?" she called out finally, "I don't know how much longer I can do this!"

"You're doing fine," a bored voice responded. "We'll be done shortly and you'll be able to get out of there. Please don't talk. Stay as still as possible."

Ronnie focused on not moving her restless legs, though she supposed it was her head that really mattered, and maybe she could shift her legs slightly without it messing up the test.

Finally, she felt the bed start to move and she slid out of the tunnel feet first.

"You did really well," said a smiling, curly-haired nurse who smiled down at her. "You can go get dressed and there is a bathroom down the hall."

Ronnie moved stiffly. She got to her feet and shuffled quickly out into the corridor to find the toilet.

Then there was another wait for the doctor to review the test results with her.

He had introduced himself earlier, but Ronnie couldn't remember his name when she sat back down in his office again, this time to look at the big computer display on the wall where he arranged the images. Ronnie studied them, looking for cracks in the skull on the x-ray, or some kind of hole or inactive area on the colored brain scan.

What would the tests show? Were her dreams about Floyd trying to bury her, injured but still alive, true? Were they memories? Something that he'd really done? If she'd been hit over the head that hard, surely it would show up on the x-ray.

"Did you find anything?" she asked.

"Well, it turns out there's nothing in there," the doctor teased. He waited for Ronnie to laugh at his joke. "Actually, everything appears to be normal. No old fractures. No lesions or tumors in the brain, nothing that might indicate an old injury or more recent trauma. As far as we can tell, your brain is perfectly healthy."

Ronnie slumped back in her chair, disappointed.

Had she really wanted to be told that she was brain injured? That Floyd really had tried to kill her or that she'd been in a devastating car accident? Did she really want an answer that badly?

She did.

"So... nothing. What does that mean?"

"I guess that it means that your memory loss is likely psychological," he said. "It's still possible that there is some physical problem that we were not able to see, something that didn't leave any scarring or other traces. If an injury had caused your memory loss, I would expect it to be pretty severe. But there's nothing here."

"So, it's back to the drawing board. Or to the couch."

"I'm sorry I couldn't be of more help. I know this must be really difficult for you."

"Yeah. Well, thanks for doing all that."

[VII]

Sleeping at the hospital was difficult, even though they gave her something before bed to 'help her settle.' Ronnie moved around restlessly, unable to find a comfortable position. It wasn't as uncomfortable as the bunk in prison, but it was still just as hard to get to sleep. Her mind kept going back to the session with Dr. Wanger. She didn't want to have her family in to visit and dredge up the past, even though she couldn't remember the past and it would be easier to function if she at least knew something about herself. She really didn't want to remember. Maybe that was why she couldn't.

Ronnie closed her eyes and forced herself to lie still, completely unmoving. Barely even breathing. If she didn't let herself toss and turn, she would soon fall asleep and then she could forget and be oblivious again, just for a little while.

When she did fall asleep, she was still restless. Slipping in an out of consciousness, her mind racing like a hamster on a wheel, spinning but going nowhere. As night wore into early morning, she started to dream.

It wasn't a dream of being buried this time, though she had dreamed that one several times and it sometimes made her afraid to fall asleep.

The noise this time was a tap running. Not a sink, but the deeper, broader sound of a bathtub being filled. And accompanying it was a whole cadre of confusing feelings. Guilt and disgust. Anger. Her body hurt. It felt bruised and raw. There were voices, a man and a woman.

"You hurt her. She's bleeding," the woman said.

"It's nothing. She'll be fine."

"It's not just a little blood. It's too much. You were too rough!"

Ronnie groaned, trying to escape the dream. Her head was dizzy and nauseated. She wanted to wake up. Maybe she had the flu and it had triggered this bad dream. Everything seemed fuzzy and far away.

"Just shut up and get her cleaned up."

Ronnie felt herself being lowered into warm water. A spasm of pain wrenched through her, starting somewhere deep inside.

"Mommy!"

"Oh, hush, Ronnie. Let me get you cleaned up and then you can go to sleep."

Ronnie was crying. "Mommy..."

"Shhh..."

"Mommy..."

She floated in the warm water. Time seemed to be suspended as well. Ronnie continued to cry, the tears flooding her cheeks and running down her throat. Eventually, she was lifted out of the water. The cold air immediately made her shiver. When she was put down, the pain got worse. As she was toweled off, Ronnie tried to roll up into a ball, holding herself and gritting her teeth against the pain. Her sobs grew louder in her own ears. It was unbearable.

"I'm taking her to emergency," Mommy said.

CHAPTER

Three

AGE 8

(I)

"Who hurt her?" the cop demanded.

Ronnie cracked her eyelids open just a tiny bit in order to look at him again. Her body didn't hurt so much now. She was tired and nauseated from the painkiller they had given her. The treatment room she was in smelled like bleach and bathrooms. Not a nice chlorine smell like at the pool, but a nasty, harsh smell that burned her nose and turned her stomach.

The policeman was talking to her mother, a sloppily-dressed, overweight, dark-haired woman who sat in the chair next to Ronnie's hospital bed. The policeman spoke politely, in a precise, even voice, but his eyes were angry and his expression grim. Ronnie let her lids close again and listened to them, feigning sleep.

"I don't know who hurt her," Mom said. "She didn't tell me that anything was wrong, and it wasn't until later that I noticed how much pain she was in. It seemed to be getting worse, and she couldn't stop crying... all curled up in pain... I thought maybe she had appendicitis."

"Who had access to her? Who else is in the household?"

"Nothing could have happened at home," Mom insisted. "It would have to be at school, or maybe on her way home... she doesn't always come home right away like she's supposed to. Sometimes it's quite late."

"And was she late last night?"

"Suppertime... several hours after school, but not after dark."

Ronnie couldn't remember anything from the evening clearly. *Had* she been late getting home? Or had she gone straight home like she was supposed to? Did she stop and talk to someone? Someone who had hurt her?

Ronnie knew she hadn't. But she blocked that thought out, barricaded it away. Maybe she had been accosted walking home from school. Or maybe she'd had an accident at home. It could have been an accident.

The cop's voice was skeptical. "The doctor says that she was bleeding quite heavily. There was a lot of trauma. If she had come home from school like that, you would have known."

"Not if she was trying to hide it," Mom insisted. "Maybe she felt embarrassed or guilty. She didn't want me to know something had happened. I didn't know what it was, not until we got here and the doctor said."

"Ma'am, that's not believable. So, why don't we talk about what really happened? I understand you are worried about what is going to happen to your husband. But you need to be thinking about your child. She was badly hurt. You need to protect her. Get him put away where he can't hurt any other little girls. You know it won't end here."

"It wasn't my husband," Mom said tightly. "He wasn't even home. Something happened at school. Or on her way home."

There was a long period of silence. Ronnie ventured another covert look, just cracking her eyelids. He was writing in a notepad, a frown crease between his heavy eyebrows. He looked up at Mom again.

"There is alcohol in her system."

"We keep a little wine for special occasions. She must have gotten into it. Maybe she thought it would kill the pain and she wouldn't have to tell me what had happened."

"Why would she think that? Why would she try to keep it from you?"

"Kids," Mom rolled her eyes. "I have five of them. Do you have any?"

He gave one nod. Ronnie closed her eyes the rest of the way as he swiveled his head toward her to look at her again.

"Then you tell me. You've never had one of them get hurt doing something he wasn't supposed to be doing and then not want to tell you he was hurt? I remember my friend falling out of a tree when I was a kid. We knew we weren't supposed to be climbing trees, and she thought that she could keep her broken arm a secret from her mother. If she just didn't tell her mother, no one would notice that her bone was poking out of the skin."

"Yes, kids cover things up," the policeman conceded.

"There you go. That's what happened. She knew she wasn't supposed to be dawdling after school and was supposed to come straight home. Or she knew she wasn't supposed to talk to strangers or go into someone's house. Maybe it was even one of her friends' parents and she didn't want to get her friend in trouble. I don't know. Kids get themselves in trouble and then try to cover it up."

Ronnie felt like she was floating behind her closed lids. It wasn't her mother's fault this had happened. It wasn't her father's fault. It was Ronnie's fault for breaking the rules. She didn't remember what she had done, but she knew it had to be true. She liked to stay out late, playing in the park. Building their play fort in the trees. Going to friends' houses when she knew she was supposed to be home for supper. She was always getting told off for dawdling on the way home from school.

When Ronnie woke up again, there was a different man beside the bed and her mother was not there. Had she been kicked out? Gone to get something to eat? Gone home to take care of the twins or to do her job?

Ronnie blinked at the man. He had a friendly-looking face and twinkly eyes. Curly, sandy-colored hair. He seemed vaguely familiar and she tried to remember where she had seen him before. The painkillers were still messing with her mental processes.

"Hi, Ronnie. I don't know if you remember me. My name is Mr. Samuels."

Ronnie reached into her memory, but everything was fuzzy. "I… don't know."

"I'm your sister Ruby's social worker."

"Oh. Oh, yeah." Of course. Ronnie should have known that. He had been by to visit her mom more than once. Mom was always grouchy after a visit with him.

"There was another social worker here to talk to you last night," Mr. Samuels said. "Do you remember that?"

Ronnie shook her head. It hurt. She winced and rubbed her temples. "No. It's all pretty blurry."

"You weren't in very good shape last night. You're a lot better this morning. So, maybe it would be a good time for you and me to talk."

"About what? Ruby?"

"No, not about Ruby. About you. You were assigned a social worker of your own last night, like I was saying, but I know you and your family, Ronnie. I'll get your file transferred over to me. In the meantime, I'd like to spend some time getting to know you. Help you tell your story."

"What story?"

"About what happened yesterday."

Ronnie closed her eyes, resting her head and thinking back. "Don't remember."

"I think you do. You might not want to talk about it, but I think you can remember what happened just last night."

A few images pressed forward out of the blur, but nothing that was clear. Nothing Ronnie could grasp hold of.

"Your dad hurt you," Mr. Samuels said softly.

"No." Ronnie could remember that much. She could remember Mom saying that it wasn't her dad. He wasn't even home. Though Ronnie didn't know where else he would have been.

"Your mom brought you in late at night. Who else was at home that could have done this?"

"I… no one… I don't know… Mom said… it was after school."

"Is that true?"

"I was… I was late getting home from school."

"Did something happen after school?" Mr. Samuels leaned forward. "Did someone hurt you?"

Ronnie nodded hesitantly. That must have been what happened.

"Who?"

"I don't remember. It's all foggy."

"You don't remember where you went? Whether it was someone at school or someone you saw on the way home?"

"No." Ronnie rubbed the space between her eyebrows, where it hurt from frowning and concentrating so hard.

"When were you drinking?"

"Drinking?" Ronnie thought of the glass of milk that she always had with her supper. Even when Mom and Dad were out somewhere, or too busy to make dinner, Chloe always insisted that each of the children have a glass of milk with their suppers. Even if all they were eating was a handful of chips or leftovers scavenged from the fridge.

But Mr. Samuels wasn't talking about milk.

"You were drinking alcohol last night. You were pretty intoxicated when she brought you in."

Maybe that was why Ronnie couldn't clearly recall the evening's events.

"I don't know. It was… for the pain."

"Who gave it to you?"

She flashed to her father giving her a cup of juice. She closed her eyes, shaking her head and trying to visualize it. She knew where the wine was. In one of the lower cupboards in the kitchen. It was strictly off-limits to the children, and none of them would ever dare touch it. Mom said that's what Ronnie had done. Ronnie would never do that. Her father wouldn't have given it to her either. Neither of them would give it to her. That was only for grown-ups and special occasions.

Mr. Samuels sat back in his chair, sighing. "You were pretty drunk, and that can make it harder to remember what happened. But I want you to work on it, okay? Really work to remember it. You wouldn't want this to happen again, would you? Not to you or to anyone else."

Once the doctor said that Ronnie was okay to go home, the other social worker said that she would take Ronnie to her new home.

"No," Ronnie objected, resisting the guiding hand on her shoulder. "I want to go to my house. Not somewhere else."

She lived in terror of being sent to a foster home. Ruby had been sent to a foster home when she wouldn't get along with their mother. That's what happened to girls who were bad. Ruby told her how bad foster care was. She told Ronnie stories about some of the foster homes she had been in and the things that went on there.

"We need to know that you are somewhere safe while we investigate," Mrs. Holmes soothed. "If everything is okay, it will just be for a few days. But you need somewhere to sleep, don't you?" She gave Ronnie an encouraging little smile, her eyes dead and cold.

"No. Everything is fine at home. I'm safe there! I don't want to go anywhere else!"

"You don't get to choose, honey. I'm sorry. The adults are going to have to decide what is best for you in this case. Social Services and the doctors agree that we need to look into this a little further before making any decision."

Ronnie looked back at the hospital bed. Only moments before, she had been happy to leave it behind. The doctor had given her instructions, told her that she needed to take it easy and get lots of rest in order to heal properly. She had pictured herself in her bed at home, warm and cozy, free from having to go to school or do chores.

"I'll stay here instead," she negotiated. "Until you decide it's okay for me to go home."

The social worker's eyes gave away no emotion. "I'm sorry, Ronnie. But you have been released. You don't need the hospital anymore, just some rest. The foster home will make sure that you are taken care of. We'll give your mom and dad a bit of a break while we try to figure out what happened to you."

Ronnie stood there, not moving. The social worker gave her shoulder a little nudge. Ronnie still didn't move.

"Ronnie, let's go," Mrs. Holmes said with iron in her voice. "Now!"

Ronnie went. She didn't think that the social worker would hit her, but she wasn't one hundred percent sure. And even if she didn't hit, she was bigger and stronger than Ronnie and wouldn't likely have any trouble dragging her out to the car by force. Ronnie couldn't fight back in her condition.

She shuffled her feet and moved slowly. The heavy painkillers had worn off and the Tylenol they gave her didn't do much to dull the pain. Every step hurt. She had to stop and rest in the hallway. Mrs. Holmes stood waiting for her, tapping her foot.

"I'm sorry," Ronnie said. "It really hurts."

Mrs. Holmes's face softened. "I'm so sorry this happened to you," she said. "It's horrible and it should never have happened. Nobody has any right to touch you."

Ronnie closed her eyes and breathed, sitting down in the worn, uncomfortable hallway chair. Nobody could touch her. Nobody would touch her again. It was a reassuring thought, even if it wasn't true.

Eventually, Ronnie had recovered enough to walk to the elevator. Mrs. Holmes had her wait on a bench outside the main doors where she would drive her car up so Ronnie didn't have to walk any farther than necessary.

Ronnie could have just run away. She could just forget about going to a foster family and run away back home again.

But she could barely walk for two minutes at a time. She wasn't going to get too far while Mrs. Holmes went to get the car.

(II)

The house was big, brick, with a rough cobbled sidewalk leading up to the door. Everything looked clean and tidy and well-maintained. Ruby had talked about families who had nothing. Who counted squares of toilet paper and needed the foster care money just to put food in their own mouths. But that didn't seem to be the case with the Dares. They seemed to be pretty well-off. It was nicer than any house that Ronnie had ever lived in.

The woman who opened the door was small, barely taller than Ronnie, with short, dark hair. She smiled at Ronnie and reached out to take her hand, clasping it between her two hands rather than shaking it.

"Hi, Ronnie. I'm so glad to meet you. I'm Mrs. Dare. How are you? Let's get you a place to lie down right away."

Ronnie breathed out a sigh of relief and nodded. Maybe she could just be unobtrusive and stay in bed until Social Services sent her back home. She didn't need to worry about how the foster parents and other foster children would treat her, she could just stay out of the way. Almost like she wasn't even there.

"Come on." Mrs. Dare kept hold of Ronnie's hand and led her into the house, up the stairs, and to a bedroom. There was a bunk bed and a single bed, three in total. Mrs. Dare led her to the single bed and helped her into it, cooing over Ronnie. "There, just get comfy. I can't believe they let you out of the hospital so soon. You should have been there for another week! Well, don't you worry, we know how to take care of you."

Ronnie sighed and closed her eyes, rubbing her cheek against the smooth, soft sheet. "Thank you. I'm..." She yawned. "I'm sleepy."

"Well, you just go straight to sleep. Sleep will help you to heal faster."

Mrs. Dare withdrew and Ronnie could hear her soft patter of footsteps walking away. Mrs. Holmes had obviously followed them to the bedroom and was waiting in the hallway outside. Mrs. Dare started whispering to her as soon as she was out of the room.

"That poor baby! I hope those people get thrown straight in jail and never get a chance to get close to a child again! I can't believe the police haven't arrested them yet."

"They need proof. So far... no one is talking. Without any evidence, there's not much that any of us can do."

"Well, you know what they did to her and you won't put her back into that home. Right?"

"I'll do what I can," Mrs. Holmes answered, as they slipped away down the hall. "I'll do whatever I can to keep Ronnie safe."

There were several other children in the home and Ronnie had a hard time keeping them straight at first. It seemed like they were in and out of the room all the time, and their names always flew by her too fast to sort them out.

She thought that the other two girls in the bedroom were Janessa and Eclipse, and the mob of boys were John, Jace, Mike, and Andrew. Or something like that.

After Mrs. Holmes was gone, Mrs. Dare told Ronnie to call her and Mr. Dare Mom and Dad. Not around the social worker, but privately. There was no need for formality. They were going to be her Mom and Dad while she was there, so she might as well call them that.

The first couple of days, Ronnie slept a lot. It was because her body was trying to heal, Mom Dare told her. But on the third or fourth day, she started to get restless and no longer wanted to stay in bed the whole time. It hurt too much to just lie there all the time. Her muscles and joints felt better being able to get up and move around. Not a lot, but out to the living room to watch TV or to sit down at the kitchen table for a healthy snack, though the kitchen chairs were hard and Ronnie couldn't sit on them for long.

"We're going to need to get you back in school before too long," Mom Dare said. "First, shopping to get some clothes and necessities. Then I'll take you to the school and get you into class."

Ronnie had only needed undies and jammies the first few days, which had been borrowed from the other girls.

"I'm going home, though," she said. "I don't need to go to school here."

"This is your home," Mom Dare said firmly. "You're not going back there."

"I am too! Mr. Samuels said. Mrs. Holmes said. They didn't have any proof that anyone did anything to hurt me."

"You *were* hurt," Mom Dare said. "You can't go back there."

"I'm going home!"

"Mr. Samuels will be coming to talk to you. Tomorrow, we will be going to get you some clothes for school."

"No, I want to go home!"

There was a creak of floorboards and Ronnie knew she'd gotten Dad Dare up out of his easy chair. She looked around in panic. She was surely in for a whipping. The footsteps continued to approach. Slowly. He was in no particular hurry.

Dad Dare moved into the doorway.

He was balding in front, a little paunchy from too much sitting and not enough activity. But he was a lot bigger and stronger than Ronnie and there was no way for her to escape.

"Are you giving your mother lip, Ronnie?" he asked.

Ronnie gulped. "No."

"It sounds to me like you are."

"I'm sorry!"

"You should be apologizing to her."

Ronnie turned to Mom Dare. "I'm sorry," she repeated. She threw her arms around the small woman and held her tightly. "I'm sorry for talking back!"

Mom Dare rubbed her back. "There, there, Ronnie. It's all right. We understand that this is all new to you and you are missing your old life. But this is where you are safe. You're a part of this family now."

"Okay." Ronnie sniffled.

"I know it's hard for you and I wish I could make it easier. I want you to try hard to fit in here and be a real part of this family."

"I will."

She could hear Dad Dare standing in the doorway, breathing. He stayed there for a few more moments, then retreated, leaving her alone. Ronnie breathed out, her body swaying as she relaxed.

"You're tired," Mom said. "Let's get you back to bed. Tomorrow will come soon enough."

"I want to go home," Ronnie told Mr. Samuels when he came to see her again. She had moved out to the living room to sit on the couch, a blanket wrapped protectively around her.

"I know you do, Ronnie. But it's not a safe environment. We can't put you back in a home where there's a danger of you being hurt."

Ronnie rubbed her eyes. She had been sure that once he had finished his investigation, she would be sent back home. He wasn't going to be able to find any reason to keep her out of the home. It would just be a few days, like he had said, and then she would be able to go home again.

"It is safe!" she insisted. "Nobody is going to hurt me. Why do you think that? What did they say?"

Mr. Samuels's mouth was a straight line. No twinkle in his eyes as he tried to formulate his answer.

"Nobody admitted that it was your father who hurt you," he said slowly. "Not your mother or your father, or even Chloe. But nobody could give any believable story about what happened to you, either. Not even you."

"I... I..." Ronnie couldn't come up with the words.

"Everybody is very clear that nothing at all is going on there... but you got hurt, and no one can tell us how. Ronnie, when someone gets assaulted on the way home from school, people don't try to hide it. They call the police. They take you to the hospital. They tell us everything they can so that they can catch the person who did it." His eyes met hers and he gave a tiny head shake. "They don't clean up the evidence and say they have no idea what happened."

"That's not what... that's not how... nobody..."

"You can't deny that you were assaulted," Mr. Samuels said quietly. "Whether you'll admit it or not, it is obvious to us that it was your father. The police may not have enough proof to charge him, but we have enough to keep you from going back there."

Ronnie sat there, stunned. All week, she had just been waiting to go back. To get back to her family and her home and her life. Sitting around in bed all day sounded good until she actually had to do it. She wanted to go back to school and see her friends. To go home and play with Chloe and the twins again. She couldn't fathom that they would keep her from home forever.

"I have to stay here? For good?" She thought about Ruby's stories of her foster homes. Even worse than the thought of staying was the thought that she would never have a permanent home again, jumping from one home to another every few months. How could she do it?

"How have things been going with the Dares?" Mr. Samuels gave her a smile, looking more relaxed with this topic. "How are you getting along?"

"Okay. But... I thought it would only be a few days. You said I could go back home."

"Mrs. Dare seems like a very nice woman," Mr. Samuels observed. "I was glad to be able to place you here. I wasn't sure they would take another child at this point."

Ronnie sniffled and wiped at her nose. "Yeah, she's nice, I guess," she admitted. So far, the woman had not hit her, yelled, or threatened. Not like some of the foster families that Ruby had warned about.

"You haven't had any trouble? No concerns?"

"No."

"You would tell me if there was anything inappropriate going on? I don't want you getting hurt again. You need to know the difference between what's safe and appropriate and what's not. You understand what I'm talking about?"

Ronnie busied herself with smoothing the surface of the blanket around her.

"Ronnie? Do you know what I'm talking about? I don't want you to be afraid of getting hugs and kisses from your foster parents, but if you're being touched in ways that aren't comfortable, you are allowed to say no and I want you to talk to me about it."

Ronnie followed a row of stitches in the blanket with her finger. "Are you my social worker now?"

"Yes, I'm having your file transferred to me. Do you have something we need to talk about?"

Ronnie stared hard at the blanket, thinking about the present and about her time with the Dares, not anything in the past. "No. Everything is good."

"You're sure?"

Ronnie nodded without looking at him. Mr. Samuels waited for a minute for her to add something or change her answer. When Ronnie didn't, he nodded. "Okay. Good. I think the Dares are a great match for you. They're good parents. But if you have any problems or concerns, you let me know."

"Okay."

"No secrets, Ronnie. I want you to be safe."

Mom Dare's face was wreathed in smiles after Mr. Samuels left. She looked at Ronnie, hands on hips.

"Well, Ronnie, are you up to going out shopping?"

Ronnie was anxious to be up and around. Shopping didn't sound like a bad idea. She nodded.

"Yeah... for a little while," she agreed.

"Let's do it, then. You get dressed and we'll pop over to the store while the other kids are still at school."

Ronnie walked back to her bedroom wrapped in the blanket and in a few minutes was dressed and ready to go.

"Why don't you grab a granola bar and an apple," Mom suggested, "in case you get hungry while we're out?"

Snacks, especially a treat like the chocolate chip granola bars Mom Dare kept in the cupboard, had not been offered at home. That was one plus of living with the Dares. Ronnie helped herself and got into the car.

"Oaf—ow!" They hit a speed bump in the mall parking lot and Ronnie cried out and grabbed the handle of the door, trying too late to brace herself against the bounce of the car. She clutched herself, holding her body rigid with the lightning bolt of pain.

"Oh, I'm sorry! I'll slow down. I didn't mean to hit it so fast. Are you okay, Ronnie?"

"Yes. Yes, it's okay. It just..." Ronnie tried to relax again. "It just surprised me. It didn't hurt that much."

"I'm so sorry. I wasn't even thinking." The woman giggled. "Actually, I was thinking about what we were going to get you. I love shopping and I can't wait to get you some cute outfits!"

Used to hand-me-downs from Chloe, Ronnie liked the sound of that. Something cute that wasn't already worn and stained. Purchased at the mall instead of the thrift store. Ronnie had always been told that her parents didn't have 'money to burn' when she asked for something nice for herself. It would appear that the Dares *did* have money to burn.

"Are you excited about getting back to school?" Mom asked as they walked through the mall. Not just looking at the clothes in the big department store at the end, but going to the little boutiques that Ronnie knew were pricey. She hadn't really noticed how the other kids in the family had been dressed. She had mostly slept and watched TV. But keeping seven kids in designer clothing couldn't be cheap. Maybe the Dares weren't just in foster care for the money. Maybe they hoped to get something else out of it. Or maybe they just really liked having kids.

"Did you ever have your own kids?" she asked.

"No, we weren't blessed to have children of our own. But our loss is your gain. I don't think we would ever have thought of foster care if we hadn't had to deal with infertility. I know a lot of families foster even while they have their own kids home, but I had never really considered it."

"Well... you're really nice folks. If I couldn't be at home... I'm glad I got you."

"And we're glad we got you!" Mom gave her a little hug. "I know you aren't happy to learn that you're going to be staying with us long-term, but I'm just tickled!"

Ronnie forced a smile, even though her eyes prickled. "Thanks."

As they walked, Mom put her arm over Ronnie's shoulder, holding her close. "We want to be able to adopt some of our foster children," she confided. "I know it's not easy, and that we're supposed to be working toward reuniting kids with their families, but in cases like yours where you can't go back because of the major risk involved, sometimes after a few years..."

"You would want to adopt me?" Ronnie looked at her, surprised.

"We would love to adopt you. I shouldn't speak for your Dad too, I suppose, because we really haven't discussed it in any detail, but you are one of the nicest little girls that we've had."

They browsed through the clothes racks, Mom occasionally holding up an article of clothing, squinting at Ronnie and deciding what she should try on.

"It's still the honeymoon, of course. But you're not going to cause us any trouble, are you? No problems with bad attitude like some of the kids that we've had."

Ronnie shook her head slowly. "No... I'll be good."

"I know you will. You've had a terrible life before now, but things will be better, I promise. You can leave all of that behind now."

"It wasn't terrible," Ronnie objected, looking up at her foster mom quickly. "It wasn't bad."

Mom's eyebrows went up. "I only know what I've been told by Social Services and that's not much. Maybe they got the wrong impression."

Ronnie nodded. "I got hurt, but it wasn't my dad," she insisted. "My mom and dad took good care of us." She looked at the pile of clothes in Mom Dare's arms. "We didn't have that much money, but that's just clothes. We did okay."

"I got the feeling that your mom wasn't around very much. Your sister watched you."

"Chloe just likes to boss," Ronnie declared. "She bossed us when Mom and Dad are home, too. We don't need much watching, we look after ourselves."

Mom nodded slowly. She looked down at the clothes. "Well, let's have you try on some outfits. I don't imagine they want you to take more than two or three things in the change room, so I'll have to hand them to you. See how everything fits and what you like."

Ronnie followed her to the change rooms and followed her instructions, stripping down to try out the various outfits that Mom Dare had chosen.

"Mr. Samuels said that you have another sister in foster care?"

"Uh, yeah. Ruby. She's a lot older. Thirteen now."

"Why is she in foster care?"

Ronnie thought about how to explain it. Ruby was rebellious and had left home when Ronnie was still just a toddler. Of course, she returned every now and then to sleep on the couch or visit with her siblings. Sometimes she was looking for money or some other kind of assistance. When she had lived at home, she had fought constantly with their mom. Ronnie could vaguely remember the screaming matches.

"She and my mom didn't get along."

"Oh...?"

Ronnie looked for more to say. "I don't know why. They just didn't."

"Sometimes kids can be pretty difficult to manage. We've had our share that we have only kept for a short period of time, before having to send them on somewhere else. To another home that can manage their behavior better or that work better with them."

"But Ruby wasn't their foster child. She was their real kid!"

"Still…"

Ronnie finished buttoning the blouse that Mom had given her and swung open the door to show her.

"Isn't that cute!" Mom gushed. "I love it. You have to tell me what you think, but I think we'll have to get that one. It's just darling." She touched Ronnie's hair. "Let me see what I can do with that."

"What?"

Mom retrieved a comb from her purse and put everything else down. She started with a small section of Ronnie's hair and carefully worked the tangles out. Ronnie stood as still as she could. She knew how frustrated her own mother would get when trying to tame Ronnie's hair. It always felt like she was going to yank Ronnie's scalp clear off her head. But Mom Dare didn't yank and complain. She just worked at it a little at a time, until she could pull the comb cleanly through a section of Ronnie's hair without snagging on any knots. Ronnie felt like it took an hour for her to get through all of it. Then she started dividing Ronnie's hair into sections, and Ronnie waited while she coaxed it into two dark, thick braids, finishing each off with rubber bands in her pockets.

"Your sisters are always losing their elastics," she said with a laugh. "There. Now look in the mirror."

Ronnie turned and looked at herself in the full-length mirror. She barely recognized the girl who looked back at her. Clean and neat, tidy braids, her cheeks a little fuller than Ronnie remembered them, but with dark circles under her eyes.

"That looks really nice."

"It does, doesn't it? It will be much easier to keep your hair tidy with the braids. The outfit is so *you*."

Ronnie wasn't sure how Mom could say that, hardly knowing anything about Ronnie.

It wasn't her. It was a stranger.

But Ronnie didn't disagree. She just nodded, continuing to stare at herself. Mom Dare was making her into a completely different person.

(III)

Ronnie's stomach was tied in knots over having to start school at a different place. She hadn't really thought until then about how she had not only lost her family; she had lost her friends, too. Her whole life had been flipped upside-down. Everything from her old life was gone.

She was allowed to go play with Janessa and Eclipse while Mom went to the office to complete Ronnie's registration. Eclipse was a very dark-skinned black girl a couple of grades ahead of Ronnie. She stood looking at Ronnie for a minute when they got to the playground.

"You're lucky," she said a little wistfully. "You're one of the keepers."

Ronnie stared at her, not understanding. Eclipse shrugged and ran off to join her own friends. Ronnie frowned, watching her go. She turned back to Janessa.

"What's that mean?" she asked. "A keeper?"

Janessa twirled her hair around her finger. "Mom and Dad pick favorites," she said. "To try to adopt. If they don't pick you, you don't stay."

"Oh." Ronnie thought about that. "Are you...?"

"They haven't decided yet." Janessa sighed. "I don't know... I mess up a lot. Maybe they'll decide they don't like me."

"Oh... I'm sorry... but you're really nice, they'll pick you, won't they?"

"I don't know. You have to do good in school, and I have trouble. You have to look like them. You know, white and all. That's why Eclipse can't be a keeper. And you have to behave, do like you're told. Call them Mom and Dad and act like you're their real kid."

Ronnie nodded. Some of this she had already picked up from Mom Dare and the behavior of the other children.

"Who are the other keepers?"

"Alex and Mike. Right now, anyway. It changes."

Ronnie felt a sense of unease. If she wanted to keep her place in the family, she was going to have to work at it.

"It depends on Social Services too," Janessa said. "Whether it looks like you might be adoptable someday, or Social Services is trying to reunite."

A couple of giggling girls ran up.

"Who's your friend, Janessa?"

Ronnie froze at the tone of the question. These weren't friends of Janessa, like she had first assumed. Their mocking tone immediately put them into the *mean girls* category.

"This is my new foster sister," Janessa said, not seeming to notice the tone, or not knowing how to deal with them.

"Is she as stupid and ugly as you?" the other mean girl demanded, and gave Janessa a shove, throwing her right to the pavement. Ronnie managed to avoid a shove by the first mean girl and the two of them ran off before any supervisor could notice what was going on.

"Are you okay?" Ronnie asked, reaching down to help Janessa up.

Janessa looked down at her legs in dismay. She had worn a skirt, and her white leotards were torn and bloody. Janessa swore, and then covered up her mouth, looking at Ronnie with wide eyes.

"Don't tell anyone I said that!"

"I won't. That must hurt. Do you want to go to the nurse's?"

Janessa stared down at the blood. "I guess I'd better. I'm gonna be in such trouble for wrecking another pair of leotards!"

"It wasn't your fault! She pushed you down for no reason."

"I told Mom I'd be careful. I said I wouldn't play tag or anything."

"She pushed you down."

"If I tell her that, I'll get in trouble for fighting."

Janessa started to limp toward the school doors. Ronnie

followed her. "You weren't fighting. I'll tell her that. You were just standing there talking to me."

Janessa looked back at her. "You'd tell her that?"

"That's what happened!"

"I don't want you to get in trouble."

"Why would I get in trouble for telling the truth?"

Janessa shrugged. "If she thinks you're lying just to cover for me."

A supervisor blocked their entrance to the school. Janessa motioned to her knees. The supervisor looked and her eyes rolled upward.

"Really, Janessa? Again? Your mom is going to be on our cases now."

"I'm sorry," Janessa said, her eyes glistening with tears.

The supervisor stepped back to let them in. Ronnie glared at her as they entered. She followed Janessa to the nurse's office, which was beside the administrative office. Despite Janessa's attempt to keep a low profile, Mom Dare was looking toward the door when they went by, and followed them.

"Janessa? Ronnie? What's wrong?"

Janessa turned to her. "I'm sorry! I didn't mean to wreck another pair!"

"It wasn't her fault," Ronnie jumped in. "A mean girl came over and pushed her down. For no reason! They tried to push me too!"

"Are you hurt?" Mom asked Ronnie calmly.

"No."

Mom turned to Janessa. She shook her head. "Take off your shoes and stockings. I'll get somebody from the office to take care of you."

"I'm sorry, Mom."

"If there's a way to ruin your clothes, you'll find it, won't you?" Mom said lightly. "You're a menace."

"It wasn't her fault," Ronnie repeated.

"I'm dealing with it, Ronnie. There's no need for you to get involved."

Mom headed back toward the office to get the nurse. Janessa swiped at her eyes, sniffling.

"See, it's okay," Ronnie comforted. She led Janessa by the hand over to the cot and helped to peel the leotards off of her bloody knees.

They both looked up as they heard Mom's raised voice through the wall. "Where's the supervision? Where is everybody when she gets pushed down in the middle of the playground?"

The answering voices were lower and Ronnie couldn't make them out.

"She's in the nurse's office now, all bloodied up. What is being done to protect my children on the playground?"

In a minute, she was coming back into the nurse's office with a couple of the staff in tow. A man in a suit who Ronnie assumed would be one of the vice principals, and a woman in a nurse's smock. She was carrying a big cup of coffee and didn't look happy at being dragged in to deal with bloodied knees before she'd had her caffeine fix.

"Hello, girls," she greeted. "Janessa. Let's have a look."

She crouched down to look.

"Oh, they're just grazed. Nothing serious."

"It may not be serious," Mom said, "but it could be! Getting pushed around the playground by a bully, no supervisors anywhere to be seen. How is she supposed to feel safe? How am I supposed to feel like she's safe here?"

"Mrs. Dare, let's not blow this out of proportion," the VP said, making a downward gesture with his hands. "A simple fall on the pavement. Grazed knees. It's nothing to get all worked up about. Janessa is fine, aren't you, Janessa?"

Janessa nodded. The nurse wiped her grazed knees with antiseptic wipes, and Janessa gasped, grabbing at them with tears streaming down her cheeks.

"No, don't touch them!" the nurse protested. "You'll just get more bacteria in them! Fingers out."

Janessa reluctantly pulled her hands back so that the nurse could wipe them again, this time slapping gauze over them immediately to keep the scrapes sterile. Janessa sat sniffling and holding on to the gauze while the nurse bandaged them up.

"You have a problem with bullying," Mom said, taking up her previous line. "What good are all of these anti-bullying programs if they aren't enforced? You've got bullies pushing younger kids down, injuring them, and I haven't heard anything to indicate that you plan to do anything about it."

The VP sighed. "Who were you playing with, Janessa?"

"I wasn't playing with anyone—"

"She was just standing there," Ronnie interrupted, "talking with me, and these two girls ran up, and one of them pushed her down, and one of them tried to push me, and then they ran away—"

The VP frowned, studying Ronnie. "Who are you?"

"Ronnie Simpson."

"Ronnie is one of mine," Mom said, "I just finished registering her. A fine impression you're giving her on her first day of school!"

The VP frowned again at Ronnie. "Do you know who these girls who pushed you are?" he asked Janessa.

Janessa stared down at her knees. "No."

Ronnie didn't believe that. Those girls had known exactly who Janessa was. Ronnie recognized an ongoing campaign when she saw it. Janessa had been fighting this battle for a while, trying to keep it quiet. If the more experienced girl believed that she needed to keep quiet about it and not do anything to make the school or their foster mother think that she was getting into fights, then maybe Ronnie should pay attention and keep her mouth closed.

"I hope this isn't an indication of the kind of student you're going to be here," The VP said to Ronnie. "Tattlers and trouble-makers are not appreciated."

Ronnie swallowed hard.

"She's been perfectly behaved at home," Mom said. "I don't think she means any harm. She won't be a troublemaker, will you, Ronnie?"

"No, ma'am," Ronnie said quietly.

"Good."

"And you..." the nurse pressed Janessa's bandages down firmly.

"You need to be more careful. Some kids are just so accident prone. Wear jeans! They're better protection."

Janessa hugged her arms around herself, nodding. The school bell rang. Mom held her hand out for Ronnie. "You don't want to start your first day by being late for class. Come on, I'll show you where it is."

"I can go with Janessa," Ronnie suggested, making a motion toward her foster sister.

"You're not in the same class. Come on then. Let's march."

Ronnie followed obediently.

Janessa seemed just as cheerful as usual after school, the morning's drama seemingly all forgotten. Ronnie was glad, because after a full day of school following her convalescence, she was exhausted and couldn't cope with any negativity.

"Did you like it?" Janessa asked. "Mrs. Slader's a good teacher, isn't she? I have her for writing and social. She makes things fun."

Ronnie nodded. The diminutive teacher was barely taller than she was. Some of the students in the class were taller than she was. But that didn't seem to undermine Mrs. Slader's authority. She had a strong voice and when it rang out, the class went silent. Even though sometimes it came from unexpected places, like the middle of a group of students.

"Did you make friends?" Janessa demanded. "Tell me who you met and I'll tell you all about them."

Ronnie sighed, looking at the ground. "I didn't really meet anyone yet. I was... sort of shy."

"Didn't you talk to anyone? Even at recess?"

"I was in at recess," Ronnie reminded her. "So she could help me with multiplication. We hadn't done much at my old school."

"Oh, yeah. That sucks. Multiplying is hard. But Mrs. Slader explains things good."

Ronnie's head was whirling from the day full of activity. Her body hurt. She wanted to lie down and go to sleep after having to sit on the hard desk chairs all day. She had felt ready to go home after the first period class. Mrs. Slader hadn't said anything when Ronnie had asked several times to be excused to go to the bathroom. Not because she had to pee, but because she was so uncomfortable sitting and needed to get up and walk around for a little while. The walking around made her tired, but she didn't get sleepy at her desk, she was too uncomfortable.

"I guess I got it," she said. "But you guys are up to nine times tables, and I don't know sixes and sevens yet." She smothered a yawn. "My brain hurts too much to think anymore. I can't do homework."

"You *have* to do homework," Janessa warned. "If you try to skip it, you'll be in big trouble."

Ronnie sighed and trudged on. It hadn't seemed like it had taken so long to get to school in the morning. Mom had driven them over, and had gone a lot farther in fifteen minutes than Ronnie had imagined. She tried to pick up her feet, but she was so sore and exhausted that she just shuffled along, dragging her feet the whole way.

"Can we stop and take a break?"

Janessa's eyes widened. "We have to go straight home."

"We are... I just need to catch my breath for a minute." Ronnie leaned against the pole of a bus stop sign for a few seconds, then sat tenderly on the edge of the hard bus bench.

Janessa was clearly uncomfortable with this. She shifted back and forth and looked around. Other children passed them on the way home to their own houses.

"If the boys see we're dawdling, they'll tattle."

"We're not dawdling. I just need a rest. I thought Mrs.—Mom doesn't like tattling."

"The school doesn't like tattling. Mom says we have to let her know if the others are doing things wrong, so that she can fix it." She shifted again, waiting for Ronnie to continue. "She'll be upset if the boys tell her we're fooling around."

Ronnie rolled her eyes and didn't point out that they weren't fooling around any more than they were dawdling.

"You go ahead, then," she said.

"You don't know the way yet. You'll get lost."

"It's that or dawdle."

Janessa stood there looking at Ronnie, clearly anxious for them to be on their way. Ronnie ignored her and breathed slowly, trying to rest and get her energy back.

As it turned out, it wasn't the boys who saw them there, but Eclipse. She was hurrying down the sidewalk at a quick pace and almost didn't see them. Ronnie wondered why she was running so late, apparently just coming from the school almost half an hour after Janessa and Ronnie had left. Maybe she had an after-school activity that she had stayed for. Or a detention that she didn't want anyone to know about.

"Eclipse!" Janessa called out, and moved to block her way.

Eclipse came to an abrupt halt and looked at Janessa, then over at Ronnie, sitting on the bus bench. Her brows drew down. "What are you doing?"

"Ronnie isn't feeling well," Janessa explained. "Do you think you could tell Mom? Please?"

Eclipse looked back at Ronnie again, considering. Ronnie wondered uneasily whether there was a rivalry between the keepers and the throwaways. Maybe jealousy would prevent Eclipse from helping, in hopes that the keepers would be sent on to other homes, giving her a chance of getting into the fold.

"Okay," Eclipse said eventually. She didn't make any demands for return favors or ask why Ronnie was having such trouble. Without another word, she continued her dash down the sidewalk, breaking into a jog. Janessa shifted her feet and looked at Ronnie, still not at ease, even knowing that Eclipse would give Mom a heads-up about them being late. Ronnie sighed and got to her feet.

"I'll try. But I can't go very fast."

Janessa headed down the sidewalk, and Ronnie followed several steps behind. Janessa kept pulling away ahead of her, then turning around to see how far behind Ronnie was and stopping to wait, scowling and fidgeting.

"Come on, Ronnie!"

Ronnie stopped. She bent over, breathing hard and leaning her hands on her legs to support her upper body.

"When Mom or the nurse tell you not to be so clumsy, does it stop you from falling down?" she demanded.

Janessa looked at Ronnie as if she had been struck, color rushing to her face. "I can't help it if I trip or someone pushes me down," she protested.

"Well, you telling me to hurry doesn't make me feel any better. It really hurts, okay?"

Janessa's lips pressed together like she was trying to avoid crying. "How did you get hurt?" she asked finally, in a small voice.

Janessa knew that Ronnie had been in bed, recovering, since she had arrived at the home. But none of the foster kids had asked Ronnie for the details of what had happened to her. Ronnie imagined that they all had their own secrets and they all had reasons that they might not want to discuss the details of for being taken away from their families and put into a foster home.

Ronnie started walking again, shuffling gingerly along. She didn't offer any explanation to Janessa.

"I'm sorry for being so mean," Janessa apologized. "I just... get worried. I don't want Mom thinking that I'm not good enough."

"She doesn't think that," Ronnie assured her. Mom Dare didn't act like she didn't want Janessa. Ronnie knew what *that* looked like. Mom was sometimes irritated by Janessa's awkwardness, but that was such a small thing. Ronnie knew that Janessa didn't talk back or fight with the Dares. She looked enough like them to pass as their biological daughter. "They like you. She's not going to send you away because you're late getting home or skin your knees."

"I don't know," Janessa said, giving a helpless shrug.

Ronnie would have walked faster for her if she could have, but there was no way. If she were going to make it home, she was going to have to take it slow and steady and take rests.

Her whole body was tired by the time the car pulled up beside them. She was holding herself tense and making such an effort to continue onward, it was exhausting. Ronnie saw the car nose up beside them, and at first was worried it was some guy trying to pick her up but, looking quickly at the car, she realized that the face peering up over the steering wheel was Mom Dare's. She rolled down the window.

"Ronnie? Janessa? Come get in."

Ronnie reached for the door handle nearest her and slid carefully in. Mom twisted around to look at her. "Are you okay, Ronnie? What's wrong?"

Ronnie took a deep breath to stifle the sobs.

"I'm just sore," she said. "Sitting on hard chairs all day and then walking… it really hurts."

Mom reached back and rubbed Ronnie's knee. "Oh, I'm so sorry, Ronnie! I didn't realize that it was going to be a problem. You've been doing all right at home, and the doctor said that once you felt okay being up and around, it was fine to resume normal activities…"

Janessa went around to the other side of the car and got into the passenger seat beside Mom.

"And how are you, klutz?" She didn't rub Janessa's knee, but put her hand over the back of Janessa's neck and gave her a friendly rub. "You survived the whole day without further injury?"

Janessa ducked her head down, getting pink. She didn't show Mom the black nail she got shutting the classroom supply cabinet too quickly. Ronnie kept quiet about it too.

"I couldn't leave Ronnie behind," Janessa said. "She doesn't know the way yet."

"No, of course not. You needed to stay with her, even if it did make you late."

"Did Eclipse tell you? Did she get home and let you know about Ronnie?"

"Yes, she told me. That's why I came to find you. I guess I'm going to need to drop off and pick up for a few days, until Ronnie's stronger." Mom looked in the mirror at Ronnie as she pulled out. "We just have to give you time to heal."

Ronnie nodded. She put her head back and closed her eyes. Even though they were only a few minutes from home by car, she was drifting off to sleep when the car pulled into the garage.

"Come on, kiddo," Mom encouraged. "If you want to sleep, go climb into bed. Homework can wait until after supper."

Homework. Ronnie's gut clenched at just hearing the word. How was she going to get through her homework when she barely understood what they had been doing in class? She didn't have a lot, but the teacher expected her to catch up on work that the class had been assigned before Ronnie got there. She didn't think that was fair.

The bed was calling to her, and Ronnie lay down with a sigh, and was asleep in seconds.

CHAPTER
Four

AGE 33

[I]

"I had a dream that I was adopted," Ronnie explained to Janessa over coffee, stirring in sugar and cream.

"You *do* know that you were adopted too, right?" Janessa asked.

Ronnie stared at her. "No."

"Sure. Just like me and Alex. Mom and Dad couldn't have kids of their own."

Ronnie shook her head, frowning. That didn't make any sense. If she were adopted, someone would have told her. Mom and Dad would have told her that first day back, when they had shown her the pictures.

"But I was just a baby," she said.

"No," Janessa laughed. "I remember when you came! You were eight or nine."

"They had baby pictures."

Janessa raised her brows. "Not of you."

"But... yes, they showed me pictures. A baby too."

"They don't have pictures of you as a baby. Not of any of us. The only baby pictures that they have are of Kent and Carrie."

Ronnie opened her mouth to argue this. Then she closed it again. Mom hadn't actually said that the baby picture was of Ronnie. Had she intended Ronnie to think that it was? She had laid the pictures out in front of Ronnie, baby picture first, then the one of Ronnie in braids, then a couple of older pictures, until the one with Ronnie and Floyd and the children, the last one before Ronnie had disappeared. Or at least, the one that Ronnie thought of as the last one before she had disappeared. Had Mom actually told her that?

Ronnie rubbed her aching forehead. They hadn't told her she was adopted. They hadn't told her that she was one of the children in foster care. The way that Mom had laid the pictures out with the baby picture first had obviously been intended to make her think that she had been a baby with them.

"Why would they try to keep that from me?"

"I don't know," Janessa shrugged. "Maybe they weren't. Maybe they thought you knew that already. Or remembered something about it."

"I told them I couldn't remember anything."

"Well, why didn't the police tell you? Maybe Mom and Dad thought that they had. I would have thought that they would have mentioned that."

Ronnie had been flooded with so much news when the police had talked to her after identifying her as Ronnie Plum. Had they told her that, and she just hadn't retained it? Or had the police themselves not known? Floyd would have known, but if he never mentioned it to the police, then would they know? Wasn't that information private, kept in sealed court records? They wouldn't know that there had been a previous birth certificate in the name of Ronnie Simpson.

Ronnie's mother was surprised when she answered the door and saw Ronnie standing there. But she didn't seem displeased by the surprise visit. Why would she object to her long-lost daughter dropping by unexpectedly to have a visit?

"Ronnie! Oh, it's good to see you," she gave Ronnie a hug around her shoulders and brushed her cheek briefly with a kiss. "How are you?"

Ronnie shrugged, looking down at the floor. She entered when Mom motioned her in. They went into the living room and sat down. Dad was in his easy chair reading the paper. He looked over the paper at Ronnie and raised his eyebrows, then went back to reading. Ronnie didn't know if she should go over and give him a kiss or offer some other greeting. She sat down.

"Mom… when I came here before, you showed me pictures."

Mom smiled. She smoothed back her hair as if she were afraid it might have blown out of place as she answered the door. "Yes. Did you want to look at more? We don't have a lot, but if you think it might help you to remember…"

"The baby picture you showed me, was that me or Carrie?"

Mom didn't answer right away. She scratched the back of her head and looked at Dad. He stubbornly refused to look up from his newspaper.

"Well… that would have been Carrie," Mom admitted.

"You wanted me to think that it was me."

"I never told you that it was you."

"You didn't tell me that I was adopted, either."

There was another pause while Mom considered her answer to this. "Didn't I? I guess it just didn't come up. I don't really think about it. Sometimes I almost forget that you *are* adopted." She laughed.

"How could you forget?" Ronnie asked. "It's not like I was a baby when I came to you."

Dad put his paper down in his lap, looking at her. "Do you remember it, then?"

"No. I was just talking to J— I was just talking to someone and she reminded me that I was adopted. Even though... I don't remember and you never told me that."

Dad gave a stubborn shoulder-shrug. "You knew the other children were adopted. What made you think you were a special case?"

Ronnie looked from one to the other. "Maybe the fact that you never mentioned it. Did you want me to think that I was your biological child? If you didn't tell me, I wouldn't know the difference?"

"How would you know the difference?" Mom queried. "You don't remember. What harm is there in letting you think that you were born to us?"

"What harm is there in letting me know I was adopted?" Ronnie challenged, frustrated. "Did you think that I wouldn't like you if I knew that you weren't my natural parents? What's the point in hiding it?"

It was Dad who answered, his voice low and reasonable. "We figured you had enough to worry about already, without having to deal with your history. You don't need *another* family to worry about."

"Does that mean they're alive? I'm not an orphan?"

"Most foster kids are not orphans."

"But you said... are my biological parents still alive?"

"We wouldn't know anything about that. We didn't have any contact with them."

"Social Services must know. They would have kept track of them."

"Ronnie..." Mom shook her head. "It's been almost twenty years since Social Services would have had any contact with them. Who knows where they are now, or if they are still alive."

"When I lived with you, they were still alive?"

"I can't tell you anything about it. You weren't an orphan. But what happened after that... I couldn't tell you anything for sure."

Ronnie shook her head, frustrated. "You must know something about why I came here to you. It's not a secret, is it?"

"We just don't think that you're... emotionally prepared to hear any of that right now. We have all worked very hard to put the past behind us, and that includes you. You worked as hard as anyone to overcome your unfortunate beginnings. We're not comfortable in discussing that with you at this point."

"It's my story!" Ronnie insisted. "How can you keep my own story from me?"

"It's for your own good," Dad said calmly.

"I'm an adult. I can... I can find out from Social Services. From their files."

"Those would have been destroyed long ago. Agencies like that can't retain records forever. Once the child is an adult, they're only kept for a few years. It was so long ago now."

"What was my name?"

Mom and Dad exchanged looks.

"Your name was Ronnie, just like it is now," Mom reassured her. "We kept your name the same."

"My last name."

There was a length of silence, and then Dad answered. "Simpson. But that was a long time ago, now, Ronnie. You're a different person than you were."

Ronnie wasn't so sure. She certainly didn't feel like Ronnie Dare. Maybe she was Ronnie Simpson.

Adah looked at the copy of the birth certificate they had on file after Ronnie explained about the adoption, and kicked herself for not seeing it sooner. The issuance date on the birth certificate was years after the date of birth, not just months. Ronnie would have been fifteen at the time of issuance. There was, of course, no reference to her previous name or parents. It was as if the Dares had always been her parents. Except for the niggling problem of the issuance date.

"Do you remember anything about the adoption?" she asked. "When it happened? Why? Do you remember anything about your... biological parents?"

Ronnie shook her head.

"No. It's all gone. All wiped out. It's so unfair!" she burst out. "I can't remember anything. They won't tell me anything. No one knows where I came from, who I was before. I don't even know if my parents are alive or dead."

"It will take some digging to find anything out. You'll have to petition the court to unseal your records. They're pretty good about it now, but it will take time. If the Dares won't tell you anything, I don't see any other way."

"They say they don't know anything."

"It's possible... but if they fostered you from the time you were eight, they must have known something. The social worker would have given them some kind of background. Something to tell them the things they would need to be aware of to watch for medical issues, behavioral problems, signs of past abuse or neglect... Surely they knew something."

"I know my name. They couldn't hide the fact they knew that. Not when I lived with them for six or seven years before being adopted. They had to know my real name."

"It's a start. You might want to do a little investigating on your own. See if you can find anything in news articles about arrests or charges against someone with the last name of...?"

"Simpson."

"Simpson," Adah repeated. She frowned. "Somebody will know something.... look for news stories around the time you entered foster care..."

"Can you search on the police computers?"

"There are privacy concerns. I can't share anything from the police database with you, even if those records have been retained. Check public records. There may be other court documents around the time you entered foster care. Or when you were freed up for adoption. There may have been criminal charges laid."

Ronnie scanned through the court files that involved Simpsons in the year before her adoption. Something had happened to suddenly free her for adoption. It was possible that her biological mother had simply changed her mind, or Social Services had just made an administrative decision, but Adah Cruz suggested that she might find something out if she were lucky. Maybe her mother had been arrested for drug trafficking or something like that, something that had made Social Services decide it was time to sever her parental rights.

The titles of the court cases didn't give her much information. What court they were filed in. The names of the parties. The city or district they were in. Ronnie narrowed it as much as she could. Only the twelve months preceding her adoption date. Only in the city, where the Dares had lived when Ronnie was placed with them. Only family court or criminal court. Simpson was not an uncommon name, but the revised search returned only a few dozen results. Ronnie glanced through them, not sure what she was looking for.

Her eye was drawn repeatedly to a criminal case against Mim Simpson and Sal Durrant. Finally deciding that her unconscious mind might know more than her conscious mind, Ronnie clicked the case.

The expanded view gave her more details, including a summary paragraph and a list of the charges against the couple. They were tagged with their years of birth to help differentiate them from any other Mim Simpson or Sal Durrant who might be around. Ronnie did a quick calculation in her head to determine that the woman was the right age to be her mother or a family member in her mother's generation. Then she read the description.

It was like a narrative of her nightmares. She felt his hands on her. Heard their conversation. The summary described in bare, unembellished sentences the charges against a mother who was accused of imprisoning and horribly abusing and neglecting her teenage daughter. She had allowed her daughter to be abused by the men that she invited into their home. She had allowed infants born to her to die, or killed them herself. Ronnie clicked further to see the text of the judgment. A guilty verdict, maximum sentences to be served consecutively. They would both be in prison for the rest of their lives. There was a victim impact statement by a Chloe Simpson, but the statement was sealed, not in the public record. She had to be the teenage daughter.

Ronnie searched for news articles using the names, but nothing popped up. Ronnie supposed that if the judge felt it necessary to seal the victim statement, he may also have issued an injunction against the media publishing their names to protect the teenage girl from gossip. She tried using more generic searches. The trial dates and a listing of the charges. Pretty soon, she started to find the news articles that described in greater detail what the horrible woman and her boyfriend had done. Any pictures of the victim were back views or else blocked out her face. She was blond, Ronnie noted. The mother hard very dark hair like Ronnie's. Chloe's figure in the newspaper pictures was thin and wasted looking, even though they were taken months after her rescue.

She examined the newspaper pictures hungrily. Were these her sister and mother? Or were they totally unrelated? They fit the picture Ronnie had drawn. They were the right ages, and as Ronnie looked at them, it seemed like they were familiar, not strangers she had never before seen.

In the end, Mim Simpson had pleaded guilty and had been sent to prison for in excess of a hundred years. She would never be getting out.

And Ronnie Simpson had been freed for adoption a short time later.

[II]

Adah hadn't said she wouldn't search the police database. Only that she wouldn't be able to share anything she found with Ronnie. And that was true. Ronnie couldn't access anything that was on the police file system without a court order.

It had been a long time since Ronnie had entered the foster care system and Adah wasn't confident that anything from that time would still be on the computers. Twenty-five years was a long time in terms of technology. They had gone through several full-blown tech changes since then.

When she searched on Ronnie Simpson, she got a hit. The record was slightly garbled; unformatted, with strings of apparently random ASCII characters interspersed throughout the narrative, artifacts of imperfect database conversions over the years. But it was clear enough for Adah's purposes. Ronnie had entered the foster care system when she was admitted to the hospital after a brutal sexual assault. Her own father had been the prime suspect.

Ronnie didn't know why she felt the need to go visit Mim Simpson in prison. It was a bad idea. Why would she want to go see this terrible woman? If she weren't Ronnie's biological mother, she would know nothing about Ronnie's history or anything she wanted to know. If she was Ronnie's biological mother, Ronnie might not like what she found out. A woman who could allow her daughter to be abused the way that Chloe had been obviously did not have a maternal bone in her body. It was a good thing that Ronnie had been removed from that home, if she had been. A woman like that obviously couldn't be trusted even with her own children.

The guard had Ronnie put all of her personal items into a small locker. She went through the metal detector and x-ray. They didn't pat her down. Having been imprisoned herself, Ronnie kept having the uncomfortable feeling that he was going to slap the cuffs on her and put her in a cell.

"Okay, ma'am. You're all clear. This way, please."

Ronnie followed him through the dismal corridors to a visiting room. It was midweek, so the room wasn't busy; only a few other people were there. The guard indicated the table that he wanted Ronnie to sit at, and she complied. She sat there anxiously, having a difficult time being still while she waited for Mim Simpson to be brought in.

There had been pictures in the paper, and Ronnie thought that

Mim had put on weight during her prison stay. She seemed even larger than she had in the papers, and she'd been obese then. She looked Ronnie over with a frown and seated herself in the metal tube chair across from Ronnie. Ronnie tensed, waiting for the chair to break beneath the woman's weight, but it held, creaking as she leaned her body forward to rest her elbows on the table.

Her eyes were sharp. "The visitor request said Ronnie Plum," she accused.

"Yes, that's my name now."

"You're Ronnie Simpson? My Ronnie?"

Ronnie swallowed. "I... I think so. I'm trying to figure it all out."

"Figure what out? You know who I am. You were old enough to remember."

"I have... some memory loss. I didn't even know my name was originally Simpson, until just lately. I'm just... trying to piece that past together."

"That foster family, they can't tell you everything?"

"No... or they won't, anyway. I've got some... emotional issues... I guess they think it would be too much for me."

Mim rolled her eyes, wrinkling her nose. "My kids are tough. They don't have emotional issues."

Ronnie couldn't think of a response to that. Did Mim think that Ronnie was not her daughter, or did she think that her words would galvanize Ronnie? Convince her to toughen up and not have a breakdown over something so minor?

"So... am I your Ronnie? Are you... my biological mother?"

Mim nodded, her eyes narrow. "You look like me when I was young. Not so much like little Ronnie, but faces change over time. You were just a little girl then, with a snub nose and red cheeks."

Ronnie's cheeks burned and she was sure that they were now much pinker and closer to what they would have been as a child. Mim chuckled.

"They took you away when you were eight," she said. "I never thought they would take you away and refuse to give you back or I wouldn't have taken you to hospital. Social Services is all too happy to stick their noses where they don't belong and make trouble for families."

"I don't remember what happened," Ronnie said.

"Somebody hurt you. I took you to emergency. They assumed that it was your father, and despite the fact that there was no evidence, refused to let you come back." Ronnie took this with a grain of salt. This was the woman who had pleaded guilty to abusing and imprisoning her own daughter. "That family who got you, they wanted you for their own. They told Social Services stories and made sure that you would never be returned to us. When I saw you afterward... it was obvious that they were doing everything they could to brainwash you and change you into someone different."

"You still saw me afterward?"

Mim nodded. "A couple of times," she said, clearly keeping the details to herself. Maybe she had snuck over to Ronnie's foster home to watch her there. Maybe she had made contact at school or somewhere else when she wasn't supposed to.

"What do you mean, brainwashing me?"

"Fancy clothes. Those Pippi braids. Acting like you were better than us. They wanted to pretend that you didn't come from our family."

Ronnie was unable to suppress a shudder. Though why that should bother her, she had no idea. Of course the family had bought her new clothes. Of course they wanted her to fit in as a part of their family. Like Dad said, they wanted her to forget the past and move forward, not back. But when Ronnie had seen a picture of herself in braids, she had immediately felt queasy, and had cut her hair into a short bob, not wanting to look like that little girl in any way.

Ronnie looked critically over Mim Simpson. She didn't feel any attraction toward her. No kinship or love for this frightening woman. Was that where Ronnie had come from? Was that really her past?

"I had a sister?" she suggested. "Chloe?"

125

"You had three sisters. Ruby, Chloe, and June. Ruby and Chloe were older. June was younger."

"What happened to them?" The news articles had mentioned only Chloe.

"Ruby went into foster care before you. About five years. June was after, a couple of years later."

"We all went into foster care? Why?"

Mim considered her answer carefully. "Ruby was oppositional. Argued and fought at every turn. We couldn't keep her under control. She was always running, drinking, getting into trouble. We needed to get her out of the house, away from influencing you kids. To put an end to the fighting."

"Drinking?" Ronnie repeated. "She must have been a lot older."

Mim nodded her agreement. "She was. And June... they said she was being abused."

Ronnie nodded and didn't ask whether it were true or not. Ronnie and June were both taken away for abuse? And after reading about Chloe's abuse that had been detailed in the newspapers, Social Services had obviously been right on the button. If they had taken the two younger girls away before they could suffer the fate of their older sister, they had been right to do it.

"And Chloe stayed with you."

Mim nodded. "Chloe is the only one who stayed after... your father died."

"My biological father? He's dead?"

"Yes. Twenty-some years ago."

Ronnie breathed, trying to loosen the tightness in her chest. She had dreamed about them. Her mother and her father. She couldn't tell if it were a memory, something true, or if it were just her brain trying to fill in the missing pieces, like the nightmare of Floyd trying to murder and bury her.

Either way, she felt relief at the announcement that her father was dead. She could only assume, after reading the newspaper articles, that Mim had allowed her spouse to abuse the children, just like she had allowed her boyfriends to abuse Chloe.

"Do you know where any of the others are now?" Ronnie asked. "I'd like to meet them."

"How would I know, in here? Do you think they come and visit me? I was surprised enough that you did."

"No, I guess not." The only reason that Ronnie had come was that she couldn't remember. She needed to get information to fill in the blank spaces. If she could remember the details of the abuse, she was sure she would have stayed far away.

At least now she had their names.

CHAPTER
Five

AGE 8

[I]

M r. Samuels came to the house after school. He greeted Ronnie and asked her how she was feeling and how school was coming along before getting to the reason for his visit.

"Your sister Ruby found out that you were in foster care and she would like to set up a visit with you."

Ronnie was surprised. Ruby was five years older than she was and they had never really gotten along together as friends. Ruby's visits to the house were brief. It wasn't like they spent any time hanging out together. But Ronnie was really missing her own home and family. She couldn't go back, but if she could see Ruby, that would at least be something.

"Would you like to see her?" Mr. Samuels asked, watching Ronnie's face.

"Yes! I'd like to get together," Ronnie confirmed.

"Great. We'll set it up for this weekend." He looked like he was going to say something more, and then stopped. Ronnie waited while Mr. Samuels composed his thoughts. He spoke delicately. "Ronnie... I don't know how well you know Ruby..."

Ronnie shrugged. "Well... not very well," she admitted. "She's been in foster care for a long time."

"Yes, she has," Mr. Samuels agreed. "I just wanted to warn you... she comes up with some wild stories, sometimes... you can't believe everything she says."

Ronnie thought back to some of the things that she'd heard from Ruby in the past, and nodded. "Yeah, okay," she agreed. She had heard some pretty outlandish stories from Ruby before. When Ronnie was little, she had believed everything. As she got older, she'd learn to dismiss many as tall tales.

"Good," Mr. Samuels said, relaxing. "I just didn't want you to think that everything she says is true."

The visit with Ruby was pretty uneventful. Ronnie felt awkward as Ruby hugged her and looked over her new clothes with a frown. The visit was short, sitting together at a picnic table in the park while Mr. Samuels sat in his car to give them some privacy. When he came back over, signaling the end of their visit, he motioned Ronnie back to the car while he stayed at the table to talk to Ruby for a minute. Ronnie wondered what they were talking about; but he was Ruby's social worker as well. He had to keep in touch with her and make sure that everything was going well at her foster home. Maybe he'd find out why Ruby was rarely actually home with them, as Ruby had informed Ronnie.

She sat in Mr. Samuels's car, watching the two of them talk. A couple of times, Mr. Samuels turned and looked in Ronnie's direction. Was he afraid that she was going to drive off with it? Get bored and leave? Get out of the car and go back, interrupting their private discussion? Eventually, he finished the conversation with Ruby and got back into the car.

As they drove back to the Dares' house, Mr. Samuels reached

over and turned off the radio, silencing the music that Ronnie had been listening to.

"So... how are things going with the Dares?" he asked.

"Okay. Good."

"You know that you can tell me if there is anything going on that you are not comfortable with."

"No, nobody's done anything to me."

"I don't just mean that... I mean... if they're saying things to you, about wanting to adopt you... that's inappropriate."

Ronnie had realized too late that she shouldn't have talked to Ruby about it. Ruby's wide, surprised eyes had shown that it wasn't normal for a foster family and Ronnie had immediately regretted having said anything. But she didn't have a lot of people that she could talk to like Ruby. She didn't really have any friends at school and Mr. Samuels wasn't exactly a confidante.

"No, it's okay. I don't mind," she said.

"It doesn't make any difference whether you mind it or not. They shouldn't be doing that. You are not free for adoption. They can't adopt you and they shouldn't be talking about it."

"Oh. Okay."

"I'll speak to them. But if anything else like that happens, I want to know about it."

"I didn't know it was against the rules."

He glanced sideways at her. "No... I don't suppose you did. You're new to the system, so you don't know how things work yet. You can ask me questions. If you're not sure about something, feel free."

"Okay."

For a few minutes, they drove in silence.

"Did you have a nice visit with Ruby?" Mr. Samuels asked eventually.

"Yeah. It was nice to see someone from my family again. I... miss them."

"Of course you do. It's okay to miss them. We'll get you started seeing a psychologist. Someone who can help you to cope with those feelings and with what happened to you. It must all be very confusing. Traumatic."

"I don't think I need to see anyone. I'm just... sort of sad."

Ronnie was working on her homework in front of the TV, something that they weren't actually supposed to do, when Jace tapped her on the shoulder. "Phone for you."

"What?" Ronnie tore her eyes away from the TV, not sure she had heard him correctly.

"Telephone. It's for you." He motioned toward the kitchen.

"Oh. Thanks." Ronnie went to the kitchen and grabbed the dangling wall phone receiver. She had no idea who would be calling her. Someone from school? She didn't have any special friends. "Hello?"

"Hi, Ron. It's Ruby."

"Ruby?" Ronnie was surprised, but happy to hear her voice. "Hi!"

"How're you doing?"

"Good. I told Mr. Samuels I wanted to talk to you again, but he said you were sick."

"Oh, I was. But I'm better now. Do you think your foster parents would let you come here to my place? To stay overnight?"

Ronnie felt a little flutter of excitement. It wasn't the same as going home, but it was the first opportunity that she had to spend more than a few minutes with someone from her family. She had never gone on a real sleepover. Their parents had never allowed it, and Ronnie hadn't been with the Dares for long enough to find out what their opinions of sleepovers were. But it wasn't a slumber party with girls from school, this was staying with family; surely they wouldn't object?

"Just a second, I'll find out. Mom?" Ronnie looked around for Mom Dare, and eventually tracked her down folding laundry. "Mom, my sister Ruby wants to know if I can come over. Visit and sleep over with her?"

Mom pressed her lips together, considering.

"It isn't that I mind you visiting your sister, Ronnie, but…" she trailed off.

"What is it, then?" Ronnie asked. She held her breath, waiting for the answer.

"From what I understand, Ruby is pretty wild. I know you'd like to be able to keep in touch with someone from your family, but I don't know if it is a good idea."

"Mr. Samuels said it was okay if I saw her. I'm not going out anywhere with her, just staying at her foster home."

"There will be supervision?"

"Her foster mom and dad, I guess. We'll just watch TV or something. I'll go to sleep in good time."

"I'd like you to spend time with our family. We're the ones who are going to be here for you, Ronnie."

"I'm here every day. It's just one night."

"Well…" Ronnie waited while Mom folded several more items. "I suppose as long as there is sufficient supervision. Her mom has to be home and say it's okay. If she's not, you can't go over."

"Okay! Thanks!"

"You need to eat supper before you go over and I'll help you to pack up an overnight bag. Then your Dad can drive you over."

"Yay!" Ronnie ran back to the phone and picked up the receiver. "She says as long as your foster mom says it's okay and is going to be there."

"Yeah, she already said it was all right."

"Okay. What's the address?"

Ruby gave it to her slowly. Ronnie grabbed the notepad beside the phone and scratched it out. She read it back carefully.

"Yeah," Ruby confirmed. "When will you be here?"

"I have to eat and pack first. Then Dad'll drive me over."

There was silence for a moment. "So, you'll be here in a couple of hours?" Ruby asked.

"Yup," Ronnie confirmed happily. "See you!"

Ruby said goodbye and Ronnie hung up the phone. She went over and checked the casserole in the oven, hoping that it was ready and they could eat right away. It wasn't bubbling yet or brown on top, and Ronnie knew she was going to have some time to wait. She quickly finished her homework—a little sloppily, she knew, but at least it was done—and then went to her bedroom to prepare what she would need for the night. Mom had said that she would do it, but if Ronnie thought of everything ahead of time and had it all ready to go, it would demonstrate how responsible she was and it wouldn't take so long.

Ronnie had been trying to stifle her yawns for at least an hour and she had no idea what was happening on the TV movie, because her eyes kept closing and she couldn't stay focused on it.

"You ready to go to sleep?" Ruby asked.

Ronnie kept her hand over her mouth as she yawned again. "I'm getting… a little tired," she admitted. Ruby gave her a little smile, not at all fooled. She got up and shut off the TV.

"Come on."

Ronnie followed her upstairs. Mrs. Winters passed them on the stairs. "Heading to bed?"

"Yeah."

"Don't stay up talking too long."

"We won't."

"'Night, Ronnie," Mrs. Winters made a particular effort to make Ronnie feel welcome.

"'Night, Mrs. Winters. Thank you for letting me come over."

"Any time. I'm glad that you two have enjoyed your time together."

They went the rest of the way up to Ruby's room, where Ronnie's backpack was on a mattress on the floor beside Ruby's bed. Ronnie delved into the bag and pulled out her nightshirt. She looked over at Ruby, who was already shucking off her pants. Ronnie's cheeks flared with heat.

"I'm just gonna… change in the bathroom," she offered, and made a quick exit.

She stood in the bathroom for a few minutes after changing, looking at herself in the mirror and suddenly wishing that she had full pajamas instead of just a nightshirt. Or that she had even just a long nightgown. She tugged at the hem of the nightshirt, but it wouldn't come down any farther than mid-thigh.

But Ronnie wasn't going to be doing any handstands. She was just going straight to bed. She went back to Ruby's bedroom and tapped on the door.

"Are you all ready?" she called softly through the door.

"Come in," Ruby answered.

Ronnie went in and headed straight for the mattress, sliding awkwardly under the blanket and then tugging the nightshirt down around her once more. Ruby was sitting on her bed. She wore an oversized t-shirt. Not a real nightshirt. It barely covered her butt, and Ronnie was pretty sure she had nothing on underneath. Ronnie averted her eyes. They were just going to sleep. She didn't have anything to worry about.

"Well... goodnight," she told Ruby.

"'Night," Ruby echoed.

Ronnie watched Ruby as she went to the door to turn off the light, and then stepped around Ronnie to get into her bed before turning off the lamp on the side table. Ronnie couldn't help noticing how much more mature Ruby's figure was than her own. All night, she had enjoyed the time together just like Ruby was a friend she was having a slumber party with. Now, Ronnie was reminded how much older Ruby was. Ronnie gathered the blanket around her uncomfortably, suddenly regretting that she had agreed to sleep over.

[II]

Despite her anxiety, Ronnie's body was tired. It was way past the bedtime that the Dares usually enforced. While Ronnie had recovered from her injuries, she still found that she wore out more quickly than she used to.

Ronnie woke up several times to Ruby moving around restlessly in her bed. Each time, Ronnie snuggled deeper into her pillow and went back to sleep again quickly. She wasn't sure what time it was when Ruby got out of bed and slid under the covers with Ronnie on the mattress. Her movements were careful and quiet, trying not to wake Ronnie up, and Ronnie gave no indication that she had awakened. Ruby lay beside her for a few minutes, matching her breath to Ronnie's, but didn't fall asleep immediately. Ronnie lay awake, her stomach tied in knots.

Ruby's arms slid around her and her body snuggled up to Ronnie's.

There was nothing wrong with sisters sleeping together. As they had grown up, if one of the little ones had a nightmare, she was always just put to sleep with her older sister. Chloe with Ruby. Ronnie with Chloe. The twins were inseparable, no matter how many times their parents put them down in separate beds. There was nothing wrong with that. It was always comforting for Ronnie to have her sister there with her in the darkness. Not to have to face nightmares alone, but to snuggle into her sister's arms and go back to sleep feeling safe and protected.

But Ronnie shifted uncomfortably, trying to escape Ruby's embrace and put an inch or two between them. She kept flashing back to a dark, uncomfortable nightmare, and Ruby's presence was making it worse instead of better. Hands on her body. A body on her body. Skin against skin, and grasping, groping hands. Pain and guilt and disgust.

Eventually, Ruby's body slackened and she was asleep, breathing heavily beside Ronnie. Ronnie swallowed a lump in her throat and tried to relax and get back to sleep herself. It was a long time before she managed to find sleep again, still stuck in a morass of memories.

Ronnie moved through the house restlessly. Her insides were all in an uproar, twisting and cramping. She wanted to either go to bed or to throw up, but it was early in the day, so sneaking off to bed would be regarded as unusual behavior and she didn't want the attention.

"Ronnie, would you help me to get some lunch together?" Mom asked

Ronnie scowled. "I don't feel good. Can't someone else help?"

"I asked you. What's wrong?"

"Nothing's wrong," Ronnie snapped.

"You said you weren't feeling well. What isn't feeling well? Your stomach?"

Ronnie put a hand over her bellybutton and nodded. "I feel like I'm gonna throw up."

Mom looked concerned. She felt Ronnie's forehead. "You don't have a fever. How long has your stomach been bothering?"

Ronnie shrugged irritably. "I dunno. Since last night."

Mom's expression cleared a little. "How much junk did you guys eat last night?"

"Not that much. Just some chips and pop." Ronnie knew it wasn't the junk food that was making her feel so sick. "So, do I have to help?" she demanded.

"I think if you're just feeling sick after eating junk, you can manage helping me to make some sandwiches."

"I don't feel good!"

"Come on. It will only take ten minutes."

"I don't want to."

"Ronnie. Come on. You're usually so helpful. Don't give me a bad attitude now."

"I just don't want to do it. Can't someone else help? Why does it always have to be me?"

"It's not always you," Mom said in a calming voice. "Now come."

Ronnie followed her grumpily into the kitchen. As she helped to get out condiments for the sandwiches, she slammed bottles down on the counter as hard as she dared without risking breakage.

"Ronnie…"

"I'm helping," Ronnie growled.

"Take it easy."

"You asked me to help and I'm helping."

"I also asked you not to give me attitude."

"I'm not doing anything."

Mom stopped complaining and they worked together in silence. When they were done, Mom thanked her politely and motioned to the table.

"Have a seat and we'll have lunch." She went to the doorway of the kitchen and called everyone else.

"I told you I don't feel good," Ronnie snarled, though the sandwiches smelled good. She stormed off to her room as the other children came in.

"What's with her?" Ronnie heard Mike ask behind her.

"I don't know," Mom sighed. "I suspect she's just grumpy from staying up too late last night. She said her stomach doesn't feel good."

Ronnie flounced the rest of the way to her bed and threw herself down.

When Dad got home from work, Ronnie felt like her heart would burst right out of her chest. It was beating so hard and so fast. She thought she must be happy to see him, but that didn't explain the knot in her stomach that, although it had loosened during the afternoon, suddenly re-knotted itself.

She walked into the living room. Dad looked over at her and gave her a smile. "Hi, Ronnie. How's my girl?"

Ronnie hugged herself. She was cold, goosebumps prickling up on her arms. "Hi." She tried to act excited, but it came out flat, barely more than a whisper.

"Come on over and give me a hug."

Ronnie hung back. He lifted his eyebrows at her and shook his head slightly.

"No hug? Come on, be friendly."

Ronnie dragged her feet on the way over to his chair, and bent down, remaining as far from him as she could while giving him the hug he requested. He didn't pull her close, just gave her a brief hug around the shoulders.

"We missed you last night," he said. "How was the visit?"

Ronnie shifted her weight from one foot to the other. "Okay. We had fun."

"You don't sound like you had fun. What's wrong? Did something happen?"

"No," Ronnie assured him. "Just watched TV and talked, and went to bed."

"You didn't stay up too late?"

"No. Later than here, but I got tired, so we went to bed."

Dad nodded slowly. "Good. Glad to hear it. This sister, Ruby... she didn't try to talk you into going out, or drinking, or anything else that you know you shouldn't be doing?"

"No. She didn't do anything like that. We just visited. She didn't ask me to go out anywhere."

Dad's eyes drifted back toward the TV. "You got any homework that has to be done by tomorrow?"

"No."

"Are you sure? You're old enough that you should be getting at least a little homework."

"I don't have any," Ronnie growled. "I don't have to do anything tonight."

He frowned. "You treat me with respect, Ronnie. Don't talk to me that way."

Ronnie hugged her arms around her body again. "I don't have any," she repeated.

"Okay. Maybe you should spend some time reading or studying, then. If you don't have any assigned homework, you should be doing some extra practice and study, to get ahead. The kids who put the most effort into it are the kids that are going to get the most out of it."

Ronnie was going to complain, but at his look, she dropped her eyes and didn't. "Okay."

"I want you to succeed, Ronnie. I'm not being mean to you. I'm trying to help you to succeed."

She nodded. "I'll... I'll go read, then."

Ronnie went back to her room, but she wasn't going to be reading. She spent as little time reading and studying as she could. At eight, they weren't going to fail her if she didn't do very well in her classes. So far, she had managed to skate by without any special attention and she intended to keep doing it.

"What's up?" Eclipse asked, when Ronnie went to her bed and lay down.

"He's getting on my case about homework."

"Ah," Eclipse made a waving-away motion. "Don't worry about that. He's that way with all of us."

"What's wrong with just relaxing when you're done? I don't have anything to do this weekend."

"Don't growl at me about it," Eclipse said. "I'm on your side."

"Nobody's on my side." Ronnie raised her voice without meaning to, but she didn't care that she had. "Everyone just keeps getting on my case. Mom and Dad. Now you! I don't have to report to you!"

Mom came walking down the hall. "Girls? What's going on?"

Ronnie closed her mouth and cut her eyes toward Eclipse.

"I didn't do anything," Eclipse said. "She's the one who's being mean."

"Ronnie, what's going on? Are you being mean?"

"No!" Ronnie shouted back. She burst into tears. She had no idea why she was crying, but she felt so overwhelmed.

"Hey," Mom moved into the room and sat down on the bed next to Ronnie. "Hey, everything is okay. I know you said you're not feeling well. You're overreacting. That's all. Everything is fine. Everything will be okay."

"Everything is never going to be okay again!" Ronnie snapped back, sobbing. "Nothing is ever going to be okay ever again!"

Mom tightened a comforting arm around her. "Come on, Ronnie. Calm down. You've done very well and no one is mad at you." She rubbed Ronnie's back. "Sh. You'll feel better once you have a good sleep. I think you were just up too late last night. Why don't you get your jammies on now and relax in bed? Read a book or play with a quiet toy. Until you're ready to sleep."

"I don't get any supper?" Ronnie protested, crying harder.

"Oh, my. Of course you can have supper if you're hungry now. You said your stomach wasn't feeling well earlier. It's better now?"

Ronnie nodded and wiped at the tears in her eyes. "Yes," she snuffled.

"Okay. Don't get changed yet. But after dinner, I want you to have a rest, okay?"

"Dad said I have to study."

"I'll explain to him that you need to sleep."

Ronnie sat on her bed with her nightshirt in hand. She stared down at it, paralyzed, those same emotions and sensations flooding over her again. When Mom came to see if she were ready for bed, she found Ronnie still sitting there, breathing shallowly and trying to push past the flashbacks.

"Ronnie? Why aren't you changed?"

Ronnie looked at her, breaking out of the fog, and looked down at the pajamas again.

"I... I don't like this. I want... I want jammies like Janessa has. With pants."

"Well, we'll have to look at getting you some. Put that on for now, and maybe we can get something else after school later in the week."

Ronnie rubbed it between her fingers, trying to understand why she felt so trapped. So strangled.

"I can't."

"Don't be silly. You've been wearing it until now. I can't just drop everything whenever you have a change of mind. We can get you something, but it won't be today. Now... I guess I can't tuck you in yet, but I'm going to say goodnight, because I have some things that I need to work on. I'll check in later at lights out, but you've been so tired today, you might already be asleep then."

"Okay."

Mom leaned over, gave her a hug, and kissed the top of her hair. "Good night, Ronnie. Sweet dreams. You get a good rest tonight so that you'll be happy and clear-headed for school tomorrow. Okay?"

Ronnie nodded. "Okay. 'Night."

Mom tucked a strand of loose hair behind Ronnie's ear, smiled at her, and left the room. Ronnie waited until she was going down the stairs, and then slid under her covers, fully clothed.

"You can borrow a pair of mine," Janessa said.

Ronnie turned around. Janessa was sitting on her bed, studying. Ronnie hadn't even registered that she was there.

"What?"

"Go ahead and grab a pair of my pajama pants and put them on with your nightshirt. Or grab a top and bottom. I don't care."

"Really? That's okay with you?"

Janessa shrugged. "Sure. Why not? Sisters can share, right? You'd help me."

Ronnie nodded her agreement. She got up and went over to Janessa's drawers, and pawed through the messy clothes until she found pajama bottoms that she liked. She went into the bathroom to change in privacy, then returned to her bedroom.

"Thanks," she told Janessa.

"Sure. They're a bit big, but they'll do. You comfy?"

"Yeah. Thanks."

Ronnie turned away from Janessa's curious, thoughtful gaze, and closed her eyes.

Ronnie had been paired with Alex for dish duty. She was clumsy with the dishes in the sink. They always seemed to slip out of her hands. So far she had been able to avoid breaking anything. Alex had been drying without much to say, but as they got toward the end of the chore, he spoke up without looking at Ronnie.

"Heard Mom talking to your social worker," he offered.

Ronnie looked over at him. "Oh…? What did she say?"

"She was all worried." He dried the pot slowly and put it away under the stove. "Says you've been acting out since that sleepover."

Ronnie knew that she had been out of sorts all week, her emotions running all over the place. "So?"

"So, she's going to put you into counseling. If you're not careful..."

He didn't finish the thought, but he didn't need to. Ronnie already knew. If she made too many waves, they would decide not to keep her and ask that she be sent to another home. It was a slap in the face with how hard Ronnie had been working to fit in and to act like the daughter they would want.

"I was already supposed to be in counseling," she reminded Alex. It wasn't just because of her behavior.

Alex continued drying utensils, sorting them all carefully into the cutlery drawer.

"Yeah, but Mom and Dad don't really like psych appointments. They won't really put you in unless they have to."

That would explain why, in spite of Ronnie's being told several times that she would be getting counseling to help her to work through the trauma she had been through, she had so far not been taken to one.

"I'm just saying..." Alex said, "be careful..."

"But... what's wrong with counseling?" Ronnie asked. "Everybody says it will help."

He rolled his eyes. "Because it makes you different," he explained. "How many of your friends at school are in counseling? None, right?" Ronnie shook her head, not explaining to him that she didn't actually have any friends at school. "It makes you different, and Mom and Dad don't want different. They want us to be just like everyone else."

"Oh." Ronnie felt around the sink for any hiding utensils, then pulled the plug and started wiping down the counters.

Alex was looking at her. "Are you telling me you actually want counseling?" he asked.

"I dunno. I wish... if it would help."

He thought about that as he shut the cupboards and doors and hung the dishtowel. "I dunno. How much could talking really help?"

"You haven't done it?"

He shrugged. "Mmm. A little. But I'm not sure it made any difference. I didn't really like talking about all of that uncomfortable stuff."

Ronnie thought about how uncomfortable it would be to try to explain what had happened to her to some psychiatrist. Maybe it was best to forget about it.

There had been a lot of arguing back and forth between Mom and Dad and with Mr. Samuels over the phone. It had been a while before Ronnie figured out that the argument centered around her and Ruby. It was Mom who sat her down in the master bedroom, away from the other kids, to have a serious discussion with her.

"When you asked me if you could go to Ruby's foster home and have a sleepover, I thought that it had been approved by everyone who needed to have a say in it."

"We asked her mom and you," Ronnie said, not understanding.

"You and Ruby were not supposed to be having unsupervised visits."

"We weren't unsupervised. Mrs. Winters was there."

"And you weren't supposed to sleep over with her."

Ronnie swallowed and looked down, the tight, anxious feeling returning to her stomach when she thought about sleeping with Ruby.

"I didn't know that. She asked, and Mrs. Winters said okay, and you said okay…"

"It wasn't okayed by Social Services and your social worker is quite concerned about it."

Dad had come into the room behind Ronnie and startled her when he spoke. "The kind of lifestyle that Ruby lives is dangerous and it's inappropriate for her to be sharing it with you or involving you in it."

Ronnie had no idea what he meant. She knew that Mr. Samuels said that Ruby was wild and that Ruby told stories. But Ruby hadn't told Ronnie any stories. Ronnie had already told them that Ruby hadn't tried to talk her into doing anything she wasn't supposed to.

"I didn't... I didn't do anything wrong," she protested.

"We're not saying that you did anything wrong," Mom said, but trailed off, looking at her husband.

"You and Ruby slept together in the same bed?" Dad demanded.

"Not at first... but she couldn't sleep and she came over later... when I was asleep."

"You obviously weren't asleep. So, what happened then?"

Ronnie shrugged. "Nothing happened. We just went to sleep."

"Did she hug or kiss you? Touch you?"

Ronnie's face got hot. She was tongue-tied. Tears started in her eyes. "We just went to sleep," she repeated finally.

"Then why are you so red?"

"It's not your fault," Mom put in, her voice gentle. "You don't need to feel bad. We're just trying to protect you."

"We didn't do anything wrong." Ronnie stared at her feet, wiping her nose with the back of her hand. "It was just a sleepover. We slept together when we were little, if one of us had nightmares or something..."

"Don't use your previous home as an example of what's okay," Dad reminded her. "You know we have different rules and expecta-tions here. To keep you safe. Your other family didn't keep you safe. Ruby isn't keeping you safe either. She obviously didn't end up in a good home where they taught her proper behavior like we're trying to do with you."

"No." Ronnie sniffled. "She's had some really mean families."

"There aren't going to be any more sleepovers," Mom said. "And you and Ruby are not supposed to be calling each other. If you want to talk to her, you have to do it through us and Mr. Samuels. Do you understand that?"

"That's not fair!" Ronnie insisted. "She's my sister. I can't talk to anyone in my family!"

"You can talk to her. You just have to go through us and get it properly approved and supervised. You're not spending any more time alone with her."

[III]

Ruby was coming over on Saturday for a visit, but Ronnie wasn't excited about it this time. Mom and Dad hadn't wanted it, but Mr. Samuels said they had to allow it. They had said they wanted it at the house where they could be the ones to supervise, rather than at a neutral location, and he had agreed.

Ronnie lay in front of the TV with the others, watching cartoons, and pretended that she didn't know that Ruby was supposed to be coming over and that everyone was upset about it. Eventually, the doorbell rang. Ronnie listened, pretending she couldn't hear.

"Where's Ronnie?" Ruby demanded.

"You're Ruby?" Dad asked

"Yeah."

"You can stay for an hour."

Ruby's voice was outraged. "My social worker said I could stay as long as I wanted."

"You can stay for an hour."

"It took me an hour and a half to get here on the bus!"

Ronnie didn't hear him give any answer to that. She heard their footsteps approaching and turned.

"Oh—hi, Ruby."

The other children looked around too, curious to see Ronnie's sister. Ronnie sat up and looked around, uncertain what she should do. Would Ruby watch TV with her like before? Did she want to do something else? Ruby's face was pink as everyone stared at her.

"Hey, Ronnie. Uh—let's go where we can talk…"

"You'll stay in here to visit," Dad said firmly.

"We can't *talk* here."

"Sorry."

Ruby made a pleading gesture to Ronnie. "Come on. Please? You and me gotta talk."

145

Ronnie looked at Dad anxiously. He wanted her to stay in the living room. But the TV was loud and that's where everybody was. They would listen in on every word.

"I was your family long before these guys, Ronnie," Ruby said in a tough voice. "I remember when you were born. I looked after you long before these guys even knew you existed."

Ronnie felt guilty. She knew it was true. Ruby was her real family. They were blood. It wasn't a temporary arrangement that could be reversed at any time. And Ronnie really loved her sisters. Ronnie got slowly to her feet and approached Ruby.

"We'll... we'll just go in the kitchen," she told Dad, without looking at his face to see how he took it. Ruby put her arm around Ronnie's shoulder, aiming a triumphant smile at the man. They went into the kitchen.

"What's he been saying about me?" Ruby demanded.

"What?" Ronnie swallowed and blinked her eyes, trying to stay calm.

"You foster dad. What's he been telling you about me?"

Ronnie shrugged, looking down at the floor. She couldn't tell Ruby about the accusations that Dad had made.

"He doesn't know anything about me—he's never even seen me before," Ruby growled. "And Chuck can't tell him anything about me, because that's confidential between me and him. So, anything your foster dad's saying, he made up himself."

Ronnie remembered that Chuck was what Ruby called Mr. Samuels.

"He didn't say anything," she told Ruby.

"I'll bet. How come no one will let me talk to you? Can you tell me that?"

Ronnie shrugged. "Mr. Samuels said I wasn't supposed to go over to see you before. With no one there."

"My foster family was there! And it isn't like I did anything to hurt you."

Ronnie fought for composure. "We weren't supposed to sleep together," she explained. Her voice cracked and she couldn't go on.

"Who told you that? There's nothing wrong with sisters sleeping together! I didn't do anything to hurt you, did I?"

Ronnie swallowed, searching for a response.

"I... don't know."

"What do you mean, you don't know?" Ruby exploded. "I never hurt you! It's no wonder I'm in trouble if you're making up stories!"

Tears were streaming down Ronnie's cheeks and her stomach quivered as she tried to control the sobs. Ruby's angry expression disappeared. She reached out and hugged Ronnie.

"It's okay," she soothed. "I'm sorry I got mad. It's not your fault."

"I didn't tell anyone." It had been Mrs. Winters who had the big mouth and told everybody that they had slept in the same bed. Ronnie wouldn't have shared that fact with anyone.

"I know, I know." Ruby rubbed Ronnie's back, holding her uncomfortably close. "It wouldn't matter if you did. You should be able to tell anyone you like. It wasn't any big secret. You didn't do anything wrong and neither did I."

Ronnie nodded, gulping. Ruby wiped at Ronnie's tears, looking stricken.

"It's okay. I'm sorry. It's your dad I'm mad at, not you."

Ronnie sniffled, trying to catch her breath. She could remember Ruby yelling at their parents when they'd both lived at home. Ruby had always been the explosive one, going off at the slightest thing. Ronnie should not have been surprised or taken it personally. Ronnie wished that they were back home. Back where everything was normal and she knew what she was going to get in trouble for. Life had not been easy, but it had been more predictable.

"I miss Mom," she said.

Ruby looked taken aback. "Yeah." She shrugged. "You could go back there, you know."

Ronnie shook her head. "I can't, 'cause of Daddy."

Ruby pulled back from Ronnie, looking down at her. "He didn't do anything really. It's just what they're telling you, isn't it? Like with me."

147

Ronnie didn't answer. The memories were so fragmented and foggy. What she thought she remembered one day was gone the next, and something different would send her into a flashback. Each nightmare was different, the details in darkness. Ruby hugged Ronnie close again, patting her back.

"Ronnie, he didn't hurt you. He couldn't have."

Ronnie tried to shut off the tears, squeezing her eyes closed. She had told everybody that it wasn't their father, but when Ruby said it to her, it felt like a betrayal. He *couldn't* have? How could Ruby know that? Ruby hadn't even lived there for five years. Had she even talked to their daddy once during that time?

"Get away from her," Dad growled, coming in the door. Ruby jumped and whirled around to face him. Ronnie stared at her feet. After the big lecture on what was appropriate and on being careful around Ruby, there Ronnie was hugging her.

"I wasn't doing anything wrong," Ruby snapped.

"Just get away from my daughter," Dad said tightly. Ronnie felt queasy at his calling her his daughter. Anxious. Ronnie moved farther away from Ruby, unable to think of how to repair the damage she had done. She didn't want to have to choose between her sister and her foster father.

"She's not your daughter," Ruby snarled. "You aren't related to her! I am. And I'd never hurt her."

"You've already hurt her—you and her father."

"Dad never did anything either."

Dad Dare shook his head. His face was pale, his mouth a tight, angry line.

"Get out of this house," he snapped.

"I don't have to." Ruby folded her arms across her chest and lifted her chin defiantly.

Ronnie could have told Dad that yelling or giving Ruby ultimatums would never work. They never had. She'd just dig in her heels.

"You get out of here, or I'll call the police," he warned.

"No, you won't," Ruby countered. "What're you going to tell them? That I came over to visit my sister, and I gave her a hug so you want me thrown out? Come on!"

"Ronnie, go on up to your room," Dad ordered.

"Stay here, Ronnie," Ruby snapped, before Ronnie could make a move.

Ronnie stood there looking at them, paralyzed. She didn't know what to do. If they would both just be reasonable, there would have been no need to have a fight. Ruby and Ronnie could just have their visit and then Ruby would go home. But Dad picked up the receiver of the kitchen wall phone and dialed. He turned his back on them and took a few steps out of the room to speak. Ruby turned to Ronnie.

"He's just blowing hot air," she assured Ronnie with unconcern. She went to the fridge and looked inside. She looked at Ronnie. "Isn't there anything to drink?"

"There's juice," Ronnie pointed out. Or milk. They were right in front of Ruby.

"Yeah, well I guess you're still drinking that, aren't you?" Ruby poured them each a glass. They sat down at the table to drink them. Ruby glanced up at the doorway, where Dad was hovering again.

"Leave us alone."

"You two are not going to be alone. Ronnie, please go upstairs. I don't want you getting hurt."

Ronnie looked at him pleadingly. He didn't budge. She wasn't going to get to visit with Ruby after all. It was over. Ronnie didn't even try to say goodbye, she just left the room and went upstairs, where she sat on her bed, numb. Her brain whirled. How had everything fallen apart so fast?

It wasn't long before the doorbell rang. Ronnie got up off of her bed and went to the window, which looked down at the street. A police car was pulled up to the curb. Dad hadn't been bluffing at all. He had called the police. Ronnie went back to the bed and lay face down, hiding her eyes in the crook of her arm.

There was no yelling and screaming. After a few minutes, she heard the front door open and then the slam of the car door. She listened for the car to drive away, but it didn't.

"Ronnie?"

Ronnie jumped and looked around. Two police officers stood in the doorway. The taller one entered the room first. He looked around and pulled over a chair from Eclipse's desk. But it was the older cop who sat down on it, inching it closer to Ronnie. His name bar said 'Cisco,' and while he appeared to be at least forty, his face was smooth and unlined.

"This must all be pretty confusing for you," he said sympathetically.

Ronnie nodded and sniffled.

"I'm Officer Cisco, and this is my partner, Officer Bentley. We're just here to help, not to get anyone in trouble, okay?"

"Uh-huh."

"Can you tell me what happened when Ruby got here today?"

"Nothing happened," Ronnie said. She sat up a little and hugged her pillow against her. "We just went into the kitchen to talk. And Ruby hugged me. That's all."

"Did you want her to hug you?"

Ronnie tried to sort out his question in her mind. She hadn't wanted Ruby to hug her. She'd been afraid of any kind of physical contact between them. But Ruby had just been trying to comfort Ronnie when she was upset. She hadn't done anything wrong. It had felt good, but Dad said it was wrong, and that made Ronnie's stomach feel sick and guilt press down on her. Ronnie shrugged, unable to give him an answer.

"Did she make you feel uncomfortable?"

Ronnie shook her head and felt her face flush. Cisco waited. Ronnie cleared her throat.

"I... I dunno."

"This is important, Ronnie. We need to know exactly what happened so that we can deal with it properly. Did Ruby touch any of your private areas with any part of her body?"

Ruby had held Ronnie close, their bodies pressed together. But she hadn't intentionally been touching any part of Ronnie, had she? Thinking about Ruby's hug, Ronnie's mind suddenly flashed back to her father. Not Dad Dare, but her biological father. She thought about his hands on her. Waves of nausea rolled over her and she closed her eyes, but that made the flashbacks worse.

Ronnie covered her eyes, pressing her palms hard against her face.

"Ronnie? Can you talk to me about it?"

"No. Ruby didn't do anything." Ronnie sniffled, trying to calm her sobs.

"But you won't answer my questions. Did she touch you?"

"I don't know... maybe... no! She didn't."

"What was your father upset about, then?" the other policeman, Bentley, asked.

"I don't know. He... didn't even want Ruby to come... He wants to get rid of her."

"Well, he's done that," Cisco admitted. "You think he over-reacted?"

"No. He just... misunderstood..."

"You don't think he needed to call the police?"

"No."

Cisco nodded slowly. He glanced over at Bentley before going on. "Now how about what happened a couple of weeks ago? Can you tell me about that?"

Ronnie rubbed her nose and sniffled, swallowing salty tears and mucus. "We had a sleepover."

"Un-huh...?"

"I went to Ruby's house, but my social worker got upset and said I wasn't supposed to without going through him. That's all."

"That's all that he was upset about?"

"Yeah."

"Your foster dad said that Ruby might have hurt you then, too."

"No, nothing happened."

"She didn't sleep with you?"

"Yes... but she never hurt me."

"She didn't touch you?"

Ronnie gave a helpless shrug. "She didn't do anything to me. We just went to sleep."

Cisco touched Ronnie's arm gently. "I understand that you don't want to get your sister in trouble. But I need you to be honest with me. If something did happen..."

151

"Nothing happened," Ronnie insisted.

"Okay... I'm going to leave my card with your foster dad. If you think about something that you need to share with me, you or he can call me. It's okay to tell me the truth."

Ronnie nodded. He patted her once on the shoulder, and the two of them left. Ronnie didn't get up to watch them drive Ruby away. She didn't understand how everything could have gone so wrong.

Ronnie looked down at her dinner plate miserably. Her stomach was in turmoil and she didn't think that she could get anything down. The food had smelled good at first, but sitting there looking at it, she couldn't force herself to eat.

"What's wrong, Ronnie?" Mom asked over the buzz of dinner conversation.

"I just don't feel good."

"You've hardly eaten a thing lately. You need to try to eat something."

Ronnie picked at the mashed potatoes. She really did like mashed potatoes. Especially the way that Mom made them. Not potato flakes mixed together with a fork, like Ronnie's bio mom made, but real potatoes, peeled, boiled, and mashed with a big masher that Mom wielded like a weapon. With lots of butter and milk in it, and a bit of roasted garlic. It was very rich, and the thought of getting it down made Ronnie's stomach squirm.

She jabbed her fork through a few leaves of the green salad and put them in her mouth. Mom watched her chew for a moment, then nodded and looked down the table at Eclipse, whose face looked like a storm cloud. Ronnie didn't know what was bothering her, but Eclipse was making no attempt to hide how she felt. Ronnie felt a little jealous that Eclipse, not being a keeper, was free to express her feelings and let everyone know just how she was feeling. Not like Ronnie and Janessa, who buried their feelings and did all that they could to behave in an acceptable way.

Ronnie caught Mike, who was sitting beside her, eyeing her plate. He was looking at her roast beef smothered in gravy. Ronnie cocked one eyebrow at him. Did he want it? He looked back at his own plate, nearly empty, and back at hers. Ronnie took a quick glance around the table to see if anyone was paying any attention, and then quickly scooped the slab of roast from her plate to Mike's. He grinned and dug in.

Ronnie felt a sense of relief. That was one less thing on her plate that she had to eat. She slid a couple of cooked peas in her mouth and chewed, looking around the table at everyone else, gauging how much they had eaten and how much she would need to clear off of her plate before she would be allowed to leave the table. She shoved the rest of the peas into the mound of potatoes, and covered them over. It looked like she had eaten both her roast and her peas. Her plate was now half empty. She speared a few more leaves of her salad.

"Is there something wrong with your potatoes, Ronnie?" Dad demanded.

Ronnie poked at them, but still didn't think she could get them down. She put the tiniest speck on her fork and into her mouth.

"It's just... my stomach isn't feeling very good, and they're so rich," she explained in a quiet voice. She flicked her eyes toward Mom, hoping she wasn't hurting Mom's feelings. "They're really good. They always are. I just... I'll eat the salad but I don't think I can eat the potatoes today..."

Everyone was looking at her. Ronnie bowed her head toward her plate and put more salad in her mouth. Her face was hot. Mom and Dad exchanged looks but apparently decided not to pursue it any further, and went back to eating, paying attention to their own plates. Mike reached over and scooped a big bite of mashed potatoes from the mound, putting it straight into his own mouth. Ronnie grinned at him.

She got halfway through the salad and had to stop. She looked at Mom for permission to be excused.

"I can't eat anymore," she explained.

Mom looked at Ronnie's plate, and nodded.

"No dessert, and no snacks later in the evening. This is it."

Ronnie nodded. "Okay."

"Scrape your plate and put it into the sink."

Ronnie got up and moved to obey.

"And you, Michael," Mom went on. "No dessert for you, either."

"What?" Mike squawked. "I ate all my dinner! I get dessert!"

"The doctor said you are getting too heavy. More exercise and less desserts."

"I'll do more exercise," Mike promised. "Enough that I can still eat dessert."

Ronnie looked over to see Mom shake her head.

"No, Michael. We'll see how much you can lose, and then add desserts back in once you've reached your target weight. But only if you're able to maintain it."

"That's not fair! Everyone else gets dessert!"

"Everyone else is not so fat. We need to take care of your health, don't we?"

Mike got up from the table, his face contorted with anger. He marched toward Ronnie and threw his plate into the sink without scraping it first. But then, he'd already scraped it clean into his mouth, unlike Ronnie. He stomped off, slamming his door upstairs when he reached his room. Ronnie felt sorry for him. She didn't think that he was particularly fat. He had a round face and a stocky build, but he didn't have a big stomach or flabby fat hanging off of his arms. Not like Ronnie's bio mom.

No one dared to say anything in Mike's defense. Especially before dessert was served. That would be a sure way of missing out.

When Mom came to tuck the girls into bed, Ronnie was changed and lying in bed ready. Mom sat on the side of the bed, studying Ronnie.

"You seem rather glum tonight. What's up?"

Ronnie shook her head. "Nothing."

"Nothing?"

"I'm just... I dunno. Feeling sad tonight. I don't know why."

"Well, you get a good sleep and I'm sure you'll be feeling better in the morning. Sometimes we can mistake tiredness for sadness. It happens to me all the time."

Ronnie accepted this, nodding. She knew that she was sad, but Mom wouldn't want her brooding. Especially if she knew that Ronnie was feeling sad about her family and being so far away from any of them.

Mom's eyes lingered on her, though, maybe sensing that Ronnie wasn't being one hundred percent honest about her feelings.

"What are you sad about?"

"Just... nothing. No reason. Just tired, like you said, I guess."

Mom stroked Ronnie's hair slowly, thoughtfully. "We all have things in the past that we'd like to forget about," she said. "Each of us has our own struggles." Ronnie closed her eyes, just listening. "I don't want you moping around, though. You can be happy if you choose to be. This is where you are now. It's a good home and you're well and safe here. I want you to just forget about everything else. Forget about the life that you had before. That will only make you unhappy. Learn to just be happy, in the present, with us."

Ronnie nodded and opened her eyes again. "I love you, Mom."

"I love you too, Ronnie."

"I'm sorry for being such a downer. I'm trying not to be."

"I know you are. It takes time. You're just a little girl, and it's hard. I have faith in you. You're a strong, smart girl. You'll put this behind you. I know you can do it."

"Okay."

Mom bent down and kissed her on the forehead. "Okay. Now off to dreamland for you. Think happy thoughts. Tomorrow is a new day."

Ronnie nodded and kissed Mom's cheek.

"Love you, Mom."

"Love you too, Ronnie."

Mom went on to say goodnight to Janessa and Eclipse. Eclipse appeared to have recovered from whatever had been bothering her at suppertime and was almost overly sweet to Mom as she said goodnight. Janessa had been in the bathroom and tripped into the bedroom just in time to be tucked in. Mom turned off the light and pulled the door shut behind her.

"You're such a goody-two-shoes," Eclipse growled at Ronnie. "Pretending that you're so perfect and are trying so hard for her." She swore. "It makes me sick, having to listen to you."

Ronnie was shocked. "I wasn't doing anything wrong!"

"No, you never do anything wrong, do you? You got them snowed, thinking that you are so perfect. Well, you're not fooling me!"

"Leave her alone, Eclipse," Janessa said. "She's new here and she's not doing anything to hurt you. It's not her fault that your skin is the wrong color."

"If it wasn't for you two, she'd have to consider me. Maybe she'd take me, if you two snowflakes weren't around."

"That's not going to happen," Janessa said primly, "so you might as well stop wishing."

"I could get you kicked out of here. Both of you. Then I'd have a chance."

"Wouldn't she just get a couple more girls in?" Ronnie asked.

"You don't know anything! It takes time. They wouldn't have two girls to transfer here right away. I could convince her, if I just had her to myself..."

"You're nuts," Janessa scoffed. "If you start making trouble for us, she'd just get rid of you. We're not the ones who are blocking you. It's Mom and Dad."

Eclipse snorted. "You think they're really going to be your mom and dad one day, don't you? They got you snowed. It's never going to happen. They're already looking for someone to replace you, klutz. I can get Ronnie kicked out too. Then it will just be me."

"And the boys," Janessa pointed out caustically.

"They don't want just boys. They want girls too. Two girls and two boys. I'm going to make sure that I'm one of the girls."

Ronnie was silent, wondering what Eclipse was going to use against her to try to get her kicked out.

"You're awfully quiet over there," Eclipse said. "I know you're not asleep yet."

Ronnie considered playing possum, but decided it wouldn't do her any good. Then she'd just have Eclipse at her bedside, trying to wake her up.

"I didn't say I was asleep."

"Just like you didn't say that you were giving Mike your dinner, so that they thought you were eating it?"

There was a little noise from Janessa. Ronnie swallowed and considered this.

"I don't think they'll care," she said slowly. "As long as it didn't all go to waste. They just don't like waste."

"You think Mike's going to be able to lose weight if he's eating your dinner too? Then *he'll* be kicked out." Eclipse sounded delighted at this thought.

"You're just mean," Ronnie said. She rolled over on her side, facing away from Eclipse, and closed her eyes to try to go to sleep.

"You're not perfect like you pretend to be," Eclipse whispered. "I know your secrets."

[IV]

Mom and Dad were happy to find out that Ruby had agreed to stay away from Ronnie if they would not pursue charges against her. They didn't tell Ronnie that directly, but she managed to figure it out from overheard fragments of conversation and from the bits that they did—and didn't—tell her.

Ronnie cried into her pillow, not in front of Mom and Dad, over the injustice of it all. She didn't let them catch her crying over it. Nor did she try to go around them and contact Ruby through Mr. Samuels.

That's why she was so startled to see Ruby on the playground when she went out for recess one day. She did a double-take, then approached her sister.

"Ruby?"

"Yeah. How's it going, Ron?" Ruby said casually.

Ronnie shrugged. She looked around for the supervisors, who surely wouldn't like a stranger hanging around the elementary school kids. Ruby put her arm over Ronnie's shoulders and escorted her partway out to the soccer field.

"Ronnie... what happened at home?"

Ronnie looked at her, frowning and trying to decide what Ruby was talking about. "What do you mean?"

"I don't remember much of what it was like. Did Mom or Dad... hurt you?"

Ronnie shook her head. Ruby's face relaxed slightly and she let out her breath.

"What happened when you went to the hospital? It was somebody else that hurt you?"

Ronnie nodded. "Uh-huh." She could hardly raise her voice enough to be heard. *Was* it someone else? Who was it that had hurt her? She'd never been able to come up with a satisfactory answer.

"Your foster family doesn't do nothing to you, do they? They don't try to touch you or anything?" Ruby pressed.

Everything was being turned on its head. Now Ruby was asking if someone else had hurt Ronnie? Suspecting her parents of the same things as they had accused Ruby of?

"No. They're nice," Ronnie told her.

Ruby sighed aloud. "Good." She nodded. "You gotta watch out, though. Sometimes folks who seem nice aren't really," she warned. "They're just waiting for a chance."

"Not my foster family. They really *are* nice."

"Okay." Ruby started to walk away without even saying good-bye, then turned back. "Ronnie—Mom and Dad never hurt Chloe neither, did they?"

Ronnie shook her head wordlessly.

"Okay. Good."

Ronnie watched Ruby walk away until she was out of sight.

~

It took a long time for Ronnie to get to sleep. She tossed and turned. Her stomach hurt. Her mind kept whirling, thinking about all of her troubles at school, and Eclipse, and how hard it was to be perfect and follow all of the rules. It didn't seem fair that she should have to work so hard to ensure she kept a place in the family. She wasn't even free for adoption yet, so what was to say that she'd ever be allowed to be part of the Dare family for good? She wanted desperately to have a place, and the only thing that she could do was to try to fit in and do what she was expected to.

When she finally fell asleep, it was a restless and dream-filled sleep. In her dream it was dark. She could barely see. Her eyes kept closing, which made it that much harder. She was searching for something, but didn't know where to find it. In the back of her mind, she knew that she was being pursued. She had to find what she was looking for before something caught up to her. Or someone. Was it her attacker? The person who had hurt her so badly? Ronnie tried her best to block out the memories, but she couldn't stop the flashbacks that came in her dreams or that came flooding back in the middle of the day triggered by the oddest things. A smell, a touch, a word.

She opened and closed cupboards and drawers, searching for that thing she had lost. She was growing more frantic. The presence was right behind her now. She had to find what she was looking for.

"Ronnie! Ronnie, what are you doing? Ronnie!"

Ronnie tried again to pry her eyes open. Why did they keep closing? She couldn't see walking around with her eyes closed. A hand shook her arm. Ronnie blinked, trying to rouse herself from the strange dream. She looked around. It was dark, but she wasn't in her bed and she wasn't in her bedroom. Ronnie rubbed her eyes, trying to clear her vision.

"What's going on?" she asked, yawning.

"That's what I'd like to know, young lady. What are you doing up at this time of night? And what are you looking for?"

Ronnie slowly realized that she was in the kitchen. What was she doing there? What was she looking for? Drawers and cupboards hung open. She remembered that she had been looking for something in her dream, but she couldn't remember what it was. The dream was fading, and she couldn't make sense of the vestiges that remained.

"Mom?"

"What's going on?" Mom demanded.

"I think... I think maybe I was sleepwalking." Ronnie looked around the kitchen, her head still feeling thick with sleep. "Was I sleepwalking?"

"Well, I suppose you might have been," Mom admitted. "What were you dreaming about?"

"I don't know. I was looking for... I forget what."

"Come back to bed now. We can't have you wandering around all night."

"No," Ronnie agreed. She followed Mom back upstairs to her room.

"Are you worrying about something?" Mom whispered, tucking Ronnie into bed again.

"No, I'm not worrying."

"Did you used to sleepwalk... before?"

"No... I don't think so."

"I guess it's just a freak thing, then." Mom laid her hand on Ronnie's forehead to make sure she didn't have a fever. "Go back to sleep."

"Okay. Sorry I woke you up."

"At least I woke you up before you started cooking down there!" Mom gave a little laugh.

Ronnie giggled at this, but was too tired to stay awake, and was back asleep before Mom got out the door.

Ronnie waited at the door for Janessa, who had tripped and taken a tumble coming up the front walk. Ronnie suppressed a laugh. Janessa had landed in the grass, so she wasn't hurt, but Ronnie knew her feelings would be hurt if Ronnie laughed at her. Janessa picked herself up, brushing off her knees. Blushing, she hurried to join Ronnie.

"Whose car—" Janessa started, but Ronnie motioned her to silence, her other hand on the door. "What is it?"

Ronnie tried to peer through the door to see what was going on. She could hear raised voices within. That wasn't normal in the Dare home.

Janessa joined her. "What's going on?" she whispered.

Ronnie looked at the car and listened with her ear pressed against the door. "I think it's Eclipse."

They both stood there, straining their ears to hear what was being said. It was definitely Eclipse's voice rising shrilly over the others.

"That's her social worker's car," Ronnie pointed out. Janessa nodded. In a moment, she could see figures moving toward the door. Ronnie stepped back and motioned for Janessa to get off of the steps. "We'd better get out of the way," she warned.

Eclipse's social worker shouldered his way through the doorway, holding on to a struggling Eclipse, her arms windmilling everywhere while she screamed and swore in protest. Eclipse saw Ronnie standing there watching and tried to kick her, eyes bloodshot and furious. The social worker hauled Eclipse past Ronnie, grimacing at Ronnie and shaking his head. They stood there and watched him lever Eclipse into the car. Ronnie half expected Eclipse to get back out of the car and make a run for it. But she didn't. She stayed in the seat, still screaming, as the social worker got in and drove away.

Dad was standing in the door. He was home from work early. Normally, he didn't get in before they got home from school.

"Come on in," he said quietly. "Show's over."

Ronnie and Janessa traipsed into the front entryway, quiet, looking at each other. Mom was inside, in the living room, wiping at her eyes with a tissue.

"You girls come in and sit down," Dad said, motioning to the living room. "The boys should be in any time as well. We'll talk to you all together."

It was awkward, sitting there in silence while Mom sniffled and dabbed at tears. Every time she opened her mouth to speak to them, she choked up, coughed, blew her nose, and went back to sniffling. It seemed like forever before the boys got home, laughing, shoving, tumbling in through the doorway like a litter of playful puppies. When they saw the somber faces in the living room, they immediately quieted, elbowing each other and composing serious expressions.

"What's wrong?" John asked. He was the oldest and, while usually quiet, took on a leadership role among the children when it was required.

"It's Eclipse," Janessa said. Dad shushed her.

The boys looked around, taking in Eclipse's absence.

"What happened? Did she get hurt?"

"Sit down, boys," Dad instructed gravely. They took their places around the room without the usual scuffle or argument. Dad sighed deeply. "I'm sure that you've all been aware of the... undercurrents... Eclipse has obviously not been happy here, and her dissension and disruption was getting worse by the day. We asked her social worker some weeks ago to look into another situation for her and nothing happened. We insisted that they had to take some action, so Eclipse was removed today." He looked at the girls. "She didn't go quietly."

Ronnie snorted. That was an understatement.

The boys' eyes flashed to her and then back at Dad.

"What happened?" Alex asked, his eyes big.

"She was kicking and screaming," Janessa contributed. "She put up a really big fuss. Her social worker had to drag her out."

There was silence around the room as they all thought about it.

"I'd never do that," Ronnie promised. "Even if I was really upset, I wouldn't act like that. I would be respectful."

"I'm sure you would, Ronnie," Dad said. "That's one reason you're still here and Eclipse is not. I'm sorry that you had to see her go like that, and even sorrier for the problems that she has been causing here. That's over and done. We won't let someone stay in the family who can't be nice and who tries to break the family up."

Jace had been quiet until now. He looked around at the others.

"She seemed pretty nice to me. What was she doing that was so bad?"

Jace was black like Eclipse, and maybe that was why she hadn't done or said anything mean to him. He was quiet and good-looking, and though he roughhoused with the other boys, he pretty much kept to himself. Maybe she hadn't had any complaints about him. Or maybe he'd just been oblivious to what was going on.

"She called me names," Mike contributed. "And she pinched and hit me when no one was around." He shrugged, his face getting redder. "I don't know what else she was saying or doing."

Mom sat down beside Mike and put her arm around him. "You should have told us that, Michael. All of you kids need to let us know if things like that are going on. We're not going to let a child who is abusive stay here and hurt you."

"She didn't hurt me," Mike protested. "I could handle it."

"None of you should have to handle it," Dad said. "You need to make sure we know what's going on in this family. If you're not sure about something, if you're uncomfortable or someone is hurting you or being verbally abusive, you need to let us know. Okay?"

They all nodded dutifully. But Ronnie didn't know what she should have done about Eclipse's barbed comments. Even with the instruction from Dad, she still couldn't see herself going to them at any time and saying that someone had hurt her feelings. She wasn't a tattler and wouldn't go to them to tell them that Eclipse was breaking the rules for anything. Let Mom and Dad figure it out themselves. Like they had.

Ronnie looked over at Janessa, who gave a little eye-roll, obviously thinking the same thing. Their job was to fit in with the family and not make waves. Not to make trouble for the others.

"The school also had concerns about Eclipse's behavior that they brought to our attention," Mom said. "We couldn't just ignore them. And we suspect that she has been stealing from us."

Ronnie's jaw dropped. Stealing from Mom and Dad?

"Stealing?" Alex echoed. "I can't believe it. What did she even need money for?"

"It wasn't just money," Mom said, "though she did take valuables. Personal things. Kids do that sometimes, when they feel like they don't have anything of their own, or stability. We won't put up with that sort of thing here. We have no tolerance for that."

Ronnie shifted uncomfortably. She wondered whether Eclipse had told tales on the rest of them, like she had threatened too. She could well imagine that, threatened with having to leave the family, she had not only told on all of them, but had probably made up some stories as well. Were Mom and Dad secretly tallying up the negative reports on each of the children, carefully weighing which ones they would keep, and which would be the next to go?

"I have homework," she said. "I should probably go and get to work on it."

Mom and Dad looked over each of them, and nodded. "Okay," Mom said, with a small smile. "All of you probably have work to do. I'll let you go and see what you can get done before supper."

They all got up and went to their rooms. Janessa whispered to Ronnie in the privacy of their room, once they were sure there was no one close enough to listen in.

"I'm glad she's gone," she confided. "She was causing a lot of trouble."

Ronnie nodded slowly. "But it's kind of scary," she confessed. "I don't want to be sent away like that. I'm not going to steal or anything like that, but... what if I do something else they don't like? Or sometimes, Social Services moves you when the family doesn't want you to. What if they took me away because Mom and Dad want to adopt me when I'm not free?"

"Or what if they decided to return you to your bio family," Janessa agreed.

"They wouldn't do that!" Ronnie gasped.

"They could. Sometimes they do."

"But they wouldn't with me. Not when they said it wasn't safe for me to go back there."

"Sometimes they do, though," Janessa said. "One social worker says no, but then her boss overrules her, or you get a new one, or something else changes. Parents agree to counseling or training,

164

and then Social Services says it's okay, it's safe for you to go back. They haven't freed you for adoption, have they?"

"No."

"Then they haven't totally ruled it out. It's still possible for them to return you."

Ronnie rubbed her head. She sat down on her bed. The room seemed empty without Eclipse and her things there. Funny how much difference one little change could make. It wasn't like she'd been able to take any more than a small backpack of stuff with her, but her absence was palpable.

"I thought you wanted to go back to your family," Janessa said.

"I did. I do. I just didn't think... it was possible."

"They probably won't. But... it happens. Their first goal is supposed to be reunification."

CHAPTER
Six

AGE 9

(I)

As soon as the lunch bell rang, Ronnie hurried for the door, trying to get ahead of the crowd. A couple of the boys got there ahead of her, but she was still at the front of the pack. There was a bottleneck in the cloakroom, but Ronnie had put her lunch bag into her desk to avoid just such a problem.

The student assigned to check lunches took up her position at the door, checking students before they exited to make sure that they had their lunches. Ronnie held up her bag and was allowed out the door. She looked for a way to ditch it, but they weren't allowed out to the playground yet and there would be someone else supervising the lunchroom to ensure that all students had healthy lunches and that no one went hungry or had junk food. Ronnie went to the table where she usually sat and waited for the room to fill up. It was only a few minutes before total chaos reigned.

The lunchroom supervisors walked around. Ronnie sat waiting as one of them hovered right behind her, obviously wanting to make sure that she had an appropriate lunch. The hairs on her arms standing on end, Ronnie took the items out of her bag, then turned her head slightly, waiting for the woman to move on to someone else. Mom Dare always sent a sandwich, a fruit, carrots or celery, and a small carton of milk. Nothing fancy, but with the number of kids that she had to feed, no one was expecting anything special.

The supervisor went on. Ronnie looked around at the other students.

"Anyone want an apple?" she offered, displaying it.

Everyone else had their own lunches and nobody jumped in to say that they wanted it. Taking a quick look around, Ronnie bowled the apple down the long table, hitting the bulls-eye when it shot off the end and landed in the garbage can. One of the boys hooted. "Nice shot!"

Ronnie unwrapped her sandwich. She didn't want it, but she needed to see what kind it was. She nearly gagged when she got the plastic wrap off of it and smelled the tuna.

"Anyone want tuna fish?" She brandished it.

"Yeah, here," Tommy, one of the boys in Janessa's class raised a hand, and Ronnie tossed it to him. "Aren't you having anything?" he queried.

"I already did. I'm not hungry."

He raised an eyebrow, and offered her back half the sandwich. "You sure? Halves?"

Ronnie shook her head. "No. Uh-uh. You have it, or Oscar the Grouch gets it." Ronnie gestured to the big garbage can.

Tommy shrugged his shoulders and started in on it. He was always hungry. Ronnie wondered whether he got enough to eat at home. He didn't look skinny or neglected, but you couldn't always tell by looking.

"Cookie?" Tommy offered, holding one up. Not a packaged cookie, but what looked like homemade.

Ronnie shook her head. She opened up the little baggic of raw carrots. As a supervisor walked down the aisle, looking at her, Ronnie put one of them in her mouth and crunched it loudly. The supervisor passed by without a word.

Ronnie knew from experience that no one would want the milk.

She put it back into the paper lunch bag and stood up for a basketball shot into the garbage can, which was rapidly filling up. It hit the rim with a clunk and then bounced inside. Ronnie ate two more carrot sticks, and shoved them over to the student next to her, Karen Parker, so that they blended in with her lunch. Ronnie got up and headed for the door. She felt like a weight had been lifted from her shoulders. With lunch out of the way, she was ready to head out to the playground. She didn't have any really close friends, but there were plenty of kids who would let her join in on a game of tag or jump rope. Unlike Janessa, Ronnie wouldn't trip and fall down at the first opportunity.

As she was walking from the lunchroom to the playground, Mrs. Hadder was talking to another teacher, and spotted her.

"Ronnie, I wanted to go over your math test with you. Are you done lunch?"

Ronnie nodded, but gestured toward the playground. "I was just going to go outside—"

"This should only take a couple of minutes and then you can have the rest of the time to play. I want to give you some extra time to make sure that you understand what we are doing."

Ronnie looked once more toward the playground, and then followed her teacher with a sigh. Mrs. Hadder motioned her over. "Come sit at my desk with me. We'll go over the test."

Ronnie sat down beside the teacher's desk, and looked with dismay at the red marks across her test.

"Did I fail?" she asked.

"You didn't do very well. That tells me you're still not understanding the work. If we can figure out where it is that you're getting lost, I'm sure we can greatly improve your marks."

Ronnie rubbed her head as Mrs. Hadder walked her through the questions on the test. Ronnie knew that there was no way she was going to make it out to the playground during the lunch break. Her mind wandered while Mrs. Hadder went through the test questions. She tried to concentrate, but most of what the teacher said went right over her head.

"What's this, Ronnie?"

Mrs. Hadder's question drew her attention back to the test paper. Ronnie looked down at the doodle at the bottom of the page.

"Oh... a rabbit," she explained lamely. That much should have been obvious to the teacher.

"It's cute. But I think you need to stay focused on math, especially during a test. Don't you?"

"I was, but it helps me to sort my thoughts out if I can draw. Makes my brain work better."

The teacher's eyebrows went up. "Hmm." She rifled through the papers on her desk and put a few sheets in front of Ronnie. "Your biggest problem right now seems to be mixing up your operations. You need to learn your times tables and I can give you some flashcards to take home for that. But if you don't know what operation you are using, you're never going to get to the right answer. So... can you draw me a picture—or two pictures—that show the difference between adding and multiplying?"

"Plus and times?" Ronnie checked.

"Yes. What's the difference between plus and times? In a way that makes sense to you."

Ronnie picked up the pencil Mrs. Hadder had provided for her and thought about it. She chewed on the end of the pencil, concentrating hard. Mrs. Hadder pulled out a binder and started working on a lesson plan, ignoring Ronnie. Putting her head down, Ronnie started drawing.

Ronnie heard Dad answer the door and strained her ears to see if she could tell who it was. A couple of minutes later, Janessa dashed up the stairs. Ronnie knew it was her because she tripped on the top step, as she almost always did. Janessa limped into the bedroom.

"Someone here to see you, Ronnie!"

"To see me?" Ronnie repeated. "Who?"

"Couldn't tell you for sure, but it looks like a couple of social workers."

Ronnie frowned. Mr. Samuels had been keeping in contact with her. Not often, just touching base now and then to confirm that everything was going well for her. Ronnie assured him that it was and she was doing her best to fit in with the family and keep Mom and Dad happy. He wasn't due for a visit and they hadn't arranged anything. She walked slowly down to the living room, as if she might figure it out on the way, or things might have changed by that time.

Janessa was right. It looked like a couple of social workers. The man was in a suit. Nondescript. Medium height for a man, not fat or thin. Medium brown hair that was neatly trimmed. He could be a doctor or a missionary. Or a social worker. In the gray suit, most likely a social worker.

The woman was a little different. Mr. Samuels had been Ronnie's social worker since the hospital, but there had been a couple of women social workers she had talked to there. Most of the Dare foster children had a different social worker from Ronnie, a woman named Mrs. Carmichael. She wore skirt suits, sometimes a tartan patterned skirt. This woman, though, was in pants and she wasn't wearing a suit jacket. Ronnie looked at them uneasily. Dad was already sitting down and, in a moment, Mom came in, wiping her hands on a dishtowel and sat down beside him, looking at the visitors uncertainly.

"Ronnie, I'm Mr. Clive. I'm your new social worker," the man introduced himself.

"Oh." Ronnie nodded, glad that it was nothing more than this. "Okay."

Everyone looked at each other for a minute. Then Mr. Clive made a small gesture toward the woman.

"This is Officer Singer. She… has some questions for you."

Ronnie's stomach knotted. "Oh…" She looked at Mom and Dad for direction. She didn't know what was going on or what to do.

"Why don't you sit down? Make yourself comfortable. You're not in trouble for anything." Officer Singer had an insincere smile.

Ronnie looked around the room and eventually went over to sit on the couch beside Mom, snuggling up to her a bit for comfort.

"Great." The woman gave her another smile. "I'm here to talk to you about your previous social worker."

"Mr. Samuels?"

"Yes. What did you think of him?"

Ronnie shrugged, unsure what Singer was looking for. "I dunno. He seemed nice."

"He was friendly to you?"

"Yeah."

"Did you like being with him?"

Ronnie frowned. "What?"

"When he came to visit you, or to take you somewhere, were you comfortable with him?"

"Uh... yeah."

"Was there any time you didn't feel comfortable with him?"

Ronnie shrugged and shook her head. "No." She looked at Mom, wondering if she understood where the questions were leading. Mom just shook her head slightly, as much at a loss as Ronnie was.

Singer looked at each of them. "Mr. Samuels is being investigated for having a relationship with one of his wards."

Mom drew in her breath sharply and tightened her arm around Ronnie.

"What do you mean, a relationship with one of his wards?" Dad challenged.

Singer and Clive exchanged looks. Singer looked Dad in the eye and spoke in a firm voice. "He had an intimate relationship with one of the foster kids that he was responsible for."

"How could something like that happen?" Dad demanded.

"It shouldn't," Singer said, "but apparently, it did."

Ronnie swallowed hard. Her mouth was sticky and dry. She looked at Singer, biting her lip. Singer raised an eyebrow and waited.

"Was it Ruby?" Ronnie asked.

Clive looked at her sharply. "Was *what* Ruby?"

"Was it Ruby? That Mr. Samuels was involved with?"

"What makes you think that?"

Ronnie looked at Mom, and then back at Clive. "I don't know... sometimes she called him by his first name. She said she wasn't at her foster family's a lot, but to call Mr. Samuels if I wanted to find her."

Singer's eyes were sharp. She nodded. "That would be suspicious," she agreed.

"So, *was* it Ruby?" Ronnie pressed, realizing that Singer still hadn't answered the question.

"I can't give you any confidential information about Ruby or any other foster child."

"It was, wasn't it?"

Singer and Clive remained silent, but everyone in the room knew the truth.

"Was there anything in Mr. Samuels' behavior that made you uncomfortable?" Singer asked. "Any of you?" She looked at Mom and Dad as well.

Dad was scowling. He looked at Mom. "He never had the opportunity to do anything around here. There were always people around."

Mom nodded.

Dad looked at Ronnie, his brow squeezing down over his eyes. "The only time he was alone with you was when you were in hospital or going to see Ruby. He didn't try anything then?"

Ronnie shook her head. "No."

"Did he ever have a conversation with you," Singer asked, "suggesting that you could meet with each other some other time? Maybe go to his home?"

Ronnie blinked. "No, he never said anything like that. He just seemed... like a normal social worker..."

"You haven't really had any experience with other social workers, though, have you?" Clive asked.

Ronnie thought about it and realized that it was true. She had known Mr. Samuels from the time she was little, because he was Ruby's social worker and came by the house occasionally to talk to their mother. While there had been other social workers at the hospital, Mr. Samuels was the one she had seen the most and who drove her home to the Dares'.

"I guess not," she admitted, "but he just seemed like... a social worker. He wasn't really friendly or anything."

Mom let out her breath. "Good. We want to keep you safe, Ronnie. You have to be sure to let us know if anyone is behaving inappropriately. Even a professional like Mr. Samuels or a doctor or a teacher at school."

Ronnie nodded and leaned her head against Mom's shoulder, seeking comfort and safety.

Later, Mom dumped everything out of Ronnie's backpack onto the bed to ensure that nothing would be missed or get lost, and started sorting through it. She separated the books and papers into piles for subjects, collecting everything that had been finished to file away. She pulled a series of papers folded in half from Ronnie's math text and shook her head.

"What's this? An art project? It shouldn't be in your math book."

Ronnie looked at the pictures of frolicking rabbits, rabbits in baskets, rabbits with carrots, and rabbits being chased away by wolves, and pulled them away from Mom.

"They are math," she insisted. "They're to help me remember what to do." She pointed out the symbols in the corner of each picture. "Mrs. Hadder says I'm really good at drawing."

"You are," Mom agreed, "but you shouldn't be drawing during math time. We'll put these away with your art projects."

"No! Mrs. Hadder told me to draw them! And to keep them in my notebook. They're to remind me what to do."

Mom looked down at the sketches doubtfully.

"She did!" Ronnie insisted.

"Okay," Mom sighed. "If your teacher thought it would help you. I suppose it can't hurt. But I don't want you drawing during math unless you're told to. You need to be paying attention."

"Mrs. Hadder says that if it helps me to focus, I can. As long as I'm listening and doing the work."

"I'll have a talk with Mrs. Hadder about it. Now you need to get washed up for supper and set the table for me."

(II)

In Ronnie's dream, she had been walking for a very long time. Her legs were tired. Her whole body was exhausted. She didn't want to keep walking, but she had to. She kept looking over her shoulder, searching the shadows. It was somewhere back there. It was following her. Chasing her. *He* was chasing her. She couldn't go fast enough to get away. She just barely stayed ahead of him with each step. She stumbled and fell to her knees.

The sharp sting of skinned knees changed everything. Ronnie blinked, looking around her, realizing suddenly that she had been dreaming. But instead of being in her bed, Ronnie was on the sidewalk. In the dark. In a pool of light beneath a streetlight. She got slowly to her feet, looking around. She didn't know what was happening or where she was. She couldn't see her house. In the darkness, everything around her looked foreign. She searched for something familiar, some landmark, panic filling her chest and making her heart pound so hard and fast that it hurt.

"Mom?" she called. "Dad?"

Maybe she was still dreaming, and if she called them, they would hear her and come and wake her up. She would find out that she was still in her bed and could just go back to sleep again.

"Mom! Help! Where are you?" Ronnie's throat choked up with tears. "Please! Mom, Dad, help me!"

She looked around for anyone who could help. The street was deserted. Not another soul in sight. Ronnie left the sidewalk, mincing over the rougher asphalt past the parked cars. There she could see up and down the road with an unimpeded view. Still, no one around. Still, nothing familiar in her surroundings.

Ronnie started walking down the street. Where was everyone? Wasn't there anyone still up who could help her find her way home? All of the houses around her were dark. Some had outside lights on, but none had lights inside their windows indicating that someone was still awake. She was too shy to start ringing doorbells, even at houses with their porch lights on.

She had been walking down the street for what seemed like a long time before a car pulled in. Ronnie faced off against the headlights and waved her arms. It was still too far away and didn't appear to have seen her. But it kept coming. The car was within a block when it slowed and eventually stopped.

The driver opened his door and stood up.

"Are you okay?" he demanded. He looked up and down and around for anyone else. "Who are you? Are you by yourself?"

He was a young man, black, wearing a baseball cap. As he approached her, Ronnie could see the stubble on his jaw and an earring in one ear.

"Are you okay?" He repeated. "What's your name?"

"Ronnie." Ronnie noticed tears running down her cheeks. She sniffled. "Ronnie Simpson."

"Where do you live? Do you live in one of these houses?" He crouched down in front of her to be closer to her eye level.

"No."

"Where do you live? Did somebody hurt you?"

Ronnie's voice was breaking up, and even though she tried to answer him coherently, she was afraid that her words were lost between the sobs and the frog in her throat. "No... I'm... I'm lost."

He stared at her, his eyes wide, the whites shining in the darkness. "Do you know where you live?"

"N-no."

"Come get in my car. I live just down the block there," he pointed. "We'll call someone to help you, okay?"

He put his big hand alongside her head, and wiped away one of her tears with his thumb. His skin smelled funny, and the smell of stale smoke clung to his clothes.

Ronnie climbed into the car and did up her seatbelt. He drove her the rest of the way down the block, stopping in front of one of the houses with a porch light on.

"Here we go. Come on in." He took her by the hand and led her up the sidewalk and let himself into the house with a key.

Ronnie looked around the strange house. It was spooky, lit only by green glowing night lights and the moonlight coming in through the windows. There was dark, spindly furniture and a thick carpet. The man fumbled for something behind her and, in a few seconds, light flooded the front entryway. Ronnie clapped her hand over her eyes to block out the blinding light.

"Mama?" the man called. "Mama, are you awake? You gotta come see what I found."

"What are you talking about?" a woman's voice threaded its way down the stairs to Ronnie's left. "You can show me what you found in the morning."

"Nah, this isn't going to wait until morning," the man said, his voice filled with mischief. "You're gonna want to see!"

There was no further answer from upstairs, but Ronnie could hear a bed creak and various other quiet noises, until the owner of the woman's voice stood at the top of the stairs, looking down.

She was a big woman, much bigger than Ronnie would have guessed from the far-away voice. She was swathed in a rich purple dressing gown and looked down the stairs at her son with her hands on her hips.

"Heaven help me!" she exclaimed. "Alvin, what have you done?"

"I haven't done anything. Found this little thing wandering around outside in the middle of the night. Doesn't know where she lives. Lost."

The woman came hurrying down the stairs, and she enveloped Ronnie in a crushing hug. "Oh, you poor darling! Are you okay? Are you hurt?"

Ronnie shook her head. "I'm not hurt. I just... woke up... and I was out there. But I don't know where *there* is!"

"Nobody hurt you? Nobody brought you here?"

"No, I just woke up."

The woman pounded Ronnie on the back. "You poor, poor thing. Come in here and sit down. Get yourself warmed up. You must be chilled to the bone!" She hustled Ronnie into the living room, and in a few moments, was covering her with thick blankets. More lights were turned on, until it looked like it was midday.

"Now, what's your name, sweetheart?"

"Ronnie."

"Ronnie. I'm Mira and my son is Alvin, as I'm sure he told you."

Ronnie nodded, wiping at her eyes.

"I'll get you some tea and that will calm you right down. What's your last name? Do you know your address?"

"Ronnie Simpson." Ronnie frowned, trying to remember the Dares' address. Sometimes, on a good day, she could remember it. She wasn't good at memorizing and, at a time like this when everything was so confused, she couldn't sort it out in her head. "I... I can't remember my address."

"Poor thing. Alvin, you go give the police a call and have them come here. They'll get it straightened out in no time flat. I'm sure your parents are missing you, Ronnie, and they'll be so relieved to know where you are and that you're safe."

The young man nodded and left the room to make the call. When he came back, nodding and saying that they were going to send a car by, Mira nodded.

"You stay with Ronnie and I'm going to get her some hot tea." She walked away from them. "The idea of letting a child that age wander around at this time of night!" She shook her head in disbelief.

When the police got there, Ronnie was snuggled up comfortably in the blanket, leaning on Mira's shoulder with the woman's arm around her, drinking a cup of herbal tea, with a little milk to cool it down. The two police officers, a man and a woman, looked at Ronnie with open curiosity.

"I was just driving home," Alvin explained, "and there she was in the middle of the road, in nothing but her nightgown! Crying and saying that she was lost and asking me to help her. So, I brought her here, and... well, Mama has made her comfortable..."

"What's your name, sweetheart?" the woman police officer asked. "Can you tell us how you got here?"

"Ronnie Simpson. Alvin brought me here."

"When I found her out there on the road," Alvin pointed out, his face getting red. "I didn't snatch her or anything!"

"How did you get out on the street?" the officer persisted.

"I don't know… I just woke up, when I fell down…" Ronnie pushed the blanket aside and her pajama pants up to show her grazed knees. "I tripped and scraped my knees."

"You woke up when you fell down? Were you sleepwalking?"

Ronnie shrugged. "I guess so."

"Have you ever sleepwalked before?"

"Yes… but not outside."

The male officer spoke. "You must live close by, then. Do you know your house number?" He turned to Mira and Alvin. "You haven't seen her on this street before? Have neighbors with kids?"

"I don't remember seeing her before," Mira said. "She couldn't tell us her address."

"Just the number," the man said to Ronnie. "Do you remember the number in your address?"

"No." Ronnie shook her head.

"I'll get a search done for Simpsons on this street and in the immediate area." He grasped for his radio.

"Not Simpson," Ronnie said.

"You said your name was Simpson."

"But I live with a foster family. Dares."

"Dare. Like in 'I dare you'? D-A-R-E?"

Ronnie nodded.

The cop spoke into his radio, turning away from them.

"You'll look at the home?" Mira said worriedly. "Make sure that she hasn't been neglected? I just can't understand a family letting a child walk off like that, wandering around in the dark in the middle of the night."

"Probably the parents are fast asleep," the woman cop said. "Granted, in some of these cases we find that the parent is off drinking and has left the children alone without supervision, but she looks like she's been taken care of. I don't think we're dealing with junkies here."

"She's so thin," Mira pointed out, cuddling Ronnie to her. "Just look at those arms, they're like sticks."

Ronnie pulled the blanket up around herself so that they couldn't look at her thin arms. The police woman wasn't deterred, though. She stepped forward and pulled the blanket away, grasping Ronnie by the wrist to pull her arm out straight and examine it. She nodded, lips pursed thoughtfully.

The male officer was back a few minutes later. "Parents have been called and are on their way. They were unaware she'd left the house."

Ronnie breathed a sigh of relief. She hadn't doubted that the police would be able to help her and get her home again; she just didn't know how long it would take, and had visions of having to spend the night at the police station or an orphanage or maybe sleeping in a police car. They might have waited until morning for Mom and Dad to wake up and discover her missing and make a report. But now they were coming. She could go back to sleep in her own bed, knowing that she was safe.

It was Mom who arrived. Thinking about it, Ronnie realized that they couldn't possibly both leave the house to pick her up, leaving the other children alone. Someone had to stay behind. Mom hurried in, expression worried, her hair combed but still sticking out this way and that, no makeup, a pair of jeans and t-shirt just thrown on. She always looked so put-together that it was startling to see her that way, looking so human and vulnerable. She dove for Ronnie on the couch.

"Oh, Ronnie! What happened? How did you get here? We didn't even know that you were gone!"

Ronnie returned the hug, patting Mom on the back. "I guess I sleepwalked. When I woke up, I didn't know where I was!"

"That must have been so scary. I'm glad that the police officers helped you." She held Ronnie at arm's length, looking her over. "You're not hurt? No one touched you? No one did anything to you?"

Ronnie shook her head. "No. I just woke up... and Alvin helped me..." She indicated Alvin, standing by looking sheepish. Mom looked at him, and looked back at Ronnie, lowering her voice to almost a whisper.

"You need to tell me if you are hurt in any way, Ronnie. This isn't something that you should hide. Did *anybody* touch you?" She obviously meant Alvin.

"No!" Ronnie shook her head. "I was just sleepwalking and he helped me."

Mom gave her another hug. "Okay. I just had to make sure that you're okay."

"Ma'am, in a case like this, we are required to visit the home and make sure that it is a safe environment with adequate supervision," the policeman commented. "We'd like to follow you back to your home and make sure that everything is in order."

"Oh." Mom's face was pale. "Well, of course. I'm sure you'll find that everything is as it should be. We are foster parents, we have regular visits from social workers. They would report if they felt that anything was questionable."

The man nodded. "Even so, we do sometimes find that things have changed, or maybe there is a situation that the social workers were not aware of."

Mom nodded, her lips tightly pressed together. She turned to Ronnie, forcing a smile.

"Well, come along, then, baby girl. Time to get you tucked back into bed."

Ronnie got up, shedding her blanket. "Thank you," she told Mira politely.

"Yes, thank you for looking after our little girl." Mom looked down at Ronnie's thin nightgown and bare feet. "I'd better carry you." She bent down and scooped Ronnie up into her arms. Ronnie put her arms around Mom's neck, and pressed her face against Mom's, feeling protected and safe.

"Do you have food in the house?" the woman officer asked, after looking in at the children asleep in their beds.

Mom look startled. "Food? Yes, of course, plenty." She led them down to the kitchen and let them look in the fridge, cupboards, and pantry. "And there is storage downstairs, too," she explained. "Staples."

"How long has Ronnie been with you?"

Mom considered, biting her lip. "Oh, how long, Ronnie? It was… what, October? Coming up on a year, now."

"Was she malnourished? Neglected?"

Mom's eyes were wide. She looked down at Ronnie. "Malnourished? No… there was possible abuse, neglect, but not as far as food went. She wasn't underweight."

Ronnie hugged herself, squirming under her gaze. Mom touched her shoulder, then pulled one arm toward her, looking at it as the policewoman had at Mira's house.

"I hadn't noticed how thin she was getting. She must be going through a growth spurt." She eyed Ronnie's height, and shook her head. "Ronnie…? Have you lost weight?" She turned back to the police officer. "We have enough food. They all get enough food. I don't understand it. I'll take her to the doctor and see what he has to say."

"We'll have her social worker follow up on that appointment."

Mom nodded, biting her lip. "I hope you understand. We haven't neglected her. They all get enough to eat. Michael is even overweight, we're trying to help him to lose the excess…"

"Maybe Ronnie felt like she was overweight too. Maybe she felt some pressure to cut back on the amount that she was eating." The woman gave a shrug. "Girls sometimes get mixed messages about their weight. Pick up the wrong things from media."

"Ronnie?" Mom's voice shook a little. "You aren't trying to lose weight, are you? You know you're not overweight."

Ronnie didn't know how to answer, standing there hugging herself, with both of them looking at her like she was a specimen under a microscope.

"I'm tired," she told Mom, covering up a yawn. "I need to go to bed."

"Yes, of course," Mom agreed. "Time to get you back to bed. We'll follow up," she promised the policewoman.

It was still the middle of the night, so Ronnie was allowed to go to bed and to sleep without any more fuss. But in the morning, Dad didn't go to work as usual and Mom sent the other kids off to school without Ronnie. Ronnie watched Dad nervously, not liking this new development. She tried to suppress the memories that flashed into her head, the days when her own father had been home from work and Ronnie was kept home or picked up from school early. There was a tight knot in her stomach. She jumped and twitched at every unexpected movement.

"We need to sit down and talk," Dad said.

They all went to the living room and despite Dad holding his hands out for Ronnie to come sit with him, she chose a seat away from them both and sat with her knees hugged to her chest, feeling exposed and vulnerable.

"We're going to have to set up some kind of alarm system and additional locks to make sure that you don't sleepwalk out of the house like you did last night," Dad said. "We don't want that to happen again. You really scared us."

Ronnie nodded. "I was scared too," she admitted in a small voice.

"I'll bet you were," Mom said with feeling. "That must have been really scary, waking up all alone, not knowing where you were."

Ronnie nodded again. "Yeah."

"Your behavior after waking up was even more dangerous," Dad said, a bite to his voice.

Ronnie looked at him, trying to figure out what he was angry about. He knew that she hadn't gone sleepwalking on purpose. She couldn't control that.

"How should you get help if something like that happens?" Mom prompted gently.

Ronnie shifted, resting her chin on top of her knees. She thought back to the night before. "I should find someone like Mira to help me," she suggested.

"It was good that you did find someone like Mira who would help you. But what you did was not smart," Mom said.

"Why?"

Dad was the one who answered. "That young man that you stopped could have hurt you. He was a stranger and you were all alone. He could have done anything he wanted to you. Nobody knew you were there. If he decided to take you away or do something to you, none of us would ever know what had happened."

"But... he was nice. He didn't hurt me. He took me home and him and his mom helped me."

"They could just as easily have locked you in the basement or murdered you."

Ronnie's jaw dropped. "He wouldn't do that!"

"Somebody else might have. It was very unwise to get into a car with a stranger."

"He was nice! He was helping me. We only went down the block. Not far."

"Once you got into his car, that was out of your control. He could have taken you anywhere."

Ronnie was baffled. Alvin could have taken her anywhere, but he hadn't. Why would he take her anywhere else? And why would he and his mother want to murder Ronnie?

"Ronnie, you can't get into cars with strangers," Mom said. "And you shouldn't be asking someone like Alvin for help."

"He's not a stranger."

"He was last night. You didn't know him and that means he's a stranger."

Ronnie shook her head stubbornly.

"When you're trying to get help, you need to be more careful who you ask," Dad told her. "You need to pick someone who isn't as likely to want to hurt you. Someone who's not going to take advantage of your vulnerability."

She chewed on her thumbnail. "Like who?"

"A woman," Mom suggested. "Especially one with kids. A policeman."

"There weren't any around," Ronnie pointed out. "Just Alvin. And he helped me."

"Then you should have kept looking. Walk to a busier street, to a store where they could call the police."

Ronnie shook her head.

Mom and Dad looked at each other. Ronnie couldn't interpret the looks that passed between them.

"Do you want to...?" Mom murmured. Dad shook his head and made a motion back toward her. Ronnie looked back and forth between them.

"The police officer noticed that you were getting really thin," Mom offered.

Ronnie clasped her knees more tightly.

"We didn't notice how much weight you have lost."

Ronnie chewed on her lip, not saying anything.

"Have you been trying to lose weight, Ronnie?"

Ronnie shook her head.

"Are you feeling sick?"

"Sort of. Sometimes."

"I'll take you to the doctor and have him do some tests to see if you're sick... So... you haven't been keeping yourself from eating?"

Ronnie hesitated, looking for a way to tell the truth without making them disappointed in her. She didn't want to chance their rejection. "Sometimes... I don't want to eat."

"How often is that?"

"I dunno."

"Once a week? Once a day? More?"

Ronnie hid her face in her knees, unable to answer.

"Ronnie?" Mom persisted. "Come on, sweetie. You can talk to us about it."

She shook her head, not looking up.

Mom sighed. Ronnie could hear Dad getting to his feet. "I've got to get in to the office. You'll take her to the doctor and let me know?"

"Yes. Get your shoes on, Ronnie. It's time to go."

(III)

At the doctor's office, the first thing that the nurses always did was to weigh and measure Ronnie. Even though it was the normal routine, she felt sick. She didn't want them commenting on how skinny she had gotten. She shivered in the paper gown. She felt heavy with guilt, and wished that she could just throw up. Then she'd feel better again. But when they gave her a cup to pee in and sent her to the bathroom, she didn't throw up. She was in there for a long time, until Mom knocked on the door asking if she were all right. Ronnie flushed the toilet and washed her hands. She opened the door and handed Mom the cup. There was barely anything in it, but Mom didn't get after her.

"Okay, come in here and wait for the doctor." Mom led the way to the examination room that Ronnie was supposed to be waiting in.

They waited in silence, Ronnie sitting on the high exam table and Mom sitting on a visitor chair in the corner, watching her but saying nothing. Occasionally sniffling and wiping her eyes. The doctor came in with a whoosh, looking at the clipboard the nurses had started.

"So, you've noticed some weight loss, Mom?" he asked.

"Yes. I didn't realize, but she's gotten so thin..."

He picked up Ronnie's arm, looked at it, pressed a thumb into Ronnie's flesh, and let it go. He looked at her eyes and her throat, and he listened to her chest with the stethoscope. He took her blood pressure twice. Then he sat down on the little wheeled stool and wrote notes on the clipboard without speaking to either of them. After noting his observations, he began to fire questions at Mom.

"She hasn't been sick?"

"No, she hasn't said anything."

"No fever? Malaise? Missed school days?"

"No."

"What does she usually wear?"

Mom frowned at this question. She looked at him, and at Ronnie. "What?"

"Describe the type of clothing that Ronnie usually wears."

"I don't know... pants, skirts, a nice blouse or sweater..."

"Long skirt or short?"

"Below the knee. Modest."

"Long sleeves or short?"

"Err... long."

"Even in the summer?"

The seconds ticked by. Mom nodded. "She says she gets cold."

"I'd like to talk to Ronnie alone." The doctor pressed a call button. "Nurse Hatch, I need some assistance," he told the female voice that answered.

"Right away, Doctor."

Mom stood, but hesitated, not wanting to leave them.

"I'll just have you wait in the waiting room for a few minutes," the doctor told her. "The nurse is here," he nodded at the nurse who joined them, "to ensure Ronnie's safety."

Mom looked at Ronnie, looking like she wanted to say something. Then she turned and walked down the hall away from them, back to the waiting room. The doctor shut the exam room door. He motioned for the nurse to stand beside Ronnie and sat back down on his stool.

"How are you feeling, Ronnie?"

She licked her lips and cleared her throat. "Okay, I guess."

"Have you ever heard of anorexia?"

Ronnie shook her head.

"Do you know what anorexia is? Do you have friends you've talked to about it?"

Ronnie shook again. Not only did she not have friends, but she didn't have any idea what that meant.

"Anorexia nervosa is when somebody starves themselves, on purpose. Maybe because they think they need to lose weight, maybe to get control when they feel like they don't have control over anything else. Maybe it makes them feel better."

She swallowed, her mouth dry as cotton.

"Do you feel better when you don't eat?" the doctor asked. "Does that help you not feel so anxious?"

Ronnie nodded. "Yeah," she whispered.

"Do you make yourself throw up?" Before Ronnie could say anything, he inserted, "Your throat is pretty inflamed, so I would guess you do."

She didn't answer. He nodded. "You're very young, and this kind of addictive behavior can take over your life pretty fast. We're going to need to get you into a program and break the cycle right away."

Ronnie could barely breathe. "What does that mean? What kind of program?"

"A feeding program."

It sounded like something for babies or nestling birds, not for a girl like Ronnie. She bit her nail, staring down at her toes.

"I'll refer you over to the ED clinic at the Children's Hospital and they'll evaluate and recommend the best program for you, whether that's a day program or residential."

"But... I can't miss school," Ronnie said, horrified. Her grades would tank. She'd miss too much instruction. They might even make her repeat the grade. That couldn't happen.

"You may need to. Your health is more important than school at this point." He touched Ronnie's arm to make her look at him. "I don't think you understand... this could kill you."

"But..." Ronnie shook her head. "I'm not going to starve to death. Most of the time I'm not even hungry. I get a stomachache when I eat. I wouldn't feel like that if I was starving, would I?"

"Your body only gives you hunger signals for so long before they shut off. You can't be guided by feelings of hunger anymore. You have to relearn how much your body needs to eat. When you start eating, you'll start feeling hunger again."

Ronnie held the paper gown against her stomach. "Look how big my belly is. Does that look like I'm starving? I'm fat!"

"That distended belly is one of the things that tells me how malnourished you are. It's not fat. It's starvation."

Ronnie shook her head crossly. He was going to tell Mom that she needed to eat more. That she needed to go to the hospital and into one of the feeding programs. He was taking away the only control she had left over her own life.

"You know you're too thin. That's what you've been hiding with your long sleeves. You didn't want your parents to notice."

"They'll just worry. Or they'll say they don't want me anymore and make Social Services find me another home. Please... don't make a big deal of it. I'll eat better. I'll quit throwing up. Just don't... I don't want them to give me away."

"They're not going to give you up because you have an eating disorder," he soothed. "This is manageable. We'll make sure that your family gets all of the resources they need. And you'll get better. Kids bounce back fast, and if we've caught it in time, you hopefully won't have any permanent damage. Don't worry about your parents being upset. Just focus on getting better."

Two 'sit down and talks' in one day. Ronnie knew that she was in major trouble. She couldn't remember any of the other kids getting two 'sit down and talks' in one day before, not even the ones who had had to leave.

The others were in their rooms doing homework, where they couldn't eavesdrop and Ronnie was again sitting in the living room with Mom and Dad, one eye on the door in case Mr. Clive were to come in. Mom had a casserole in the oven. Ronnie could smell it as it baked and she knew that she was going to have to eat it. There would be no way to hide the fact that she wasn't eating from Mom and Dad after her appointment with the doctor. They were going to be on the lookout.

But they couldn't stop her from going to the bathroom.

Anxious, Ronnie scratched her arms, letting her nails dig in, leaving long scratch marks under her sweater.

"Your mom told me about the visit to the doctor today," Dad said.

Ronnie nodded.

"The doctor said that you have anorexia. An eating disorder. He explained to you what that was?"

"Uh-huh."

"You probably didn't understand what was going on before that, did you?"

"No. But now I do... so I'll do better. I'll make sure I eat enough," Ronnie promised.

A car pulled up outside and she watched to see if it was Mr. Clive's car. But someone got out and went up the walk to the neighbor's house. Ronnie was still safe. For the moment.

"He gave us information on eating disorder clinics, so that we can get you into a program that will help you out."

"I don't need to go into one of those programs. I can do it at home here."

"You've damaged your body by starving it like this. We need to make sure that you get better. Just like if you had cancer, we'd need to get you into a cancer clinic to get the proper treatment. You wouldn't just cure yourself of cancer at home, would you?"

"But... it's not the same. I don't need medicine or chemo or anything. I just need to eat more."

"There's more to it than that. They'll need to help you to get past the issues that are making you do this."

"I can do it at home," Ronnie persisted. "I don't want to miss any school. I want to move up with my friends. Trust me, I can just do it at home. I don't need a feeding program."

Even the sounds of the words 'feeding program' made her feel sick. She pictured them using a syringe or a tube to put food down her throat and into her stomach, whether she wanted it or not. There should be a law that said they couldn't do that to her. How was it any more right to force someone to eat than it was to withhold food and starve them? It wasn't fair. They shouldn't be allowed to do it. She should be able to decide how much she was going to eat by herself. Or for Mom and Dad to say what she had to eat. She didn't want someone at the hospital force-feeding her.

"We love you, Ronnie," Mom said quietly. "But we can't trust you to just get over this by yourself. The doctor said that it's like an addiction. Like being an alcoholic or drug addict. It's not a cycle that you can change by yourself. You need the proper professionals showing you what to do, helping you through it."

"I'm not addicted. I can do it by myself."

Mom shook her head. "No, Ronnie. It's not a matter of not trusting you. We love you and we want to help you. And there's only one way to do that. We need someone who is experienced in these things and can show you what to do."

Tears started to run down Ronnie's face. She wiped at them, but didn't try to stop them. They would give in if they saw how upset she was, wouldn't they? If they thought that she was remorseful, they would back off. Not force her into anything.

Mom looked at her watch. "Supper in ten minutes," she said briskly. "Why don't you go wash your face and blow your nose, and then you can help me to set the table and get everything out?"

Ronnie snuffled and nodded, swallowing hard.

The other kids didn't know what was going on, but they could see that Mom and Dad were focused on Ronnie, and they knew that something was up. Janessa tried to catch Ronnie's eye a few times, but Ronnie couldn't explain to her what was going on. There wasn't some signal that she could give Janessa to explain what she was in trouble for.

Mom's eyes were on Ronnie as the casserole and other dishes went around the table. Ronnie took one small serving of each item and waited for the watching eyes to leave her. They kept watching her, even after she had dished up. There wouldn't be any putting her food on Mike's dish. He seemed to pick up on this, looking at Ronnie and looking at Mom and Dad, a frown of concern on his face.

It was hard enough to eat when no one was watching and she

didn't have to eat a certain amount. Just a few bites here and there. But with everyone looking at her, there was a huge lump in Ronnie's throat that made it almost impossible to swallow. She sniffled and tried to keep from crying again. No one was going to be impressed if she were crying at the table. What a scene that would make.

Ronnie's stomach hurt. She couldn't eat anymore. It rumbled and writhed, pain and nausea combining.

"May I be excused, please?"

Mom eyed her plate. "You need to eat more, Ronnie."

"I can't. I don't feel good. I swear, I would, I just feel sick." She put a hand over her stomach. "I must have a bug. The flu."

"You saw the doctor today. You don't have the flu. Now finish up what you took. You need to eat more than that."

Ronnie eyed it. She wasn't going to be able to artfully hide that she had barely eaten. Not with them looking at her, undistracted by the antics of the other children, who were all getting restless and silly with Ronnie getting all of the attention of their parents.

"I... I can't," she protested again.

"We talked about this before supper." Mom's eyes darted around the table at the other kids, not wanting to say too much in front of them. Though by the end of the day, Ronnie had no doubt everyone would have all the details.

"I tried. I'm just not feeling good."

Mom looked at Dad, and eventually Dad gave a little nod. Ronnie stood up and quickly scraped her dish before putting it in the sink. She hurried upstairs, as if she were eager to get her homework done. Except that she hadn't been at school to get any homework and she wasn't headed for her bedroom. She darted into the bathroom, the urgent twisting and turning of her stomach getting unbearable. She didn't have any time to lock the door, but simply pulled it shut behind her on the way to the toilet. Ronnie barely made it in time. She steadied herself on the cold porcelain and got down to her knees. She closed her eyes, her stomach just about turning inside out with the violence of her illness.

The door opened mid-puke. Ronnie couldn't turn her head to look. There was a soft hand on her shoulder.

"Ronnie."

She couldn't stop to pay any attention to Mom. The hand rubbed her back gently, soothingly.

"Shhh, it's okay," she murmured. "It's okay, Ronnie. We're going to get you help."

When the heaves subsided, Ronnie reached over to flush the toilet, and wiped her face and blew her nose.

"I didn't make myself throw up," she insisted. "I didn't try to. I just... I ate too much, it wouldn't stay down."

Mom nodded, still rubbing Ronnie's back. "The doctor said that you wouldn't be able to eat very much at a time. The feeding clinic will be able to get you used to eating again."

Ronnie looked at Mom and saw her wiping away tears. "Don't cry, Mom. I'm sorry! I'm sorry."

"I know, Ronnie. It's just... I don't know how we let this get so bad, right under our noses. I saw how much you ate tonight. It was hardly anything... but it was too much for your poor stomach. It just makes me... so sad."

Ronnie patted Mom's knee. "I didn't mean to make you cry. I didn't want you to be sad. I'm sorry."

"It's not your fault. We'll fix this, honey. We'll get you into the clinic and it will all be okay."

Ronnie nodded. She knew that it was going to take more than willpower to overcome the anorexia. She couldn't just decide to start eating again.

"Will you still keep me?" she begged. "Please don't send me to another home."

She wanted Mom to say, 'of course not' or to express how much they loved her and could never let her go to another home. But Mom just shook her head slowly with a sad frown.

"We need to do what's best for you," she said. "I don't know yet what that will be. We'll need to talk."

Ronnie scrubbed her eyes with her fists, the sobs escaping her burning throat.

~

Mom and Dad hadn't been able to get Ronnie into the daytime feeding clinic. The staff explained that her condition was too serious to be able to be in the day program. She had to do residential, which meant that she would be there all day and night until she was out of the program. Ronnie was terrified that putting her into a residential program meant that she wouldn't be going back to the Dares again afterward. They'd have lots of time to distance themselves and for Mr. Clive to find her another family while she was away. Then Mom and Dad wouldn't have to worry about Ronnie's problems any longer and could focus on the other children in their home. Ronnie would become disposable and someone else would become the keeper.

Mom took her to the clinic, which was run out of the Children's Hospital, and signed all of the forms to get Ronnie registered in the program. Ronnie had to say goodbye and was led to another room, a small office where a woman with a W-shaped frown line between her eyebrows even when her face was at rest met her with a clipboard.

"I'm Mrs. Wood," she said. She waved a thin hand with glossy red nails at the seat across the table from her. "Have a seat, Ronnie."

Ronnie did was she was told, forcing her body into the hard chair. She shifted a little, trying to get comfortable.

Mrs. Wood's black hair peppered with gray was pulled back into a bun. She had a pair of glasses on a chain around her neck. She looked like the grouchy librarian from a movie.

"The chair is hard, isn't it?" Mrs. Wood observed.

Ronnie nodded. She tried to avoid shifting again, but the chair was so painful, and Mrs. Wood's attention just made it worse. Focusing Ronnie's discomfort instead of distracting her.

"One of the reasons that you are so uncomfortable sitting there is that you don't have enough body fat to cushion your tailbone. When you are eating better, you'll be more comfortable sitting on chairs like that." She waited for Ronnie to give some sort of response. Ronnie just nodded. "Won't that be a nice benefit? To feel better sitting down again?"

"Yeah, I guess."

"Having such a low body fat doesn't make you feel good. You're cold all the time, you can't sit comfortably, and you hurt all over. You can't see or feel what it is doing to your liver and other internal organs, but it does cause damage."

Ronnie shrugged and nodded, unsure how she was supposed to respond.

"You will be weighed every day on this program, but you will not be allowed to see what your weight is. That number is only for our doctors. Do you understand that?"

"Okay."

"Every meal will be supervised. If you're going to make yourself throw up, you will lose your bathroom privileges and will have to use a bedpan. If you don't start putting on a little weight in the first two days, you will be tube-fed until you start gaining. It's uncomfortable and it means that you lose control. You don't want that, do you?"

"No," Ronnie agreed. She swallowed. What would it feel like to have a tube put down her throat and food pumped into her? The thought made her feel sick.

"Have you had anything to eat today?"

"Um... a little toast."

"How much is a little?"

"A few bites."

"Mouse bites or big bites?" Mrs. Wood asked, with half a smile. "A quarter of a slice of bread? A half?"

Ronnie shifted. "Maybe between a quarter and a half."

The woman nodded and noted it down. "Good. You will eat a snack at ten-thirty, and lunch at twelve-thirty. You may take a small portion, but you are expected to eat something."

"Okay."

"You must have questions for me. What would you like to know?"

"How long do I have to stay? I told Mom I'd eat. I don't need to be here." Even though Ronnie knew deep down that she couldn't do it on her own, that didn't stop her from trying.

"Most of the children who come here don't think they need to be here. But eating is not the only issue. The center of this disorder is not how you eat, it's how you think, and that's what we need to work on the most."

"So, how long?"

"However long it takes. The initial treatment cycle is six weeks."

"Six weeks?" Ronnie was horrified. More than a month. Missing school for six weeks. A constant reminder to Mom and Dad about how inadequate Ronnie was as a daughter for six solid weeks.

"It will go a lot faster than you think. At that point, we'll evaluate whether you are ready to manage on your own or whether you need further treatment or counseling. You will need long-term support."

"What if I do really good, can I get out early?" Ronnie pressed.

"We don't do that," Mrs. Wood said firmly, leaving no room for negotiation, "but you won't be away from your family for that long. They will be able to visit."

Ronnie put her face in her hands. "I can't do this for six weeks!" She tried to keep the tears from coming, but they leaked into her fingers. "I can't, they won't want me anymore! They won't want to keep me."

Mrs. Wood touched her on the shoulder, fingers gentle.

"Ronnie. It's okay. I know you're scared. But nobody's going to kick you out. You're here to get help."

"I can't do this. I can't."

Mrs. Wood sighed. "Come on. Let's just jump right in and get you going. It won't be nearly as bad as you are imagining."

"What?"

"First weigh-in. Come with me."

Ronnie got up and followed Mrs. Wood, her stomach tied in knots. The woman led her through the corridors to what looked like a doctor's office, where she was given a hospital robe to wear—

cloth, not paper—and as Ronnie shivered, they measured her height and then took her to a scale. When she stepped on the scale, the nurse went around a desk to a display that Ronnie couldn't see and noted her weight. She gave no sign as to what she thought of it.

Mrs. Wood took her on to a doctor's exam room. Ronnie sat on the exam table and waited, just as she had at her own doctor's office. Mrs. Wood sat in the visitor's chair where Mom should have sat and didn't try to engage Ronnie in conversation.

The day that Ronnie was finally released from the ED program and Mom came to pick her up and take her home was one of the happiest days of her life. She had her bag packed first thing in the morning, as soon as she woke up and changed into her day clothes. No more uniform. No more hospital gowns. No more weigh-ins. She had graduated. She was going home. And she was never, ever going back to the program again. She wasn't going to be a repeater, going back into the program again and again, until she succeeded in killing herself. She was going to be strong and healthy and not give in to the temptation to withhold nourishment from her body. There were other ways to deal with problems. She had lots of new strategies and she was strong. She would succeed where others had failed.

She stood in the front lobby, watching out the glass doors for Mom's car to pull up. The receptionist at the desk was watching her.

"You can't leave until you're properly checked out," she warned, "so don't just go running for your car when you see it pull up."

Ronnie had to admit that that was exactly what she was hoping to do. Spot the car, and then just fly out of there, jump into her seat, and never have to look back again.

"Okay."

Even though she had said it, she still had to keep a tight grip on herself when she finally saw Mom's old blue sedan pull into the parking lot. She put her hand on the door, and stopped there, watching it.

"There she is," Ronnie reported. "She's coming."

"Just relax. We'll need a few minutes to sign the release papers and give your mom post-clinic care instructions. It's going to take a bit."

Ronnie didn't sit down. She stayed at the door, one hand on the handle, until Mom came up the walkway. Then she pulled it open for her. Mom looked surprise.

"Ronnie! Oh, it's good to see you!"

She held out her arms and enveloped Ronnie in a hug. It was different from the hugs that she gave Ronnie on Visiting Day. It was a welcome-home hug. A hug that meant she didn't have to stay there any longer. Ronnie squeezed her hard.

"Me too, Mom," she squeaked out.

"Oh, you're holding me too tight! How could someone so skinny be so strong?"

They both froze for a moment, looking at each other. Mom wasn't supposed to use the word skinny. It was one of those words that they weren't allowed to use in casual conversation anymore. Skinny. Thin. Eating disorder. Anorexia.

"Sorry," Mom apologized. She released Ronnie from the hug and approached the receptionist. "The doctor said that there would be some documents for me to sign. Release papers."

"Yes, ma'am," the receptionist agreed cheerfully. She walked Mom through each of the forms, and gave her several papers and pamphlets to take home, emphasizing the fact that the family needed to do follow-up to stay on top of Ronnie's *condition* and make sure she didn't have a *relapse*. Mom nodded, looking through the various papers in confusion.

"Yes, I'll look at these when I get home. There are an awful lot of instructions, aren't there?"

"Just things that you can be doing to help Ronnie succeed in the future. She needs the support of her family."

Mom nodded. "Of course. We'll take care of all of this."

Then she was done, and she turned to face Ronnie. "I guess that's it, Ronnie. You ready to go home?"

Ronnie nodded, her eyes tearing up. "Yes. Please."

Mom reached out to take Ronnie's bag from her. "Let me take that. It looks heavy."

"I can do it," Ronnie insisted. "I'm strong."

A moment of silence passed between them, during which Ronnie prepared her arguments about how strong she was, what good shape she was in now that she was properly nourished, and how Mom didn't need to be babying her at all. She could do all of the things that were expected of her. But Mom didn't point out how frail Ronnie looked or say that her muscles had wasted too much to be carrying such a heavy bag. She just nodded and led the way out to the car.

Ronnie was almost as excited for Janessa to come home after school as she was to get out of the ED Clinic in the first place. While Mom had come to visit her at the clinic on Visiting Day, and Dad had joined her on a couple of occasions, Ronnie hadn't seen any of the other children in six weeks. It seemed like forever. She had been afraid to ask whether everybody was still there, or if some of them had gone on to other homes. But when she got back to her bedroom, she could see that all of Janessa's personal items were still there. Janessa hadn't been kicked out. Ronnie had made it through the program at the ED Clinic, so she was cured and the Dares hadn't asked for her to be put into another family. Ronnie could rejoin the family, and everything would be as it had been before she had left. It would be as if she had been there the whole time.

She watched out the front window for Janessa, pacing like a caged animal. Mom tried a couple of times to get her to do something else. But after she completed each chore, Ronnie went back to the living room and watched for the first sign of Janessa. The hands on the clock kept moving forward at a super-slow pace, but eventually, it was time for Janessa to be home, and Ronnie waited for her to come into sight.

She finally saw Janessa make her way around the corner, and Ronnie was out the door in a flash, screaming. "Janessa!"

Janessa looked as if she didn't know whether to run or to drop her books, and in the end, just froze in place. Ronnie threw her arms around Janessa, hitting her with such force that they both fell to the grassy boulevard on the other side of the sidewalk.

CHAPTER
Seven

AGE 10

[I]

R onnie knew that something was wrong when she saw Mr. Clive's car parked outside of the house when she got home from school. He knew what time she usually got home and never set up appointments for earlier.

With her stomach and chest tight with tension, she walked up to the door and stepped inside, looking around for Mr. Clive.

Mom appeared to greet her and make sure she put her shoes away properly. "He's in the living room," she whispered to Ronnie.

"What's going on?"

"He'll tell you. Come on."

"Is he taking me away?" Ronnie asked, thinking of Eclipse.

"He's not taking you away."

Breathing a sigh of relief, Ronnie preceded Mom into the living room. Mr. Clive was there, his mouth a thin line, downturned at the corners. He motioned for Ronnie to sit without attempting a smile.

"Ronnie... I have some upsetting news for you..."

Ronnie didn't like the sound of that. She waited, wordless.

"Ronnie... your father has been killed."

Ronnie's eyes went immediately to Mom, her jaw dropping at the shocking news. Mom looked far too composed for Ronnie to have understood Mr. Clive correctly.

"Not Mr. Dare," Mom said. "Your biological father."

"Oh!" Ronnie looked back at Mr. Clive, the air going out of her lungs. "My... why? What happened?"

She supposed it had been some sort of accident. Some industrial accident at work, or a car crash.

Mr. Clive sighed. "That's the really difficult part," he said. "He was shot." He gave that a couple of seconds to sink in. "By your brother, Justin."

Ronnie stared at him. "What? Justin is just little! He's only... eight."

"I know."

"How could he shoot anyone?"

"Accidental shootings happen all the time, when guns are left where children can reach them," Mr. Clive pointed out.

Ronnie shook her head in disbelief. "Justin must feel awful. Is he okay?"

"I said that accidental shootings happen, not that this was an accidental shooting."

"What does that mean?"

"It means..." Clive looked at Mom Dare as if for support. "That it wasn't an accident. Justin shot him intentionally."

"But... why would he do that?"

"Ronnie," Mr. Clive's expression was serious. "I know it must seem like a long time since you were brought here. Two years ago, you were eight. June and Justin are eight now."

"They're two years younger than me," Ronnie agreed. That was obvious.

"How much do you remember about what happened to you two years ago?"

Ronnie swallowed and looked at Mom, who gave her a little squeeze.

"We try not to talk about that," Mom said quietly.

"I understand... you want to put it behind you and not to keep going over it again. But this is important. It will be important to Justin's defense. Do you remember what happened to you?"

Ronnie shook her head slowly. "It was a long time ago. I don't remember much now. I got hurt. I went to the hospital."

"Do you remember who it was that hurt you?"

"It wasn't my daddy," Ronnie shot back. "He wouldn't do that."

"Social Services investigated at the time and they were pretty sure that it was him. There wasn't enough evidence to convict him, but they determined that it was too dangerous for you to be put back into that situation again."

"They were wrong," Ronnie insisted.

"Justin said that he was protecting June. That she was being molested by your father."

Ronnie felt all the blood drain from her face. She was suddenly cold and empty. She had done all she could to suppress the memories, but they were trying to force themselves to the surface. Could it be true that her father had hurt June too? Not *too*, Ronnie corrected her thought processes. He had never hurt Ronnie. He couldn't have hurt June. Justin was just making up an excuse to try to get himself out of trouble. It had been an accident. He had carelessly picked up a loaded gun. In accidentally shooting their father, he had to come up with an explanation. He was just covering himself with the claim that he was protecting June.

"Just take it easy," Mr. Clive said. He was sitting on the couch on Ronnie's other side, feeling her forehead with one hand and taking her pulse on her wrist with the other. "Keep your head down for a minute. Don't try to get up too quickly."

She pushed his hands away, shaking her head. "What's going on? Just leave me alone. I want... I don't want to talk about this. I need to go to my room now."

"Sit," Mom insisted, pressing Ronnie's shoulder down. "You fainted for a minute. We want to make sure you're okay."

"I didn't faint. I just want to go to my room."

"Ronnie. You're going to need to testify. At Justin's hearing. Because the same thing happened to you and June, your story will confirm the accuracy of June's. The jury will understand Justin's reasons for doing what he did."

"I can't do that! I can't tell you anything. Nothing happened to me."

"We know that's not true. You were hurt. You may not want to talk about it. You may not remember everything clearly, but you know what happened."

"No. I don't remember anything. Nothing."

"You were eight and June is eight. You were both assaulted. In your own home. June was under the influence. A high concentration of alcohol in her blood. Just like you."

Ronnie's head whirled dizzily and she was afraid she would pass out again. She couldn't believe what was happening.

"Ruby was eight," she said suddenly.

"What?" Mr. Clive and Mom both spoke at the same time.

"Ruby was eight when she went into foster care too. But she never said anything happened to her. She just left because she was always fighting and acting out."

Clive gave a little nod. "Those could have been ways of dealing with what was happening to her. Not everyone who is abused tells about it. In fact, most don't." He looked down at Ronnie, reminding her that like Ruby, she had never admitted to any abuse.

"But what about Chloe? Nothing ever happened to Chloe when she was eight," Ronnie said triumphantly. "So nothing happened."

"Saying that nothing happened doesn't make it true. You know what happened to you. And as far as Chloe goes... you're right, she's always denied any abuse as well. But there are still some clues..." he trailed off.

"What?"

"I can't talk to you about it. That's information that only her social worker knows. It's private."

203

"She's my sister! You can tell me. Especially since it's something to do with me. Or you think it is."

"I'm sorry, but I can't. Chloe won't admit anything, so there's nothing that I can do, but there are enough indicators to make me wonder. Even if she wasn't abused, that doesn't mean the rest of you weren't."

"Well, I wasn't," Ronnie said firmly. She looked pleadingly at Mom. "Can I go to my room now, please? I don't want to talk about this anymore. It's making me sad."

Mom nodded. She gave Ronnie a squeeze and gave Mr. Clive a hard stare. "She's had enough. Thank you for coming to let her know what was happening."

"I'll let you know the funeral arrangements," Clive said, rising to his feet.

"Ronnie won't be going to the funeral."

Ronnie looked at Mom in shock. "I have to! He's my daddy!"

Mom hesitated. "We'll see," she said. "I'll have to talk to Mr. Dare about it."

Clive looked at her. "This is one decision that Social Services is going to insist on. You can't keep Ronnie away from her father's funeral. She needs to attend."

Mom got a stubborn look on her face and looked away from Clive. Ronnie looked at Mr. Clive for reassurance. What if Mom and Dad did something to prevent her from going? If they pushed it, could they keep her away?

Ronnie supposed that if they did, Social Services would take her away, or at least threaten to. Mom and Dad didn't want that.

The funeral wasn't right away. Ronnie had seen enough cop shows on TV to know that they must have to autopsy the body and finish their investigation before her father's body could be released. But eventually, Mr. Clive informed her that arrangements had been made and told Mom and Dad the details so that they could get her there.

"I will be picking up Ruby," he told them. "If you like, I can pick up Ronnie as well. Save you the trouble of having to take her."

Mom shook her head. "Oh, no. We need to be there for her. It isn't going to be an easy thing for her. She'll need Mr. Dare and I with her to give her support. I wouldn't send her to something like that all by herself."

Dad nodded his agreement. "I'll take the time off work. It's during school, so the other kids are taken care of."

Clive nodded. "I'll see you there, then." He looked Ronnie in the eye. "How are you doing, Ronnie? I know this must be very difficult for you."

So far, it hadn't been. Ronnie didn't really believe that any of it was true. It had been two years since she had seen Justin or her father, and she felt like they were still living at the old house, everything just as it had always been. She hadn't cried about it, though she had tried.

"I'm okay," Ronnie said, looking down so he wouldn't see that she wasn't sad about it. Let him think that she was. Ronnie was a caring person, it didn't make sense for her to act so coldly about her father's death.

"It wouldn't be a bad idea to increase Ronnie's counseling sessions," Clive said. "Just to help her to get through this. It must be bringing up a lot of old memories. Lots of conflicting emotions to work through."

Ronnie opened her mouth to point out that she wasn't going to counseling. She didn't need anything. But Mom gave her head a little shake, silencing Ronnie.

"We'll certainly look into it," she agreed.

Ronnie knew that Mom and Dad didn't want her discussing what had happened to her before she came to the house with anyone else. Not even with them. They believed that she would be healthier and happier if she just moved forward, not looking back. That old life was over. Whatever had happened there was gone. Ronnie wasn't that person anymore.

The morning of the funeral, Ronnie woke up feeling a little sick. She toyed with the idea of telling Mom that she was ill and just wanted to stay in bed and wouldn't be able to go to the funeral. That would make Mom happy enough. But in spite of her nervousness, Ronnie wanted to go to the funeral. She wanted to see her family again and to say goodbye to her father. She had never had a chance to say goodbye after that last day. Not to any of them.

She eventually dragged herself out of bed and got ready with everyone else going to school. Like it was just a perfectly normal day.

She didn't usually wear a dress for school except on special occasions. She didn't have a lot of use for the crisp, clean dresses that hung in her closet. Sometimes she went out to tea with Mom or waffles with Dad on their one-on-one dates. And on the occasional trips to church, which were few and far between.

The funeral wasn't until eleven, so after the other kids left for school, Ronnie was left there by herself with Mom and Dad, kicking around the house trying to find something to keep her occupied. She couldn't focus on reading a book, and there was nothing good on TV, just daytime soaps, talk shows, and game shows.

Ronnie tried to calm herself. There was nothing for her to be afraid of. She was going to see her family. She'd been missing them ever since going into foster care. She had only seen Ruby those few times, and no one else. She was sorry that the trouble between Dad and Ruby meant that she couldn't see her older sister anymore. Mr. Clive had told her about Ruby having had a stroke. Even then, Ronnie hadn't been allowed to go see her. She had wanted to go and make sure Ruby was okay, but Mom and Dad vetoed any such thoughts. Mr. Clive said that Ruby was getting better. Her speech was easier to understand and she was walking on crutches instead of using a wheelchair or walker. That was good progress. But Ronnie had still wished that she could see Ruby with her own eyes to make sure she was okay. She'd have the chance to see Ruby at the funeral. And everyone else.

"Is Justin in prison?" she asked Mom, who had come into the living room to pick up anything that didn't belong there.

"Hmm, Mr. Clive hasn't said exactly. I got the feeling that he and June are together. In foster care. I don't know whether they're in a group home or institution. I don't think he's allowed to say very much."

"I hope he's not in prison."

"Well, he did shoot your biological father. That's a crime."

Ronnie didn't know how to respond to this. She wanted to justify him, to say that it was right if he had been protecting June. But that would mean that her father had been hurting June. If he had been hurting June, had he been the one who hurt Ronnie? Either Justin was a criminal, or her father was. It wasn't much of a choice.

"I'm sorry," Mom said, watching Ronnie's face. "I know that you must love your little brother very much. It must be hard for you to hear about it. We won't talk about it anymore."

She closed the conversation, giving no thought to the fact that Ronnie was the one who had started it.

Ronnie *did* want to talk about it. She wanted to talk about a lot of things.

(II)

Eventually, Dad broke away from his computer work and went looking for Ronnie while tying his tie.

"Ready to go, kiddo?"

Ronnie nodded. "Yeah, all ready."

"Head out to the car. We'll be right there."

She wasn't waiting in the car long before Mom and Dad were out, discussing the location of the church and the traffic patterns to determine the most efficient way to get there. Neither one spoke to Ronnie.

When they arrived at the chapel, a tall man asked if they were family, and Mom launched in on a detailed description of Ronnie's place in the family and how she was their foster daughter. He nodded politely and took them to a visiting room where the family was assembled.

Her mother and Chloe stood near the casket. Her mother was crying, wiping tears, and Chloe had her arms around her comfortingly. Both Chloe and her mother were heavier than Ronnie remembered them, but very recognizable. Chloe was wearing a yellow cotton dress that set off her blonde hair. She was thirteen and had a full figure, much curvier than Ronnie remembered Ruby being two years earlier at the same age.

With Mom and Dad close behind her, Ronnie advanced into the room. She could barely remember what her father looked like, but looking at his body, it all started to come back. His black brows. His red lips. His eyes were closed, but she remembered how he looked at her and waves of dread rolled over her. She looked over her shoulder at Mom and Dad. Mom reached forward and gave her shoulder a little squeeze. Ronnie took a couple of deep breaths, trying to push the images filling her mind away. If her father had ever done anything to her, that was over now. He was gone and would never come back. He really was dead.

She willed her feet to take her to Chloe and her mother. She hugged Chloe uncertainly. They weren't a family of huggers. Her mind went back to Ruby hugging her at the house, the day that Dad had tried to have her arrested. She glanced over her shoulder at him, making sure that he wasn't upset by the embrace.

"How are you, Ronnie?" Chloe asked.

Ronnie nodded. "Okay."

She moved on to her mother, giving her a kiss on the cheek.

"Thanks for coming," her mother said. Her eyes went to Dad and Mom Dare, and Ronnie didn't know if she was supposed to introduce them. But they stepped up, introducing themselves and offering whispered condolences.

It wasn't until then that Ronnie looked past her mother and saw Justin standing with an armed and uniformed police officer, June beside him. Ronnie navigated around the policeman and a woman whose clothes screamed 'social worker' to Ronnie.

Ronnie smiled. "Hey, Justin. Are you okay?" She reached out to hug him and the policeman put out his baton, stopping her.

"You can shake hands," he said sternly.

Ronnie swallowed, feeling her eyes widen in her anxiety. She shook hands with Justin, taking in his long, lean face, no longer the round face of a baby. He and June had both changed a lot since she had seen them last. Justin shook hands, but couldn't seem to find any words for her.

Ronnie kept moving, looking back at Mom and Dad before giving June a hug. June's face was white and pinched. Ronnie wondered belatedly why they were there. Why would Justin come to the funeral of the man he had killed? Why would June come to the funeral of the man who had assaulted her? Had they been forced? Or had they wanted to come, like Ronnie had, against their guardian's wishes?

"Thanks for coming," June whispered. "We gotta talk."

Ronnie hesitated. Talk when? Where? There wasn't exactly any way they could go off somewhere private to talk. The receiving line was still moving and Ronnie couldn't stop to say more than a few words to June.

"Are you okay?" she whispered back.

June nodded and gave her one last squeeze and then Ronnie was moving on past her. She wondered if she should stand at the end of the line with June and greet people as they came in. Dad took her by the elbow and guided her to a chair. They sat down.

"Shouldn't I stand up there?" Ronnie asked, motioning to her family.

"It's better if you sit here. We'll go in with the family. You don't need to be up there, on display."

Ronnie wound one of her braids around her finger, feeling the smooth, woven texture. She didn't want everyone looking at her, but she wanted to be with her family.

A funeral worker came in and the casket was shut for the last time. They were given instructions on the procedure for entering the chapel, and then followed the casket out. The family sat on the front row, her mother and Chloe sitting on one side and Justin and June on the other. Mom and Dad slid into the second row. Ronnie hesitated, looking at them. Biting her lip, Ronnie stepped up to the front row, and went over to sit beside June. June gave her a little smile. After everyone sat down, the preacher got up at the front and started to speak. June leaned over to whisper to Ronnie.

"You have to speak at the trial. You need to tell everyone what Dad did, so they believe me and Justin."

"I... I don't remember," Ronnie protested.

"I know," June put her hand on Ronnie's arm. "It's hard, because of the wine. And... because... you don't want to think about it..."

Ronnie forced herself to breathe evenly. She closed her eyes for a minute. First seeing her father's face, and then having June whisper those words in her ears, the flashbacks grew stronger. She tried to repress them. To keep from remembering. June grabbed her hand and squeezed it.

"I know," she sympathized. "Me too. You should see Dr. Summers. She's really good. She helps me talk about it."

"I don't want to talk about it."

"But you need to. You have to tell what happened or no one will believe Justin. Chloe and Mom are going to testify against him. You need to be on our side."

Ronnie looked up at the preacher, pretending that she was listening to what he was saying. But it was all just gibberish, not even anything about their father.

"Ronnie." June nudged her. "You'll talk, right? You'll tell what happened to you. Then they'll understand. They'll know what... what he was doing to me."

Tears squeezed out the corners of Ronnie's eyes. And it wasn't because of what the preacher was saying or because she was upset about her father dying.

It was the memories bubbling up to the surface, refusing to be denied. His face, his eyes in her mind. His whispered words in her ears.

But there was more to it. She was hearing her mother's voice too. Why was she hearing her mother's voice?

Both of them together, talking, arguing before her mother decided to take Ronnie to the hospital.

Ronnie put her hands over her face, trying to shut it out. Or sort it out. To keep it from overcoming her.

Ronnie knew that she was in trouble before Mom and Dad said anything. Abandoning them to go and sit with June had been a major infraction. Ronnie's stomach tied in knots when she thought about it. What if they decided that they didn't want her anymore? She had betrayed the family.

"You can make yourself a sandwich when you get home," Mom said.

Ronnie put her hand over her stomach. "I don't feel good."

"You need to eat something. You barely had anything for breakfast."

"I'll… I'll try. I'll have something little." Ronnie didn't know if she would, though. The funeral had been so overwhelming, and now despite his silence, she knew Dad was angry at her for her behavior. "I had to go sit with June," she said. "She's my sister, and she needed me." To say nothing of Ronnie needing June. They were sisters and they should be allowed to see each other.

"You have sisters in our family," Dad pointed out.

"I know. And I love them. But… I still have my own sisters, too. My biological sisters."

"They are still your sisters," Mom admitted. "I can understand why you would want to see them, especially at a time like this. But you could still have supported them and sat with us."

Ronnie felt like she was trying to sit on an out-of-control sled, holding desperately to it as it raced down the hill straight toward the trees. She couldn't steer. She couldn't hold on. She couldn't let go. With her elbow resting on the car door, Ronnie hid her face in the crook of her elbow. Mom and Dad were silent, not pursuing it any further. Ronnie didn't cry. But she didn't not cry, either.

When she got home, Ronnie obediently made herself a sandwich, but the smells of the cold cuts, mayo, and mustard nauseated her. She forced herself to nibble the edges of the bread, but she hated the dry crusts. And they had said on TV the other night that the crusts had stuff in them that could cause cancer. So did the preserved meats. Ronnie went back upstairs to go to her bedroom, stopping in the bathroom on the way to try to settle her sick stomach. She felt better after throwing up. The pain and nausea disappeared and the feeling of impending doom gradually eased.

She went into her bedroom to try to read and study until the other kids got home from school.

(III)

Ronnie remembered his eyes. His hands. The horrible feelings, and then the pain. She heard her parents arguing through the red haze of pain. She fought off the hands, rejecting any attempt to help or move her.

"No! No, stop!"

There was a hand on her arm, shaking her. The pain increased and Ronnie fought harder.

"Leave me alone. Don't touch me!"

"Ronnie. Ronnie, wake up."

Ronnie continued to try to pull out of the grasp, but the words worked their way into her brain. *Wake up*. She was dreaming and she had to wake up to escape the nightmare. She tried to force her eyelids to open. She shook her head and tried to force her way to consciousness.

The house was dark. She couldn't see Mom, but she knew that was who was holding on to her arm and speaking to her.

"I was dreaming?" Ronnie asked, trying to catch her breath.

"You're sleepwalking. Are you awake now?"

Ronnie rubbed her eyes, trying to focus on her surroundings. She was in the living room, all turned around.

"I was sleepwalking?" she repeated.

"Come on, let's take you back to your room."

Ronnie let Mom lead her back to the stairs and up to her bedroom. She pulled out of Mom's grip to climb into her bed.

"Sorry," she apologized. "I guess I was dreaming."

"It's not your fault. The other girls are supposed to wake up if you're wandering around."

Janessa and Devaughn were obviously deep asleep, not stirring at their conversation and movements. Ronnie snuggled under her blankets. "I wasn't loud enough to wake them."

"I could hear you downstairs. They should have woken up." Mom peered at the alarm sensor on the door, unable to see it in the dark. "You're supposed to set the alarm when you go to bed. So it wakes the girls up before you get to the stairs."

"I didn't think I was going to sleepwalk tonight."

"So soon after the funeral? It obviously stirred things up. You're supposed to arm it whether you think you're going to sleepwalk or not. You can't know that when you go to bed."

"Sometimes…" Ronnie yawned. "Sometimes I can."

"Well, I'm going to arm this when I leave. In case you get up again. Try to think happy thoughts as you're going to sleep. Lay all your worries aside, everything is fine."

Easier said than done. It sounded like a simple solution. But Ronnie didn't know how to get rid of the worries or the dreams. Everything *was* stirred up, and she knew she would continue to dream when she fell asleep again.

"I'll try," she promised.

Mom nodded. She went over to the bed and gave Ronnie a kiss on the forehead. "Sweet dreams, honey."

Mom left, pausing to turn on the door sensor before walking out and shutting the door. There was a thirty-second delay on it to allow her to leave the room before it kicked in.

Ronnie closed her eyes, rolled over, and tried to clear her mind to go back to sleep.

Ronnie struggled to free herself from the grasping hands, fighting desperately. She didn't want to be hurt again. She didn't want to do the things he said. She could hear his voice in her ear, whispering to her.

"No! Let me go!"

"Ronnie. Ronnie, you're okay. Come back to bed."

"No!" Ronnie fought harder. She didn't want to go to bed with him. She didn't want to be with him.

"Ronnie!"

The dream images dissolved and gradually the room around her resolved into the kitchen. The back door. Ronnie fighting to turn the locks and escape and Dad holding on to her, preventing her from moving.

"Where am I?" Ronnie demanded, trying to process it.

"You're safe, Ronnie. You need to go back to your bed."

"Am I home? Where am I?"

"You're home. You're safe from any harm."

She grasped his wrists and tried to see him in the dark. Dad Dare. Not her father. Her father was dead, wasn't he? He couldn't come back to hurt her again.

"Okay," she said softly.

"Good girl. Now come on. Back up to bed."

He stayed with her, following her up the stairs and into the bedroom. Mom was waiting in the hallway, rubbing her eyes and frowning at the two of them.

"Where was she? The alarm didn't go."

"Down at the back door. Lucky we didn't have her wandering the streets again." Dad followed Ronnie into the bedroom and checked the light on the door sensor. It was a solid green. "The sensor is not activated."

"I armed it last time!" Mom's voice was frustrated and impatient. "Ronnie, you saw me do it. You saw me turn it on before I left last time."

Ronnie rubbed her eyes. "Yes. She did," she agreed.

Dad looked at Mom, and looked at Ronnie. The other girls slept on, undisturbed by the conversation. "Then someone turned it back off again. It couldn't be you. So, it must have been Ronnie."

"Ronnie was asleep. She couldn't turn it off while she was sleep-walking."

Dad grunted. "You hear about people doing all kinds of things while sleepwalking. Cooking meals. Driving cars. If she knows how to arm it and disarm it while she's awake, I guess she knows how when she's sleepwalking."

Ronnie felt guilty about this, even though she hadn't consciously made the choice. "I'm sorry. I didn't mean to..."

"We'll have to try to sort out another solution," Dad said, shaking his head. "Meantime, you need to go back to sleep, kiddo. Think you can stay down this time?"

"I'll try..."

Mom gave her a brief hug. "Don't stress yourself out about it, that will just make it worse. Try not to worry."

It was just as hard not to worry as it was not to sleepwalk. How was she supposed to do that? But Ronnie nodded. "Okay, Mom. I won't."

"Back in bed. I think... we'll arm the alarm anyway. Maybe you won't disarm it again."

"Yeah, okay."

The next time Ronnie awoke, it was to the door alarm. She was still in bed, but the alarm was going.

Devaughn swore and pushed the buttons on the alarm, trying to turn it off, swearing the whole time. In her panic, she couldn't get the alarm to stop. Mom crossed the hall and entered the room, nudging Devaughn out of the way in order to silence the alarm.

"You need to pay attention to whether it is armed before you open it!" she scolded Devaughn.

"I know, I know. I'm sorry. I was in a hurry and still half asleep." Devaughn danced around uncomfortably. "I gotta go to the bathroom!"

"Go then!"

Devaughn ran down the hall. Mom looked at Janessa and Ronnie. "It's about time to get up anyway, so you may as well quit playing possum and get up," she advised.

Ronnie opened her eyes again, grinning at being called out. Janessa continued to lie with her eyes closed, not stirring. Devaughn was back from the bathroom in a couple of minutes, and headed back toward her bed.

"It's time to get up," Mom repeated. "Don't go back to bed."

"Just for a couple more minutes…"

"No, Devaughn. You're first up, why don't you go have a quick bath, so it's free for everyone else? Warm water. Go on."

Devaughn groaned, but turned around and headed back to the bathroom again. Ronnie sat up, holding the blanket around her like a robe. "I get it next."

"You get it next. Get your schoolbooks ready while you're waiting."

"Okay."

[IV]

Ronnie sat looking at the toast on her plate, wondering how she was either going to force it down or to throw it out without Mom noticing.

The boys had gotten the bathroom late, so there was an uproar when they rushed down to get their breakfasts and make their lunches, and Ronnie watched for her opportunity.

"Eat up, Ronnie," Mom advised, touching her on the shoulder. "You have an appointment to get to this morning, after the others are on their way to school."

"What?" Ronnie looked up. "What appointment?"

She hated the dentist, and that was the only appointment she could think of that Mom might have set up.

"Psychologist," Mom said. "Eat up."

She moved over to the counter to make sure that the boys were preparing healthy, well-balanced lunches. Janessa raised her eyebrows at Ronnie.

"What did you do?" she whispered. "Why's she making you see a shrink?"

Ronnie shook her head, her heart thumping. "I don't know!"

"Because you're sleepwalking," Janessa suggested. "Or because of the funeral?"

"I don't know." Ronnie bit her nail. "I didn't ask her for it."

Janessa ate a few bites of her Cheerios, cutting a glance over to Mom. "After, just tell her you feel a lot better. Say it really helped."

Ronnie nodded. A ruckus broke out among the boys, and when Janessa and Devaughn looked over to see what was going on, Ronnie folded the piece of toast in half and slipped it into her pocket. When Janessa looked back at Ronnie, Ronnie was chewing and wiping her lips with her napkin. Janessa's eyes went down to Ronnie's empty plate and a frown crossed her face. Ronnie kicked Devaughn under the table and Devaughn let out a squeal, clutching at it.

"Quit making faces at me!" Ronnie told Devaughn.

"I didn't do anything!" Devaughn protested.

Mom hurried over. "Girls! What's going on with you kids this morning? Are you trying to give the boys a run for their money? What's going on?"

"Ronnie kicked me!" Devaughn howled.

"She was making faces at me," Ronnie insisted. "Making fun of me because I have to go see the psychologist."

"I was not! I wasn't even looking at you!"

"She was too. She was going like this!" Ronnie made a face for Mom. "It hurt my feelings!"

"Devaughn, you know better than that. If one of us has to see a therapist, it's not something to make fun of. You need to be kind and supportive."

"I am, I wasn't making fun."

"And Ronnie, we don't kick! If Devaughn is bothering you, tell me. Violence is not the answer."

Ronnie stared down at the table. "I'm sorry, Devaughn. Sorry I kicked you," she said contritely.

Everyone looked at Devaughn for her apology. Devaughn's face got red. "I didn't do anything."

"Ronnie has apologized. Don't you think you can too?" Mom encouraged.

"But... fine!" There were tears in Devaughn's eyes. "I'm sorry!"

"That's better. Now you girls get along. No more fighting. Ronnie, it looks like you're done. Please start in on the dishes."

Ronnie nodded and picked up her plate as she stood.

Dr. Swanson was an old man, older than Mom and Dad, almost completely bald, with just some white fringes around his ears. But he wasn't a wizened, frail old man. He was tall and well-built, and seemed to have plenty of energy.

"I'm glad to meet you, Ronnie," he said pleasantly. "How are you feeling today?"

Ronnie shrugged. She looked around the office. It wasn't like a doctor's office, all white and steel and clinical. It was more like a businessman's office. There were even some toys on the shelves, his desk, and in a wooden box in the corner.

"Okay, I guess."

"You're a little anxious today? This is something new, that's going to take some getting used to."

Ronnie nodded.

"Well, remember that I'm here to help you. You've got a lot of difficult stuff going on right now. I'm just here to help you to work through it."

"Yeah, okay."

"Your mom says that you've been having nightmares and sleep-walking. They're concerned about you."

Ronnie felt her face flush. "I know."

"Why don't you tell me about the dreams that you have been having? Is it a recurring dream, or different dreams?"

Ronnie studied the pictures and certificates that Dr. Swanson had on his walls. "You've been a doctor for a long time."

Dr. Swanson looked at her, not answering. Ronnie shifted uncomfortably.

"What do you dream about?" Dr. Swanson asked after an interval of silence.

"Um... different things, I guess."

"Did you dream last night?"

"I don't remember."

"I'll let you think about it for a minute."

Ronnie felt the silence growing. She swallowed. She didn't have to think about it, she already knew that she'd been having nightmares and sleepwalking the previous night. She didn't want to talk about it, which was silly, since that was what Mom and Dad were paying for. They might not like her talking about her past, but they didn't want Ronnie to be miserable.

"I guess I did," she admitted. "I was sleepwalking again."

"There's nothing wrong with you," Dr. Swanson said, brushing a hand over his scalp as if to smooth down the hair that was no longer there. "Your body is just responding to your state of mind."

"Mom and Dad are afraid I'll get out of the house and something will happen to me."

"Well, that's pretty rare. Most people would wake up before they got outside, or once they stepped out in their bare feet."

"I did once, though. And I didn't wake up."

"Oh, did you? Well, if we're not able to improve the sleepwalking with counseling, you might need a sleep study to see if there is an underlying physical condition."

"I didn't used to sleepwalk. When I was... at home."

He looked momentarily confused, but his answer was calm and unhurried. "Where are you now and how is it different from home?"

Ronnie twisted her fingers together, composing an answer. "I'm with a foster family. They're not my real—my biological Mom and Dad."

"I see. How long have you been with your foster family?"

"A couple years. Almost three, I guess."

"Oh. So, this isn't a new situation."

"No."

"When did you start sleepwalking? As soon as you moved?"

Ronnie shook her head. "I don't know. Not this bad. A little bit…"

"How long ago was it you sleepwalked outside?"

Ronnie lifted her shoulders in a shrug. "Maybe… a year."

"And when did it get 'this bad'?"

She sat there, staring at what looked like a little toy with silver balls on his desk. Dr. Swanson reached over to it, pulling out one ball and letting it swing down to hit the others. Another ball bounced out at the other end, swung back, and hit the row again. Balls continued to click together, back and forth, in a steady rhythm. When the bounces were getting too small, Dr. Swanson pulled back two balls, and when they hit the row of balls, two balls bounced out the end, and the reaction went on as before.

"Cool," Ronnie said, giving him a little smile.

"Each reaction is equal, more or less," Dr. Swanson observed. "You drop one ball, and one ball comes out on the other end. You drop two balls, and two come out on the other end. They keep going back and forth, the same number of balls each time."

Ronnie nodded.

"It's like our lives. You put something new into the system," he lifted up one ball, and dropped it, "and there is an equivalent reaction."

She considered this, chewing on her thumbnail.

"When I hear that you are having nightmares and sleepwalking, I know that there's something new in the system. Something happened to cause this reaction. It didn't just come out of nowhere."

"But I don't know—"

"Something changed. Something started them. And something made them worse. I want you to think about what happened lately, before the nightmares got worse. What was happening in your life? Big or small, it doesn't matter. Just think over it."

"My daddy died. My biological father."

Swanson nodded. "That could certainly be traumatic. Was it expected? Was it sudden?"

"He wasn't sick."

Swanson continued to nod.

"He was shot."

"Well, I could see how that would give you nightmares! How awful. How do you feel about that?"

"Confused. It's all mixed up."

Swanson waited for more, but Ronnie wasn't sure what else to say.

"I never got to say goodbye to him. I haven't seen him for two years. It was... kind of spooky, seeing his body like that."

"Yes," Swanson encouraged. "What was spooky about it?"

When Ronnie closed her eyes, she could see his face. Not still and dead like it had been. Eyes open, Animated. Speaking to her directly.

"I kind of forgot what he looked like until I saw his... body... again. It was like he'd already been dead for two years. But when I saw his face... I started to..." Ronnie trailed off, trying to pull her thoughts together.

"What started when you saw his face?" Swanson prompted.

"I don't know. I started to see things in my head."

"What kind of things? Memories?"

Ronnie scratched at a snag in her pants. "I don't know if that's what they are. I see things. I try to make them go away but I can't forget them..."

"Repressing memories doesn't make them go away," Swanson said.

He was more accurate than he knew. She nodded without looking at him.

"There are better ways to deal with memories. Talking about them, for instance."

"I don't want to talk about them," Ronnie replied instantly.

"Talking can be hard. But it will make you feel better, in the long run. Maybe we can get rid of the nightmares and sleepwalking. Or at least bring them down to a more manageable level. Wouldn't you like that?"

"I guess. Maybe. It bothers Mom more than it bothers me," Ronnie said with a bit of a grin. Mom was the one who was trying to keep her from leaving her room or the house. Ronnie didn't really worry about that. Just about pushing the pictures away.

Swanson chuckled. "Moms worry about everything. Your foster mom is obviously very worried about you and your well-being, or she wouldn't have brought you here. Do you believe that she wants to help you?"

"Yeah, sure." Ronnie knew that Mom loved her and wanted her to be happy. She said so all the time.

"If you can trust that she loves you, maybe you can trust me and what I suggest. You know that she wouldn't bring you here if it was something that would harm you. She knows this is the right thing for you."

"Uh-huh."

"Maybe we can talk a little about these memories."

"Pictures," Ronnie corrected, not wanting to call them memories.

"Pictures, then. What kind of pictures do you see?"

Ronnie sighed, and closed her eyes, trying to focus. "I see his face. My daddy's."

"Yes…? Go on."

"Not like when he was dead. Like he was still alive."

"Do you miss him?"

"Yes."

"And wish that he was still alive?"

"Yeah. I wish Justin hadn't shot him. It's bad for Justin too."

"I… would guess so. Who is Justin?"

"My brother."

"You have an older brother?"

"Younger. I know, it's crazy, right? But it's true. He's just little… and he shot our daddy. He's going to prison. Or probably. He wants me to testify."

"Yes…?"

"I can't, because I can't remember. I don't remember any of the stuff they say happened. I really don't."

"Maybe it's there, in those picture and nightmares."

Ronnie swallowed. "Uh-huh."

"It's okay if you don't want to call them memories. Let's just call them impressions for now. What kind of impressions do you have about your father?"

"He was big. All adults are big, and I was only eight. My *impressions* are... of him talking to me. And holding on to me. That's all."

"And in your impression, why is he holding on to you? Is it like holding you in his lap on a playground ride? Or holding on to your arm to prevent you from doing something?"

"I dunno. Both. He does both. Holds me in his lap. Holds my arms. Grabs me so I can't walk away."

"When he's holding you, how do you feel?"

"Scared. Little." Ronnie shifted uncomfortably in her chair, trying to identify the feelings and images in the impressions, without having to feel the emotions. She didn't succeed. "I don't like it. I don't like what he's doing."

Dr. Swanson waited for a while without saying anything.

"What happens when you don't like it?"

"What do you mean?"

"What do you do?"

Ronnie got up. "How much longer do I have to stay here? Mom said it wouldn't be very long. Will you tell her that I answered all of your questions and I'm feeling better now? I don't need to come back next week."

"I think you need more than forty-five minutes of therapy."

"I really am feeling better."

Ronnie was lying. Her emotions were stirred up worse than ever. She didn't know what to do with herself. She didn't want to look at the pictures. She didn't want to talk about them. She wanted to take that big hot ball of feelings and throw it away. She didn't want to have to keep thinking about it. Not any of it.

"I'm glad you're feeling better. But I don't think we're done."

"Just tell her you don't think that I'll sleepwalk anymore. I'll try to stop. I'll really try this time."

"Trying to stop sleepwalking isn't going to have any effect. It isn't something that you can control by will. In fact, the harder you try to suppress these... impressions... the harder you are going to struggle with the nightmares and sleepwalking. Your brain has to deal with it somehow."

Ronnie paced back and forth. She looked at the toys on the shelf, but she couldn't stop and be still.

"Why don't you give me a pill? Can't you give me a pill to help me to sleep better? Or to make me feel better. Just give me a pill and it will be okay."

"There are some prescriptions that we can consider to help you sleep better. But that isn't the same as dealing with the emotions. Those are not going to go away. They're still going to be there, no matter how many pills you take."

"Unless I OD'd," Ronnie pointed out. "If I OD'd, I wouldn't have any more memories or any more trouble sleeping!" She gave a little laugh at her own cleverness.

"Ronnie..." Swanson's serious tone of voice compelled her to look at his face. He wasn't laughing at her joke. He looked very somber and concerned. "Joking about overdosing is not funny. In fact, it really concerns me. Have you considered suicide?"

"No," Ronnie brushed it away. She shook her head and paced across the room again. "I'd never do that. You have lots of certificates. That means you had to go to school for a really long time, right?"

"Longer than you've been alive," he agreed.

Ronnie rolled her eyes at this. Obviously he had gone to school longer than she had been alive. Even if he only went to high school, that was longer than she had been alive. He'd probably gone to school twice as long as she had been alive. Or more.

"How do you think the people who love you would feel if you committed suicide?" Dr. Swanson asked.

"I guess they'd be really sad. But they could adopt another kid. They don't have to have me," Ronnie pointed out.

He rubbed his chin, looking at her. "You think you're disposable? Any kid would do just as well?"

"Well, maybe not any kid, but there are lots of them to choose from. They could find someone else. They replaced Eclipse with Devaughn."

"That must have bothered you."

Ronnie looked at him, thinking about it. *How did she feel about Eclipse?*

"We weren't that close."

"Even so... we aren't used to just losing our family members. Maybe that was more traumatic to you than you realize, after losing your association with your birth family."

Ronnie walked up the side of the room to look out the window behind Swanson. "No... I was okay with it. I understood. She didn't fit in with our family. We were just helping her out for a little while by giving her a home."

"Did you understand from the start that she wasn't a permanent member of the family?"

"Yes."

"But you're hoping to be adopted. You're hoping they are your permanent family."

"Uh-huh," Ronnie agreed cheerfully. She was doing a good job of it, too. She felt like she had a pretty good grip on the position. As long as some little thing like school grades or sleepwalking didn't become an issue.

"Do you worry a lot about having to leave and go to a different family? About not being adopted?"

There was a smudge on the window. Ronnie rubbed it with her sleeve. "Not a lot. I know they want to adopt me."

"Did your nightmares get worse when Eclipse left?"

"Uh..." Ronnie thought about it. "No, it was after that."

"Was it when your father died?"

"Maybe."

Dr. Swanson made a note on the file in front of him. Ronnie couldn't read his writing over the distance she was standing from him.

"Could you come sit back down, Ronnie? Maybe you could tell me some more about your father." He looked down at his notes. "Let's go back to those impressions of him. Of being held, and not being comfortable with it. What would you do, if he was holding you and you didn't like what he was doing?"

"I don't know. I wouldn't do anything. He was my daddy."

"How did that make you feel? You didn't like him holding you, but you couldn't do anything about it?"

Ronnie walked back over to her chair, but was too anxious to sit back down. At least when she walked around, the knot in her guts loosened a little and she felt like she could breathe again. She didn't like Swanson's questions. They made the pictures more clear. She really didn't want to think about them. She didn't want to think about how she felt, or would have felt, if he were hurting her and she couldn't do anything about it. She felt sick and trapped and helpless, just like in the dreams.

"How long do we have? Isn't the time almost up? When do I get to play with the toys? Could I take a break?"

"If you see something you want to play with, please help yourself. I think we'll keep talking, though."

Ronnie looked through the toys in the chest that she had noted earlier. There wasn't really anything that she wanted to play with, but she pulled out a baby doll and went over and sat back down with it. Swanson watched her for a minute.

"How would that baby feel if you were holding her and wouldn't let go?"

Ronnie sat the doll in her lap and put her arms around it, pinning it in place. She closed her eyes. "Trapped. Scared. But if I'm her mommy, she knows I wouldn't hurt her."

"I see."

Ronnie released the baby and opened her eyes. It had plastic head and limbs, but a soft torso. She laid it on its back in her lap and pulled up the dress. She looked at the doll's body in surprise.

"I've never seen a doll like this before! It's a girl and it has all of the girl parts!" She fingered it, exploring all of the parts to make sure they were complete. "That's cool. Where did you get it?"

Dr. Swanson was watching her and it suddenly occurred to Ronnie that maybe she shouldn't be poking her fingers into the doll's private parts. She put the baby's dress down again and smoothed it down. "There. All better. You should get a diaper for her. Then people wouldn't touch down there."

"That probably wouldn't stop anyone. You can take a diaper off just as easily as pulling up the dress."

"Why would anyone do that?"

"Maybe people need to show me what happened to them and it's easier with a doll."

"Nobody would do that to a baby. Not if they loved it."

"It can be pretty confusing, can't it? Sometimes people say they love you and then their actions say something different. Or sometimes we feel loved by them and sometimes we feel hurt or used."

"Or guilty," Ronnie contributed.

"Oh, yes. Definitely," Swanson agreed.

Ronnie smoothed the doll's dress. "You have to be careful... you could accidentally hurt someone."

"People don't always realize that, do they? How fragile a baby might be."

Ronnie nodded. She stared off into space, trying to sort out the images and the feelings. "They said it was my daddy that hurt me."

Dr. Swanson nodded. He gave her time to say more, but Ronnie floundered, not knowing what else to say, where else to go with it.

"What do you think?" Dr. Swanson asked. "Are they right?"

"I thought my mom and dad loved me. Moms and dads are supposed to love their kids. That's what everybody says, right? Nobody loves more than a mother... But..." She shook her head. "I don't think they ever said they loved me. Only when he..." Ronnie trailed off and shook her head. She slapped her hand down hard on the baby doll in frustration, making her hand sting. "Hurting someone, that's not love, is it?"

Swanson ran his hand over his scalp again. "Sometimes in relationships there are accidental hurts. Hurt feelings, knocking into each other by accident. But not abuse. Not inappropriate touching or hurting someone's body. Or threatening or demeaning behavior.

That's not showing love. We need to protect ourselves from people like that."

"He's dead now so I don't need to be protected. I could go back to my family. Or to my mom."

"Is that what you want? Did Social Services suggest it?"

Ronnie stared at her feet. "No. They wouldn't let me go back, I don't think. Because my mom…"

He raised his eyebrows and waited. His eyebrows were darker than the white hair over his ears. Sort of a silvery gray.

"Do they not think that your mother is safe either?" he eventually asked.

"No. She shouldn't have let him. She shouldn't have… helped him."

"So, maybe it wouldn't be safe to go back there. Maybe you still need to be protected from your mom too."

"She wasn't the one who hurt me, though. She's the one who took me to the hospital. So, she took care of me, she would look after me and protect me."

"Did she try to protect you from you dad? I thought you just said that she didn't. She helped him."

"She didn't do it. She didn't touch me. I just mean… she…"

"Enabled it?"

Ronnie frowned at this. "What does that mean?"

"It means that she did things to allow him to hurt you, or to cover up what he had done to protect him from being punished."

"Yeah. That's what they say she did. Enabled."

"And what do *you* say? Did she?"

"I don't remember." But she did remember her mother bathing her, washing away any evidence.

"Do you have nightmares about this?" Dr. Swanson asked.

"Sometimes."

"How about when you are sleepwalking? Do you remember what you dream about when you are sleepwalking?"

"Him holding me…" Ronnie said. She shuddered a little, goosebumps sprouting up on her arms. "He wouldn't let me go. But it's just a dream. I just dream it because they keep saying he did that. Not because I remember."

Mom talked to the therapist and paid for the session and they took the elevator back down to where the car was parked without saying anything to each other.

"Are we done now?" Ronnie asked as she buckled herself in. "I don't have to go back there again?"

"Is that what Dr. Swanson told you?"

"Well... no. He thought I should keep going back," Ronnie admitted. She was sure he'd told her that anyway. There was no point in hiding it. "But I don't think I need to go back. I think I'm okay. This helped a lot, and... I shouldn't have to go back again."

Mom started the car and pulled out. She looked over at Ronnie and then back at the road again. "The doctor thinks that you still have a lot left to process. This is just the beginning."

"But... doctors always want you to go back again," Ronnie said, echoing one of her mother's frequent complaints. "They always say that you have to go back to follow up, just so they can bill you again. So, you have to pay to say there's nothing wrong with you."

Mom nodded her head a little, betraying her agreement. "I don't think that's what Dr. Swanson is doing. We're all very concerned about you, Ronnie. Worried about how you are handling all of this."

"I'm okay. I just sleepwalked a few times. That doesn't mean anything."

"Your father's death has obviously had an effect on you. And... Mr. Clive and the prosecutor both want you to see a therapist to see if they can help you to talk about... your testimony at Justin's trial."

"I don't want to testify."

"We don't want you to have to. But it isn't within our control. If they subpoena you, there's nothing we can do about it. Even if we tell them it's a potentially harmful situation, that it could cause even more emotional problems for you... it doesn't seem to matter."

"They can't make me talk about anything. If I can't remember…"

Mom looked sideways at Ronnie. "Are you sure you don't remember?"

"It was a long time ago," Ronnie brushed it off. "I don't know what happened. I don't remember who hurt me. I don't want to. I don't want to think about it and I don't want to have to go back to Dr. Swanson's again. I just want to… be normal. Like everyone else."

"You are normal, Ronnie. There's nothing wrong with you."

Ronnie turned to look out the window, making a face when she was turned away so that Mom wouldn't see it. If Mom said she was normal, that meant she was doing her job. She was fitting in. But she didn't feel normal. She felt like an alien just trying to pass herself off as human. All of her experiences and feelings and reactions were different from those of anyone else around her. She had come from a completely different place. She didn't fit in, no matter how hard she tried. Those differences were just magnified by her trip to Dr. Swanson's. If they kept taking her there, it was just going to confirm to the Dares how different and damaged she was, and she couldn't afford for them to think that.

(V)

The date of Justin's trial had initially been months away, but it came all too soon. Ronnie had tried not to think about it. She tried not to worry about what was going to happen. Justin's lawyer, Thorne, had called several times to say that he would like to go over things with her to help her to prepare for her testimony, but Mom and Dad had said no. The prosecutor, Voychuk, had demanded that she come in to talk to him several times, but Mom and Dad said no to that, too. Both of them made Ronnie nervous. They both wanted her to tell them what she was going to stay when she got onto the stand at the trial. Ronnie had no idea what she was going to say. She couldn't get up there and accuse her father of doing such awful things to her. It was wrong, and she would feel naked, stripped in front of the world and baring all of her secrets like that.

Voychuk knew that Ronnie had maintained it wasn't her father who hurt her, and that was what he expected her to say on the stand. But Ronnie didn't know if she could say that, either. The nightmares were becoming worse. She was sleepwalking every night. The impressions were asserting themselves and Ronnie couldn't forget them during the day like she had before. They were with her all the time. Therapy wasn't making them go away.

Ronnie couldn't eat before the trial. Her stomach didn't just have butterflies, she felt ready to throw up. Mom encouraged her to eat a few times, but she couldn't even look at food and spent most of the time in the bathroom until they had to go to the courthouse.

"It's time to go," Mom called through the door.

When Ronnie came out, Mom gave her a hug. "I know it's hard, sweetie. After today it will be done. Then you don't have to think about it anymore."

"I don't understand why I have to go," Ronnie complained. "I've told everyone I can't remember what happened. It wasn't my daddy. So, why do I have to go?"

"They subpoenaed you. We've objected, but there's nothing we can do. You have to go. You can tell them you don't remember anything. Then you can come home. Okay?"

Ronnie nodded, trying not to let the tears that filled her eyes escape. She could do it. Just a few minutes on the stand to say that she didn't know what they were talking about. That they were wrong. Then she could go home and forget all about it.

It was early when they got there. Justin was already sitting up at the front with his lawyer. He kept twisting around to see the courtroom behind him and was watching as Ronnie and Mom and Dad came in. Dad motioned to one of the back benches, but Ronnie shook her head.

"I want to sit with June," she said, pointing at the bench up at the front, where June sat as close to Justin as possible.

"You need to sit with us."

"Then come up to the front," Ronnie pleaded. She remembered

how upset they had been after the funeral, when she had sat with June instead of with them. Then she'd only been separated from them by one bench. But she had to be with her little sister. She had to be as close to her as possible. Ronnie didn't understand why she felt so guilty about June. She hadn't done anything to hurt June. She couldn't have stopped June from getting hurt. But deep down, she felt like if anything had happened to June, it was Ronnie's fault. She could have put him in jail before June was ever hurt, if she'd just been able to tell them what happened.

"You two can't be chatting during the trial. You have to sit quietly."

Ronnie nodded. "I will. I promise."

Mom and Dad looked at each other and then moved toward where June was sitting. Ronnie slid in next to her. June was wearing a simple white t-shirt and no makeup. Her hair had been neatly combed, unlike Chloe's. Chloe and their mom sat on the other side, with the prosecutor. Voychuk. Even his name made him sound like a villain from James Bond or Dracula. Chloe looked unkempt, as if she'd been dragged out of bed to testify. She was wearing makeup, but it didn't make her attractive.

"Thanks," June said, touching Ronnie's hand tentatively. "You're going to tell them what happened, right? About how he hurt you."

Ronnie looked over at the Dares and found Dad glaring at her already. "We're not supposed to talk."

"Oh. Okay."

Ronnie sat back, looking at Dad again to make sure he saw she was sitting quietly and not talking. He nodded. Ronnie looked around, watching for anyone else she knew. But who would there be? None of her old school friends would be there and she didn't know any extended family. Most of the people there seemed to either be professionals who expected to testify or reporters or other curious onlookers just there to see someone else's life ruined. The courtroom was nearly full when Ronnie saw Ruby being escorted in by a police officer. She had missed Ruby at the funeral, but Mr. Clive said that she'd been there sitting in the back. Ruby walked with the assistance of crutches, short ones she held in her hands, with cuffs around her wrists. Mr. Clive said she was recovering from her stroke, but her speech and mobility were still affected. Like Ronnie, she had been subpoenaed to ensure her attendance. Ronnie didn't know if the policeman was there because Ruby had refused to come, or because she was still supposed to be in custody. Since the courtroom was almost full, Ruby didn't have much choice as to where to sit, so she didn't get the back row. She ended up sitting at the front behind Chloe.

The attorneys made their opening statements. Justin wrote notes to his lawyer on the legal pad on the table. Ronnie wondered what he was writing about. Then Justin was called up to testify. He spoke clearly, relating his story of what had happened and then answering the prosecutor's questions in a matter-of-fact way. Ronnie felt cold listening to him. His words seemed impossible, but she couldn't dismiss them. Everything he said sent impressions flooding through Ronnie's head. She could see exactly what he was talking about. It was as if he'd opened a curtain to look straight into her brain, flooding it with light so that she could see it as well. Ronnie didn't want to see. She closed her eyes, but that didn't shut off the images.

June grasped Ronnie's hand and gave it a firm squeeze. "It's okay," she whispered. "It's okay, he's gone now. He can't hurt you."

Ronnie squeezed back, hanging on for dear life. She thought that June was giving her comfort, but maybe it worked both ways, because all too soon it was time for June to go up to the witness box and answer questions. She reluctantly let go of Ronnie's hand and walked up to the front. Ronnie suddenly really had to pee. She was sure that they would call her up next. She glanced down the row to see if there was any way that she could make her way out of the courtroom and to the bathroom without anyone noticing her. It was impossible.

Ruby was shifting around and Ronnie wondered whether she had to go to the bathroom too. But looking sideways without turning her head too much, she could see Ruby rubbing and read-justing her legs, obviously cramped in the tight rows of the courtroom.

June started off strong. Her voice was steady and even though her hands fidgeted with her hair and face, she looked as comfortable as seemed possible on the stand. As Voychuk questioned her about the abuse and her failure to report it to her mother, school teachers, or any other trusted adult, her voice wavered. She swallowed a lot more. Her face flushed and tears started down her cheeks. She didn't sob aloud, but everyone could see the tears sliding silently down her face and soaking into her t-shirt.

There was a lump in Ronnie's throat. Justin's testimony had made her see images, to see it all played out around her, but June's testimony made her *feel* it. Helpless, alone, frustrated, and guilty. Caught in a trap there was no way to get out of. She wished that June were still sitting next to her so that she had someone's hand to hold. Mom, on the other side, didn't seem to know that Ronnie needed anything. June was crying in earnest by the time Voychuk was done with her. So were several of the jurors. Ronnie was struggling to keep her emotions under control, the walls of the courtroom closing in around her.

Then June was done and it was Ronnie's turn. Ruby got up and walked down the aisle and for a moment Ronnie thought she was leaving and that the policeman would have to wrestle her back to her seat by force. But Ruby walked unsteadily, stopped and rubbed her legs, and stretched them out. Not running away, just trying to get comfortable.

Ronnie sat down in the hard chair of the witness box. She looked out at the audience, able to see everybody's faces clearly for the first time. Justin, watching her intently, looking like he would bound over the table and come to her side if she asked for it. June sniffling and wiping her eyes, nobody sitting beside her to comfort her. Ruby hobbled back to her seat, a scowl across her face. Chloe and their mom were staring daggers at Ronnie. Ronnie felt that familiar fear in the pit of her stomach. When their mom got mad about some misbehavior, Ronnie hadn't been faced with the threat of being disowned, but with swift physical reprisal. No one messed with Mim Simpson.

Ronnie looked away from her, back toward Justin and June. And her Mom and Dad. They were all there, rooting for her. Supporting her.

One of the court clerks adjusted the mike, moving it closer to Ronnie's mouth, and prompted her to speak up several times as he swore her in and she answered Voychuk's preliminary questions. Ronnie fought back tears of frustration as she tried to speak loudly enough that everyone would be able to hear her.

"You were admitted to the hospital after being assaulted when you were eight," Voychuk stated, and gave the date of her admission.

Ronnie nodded.

"Is that correct?" Voychuk asked. "I need you to give your answers out loud. The court reporter can't record head-shaking," he said with a teasing smile.

Ronnie nodded again and swallowed. "Yes."

"At that time, you told the police that it was not your father who assaulted you."

"Uh-huh."

"And since that time, you have never claimed that it was your father who hurt you."

"No."

"*Was* it your father?"

Ronnie swallowed and cleared her throat. She nodded her head. She could see the surprise in his eyes. He waited for her to answer aloud. Ronnie tried to speak, but no sound came out. She cleared her throat again.

"Yes."

"You've had every opportunity to accuse him since then. Why would you change your story now?"

When Ronnie opened her mouth to answer, he talked over her.

"It wouldn't be just because you want to keep your baby brother out of jail, would it?"

"No. I don't want him to go to jail, but I wouldn't lie."

"You *have* been lying for years, and now you're telling the truth."

Ronnie nodded. There was a long pause and she remembered to speak. "Yes."

"When did this alleged abuse begin?"

"I guess when I was eight… about eight…"

"Did you tell anybody about what was going on?"

"No."

"Why not?"

"I didn't understand… I was confused. And I didn't know who I could talk to."

"Why not talk to a teacher at school?"

"My mom… my mom always said we weren't supposed to talk about family stuff. She said if we did, we might get taken away. Like Ruby did." Ronnie flashed a glance in Ruby's direction and gave her an apologetic smile. Ruby stared right through her.

"You thought that if you told, you'd be removed from the home."

"Yeah."

"But then you would be away from the abuse. Didn't you want to be taken away from the abuse?"

"No."

Ronnie's voice was so small that he had to ask her to repeat herself.

"No."

"Why wouldn't you want to be taken away?"

"I loved my mom and dad. I didn't want to have to go away. I wanted to stay with them and my brother and sisters."

Justin's fists were clenched as he looked from Ronnie to Voychuk. He nodded at this, probably unconscious that he was doing so.

"You'd rather be abused."

"No… I didn't know what to do. I wanted to stop it… but I didn't know what to do."

"Previously when you were questioned about this." Voychuk was flipping through pages on the table. Then he stopped and put his index finger in the middle of one like he had found the reference that he was looking for. "You said that you were too confused and couldn't remember what had happened."

"Uh-huh."

"The hospital reports say that you were intoxicated. Drunk."

"Yeah."

"You don't really remember what happened, do you?"

"I don't remember much about what happened the night I went to hospital." The images were rushing back to Ronnie even as she said it. Overwhelming her with detailed images, sensations, and feelings. She could barely go on. "But I remember some. And there were other times too." She had been about to say 'other nights,' but something tickled at the back of her brain. Had there been daytime episodes too? While the other children were at school? That didn't make any sense, why would she be home when the others were at school? But she couldn't escape the feeling.

"Isn't it true that you were late getting home from school that day?"

Ronnie was confused by the change in direction.

"Yes."

"And you were, in fact, late getting home from school many other days?"

"Yes."

"Isn't it true that you were assaulted after school, during the time before you got home? And that you've never accounted for what happened during that missing time?"

Ronnie grasped the arms of the chair, feeling like she was going to faint and slide right out of it. Her heart was beating so fast it hurt. Her face was hot and sweaty.

"No."

"What were you doing after school, then?"

"I just... sometimes my friends, we went to play in our fort in the park. Or sometimes I went to other girls' houses. Just to play games or watch TV."

"What about that night? Where did you go that night?"

"I don't know... it wasn't night, only afternoon... we went... to the park."

"Are you sure of that?"

Ronnie fought to remember. She bit her lip. "No."

"I would think that on the night that something like that

happened to me, I'd remember what I had been doing. Isn't it true that you went to your play fort? And there was a man in the park watching you? And that's who assaulted you?"

"No!"

"Your friends said that you weren't with them."

"I... I was... I think."

"Don't you remember? I would remember who assaulted me."

Just when Ronnie felt like she couldn't go on, she couldn't say or remember anything more, it was like her body decided to shut the anxiety and fear and frustration off. Her heart started to slow. Like she had broken over the top of the hill and was now coasting down the other side.

"I remember who did it," she said softly.

"Speak up, Ronnie. You've got a microphone, but we can't hear you."

"I remember who hurt me. It was my daddy."

"Explain to me what you think you remember."

Ronnie took another calming breath, the emotions continuing to evaporate.

"I was okay when I came home. I wasn't hurt at the park. I had supper with everyone. Everything was normal."

Voychuk stood there, eyebrows raised in disbelief.

"Mom sent everyone off to bed. Except for me. She said that they needed me for something."

Still Voychuk said nothing. Ronnie breathed. For an instant, her eyes locked with Justin's. He believed her. He believed every word. She glanced at June, who was nodding in agreement. She mouthed something at Ronnie, but Ronnie wasn't sure what it was.

"I was supposed to sit on the couch and watch TV with Daddy while Mom got everyone off to sleep. He got up and got me a cup of juice." Ronnie paused. She waited for Voychuk to ask a question. "It tasted bad. He said I needed to drink it all. Like cough medicine. So, I did. He put his arm around me and said he wanted to cuddle. It felt nice and I was getting tired. He pulled me onto his lap and I cuddled there, but he kept moving around, not letting me fall asleep like I wanted to."

Ronnie licked her lips. Her mouth was dry. She didn't need to pee anymore. She kept talking, telling them what had happened. The courtroom receded far away. She described it like it had happened to another person and didn't affect her. Bare facts. Not a tear or a sob when she told how badly he hurt her. Not like he had before. Much worse. She wondered fleetingly if he'd been angry with her for resisting. Or angry at her mother for something she had done. There had to be a reason he'd hurt her so badly. Ronnie related the bath, the argument, the agonizing trip to the emergency room, shivering in her nightie, her body clenched with pain.

She was barely conscious of the questions that Voychuk was asking her. One part of her brain answered while the other part segregated the pain. She was exhausted when Voychuk said he was done. Thorne didn't have any questions, so the judge told Ronnie that she could step down. She went back to her seat like a sleepwalker. She had to shuffle past Mom and Dad and neither of them said anything to her. Ronnie sat back in her spot beside June. June reached around her shoulders and gave her a squeeze.

"I'm sorry," she whispered. "That must have really hurt."

Ronnie swallowed and closed her eyes and didn't answer.

Ronnie's mother and Chloe testified after the lunch break. Their testimony was about as expected. Insisting that nothing had happened to June and that the shooting was therefore unjustified and unprovoked. Ronnie tried to listen to it with the ears of a juror. Did they sound like they were telling the truth? Were they believable? They both sounded so sure of themselves. The idea of their father touching June or Ronnie or anyone else was ridiculous. The jurors were no longer crying like they had been for June's testimony.

Then it was Ruby's turn. Ronnie had been wondering if they were actually going to call her or not. But with Ruby testifying for the prosecution, the two sides were balanced, with three family members for each. They needed her testimony, particularly as one of the children, to add weight to their case.

Ruby struggled up to the front and settled herself into the witness seat. After managing to get her sworn in, only with the intervention of the judge, Ruby gave short, stuttering answers to the questions directed at her. It took her a while to get the words out, but once she did, they were understandable.

She seemed puzzled by the suggestion that, like Ronnie and June, she had been molested by their father. Her eyes went from one face to another, intense, trying to read each of them. She denied any abuse. Denied drinking or being given alcohol. Ronnie studied her carefully, wondering if she had nightmares. Did she have impressions too, or had she succeeded where Ronnie had failed and completely repressed the memories? She had had five years more than Ronnie to completely wipe them out before having testify.

Mr. Clive had said that the jury could be deliberating for days before they came back with a verdict one way or the other. But it was just the next day that he called back to say the jury was coming back in.

"I don't think we need to go back," Mom said, taking plates from the drying rack and stacking them in the cupboard. "Mr. Clive will call and let us know the verdict when he hears it. You don't need to be there for that."

Ronnie wasn't sure how she felt about that. She'd like to go, to hear for herself, and see her siblings one last time. But it wasn't worth arguing about. Even if she went, she wouldn't be able to talk to any of them again. She wasn't sure how she would handle it if they convicted Justin and sent him to prison. She kept repeating to herself that they couldn't send an eight-year-old to prison, but she didn't one hundred percent believe it.

She helped with putting away the dishes, and then with sorting laundry. Mom had let her stay home when she said she wasn't feeling well after all of the upheaval of the trial. Ronnie hadn't slept well, which meant that Mom hadn't either, and they both had a morning nap after the other kids were off to school.

Ronnie watched the clock. How long did it take for the jury to stand up and say guilty or not guilty? Still, the phone startled her when it rang. She and Mom exchanged glances. Mom answered it, greeted Mr. Clive, and listened. She told him thank you and hung back up again.

"Did they convict him?" Ronnie asked worriedly, heart beating hard.

"No... the jury hung. The judge declared a mistrial."

"What's that mean? He doesn't have to go to jail?"

"Not unless they try him again. Mr. Clive says he doesn't think they will. Not without something a lot more convincing."

"So he's okay. He can just go to a foster family now."

"It looks that way."

Ronnie let her breath out in a long whistle of relief. "Good. That's really good."

Mom was frowning. "Mr. Clive asked before if we'd consider taking the twins if things turned out okay."

"Really? So we could be together? That would be cool! Are you going to do it?"

"We need to discuss it. I'm not sure it's the best course. They're different than you, Ronnie."

Ronnie scratched the back of her head. "What do you mean?"

"Justin has already resorted to violence. I don't want to put any of you kids at risk, if he should blow up over something else. From what I've gathered from Mr. Clive, there has been fighting at school as well. He's not the kind of child I would normally agree to take."

"But he's my brother! And June needs him. They can't split up twins."

"I don't want to split up twins," Mom agreed. "I'm just not sure that we're the right family for Justin or June."

"Why not June?"

Mom chose her words carefully. "June seems to have some... more serious psychological issues... She has a lot of problems with school, both with the work and getting along with other students and following the rules. She's not like you, Ronnie. She's not willing to follow rules and fit in. With Justin being so oppositional and prone to violence... I just don't think it's the right situation for us. They need a family that's more experienced dealing with... delinquents."

"They're not delinquents." Ronnie was outraged. "They're just eight!"

"I'm not calling them names," Mom soothed. "I'm not judging them. I just don't think it's the right situation for our family. I think they need a different kind of care. We're not prepared to take two children who are going to be such a disruption and a potential danger."

"That's not fair!" Ronnie complained. She stormed off to her room and shut the door. She threw herself down on the bed and buried her face in the pillow. For an instant, she'd been happy about Justin not being convicted and having to go to jail, and then about the possibility of them moving in to the Dare family. Just to be crushed by the announcement that June and Justin were too badly disturbed for the Dares to take them.

Did Mom and Dad regret taking Ronnie? With Ronnie's sleep issues and having to testify at the trial, did they wish that they had never taken her in? Were they watching her marks at school, deciding what average she needed to maintain for them to keep her in the family?

Ronnie wiped at her tears. If she were concerned about maintaining her position in the family, she'd better quit whining and crying and buckle down. Crying wasn't going to win her any popularity contests.

[VI]

Ronnie shook off the hand that shook her shoulder, groaning that she wanted to go back to sleep. She knew that it wouldn't actually get her any more time to sleep, but she felt too exhausted to even open her eyes.

"Ronnie. Up and at 'em. You haven't been at school for two

days, you need to get back to it or you'll have problems keeping up."

Ronnie turned over and lay there, blinking. The woman decided that she was up and moved on. Listening to her progress, Ronnie looked slowly around her, taking in all her surroundings. Nothing was familiar. She was disoriented, but not upset by this. She thought that maybe if she lay there for a while, she would wake up enough that it would all start making sense.

"You'd better get up!" one of the other girls warned. "Mom will get mad if she has to come back!"

Ronnie forced herself to sit up. She looked around to see if this changed perspective would help at all. She slipped out of bed and joined the girls getting dressed.

"Hey, that's mine!" The pair of pants that Ronnie had picked up at random was snatched out of her hands. "You can't have it!"

Ronnie looked at her for a moment, then looked back at the dresser drawers, floor, and closet. She had no clue what was hers and what belonged to the other girls. She couldn't see any sense of order that would help her to sort it out.

"I don't know what to wear."

"You should wear that new blouse," the third girl suggested. At Ronnie's blank look, she grabbed it out of the closet, and then grabbed a pair of pants for Ronnie as well. Relieved, Ronnie dressed.

"Where's Ronnie?" Ronnie heard Mom ask. "Ronnie, quit dawdling!"

Taking another minute to look at herself in the mirror to make sure she looked okay and hadn't forgotten something, Ronnie headed down the hall, then down the stairs toward the sounds of activity. The kitchen was a bustle of activity, everyone moving around to get breakfasts and bagged lunches ready.

Mom looked up from the lunches she had been expecting to look at Ronnie as she came in.

"Ronnie, your hair!"

Ronnie touched it uncertainly. "What?"

"You need to get ready."

Ronnie stared at her, trying to discern her meaning.

"Come here. Sit down," Mom barked, motioning to a kitchen chair. Ronnie sat down and was still as Mom grabbed a comb and elastics and moved quickly to braid Ronnie's hair into two long pigtails. Ronnie had combed her hair, so the comb didn't snag, but the speed with which Mom moved to whip the braids into shape made her pull and hurt Ronnie's head. Mom snapped elastics onto the ends. "There. Now get yourself some breakfast. I don't understand why you'd being such a slowpoke this morning. Are you worried about school?"

Ronnie didn't move from the chair. She pulled a bowl over in front of her and poured granola into it.

"I can't remember anything," she said.

"Do you have a test?"

"I don't know."

"What are you worried about remembering? Are you worried about getting behind because you missed?"

"No." Ronnie poured milk over the oats. "I can't remember anything."

"What are you talking about?"

Ronnie took a bite and started chewing, while Mom moved around the kitchen like a little tornado, trying to be everywhere and do everything at once. She dealt with lunches, permission slips, and the rowdy boys, who kept poking each other and causing other disruptions. Ronnie ate slowly, figuring that eventually everyone else would head off to school and she could explain her dilemma once it was peaceful.

"Ronnie, you haven't even started on your lunch. Quickly finish eating breakfast and make yourself a sandwich."

Ronnie continued to chew her granola. In a couple more minutes, Mom was there, pulling the bowl away.

"You're done. Fix your lunch."

Ronnie got up. She moved slowly around the kitchen, assembling a sandwich with the makings left on the counter. The boys headed for the door, and the two girls were looking at Ronnie with impatience.

"Go ahead," Ronnie said. "Don't wait for me."

"You're going to school today," Mom said firmly. "You can't afford to miss another day."

The girls whispered and elbowed at each other, then with another look at Ronnie, headed for the door. Mom hovered over Ronnie.

"What's gotten into you today, Ronnie? You need to get going."

"I can't remember anything."

"That's what you said. What do you mean, you can't remember anything?"

Ronnie looked at her. "I can't remember anything... not you, or this house, or the others... or anything."

"What are you talking about?"

Ronnie just looked at her.

"Ronnie, quit playing around. I need you to get to school."

"I don't remember where school is. Or where my class is. Or who the teacher is, or my friends. I don't remember."

"You're being silly."

Ronnie gave a shrug. Mom studied her, looking for a smile or some indication that she was joking. When Ronnie didn't give it, she frowned.

"You aren't serious."

Ronnie nodded.

"You are telling me that you don't remember anything? You don't remember me?"

"No."

"Or your sisters? Or this house?"

Ronnie shook her head. "I can't remember anything."

Mom's eyes widened in alarm. "We need to take you to the hospital! Did you hit your head? What happened?"

"No." Ronnie felt the back of her head, then all over it. "No, I don't think so. Nothing is hurt."

"Why didn't you tell me sooner? Get your coat and shoes on and get in the car. I'll just put a few things away here..." Mom started flitting around the kitchen, putting away the mayonnaise and anything perishable. She looked back up at Ronnie. "Ronnie, I said..."

She trailed off. Ronnie looked out the doorway that led to the stairs that she had come down. She looked up and down the hall. Front door or back? And would her coat and shoes be at the door? Would she recognize them when she saw them? She assumed not, since she hadn't known which clothes were hers.

"Where do I go?"

"To your right. The back door. Your things are in the closet."

"Okay. Thanks."

She could feel Mom's eyes on her until she was out of sight of the kitchen. She found the back door and a sort of a mudroom where everything was carefully organized, but she still couldn't tell which things were hers and which belonged to the other kids.

CHAPTER
Eight

AGE 33

[1]

Ronnie rang the doorbell, pounded on the door, then opened the door and stepped in before it could be answered. Mom was hurrying toward the door, eyes wide.

"Oh, Ronnie! What's wrong? What's going on?"

"This has happened before!" Ronnie accused. "Why didn't you tell me this has happened to me before?"

Mom stopped short. Her eyes went from one side to the other as if she were looking for the answer. She opened her mouth and nothing came out. She approached Ronnie again, her hands going up in a calming gesture. She looked as if she didn't know whether to defend herself or give Ronnie a hug. Ronnie stepped back, angling her body so that she was perpendicular to Mom.

"You're starting to remember?" Mom asked, offering a tentative smile. Ronnie didn't think that Mom was really happy about it.

"Why didn't you tell me that this had happened before?" Ronnie demanded. It took everything she had to keep from facing off against Mom, hitting her or shoving her back. Her fury was boiling over, erupting like a volcano, threatening to burn everyone around her.

"I... we didn't know what was the right thing to do... How would it have done any good, telling you that?"

"Maybe I wouldn't feel like no one believed me. Everyone keeps acting like I'm just putting on an act. But I'm telling the truth and you know it! You know it because it happened before!"

Mom got closer and reached out her hand for Ronnie's. "Even before... there were never any real answers. I can't tell you anything, because we never got a good explanation before. We didn't know before... how much was real, and how much was just... anxiety... or attention-getting..."

"It was real!" Ronnie snarled. "Just like it's real this time! I wouldn't put on an act! I wouldn't make believe that I couldn't remember! Why would I? What kind of person would do that?"

"I don't know. No one knows. They couldn't tell us why you couldn't remember."

"*Why?* After everything they did to me and being forced to remember it all and tell it to everyone in court? How could I just go on after that?"

"Are you saying that you chose not to remember?"

"No, I'm saying it was too much for me. I couldn't handle it."

Mom sighed. "Then how would telling you all about it be helpful? It would just make things worse."

Ronnie looked for an argument to this, but couldn't find one. "You've been keeping everything from me. You didn't tell me this had happened before. You didn't tell me that I was adopted. You didn't tell me about what happened to me before I came here. Why not?"

"Before... the doctor said to try to stay away from topics that might upset you. They said not to push you to remember. Just to try to keep things normal, and you would remember gradually. That's just what we tried to do this time... just be normal. And... you're remembering...?"

Ronnie scowled. "Yes."

"It must be hard... learning it all over again," Mom said tentatively.

"Yes, it is."

"Do you want to come in?"

"No." Ronnie turned to go, putting her hand back on the door-knob. She hesitated. "What happened to my sisters?"

Mom shook her head. "You met Janessa already. Do you mean the other foster children?"

"No, I mean my real sisters. Ruby and Chloe and June. Did you ever hear anything?"

"No. We couldn't take any of them. I don't know who eventually did. Ruby didn't stay in foster care, I don't think. She was always so wild."

"It wasn't her fault," Ronnie protested. "Not with our daddy hurting her and then her social worker messing around with her too. It's not her fault she was like that."

Mom sighed. "People can react differently to the same thing. You are not like Ruby or June, even if the same things happened to you. You are the child that we wanted. I don't know what happened to them where they eventually ended up. Prison, probably."

Ronnie looked for Chloe first. She and Chloe hadn't been best friends, but they had been close enough in age to play together and to share a room when Ruby was gone. When Ronnie had read about what had happened to Chloe, her heart had ached. Her sister who had been hurt so badly. Those scars had to run deep. Ronnie wanted to make sure that Chloe was okay. And to give her a hug. But none of the searches she tried produced any matches. Chloe Simpson, or at least Ronnie's Chloe Simpson, had disappeared off the face of the earth. Maybe she had changed her name because she didn't want people to be able to track her down. Media and weirdos who wanted details of exactly what sick things had been done to her.

Ronnie went on, putting Chloe to the side for a while. There

P.D. WORKMAN

were a number of promising hits on Ruby Simpson. One kept popping up, and all of the details seemed to fit. Ronnie took a deep breath and picked up her phone. She punched in the number. It rang a couple of times and then was picked up. But it was a male voice that answered.

"Hello?"

"Uh—I'm looking for Ruby Simpson."

There was a slight hesitation before the man spoke, and then his tone was cautious. "May I tell her who is calling?"

Ronnie cleared her throat. "It's Ronnie."

"Hold on." He muffled the phone, but Ronnie could still hear him repeat it. "Ronnie."

"Hello?" Ronnie felt a little thrill at hearing Ruby's voice as she took the phone. "Ronnie?"

"It's Ronnie Simpson," Ronnie said, wanting to make sure that Ruby didn't mix her up with some other Ronnie.

"Ronnie! I can't believe it's you! How are you?"

"Uh—I'm good. How about you? I haven't seen you... forever. I think... at the trial."

"Yeah. I know. It's been a long time. I couldn't exactly call you, after all the trouble your foster parents caused. I said I wouldn't call you so they'd drop the charges. Once we were both adults... I didn't think you wanted any contact."

"Things were pretty weird," Ronnie said, aware that her words didn't begin to describe the situation. "But now..." She wasn't sure how to say that she wanted to meet her siblings, wanted to be a family again.

"I'm so glad you called. I've missed you."

Ronnie breathed a sigh of relief. "I miss you too." She was careful not to say that she *had missed* them, since for the past eleven years she hadn't even had one thought of them. "And the others. Did you... keep in contact with the others? Do you know where June or Chloe are?"

"June and Justin ran away years ago, but we got back in contact again two years ago. When Michelle and Kenny, their—June's children—ran into Charlie." Ruby chuckled.

"Who is Charlie?"

"Oh—Charlie is my husband. He's a police officer. He happened to run into the kids on a drug bust." She laughed again.

"On a drug bust?" Ronnie was picturing little kids, and couldn't fathom how they could be involved in a drug bust.

Ruby's voice became more serious. "I'm sorry. This is too much information all at once. You don't know anything. June's kids, Michelle and Kenny, they ran away. And they fell in with the Jags, my old street gang. They're doing a lot better now, getting their lives straightened around."

"How old are they?" June was younger than Ronnie. She couldn't imagine that June's kids were as old as Ronnie's, and Kent and Carrie were only fifteen and thirteen.

"Seventeen and eighteen, can you believe it? I can't believe that June's old enough to have teenagers. But then, my Sheree is in college!"

"Oh. Wow."

"How about you, any kids?"

Ronnie hesitated. "Well... it's a long story."

There was a pause while Ruby took this in. "Okay. Maybe you can tell me about it sometime."

"Yeah. Sometime."

CHAPTER

Nine

AGE 12

(I)

"Phone for you," Devaughn offered, waving the wireless receiver at Ronnie.

Ronnie looked up from doing her schoolwork on the bed. "Mmm. Who is it?"

She didn't have any close friends, so any phone calls tended to be from teachers or professionals who wanted to check up on her or talk to Mom and Dad.

"I dunno. I think maybe it's that sister of yours."

"June?" Ronnie grabbed at the phone. She put it to her ear and spoke softly. "Hi."

"Hey, Ronnie." It was June's voice. She sounded upset. Or maybe lonely.

"Hi. What's wrong?"

"Who said there was something wrong? I just called to talk to my sister."

"Okay. So, what's up?" Ronnie tiptoed over to the door and

pushed it shut. She didn't want to be overheard talking to June on the phone. Mom and Dad wouldn't like it.

"We got moved again," June informed her. "Different family. I have a new number now."

Ronnie took the little address book out of her backpack pocket and thumbed to the well-worn page. Lots of numbers crossed out. She'd never actually called June. But she could. Maybe someday she would call June instead of the other way around. She would find a time when Mom and Dad couldn't overhear her. Initiate a call to let June know that she was still loved by someone in the family. Ronnie always felt good when June called her. She should return the favor.

"What's the new family like?" she asked, after writing down the new phone number.

"I dunno yet. Lots of other kids. Probably won't be here long anyway."

"I wish you could find a family like mine. Where you could stay. Maybe get adopted someday."

"No one wants us," June sighed. "We're too old. And twins. Once they hear about our history..." she trailed off.

Ronnie thought about it. The molestation. The murder. The hung jury. Ronnie didn't think about it as being her past too, just June and Justin's. As sad as it was, it made sense that no one wanted to adopt the boy who had intentionally killed his own father, even if there were justification. And no one wanted to split the twins up. So, both became unadoptable.

"I'm sorry," she said lamely.

"It's okay," June sighed. Then with forced brightness, "It doesn't matter to me anymore. Me and Justin are together and that's all the family I need. I have you too, even if we're not together."

"At least they've kept you two together."

"Yeah," Ronnie could hear June's gulp. "I couldn't live without Justy."

"How is he? Is he okay?"

"Sure. Justy's always fine. I'm the one who's always messing up. Who's damaged."

Ronnie chewed on the knotted tie of her hoodie. She knew from what June said that Justin was her support. He was always the strong one. Still protecting June. Ronnie wondered if Justin had buried his own issues, like Ronnie tried to do with hers. Somehow they kept rearing their ugly heads, no matter how hard she tried to push them down. The day that Justin's suppressed troubles reared back up... she imagined a fireball going up in the sky. A big mushroom cloud of smoke and debris. That's what would happen when Justin let go.

"Are you still seeing your counselor? Dr. Summers?"

"Yeah. Sure. Do you think I could come visit you one day, Ronnie? Could I come to your house and see you?"

Ronnie remembered the visits with Ruby and how disastrously they had turned out. She wouldn't want June ending up in trouble for something that she didn't do.

"No... I don't think it would work out," she said. "If they even knew that I was still talking to you..."

"What do they have against me?" June whined. "I haven't done anything."

"I know... but they didn't like Ruby and really made trouble for her. I don't want them making more trouble for you. I'm sorry, okay...?"

"Whatever. Did you know we turn ten next week?"

"Really?" June and Justin had been six when Ronnie was taken out of the home. Eight during the trial. Now they were turning ten. Time was flying by. How old would they be when Ronnie would be able to see them again? Adults? "What are you going to do for your birthday?"

"I dunno. Nothing special. I don't know if they'll even know it's our birthday."

The thought made Ronnie sad. She always celebrated her birthdays with the Dares. What would it be like to not even have a birthday? She wished again that the Dares had considered letting June and Justin live with them. But she knew that the twins would never have been able to live by the Dares' rules.

"Well... happy birthday anyway. I wish I had a present to give you."

"Thanks. I'll tell Justin you said happy birthday too."

CHAPTER
Ten

AGE 15

[1]

M rs. Finney leaned over Ronnie's shoulder as she handed their latest art assignments back to them.

"See me after class, Ronnie."

Ronnie looked up at her, worried. What had she done? Had she forgotten to turn something in or been careless and torn or spilled on a project—hers or someone else's? Did Mrs. Finney think that she'd been acting up when she hadn't? Maybe when Mrs. Finney had stepped out into the hallway to talk with the principal the other day, leaving the room unsupervised, she had caught a glimpse of Ronnie monkeying around.

But Mrs. Finney's face was kind and smiley, not stern, so Ronnie breathed out and tried to relax. Art was Ronnie's favorite subject, and she didn't want to be in trouble with Mrs. Finney for anything. Mrs. Finney continued handing other students' projects back. Ronnie watched her covertly and didn't see her bend down to whisper anything to anyone else. Whatever it was, it was only Ronnie.

She soon lost herself in her work, not thinking about Mrs. Finney or about problems at home or in her past. Working on her art was one of the only times that she could actually be comfortable and leave all of her anxieties behind. When she was lost in an art project, she didn't even think about getting the rest of her homework done, which could be a problem. But in art class itself she wasn't supposed to be doing anything else. Just immersing herself in her work.

Ronnie was so focused on her drawing that she didn't even hear the dismissal bell. Ritchie, who worked at the workstation to her right, nudged her shoulder.

"Time to go," he pointed out. "Didn't you hear the bell?"

Ronnie looked around and saw everyone else cleaning up their stations. "Oh—thanks. I didn't."

He rolled his eyes. Ronnie carefully put her drawing into the stiff-sided portfolio so that it wouldn't get crumpled or bent. She picked up her pencils.

"Ronnie...?"

Ronnie looked over at Mrs. Finney's desk and remembered the instruction to stay after. She left her workstation and approached the teacher.

"Yes, Mrs. Finney?"

"Come over here, I have something to show you."

Mrs. Finney moved some books around and pulled out a small black folder as Ronnie came around to her side of the desk.

"This is a special award," she said in a low, reverent voice, as she sat with the folder in her hands, not opening it. "It's given to students who show a special aptitude in art. I haven't ever had a student receive it before, although I have made submissions in the past. I gave them some of your work."

She opened the black folder to show off the certificate displayed inside it. The certificate had a big shiny gold embossed seal on it and it had been filled out by hand in calligraphy. It was made out in Ronnie's name.

Ronnie gasped. "Really? I won an award?" Tears pricked her eyes with sudden emotion. Sometimes the other children had earned awards for academics, but they didn't come easily for Ronnie. It was a struggle for her just to keep up passing grades. She had never won anything before and she'd had no idea that Mrs. Finney had submitted any of her work for the award.

"You did." Mrs. Finney gave her a warm, happy smile and handed the folder to her. "This is really special. I'm so glad that you won. You do such a good job."

"Wow." Ronnie felt the weight of the folder in her hands. It was thick and substantial, with a velvety fabric on the inside that cushioned the certificate. "Wow! I can't believe it!"

"Your work has been passed on to the national art competition. If you were to win at the national level—one of the best young artists in the country—there's actually a cash award and a bursary that go along with it. Something to help toward your post-secondary education."

Ronnie wasn't sure that she understood what all of that meant. But she understood that it was a competition all the way across the country and that she could win money. For her art!

"Do you think I can win?" she asked breathlessly.

"I don't know." Mrs. Finney bit her lip. "I don't want you to get your hopes up. There are lots of other entrants. But it's always possible. Your work is as good as anyone's."

"Thank you so much!" Ronnie hesitated, then threw her arms around Mrs. Finney. "Thank you so, so much! I can't wait to show my mom!"

She finally had something to show for all of the work that she had been doing. Something to prove to Mom and Dad that she was worthy to be part of their family.

Ronnie hurried into the house, eager to tell Mom about the art award. Mom was not in the living room or kitchen as she usually was when Ronnie got home, so Ronnie went upstairs to look for her.

"Mom?"

"In here."

Ronnie changed her destination from the master bedroom to the girls' room. "Mom, guess—" she cut herself off, looking at the new girl sitting on the third bed.

"Hi, Ronnie. This is Stacey," Mom introduced.

Ronnie looked the girl over carefully. She was close to Ronnie in age, maybe a little older. Teens in foster care had to be tough, and she looked that. Stacey had a short cap of black hair and a perma-nent sneer across her pinched, heavily made-up face. She had a row of earrings down one ear and one in her lip. She was shorter than Ronnie, more solidly-built but not fat.

"Oh, hi," Ronnie greeted. She didn't understand why Mom and Dad continued to foster. They were getting older and none of the kids that they had taken in lately had been good prospects for adop-tion. Even though they only wanted long-term kids with prospects for adoption someday, Social Services kept giving them emergency and short-term placements that were disruptive to the family. Every time they took on a new kid, Ronnie had to worry over her position.

Stacey looked Ronnie over, scowling. "Hi."

Ronnie stood there awkwardly, not sure what to say. She should engage Stacey in conversation. Ask her questions. But nothing came to mind.

"Did you have something to tell me?" Mom asked after a few seconds of silence had dragged by.

"Uh, no. Nothing."

"Is Janessa on her way?"

"Yes. She stayed for tutoring, but it's only half an hour."

"You could use some tutoring yourself," Mom commented, raising one eyebrow.

Ronnie knew she probably should have stayed with Janessa, but she'd been excited to tell Mom about the award. Now it seemed like such a small thing. Mom wouldn't make that big a deal of it. They were more interested in academics than in Ronnie's little pictures. Dad had mentioned more than once that he felt Ronnie's drawing

took up time that she should have been spending on more important subjects.

"Yeah, probably should have," Ronnie agreed. "Do you want
help with supper?"

Volunteering for housework should earn her points, making up
for some of what she had lost by not staying after school for
tutoring.

Mom smiled. "Actually, that would be great. Stacey's arrival
disrupted things a little and I haven't had the time to spend on it
yet. I threw a frozen casserole in the oven, but if you could check on
it, start some veggies cooking, and make a salad, that would be
wonderful."

Stacey eyed Ronnie. "I can cook," she said. "I'm really good."

"Well, we'll get you to help out too, but not on the first day. We
still have to get you all settled in."

"Mr. Clive said I'm a really good helper. He told you that,
right?"

"I'll be very glad for the assistance," Mom assured her. She
looked at Ronnie and nodded a pointed dismissal.

Ronnie left her schoolbag on her bed and went downstairs to
work on supper. What was Stacey being so helpful for? Had Mr.
Clive told her there was a chance that she could be adopted by the
Dares? He had never particularly approved of the fact that the
Dares intended to adopt Ronnie, when she wasn't even freed for
adoption. He wouldn't have told Stacey that, would he? Or had
Mom told Stacey?

Ronnie dug into the fridge, trying to shake the thoughts off.
Stacey was just being helpful because she liked to cook. Or liked to
be helpful. Not because she was competing with Ronnie or thought
that she had a chance at a permanent family. She was just being
nice.

All through dinner, Stacey kept making faces at Ronnie, wrinkling
her nose over the food and making comments about how good she

herself was at cooking and housekeeping. When Mom asked Janessa about her schoolwork and tutoring, Ronnie expected Stacey to jump in with comments about how stellar her marks were and how well she did at school, but Stacey didn't. Instead, she shook her head, expression dark. "I have learning disabilities," she said. "So, I don't do well at school. I don't get good marks. But that's not because I'm stupid. I'm really smart. I just have trouble getting good marks because of my disabilities."

Mom nodded understandingly. "It can be hard to get marks that are a reflection of your real abilities," she agreed. "But the school does offer special tutoring and they have a really good alternative stream for those with disabilities. Focus on trades, special accommodations for kids with dyslexia, things like that."

"I don't need to be in a program like that. I'm really smart. I'm going to university, not some welding shop. And they don't call it dyslexia anymore. They call it a reading disability. Because dyslexia makes people think that you just see letters or words backward and that's not what it's all about."

"Well, whatever they are calling it," Mom said, with a nod.

Janessa looked sideways at Ronnie with a questioning look. Ronnie just shrugged and stared down at her plate, pushing a piece of lettuce around.

"Ronnie?" Mom said. "Is everything okay? Aren't you hungry?"

Ronnie hated that worried tone. That 'are we going to have to send you back to the ED clinic' tone. Ronnie forced herself to take a bite. "I'm fine. Just… I was picking a bit while I was making dinner, so I'm already mostly full."

Mom gave a little sigh and nodded.

"Maybe it's because she didn't do a very good job of cooking," Stacey pointed out. "It's not that good. The lettuce is wilted and mine had brown spots. The tomatoes got all smushed when she cut them. It's not a very interesting salad. I would have put almond slivers in it. Or maybe croutons."

"I'll get your help another day. Ronnie did a great job helping out."

Dave suddenly howled and punched Alex in the arm for something. Chaos ensued, with Mom and Dad both hurrying over to break the boys up and broker peace again. Dave ended up getting sent to his room, stomping up the stairs like an elephant. The door slammed upstairs. Mom grimaced and rolled her eyes.

"Boys. Sometimes I just don't know what to do with them."

[II]

Stacey volunteered to help with clean-up and Janessa was on dish duty, so Ronnie went back up to her bedroom by herself to get a head start on homework while it was quiet and distraction-free.

She picked up her book bag and looked at it, frowning. She had the weird feeling that it had been moved or tampered with. She looked it over, but couldn't see anything out of place. Ronnie sat on the bed and pulled it into her lap, looking through it and pulling out her homework. She arranged everything in piles and started in on her math. As she worked through the exercise, her mind was drawn back to her bag. Why would anyone touch it? It was her own property. Mom might take her work out and help her sort it if she thought Ronnie was being too messy or not keeping on top of her work, but she hadn't done that for a while, and if Mom had looked at it, it would have been carefully sorted out and there would be no more loose or crumpled papers inside. Ronnie pushed apart the zippered opening again to look at the contents, frowning and shaking her head.

She was ten minutes into her work before she was hit with a bolt of lightning.

"Oh, no!" she said aloud, and opened the bag again, looking for something specific this time.

Ronnie stormed down the stairs into the kitchen, where Stacey was still helping Mom tidy up, though it looked like she was talking more than cleaning.

"Where is it?" she demanded.

"Where's what?" Stacey responded with cool unconcern.

"My award! You stole my award!"

"Ronnie!" Mom remonstrated, her voice shocked. "I'm sure Stacey hasn't done anything with your things. What award?"

"I got an award in art," Ronnie explained. "It was in a special folder and there was a gold seal and everything. Mrs. Finney said that she was going to submit some of my work into a contest. A national contest, all the way across the country. That's how good she thought it was!"

"Wow, that's very nice," Mom said, smiling.

"But *she* took it! It was in my bag and it's not there now. Stacey took it."

"You've lost things before without Stacey's help. I'm sure it's in there somewhere, caught between some papers or inside a binder. That, or you left it at the school without realizing. You know how easy it is to forget something like that."

"I didn't forget it! I wanted to show you when I got home. I put it in my bag right before I left school. I wanted to show you as soon as I got home. But then *she* was here and I didn't show you then. If I did, you'd know I didn't forget it!"

Ronnie's fury was bubbling over. She could barely speak, she was so angry. Her face was hot and she knew that she was red in the face.

"That doesn't make it Stacey's fault that you lost it," Mom said. "Now, you apologize for accusing her. That's not a very sisterly way to behave! And this is Stacey's first day!"

"I didn't lose it! I told you, she took it!"

"Stacey wasn't alone with your bag. She was with me. She didn't get into your bag."

Ronnie took in a breath to protest, but couldn't think of anything to say. If Mom had been with Stacey the whole time, then how had she accessed Ronnie's bag? Ronnie knew that she had taken the award folder. She couldn't just have missed it or left it at school.

"You need to apologize to Stacey," Mom prompted.

"But—"

"No buts."

Ronnie stared at Stacey, wishing that she had lasers for eyes and could just stare a hole right through Stacey. She swallowed and steadied her voice.

"I'm sorry."

"What for?" Mom encouraged.

"For... accusing you of going into my stuff."

"Thank you. Now the both of you head upstairs. Ronnie, how much homework do you have left?"

"Still a bunch."

"Get to work, then."

Tears started down Ronnie's cheeks. Stacey started to walk back up to the bedroom, but she was going slowly, not wanting to miss anything. Mom stroked Ronnie's cheek.

"What is it, Ronnie?"

"I wanted to show it to you. It was really cool. And now it's gone!"

"It will turn up. You need to take better care of your things. I've told you before."

"I did take care of it. I put it in my bag. I didn't lose it."

"Go on up and do your homework. You're tired. Need to get to bed in good time today."

When Ronnie walked back into the bedroom, Stacey smiled at her.

It wasn't a very nice smile.

(III)

"Are you going to tell them?" Janessa asked, walking close to Ronnie, keeping her voice low. She looked around to make sure that none of the others were around who would overhear them and maybe make trouble.

Ronnie shook her head. "I'm just supposed to get it signed. They didn't say they'd call. I can do that..."

"You don't think they'll find out?"

"I hope not." Ronnie let out a pent-up breath. Her stomach was tight and her breathing shallow. She couldn't afford to get into trouble. If the Dares got rid of her now, who knew what kind of place she'd end up in. No one wanted a troubled teen. They'd end up putting her in a group home or worse.

They both stopped talking when they got inside the door. Mom heard the door, and came out to the front to greet them.

"Hello, girls. How was school?" she inquired cheerfully. No sign of a storm brewing. In fact, she seemed more upbeat than usual.

"Great," Janessa offered, kicking off her shoes. "I got my social test back today and I got an A. I did really well, it was hard test!"

"Good for you," Mom praised. She looked hard at the shoes. Janessa picked them up and put them neatly in their place in the shoe cubby.

"How about you, Ronnie?" Mom turned to her. "How did you do on your math test?"

Ronnie looked at Janessa. Then back at Mom, as she pried her shoes off without untying the laces.

"Okay," she said. "I didn't get an A... but I passed."

Mom raised her brows. "So, what did you get?"

"Sixty-nine."

"A C? Ronnie," Mom's voice dripped with disappointment. "You know that's not good enough."

Ronnie nodded. "I'll do better on the next one," she promised. "I'll bring it up. This one just had a lot of algebra on it and... it was a really tough test."

"There will be just as much or more algebra on the next test. You need to spend more time studying. And get some tutoring too. You need extra help."

"Okay. I'm sorry."

Mom nodded. "I made snacks. Come on in to the kitchen and you can tell me about the rest of your day."

Both of them were obviously included in the invitation. Ronnie hurried to the kitchen, determined to have her snack before any of the others got home. They walked into the room and saw, not apples and cheese or another of the usual healthy snacks that Mom insisted they needed after school, but chocolate chip cookies. They were not even from a package. Irregularly-sized, dark-at-the-edges, homemade cookies. Janessa and Ronnie exchanged incredulous looks.

"Those look great," Ronnie gushed. "Wow! Can I have three?" Two was the usual limit.

Mom laughed. "Yes, you can have three," she agreed. She went to the fridge to get out the milk and pour them each a glass.

"Wow, what lottery did she win?" Janessa murmured. Ronnie grinned in agreement.

They were done by the time the boys got home and as Mom went to the door to greet them, Ronnie and Janessa hurried upstairs to get started on their homework. Janessa snagged another cookie as they walked past the plate, but Ronnie didn't.

Things were quiet during homework time, and the conversation at dinner seemed normal. Ronnie was starting to relax. Obviously, the school had not called home and her parents were oblivious to any trouble that Ronnie was in. She exchanged a few glances with Janessa at the table, and neither of them said anything that might clue Mom and Dad in. The boys either hadn't heard anything or had decided not to bring it up, maybe planning to blackmail her later.

When dinner was finished and everyone stood up to leave, Mom spoke to Ronnie.

"Ronnie, you can help clear and wash dishes," she instructed.

Ronnie froze. "It's not my turn today," she protested. "Today is Michael's—"

"Michael can take it tomorrow. We want to talk to you today."

The other children skedaddled, eager to be out of the way if there were going to be trouble. Michael especially didn't want to be around if Ronnie won the argument and they decided it was his turn to clear. Ronnie watched them go, her heart sinking. She started to scrape the dinner plates over the garbage, but her mind wasn't on the job.

She didn't ask them what they wanted to talk to her about.

"I'm sorry," she said, hoping that by coming clean, the punishment would not be as severe.

"Sorry for what?" Mom's expression was bemused.

Ronnie looked at her for a moment and saw no knowledge there. They didn't know? What did they want to talk to her about, then? Surely they hadn't decided that Ronnie simply wasn't going to work out. She'd been with the family for seven years now, almost as long as she had been with her biological family. Had they finally made the decision to rehome her?

"Uh—sorry for talking back. About the dishes. I thought maybe you didn't read the chart and just forgot whose turn it was..."

Mom shook her head. She and Dad looked at each other, gauging how to begin. Finally, Mom took up the thread.

"Ronnie... you've been with us a long time now. Seven years. You've had a lot of ups and downs in that time, but I think we've weathered the storm pretty well."

Ronnie stood there frozen. It sounded like the beginning of a 'we can't do anything else for you' speech. How was she going to adjust to a new home now? They wouldn't turn her out into the street, but they might as well. Instead of having a family to guide and support her into her adult years, she would have nothing and no one. She knew what happened to foster kids who aged out.

Mom was looking at her expectantly. Ronnie realized she'd zoned out. "I'm sorry," she blurted. "I'll do better. I'll try harder. I really will."

"Did you hear what I said, Ronnie?"

Ronnie swallowed and shook her head.

"We got the call that you've been freed for adoption."

Ronnie felt like she'd been kicked in the chest. She suddenly couldn't get any air. Freed for adoption? Did that mean that the Dares were going to adopt her now, and there would never again be any threat of their disowning her? She could be a permanent part of the family, like Janessa and Alex?

Dad laughed, a deep, rolling chuckle.

"You look like you just got slapped in the face," he said. "It was a bit of a shock to us too!"

Ronnie sputtered, trying to say something to fill the silence.

"Really? Are you really going to adopt me? Now?"

"It won't be today," Mom said with a gentle smile. "You know how slow Social Services is about getting things moving. But sometime in the next few months... we'll have a brand new baby girl of our very own!"

"Me?" Ronnie had to hear it. She had to understand that they were telling her the truth, that she was really going to be adopted into the family permanently.

"Yes, Ronnie, you! We're going to adopt you."

"Oh, thank you!" Ronnie gave Mom a tight hug. She turned to Dad and, after an infinitesimal hesitation, gave him one too. He gave her a pat on the back and let go. "Thank you!"

"It's been a long time in coming," Mom said. "I was beginning to wonder whether they were ever going to free you, or whether we would have to wait until you were an adult. But now you'll be ours. You'll be a permanent part of our family."

Ronnie nodded. A little choked up, she continued to scrub the dishes. She would remember every movement. Every sensory impression. It was the moment that she found out she would be a permanent part of the Dare family.

When she was finished the dishes she went upstairs to the bedroom.

"Did you get in trouble?" Janessa asked.

Ronnie glanced over at Stacey. She tilted her head for Janessa to follow her out. Janessa raised her eyebrows and complied. There weren't very many places to have a private conversation in the house. Ronnie motioned to the bathroom and they both went in. Ronnie locked the door and turned on the water.

"They're adopting me!"

"What?" Janessa squealed and gave Ronnie a hug. "Really? I didn't think they could!"

"Social Services called today."

"Does that mean that your bio parents agreed to it?" Janessa asked. "I thought before your bio mom wouldn't relinquish her rights and Social Services wasn't going to force it."

"I don't know." Ronnie shrugged. "They didn't say what happened. Just that I was free now."

"That's awesome!" Janessa gave her another hug. "Now you'll be my sister forever!"

Ronnie nodded.

"So, they didn't... find out?"

"No." Ronnie breathed out. "They won't change their minds, will they?"

"They never have," Janessa pointed out. "It's been seven years. They said right from the start you were a keeper. You're a lot better than me at fitting in and they still adopted me."

"Yeah." Ronnie turned the water off again. "I don't have to worry. They're really going to adopt me."

"Congratulations." Janessa gave her shoulder a squeeze. "Sis."

(IV)

Even though they hadn't said anything in front of Stacey, the other girl obviously figured out what was going on. Maybe she'd eavesdropped when they were talking in the kitchen or had asked Mom what was up. When Ronnie and Janessa climbed into bed, Stacey wasn't there. Ronnie tensed up and, rather than crawling into bed, she went to the door and looked down the hallway to see if Stacey was in the bathroom. She wasn't. But the door to the master bedroom was closed. Ronnie walked back into the bedroom and got into bed.

"What's wrong?" Janessa asked.

Ronnie looked over at her and didn't say anything. She pulled up her blankets and tucked them around her, making a little cocoon. They left the bedside lamp on for Stacey and for Mom.

"Is she in the bathroom?" Janessa questioned.

"No."

"Then what's she doing? We've got to get to sleep if we're going to be up in time tomorrow."

"I don't know."

The minutes dragged on. Ronnie kept looking at the clock, expecting it to be much later than it was. An eternity passed before she heard the door down the hall open, and Stacey padded past the room, glancing in before she went into the bathroom. Mom was a few steps behind her and entered the room, first saying goodnight to Janessa, and then sitting on the side of Ronnie's bed. She looked at Ronnie, her head cocked slightly.

"In all of the excitement about our big news, it occurs to me that you didn't get a chance to tell me if anything happened at school today that you needed help with." Ronnie was shaking her head. "Maybe a problem with homework or something that you needed to share with me?"

Ronnie continued to shake her head. Mom sat up a little straighter, her mouth turning down.

"Ronnie... do you have a note for me, or do I need to call the school about it in the morning?"

Ronnie groaned. She brought her hands up to her face. "Mom... I'm sorry... I screwed up..."

"Yes, it certainly sounds like it."

Ronnie motioned to her school backpack. Mom picked it up and handed it to her. Ronnie dug out the report and handed it to her. Mom's eyes went back and forth as she read it.

"Oh, Ronnie! An in-school suspension... loitering in an out-of-bounds area. With a boy?" She looked at Ronnie and raised an eyebrow.

"It wasn't like that," Ronnie protested. "We weren't making out or something! We were just—" she stopped herself. "We were just... talking."

"Talking," Mom repeated.

Ronnie looked down at the report. She hadn't even read it through. Mr. Stivek's spidery handwriting was nearly impossible to read and Ronnie had never intended for it to get into her parents' hands. She had intended to just forge Mom's signature and hand it back in.

"It doesn't say you were just talking," Mom said.

"Well, we were. That's what we were doing. Ibri, he's been going through a really tough time with his parents and he just needed someone to talk to. I was just trying to help him out…"

"And how did *smoking* help him out?"

There was a snort from Janessa's direction. Ronnie paid no attention. "Does it say I was smoking? *He* was smoking…"

Mom looked Ronnie directly in the eye. "*Were* you smoking?"

Ronnie held her hands up pleadingly. "Mom…"

"Just answer the question. Were you smoking?"

Ronnie nodded, unable to answer out loud.

"Why would you do that?" Mom demanded. "You know how bad it is for you."

"I don't know why!" Ronnie clenched her hands into fists and held back tears. "I was just stupid! I knew I shouldn't, but…"

"But a boy was doing it and you thought it was cool."

"No, I knew it wasn't. I knew it was stupid and can cause cancer, but I just wanted… to be with him and help him. I was just… trying to make him comfortable with me. I know… it's stupid…"

"You don't have to do something you know is wrong to be friends. If you do, that person is not worth having as a friend."

Ronnie bristled at this. "You don't know anything about him! He's worth having as a friend!"

"Not if he changes you. Not if he encourages you to do things that you know are wrong. Things that are dangerous to your health."

"It was just once," Ronnie insisted. "It's not going to give me cancer if I only do it once."

Mom was silent for a time. She took Ronnie's hands in hers. "I'm very disappointed in you."

Ronnie looked down, a pain in her chest. "I'm sorry, Mom," she said sincerely, letting the tears fall, "I really am. You won't… you'll still adopt me, won't you?"

There was a long pause as Mom thought this through. Ronnie could hear Janessa moving restlessly in her bed. There was a movement in the bedroom doorway, and Ronnie could see, in her peripheral vision, Stacey listening in.

"You have to promise me that you will never smoke again," Mom said sternly. "Or drink alcohol or take drugs. You can't do things like that just to fit in. If you get addicted it could ruin your entire life."

Ronnie nodded.

"As for this boy... I don't want you seeing him again."

Ronnie sniffled. "But he's at school. In my classes. I can't help seeing him."

"You know what I mean. Hanging around with him. Spending time with him outside of classes. Hiding behind the school to smoke. You may not see him outside of your classes."

There was a big, hot lump in Ronnie's throat. She and Ibri were just friends, as she had said, and nothing more, but it still hurt to have to agree not to see him again. He would be hurt. She really had wanted to help him. He was having such a difficult time and needed someone to lean on and to pour his heart out to. He wouldn't understand how she had to promise not to see him anymore. How her Mom could coerce her into agreeing.

"He's my friend," she protested again.

"Not anymore. If you're going to be a part of this family, there are rules that you need to follow. You know that. I won't have you hanging around a bad influence like that. Who knows where it could lead."

Ronnie wiped away tears with the back of her hand. "Nothing would happen. I wouldn't do anything else wrong."

Mom shook her head emphatically. "No, Ronnie. I don't want you to see him again."

Ronnie nodded, letting her breath out in a long, strangled sigh. She didn't feel better for making the promise. She hated what she had done. How she had betrayed Ibri.

"Good. Do I have to explain to you the danger of being with a boy alone and isolated like that? You've been hurt before. You know how traumatic it would be if things got out of hand. A boy won't necessarily stop because you tell him no. If you're all alone there, there's nobody to help you. Promise me you won't do that again."

"Okay." Ronnie snuffled, swallowing tears. She had been successful in suppressing the memories most of the time, but they came flooding back at Mom's words. *There's nobody to help you.* She remembered that feeling more clearly than anything.

"I want you to protect your virtue." Mom patted her hand. "Make good choices. Save it for after you are married. When it's safe, and something special between you and your husband. That's the only way you'll feel good about it."

She nodded, her face heating with embarrassment. She didn't really mind Janessa hearing what Mom had to say. Ronnie would probably have confided in her about it anyway. But she hated Stacey, an outsider, hearing the intimate details. What if she spread it around at school? Told all of her friends how Ronnie had gotten in trouble and what she had agreed to? Even if all she did was taunt Ronnie in private, it was still humiliating.

"I'll talk it over with your Dad," Mom said. She leaned over and kissed Ronnie on the cheek. "You get some sleep and don't fuss over it tonight. Tomorrow is a new day, and you can start out fresh. I'll sign this now, so you don't have to ask me in the morning." She leaned over and got a pen out of Ronnie's bag, and used one of her notebooks to form a hard surface behind the note. She signed the report and slid it carefully back into Ronnie's bag, sandwiched between two books to keep it from getting crumpled. "Now go to sleep."

Ronnie lay back down. Mom got up to leave and Stacey walked into the room. Mom said goodnight to her and left the room. Stacey headed to her bed, sneering in Ronnie's direction. None of them said anything to each other.

Ronnie was slow getting her books out of her locker and walked into the classroom an instant after the final bell rang. Mr. Vick glared at her, but there was no point in writing her up for being one second late, so he just called for the class to settle in and get their notebooks out for a pop quiz. Ronnie sat down without looking at Ibri, though she knew that he would be trying to catch her eye, just to smile a greeting. She hurried to assemble her notebook and writing materials and looked steadily at Mr. Vick. His brows drew down slightly looking at her and he went on.

It was the longest period in Ronnie's life. She was hyper-aware of Ibri the whole time, hearing every movement that he made, but refusing to turn her head even an inch to look at him. She tried to dash out the door ahead of him as if she needed to get to her next class quickly, but he was right behind her, grabbing her arm.

"Ronnie! Ronnie, what's going on?"

She pulled out of his grasp. "I can't talk."

"Wait! Hold on! Are you mad at me?" he hurried to keep up with her brisk pace.

Ronnie bit her lip and tried to ignore the hot lump in her throat.

"Ronnie! Please!"

She stopped and he bumped up against her, unable to stop himself in time. Ronnie turned to him, taking a step back to establish personal space. "I'm not mad at you," she said briskly. "I got in trouble for yesterday and I'm not allowed to talk to you."

His eyes widened and his mouth dropped open. "Not allowed to talk to me? They can't do that. No one can stop you from talking to me."

"Yes, they can. Trust me, Ibri," she looked around to ensure that none of her siblings were around. "They can."

She turned away from him again to go on to her next class. He put his hand on her shoulder, stopping her. He was gentle, not keeping her still by force.

"For how long?"

She looked over her shoulder at him and swallowed. "Forever."

He let her go. Ronnie hurried on, his hurt-puppy expression branded into her brain forever.

(V)

Ronnie and the family waited in the lobby outside the courtrooms. There was an upholstered bench to sit on, but every time she sat down, she got too squirmy and had to jump up again and pace up and down. She had been to both Alex's and Janessa's adoption ceremonies, but they had both been free for adoption much earlier than she, and she couldn't remember much about them. Long waits, listening to the judge talk on and on, and then a party afterward. She remembered the parties, but not the important part. Not the instant where they actually became part of the family.

Finally, it was time. The courtroom door opened, the people who had been in there before her started filing out, and Ronnie's name was called out by the court clerk. She fought her way into the courtroom ahead of everyone else, against the tide of people coming out. She went to the chairs at the front of the courtroom and turned around, waiting for Mom and Dad and Alex and Janessa.

There were no other children. Mom and Dad had decided that with the adoption of Ronnie, their family was complete, and from that point on, there would be no more foster children. They had always wanted two boys and two girls, but they would be satisfied with just the three of them. Stacey and the other two boys had made a quiet exit.

"Calm down," Mom said with a smile. "You can't make it go any faster by pacing back and forth. It will happen."

"I know. I just... I'm so excited. I can't wait until it's actually done and I'm part of the family."

They wouldn't be able to just call Mr. Clive and have her taken away. It would be forever. Just like she'd always dreamed.

She didn't have to wait long. The judge was handed a stack of papers and called the court session to order. After a minute, he looked up at the family and gave a thin smile.

"Looks like you've been waiting a long time," he commented.

"Yes, we have," Mom acknowledged.

Ronnie nodded vigorously.

"Does anyone have anything they'd like to say before I sign the papers?"

They all looked at each other. Ronnie hadn't thought about preparing an acceptance speech, like she was an Oscar winner. She just wanted to be a part of her family forever. Mom shrugged, looking a little embarrassed.

"We're just so excited," she said with a little shrug.

The judge nodded and started signing. He looked up again. "That's it. It's done." He handed the order to the court clerk.

Ronnie looked at the Dares, feeling a little let down. That was it? That was the big event? It was all so anticlimactic. Mom gave her a big hug.

"Welcome to the family, Ronnie. You're officially a Dare."

Ronnie breathed out. She had been looking forward to it for so long. She didn't quite believe it had really happened. Two minutes of ceremony and she was finally safe.

Outside the courtroom, they took pictures. They went home and had pizza and ice cream. Then it was time to do homework, just like any other night.

CHAPTER
Eleven

(I)

J anessa and Ronnie had their heads together, discussing Janessa's plans for college and what she needed to pack to take with her, when Mom tapped on the door and came into the room.

"How are my girls?" she greeted.

"Good." Both girls looked at her to see what she wanted.

"Ronnie, I just wanted to let you know that we'll have company for dinner on Saturday," Mom said.

"Oh. Okay. Who is it?"

"A fellow that your father knows from work. He's on his own, so we thought we would treat him to a family dinner. Do something nice for him."

Ronnie and Janessa exchanged glances. This was odd behavior; not the type of thing that they normally did. But that didn't prevent them from doing so now.

"What's his name?" Janessa asked.

"Floyd Plum."

"Floyd Plum," Janessa repeated in an attempt at a British accent. "Sounds very plummy!"

Ronnie giggled. It *was* sort of a funny name.

"Now don't make fun of him," Mom said. "Dad says he's a very nice young fellow."

"Oh, he's a young fellow." Janessa said in a knowing tone. She smirked and nudged Ronnie. "I guess that means you're doing the entertaining."

Ronnie rolled her eyes. She didn't look directly at Mom, but glanced at her sideways to gauge her reaction. Was she the one who would be expected to keep the conversation flowing? How young was Floyd Plum? Would he relate better to Ronnie or to Mom and Dad? Mom didn't give her any clue one way or the other.

"Just be nice," she repeated.

"Okay," Ronnie agreed.

Mom nodded and withdrew. Ronnie looked at Janessa, frowning.

"What do you think is up? I wish you were going to be there."

"I know. Me too. But I'll be getting settled at the dorm."

Ronnie sighed noisily. "Well, Alex will be here at least, right? It won't just be me."

"You'd better talk to him about it, not me. I don't know what his plans are."

While Alex was still home and not off to college like Janessa, he was working and had a social life of his own, so he wasn't at home as much as he used to be. Ronnie was a little bit afraid of how lonely it was going to be with Janessa gone, and just her and Mom and Dad home most of the time. While she loved her parents, she didn't want to be their sole focus. It was weird, after so many years with four or five other kids in the house to think of it just being her.

"I'll tell him he has to stay home," Ronnie decided. "I don't want it to just be me when we have company."

Ronnie smoothed down her shirt, examining herself in the mirror. She didn't want to end up going down to dinner with company with a spill or smudge. Mom poked her head in the door.

"You look nice," she approved with a smile.

"Thanks."

"You're so pale. How about a little color in your cheeks?"

Ronnie stared at her, not understanding. Was Mom worrying that she was sick? That she wasn't eating or taking care of herself properly?

"Come with me," Mom said, beckoning.

Ronnie obeyed, following her into the master bedroom. Mom motioned to her dressing table. "Sit down. Let me see what I've got."

Ronnie slowly sat herself down at the table, looking over Mom's array of makeup, moisturizers, and scents. Makeup had always been forbidden, even though all of the girls Ronnie's age were wearing it. Ronnie had a secret stash that she used sparingly while she was at school, carefully cleaning it off before she went home.

Mom seemed cheerfully oblivious to Ronnie's confusion over the sudden offer of cosmetics. She applied moisturizer cream, and then started testing out foundations to find one that was light enough for Ronnie's skin. Ronnie watched in the mirror in silence. She didn't smile. Not just because she didn't want to move her face while Mom was working on her, but because she had no idea whether to be happy about this new development.

Mom only took a few minutes and only put on the minimum of a little blush and lipstick. She smiled and patted Ronnie's cheek.

"There, that's lovely. You can start wearing a little make-up if you'd like. Just like this, nothing obvious. Not like some of those teenagers I see!"

Ronnie nodded and forced a smile. "Okay. Thanks."

"Now, we'd better get downstairs and start getting everything ready, so it will be on the table when your dad and Floyd get home."

Ronnie went downstairs with her, and they worked together to pull dishes out of the fridge and oven, to fill a pitcher with ice water, and to make sure that everything on the table looked just right.

~

Everything was ready and on the table when Dad walked in the door. Ronnie looked behind him, curious to get a glimpse of the man that he was bringing home with him.

Floyd Plum had short, blond hair. He was a young man, twenty-something. Taller than Ronnie, but not so much that he would tower over her. He looked a little anxious, his movements awkward and a bit jerky. He nodded at Ronnie and smiled at Mom.

"Uh—hi, Mrs. Dare. Thank you for inviting me into your home."

Mom gave him her hand. "Floyd, it's good to meet you. You can call me Cynthia. This is our daughter, Ronnie."

"Hi," Ronnie greeted shyly. She wasn't sure whether she was supposed to shake his hand too, but she didn't offer it and they just stood there looking at each other awkwardly.

"Hi," Floyd said. His smile seemed forced and his face was getting pink.

"Let's all sit down," Dad suggested, motioning to the table. "It looks like everything is ready?"

Mom nodded. "Yes, please. Have a seat. Ronnie, would you pour the water?"

Ronnie moved around the table, trying to avoid touching Floyd as she leaned over him to reach his glass. She could hear Janessa's voice in her head, making observations about Floyd. He was not bad looking. Maybe even cute. He was older than she, but young enough to be of interest. There was no ring on his finger and he didn't look like he was the type who was into partying or other unsavory habits. He was clean-cut and neat with no piercings or tattoos. Dad wouldn't have brought home someone who was a bad influence.

Mostly, Mom and Dad kept the conversation moving forward and didn't allow for awkward pauses. Floyd was pleasant and well-mannered.

"What are you studying in school, Ronnie?" he asked, looking across the table at her.

Ronnie tried to formulate an answer, taken off-guard.

"Ronnie is still in high school," Mom advised, patting her mouth with a napkin. Floyd looked taken aback.

"Oh, you look older," he apologized. "I thought you were in college. Chris had mentioned his daughter was starting college…"

"Janessa," Ronnie said. "She just left for school."

"Oh, okay. I was confused."

"No harm done," Dad said heartily. "I'm not sure if Ron will be going on to college… marks aren't quite what they should be, are they sweetie?"

Ronnie's face burned. Not just at his pointing out that she was doing poorly at school and limited in her future, but also over his treating her like a child in front of Floyd.

"They could be better," she muttered, looking down at her plate.

"Not everyone is cut out for academics," Floyd allowed generously. "Maybe there's something else Ronnie is interested. Another direction she'd like to go."

They were all silent, considering. Nobody jumped in with any particular talent or passion Ronnie had. She didn't know what she was going to do after school. Maybe find a retail job. Something she didn't need a high school diploma or 4.0 grade point average to get. Those positions had to be filled too.

"Ronnie's so good with children," Mom suggested. "I think she'll be a great mother."

If anything, that just made Ronnie feel even more awkward. The only thing that she was good for was reproducing? What a thing to say in front of a man who was basically a stranger to them.

"What is it you do?" Ronnie directed the question at Floyd, hoping to take the heat off of herself.

"I'm a CPA," he said. "Accounting."

Ronnie nodded. "That sounds good,"

"He'll be a good provider," Mom pointed out.

Ronnie scooped a forkful of lasagna into her mouth and chewed, barely tasting the zesty sauce. She looked sidelong at Mom, starting to get an inkling of what was going on.

(II)

After supper, Ronnie looked for a graceful way to excuse herself and get away from whatever else was planned for the evening.

"Well, I have homework," she said, looking pointedly at her watch. "It's been fun, but if I'm going to bring my grades up…"

"Oh, you can stay for a little longer," Mom said. "There's time for homework later."

"No, there's really not," Ronnie said. "I have quite a bit that I have to get done tonight."

"Well… I suppose,"

Ronnie nodded and stood up. She looked in Floyd's direction. "It was nice meeting you, Mr. Plum."

"Oh, no. Call me Floyd," he protested. He stood as well, as if to escort her to the door. But Ronnie was just going upstairs to her room. "I wonder if we could see each other again. Do you like movies?"

Ronnie opened her mouth to break the news that she wasn't allowed to date, but Mom jumped in ahead of her. "I'm sure Ronnie would love to go out with you sometime."

Her mouth open, Ronnie stared at Mom. First, she was allowed to wear makeup, and now she was allowed to date? All because of Floyd? She looked from one parent to the other and they just looked at her and nodded. She eventually dragged her eyes back to Floyd, who they'd all left hanging. He was still standing there, looking at her.

"Uh, yeah," she agreed. "A movie. That sounds nice. Um. Give me a call."

Floyd gave her a broad smile, maybe the first genuine one of the evening. "Great! I will," he promised.

Ronnie retreated to her room, but she didn't pull out her schoolbooks. She sorely missed having Janessa there to discuss everything with. She knew that she could call her, but it wasn't the same. Janessa was gone, and it was time for Ronnie to grow up and deal with it herself.

The first official date with Floyd wasn't awful. They agreed on a movie ahead of time, over the phone. Ronnie had no idea how she should dress, but gave it her best shot, going for neat casual. As if she had anything else in her closet. There were a couple of skirts and dresses, but she wouldn't wear those to a movie theater.

Floyd picked her up in his car, and he didn't sit at the curb and honk the horn, but went up to the house and greeted Mom and Dad politely and filled them in on the movie times so they would know when to expect Ronnie home. He went back to the car with Ronnie, opening the door for her like a gentleman. That was one bonus of dating an older man. He actually had his own car and it wasn't a rusted-out old wreck.

Ronnie's heart was pounding hard as she got into the car. Her first date. Her first real date. Approved by Mom and Dad and everything. She had begun to think that they would never let her date, or have anything to do with boys. Mom didn't let her forget getting in trouble with Ibri. It seemed like years ago, but they weren't going to let it go that easily.

Floyd got into the car beside Ronnie. He adjusted the air and asked her whether she were comfortable. He turned on the radio and asked her what she liked to listen to. He found a station that they both liked. He shifted into drive and they were off to the theater. While he was driving, Floyd took his hand off of the wheel and put his hand gently over Ronnie's. They drove like that for a few minutes, his warm hand over hers, until he needed the use of both hands again and removed it.

Floyd chatted mostly about the movie. He knew the leads and asked her if she liked them and talked about what other movies they had been in. Ronnie watched him as he talked. He had a dimple in the center of his chin. Not a cleft. Just a little bit of a dimple.

As one would expect in a family with so many children, movie tickets and theater food were expensive, and it was very rare that they had gone to movies together. When they did, it was one large popcorn shared among all of the children, and a large pop shared between the girls and one between the boys. It was nice of Floyd to buy her a drink of her own, a jumbo sized popcorn between the two of them, and her favorite sweets.

"This is really great," Ronnie said, as the two of them sat down and made themselves comfortable. "Thank you for inviting me."

"You're welcome," Floyd said politely. "I hope it's a good movie."

Ronnie was watching him carefully, waiting for him to make a move. She knew that most of the teens who came to the movie theater on dates didn't go to watch the movie, but to make out once the lights went down. But she didn't know what Floyd's intentions were. He was older. Maybe he was past that scene. Maybe he was too nerdy to even realize that's what the expectation might be.

As they got settled, Floyd put his arm behind Ronnie. She didn't flinch or pull away, just turned her face toward him, waiting.

"Do you go to the movies a lot?" he asked casually.

"No. I'm not allowed to da—my Mom and Dad—before they haven't let me... go out."

His eyebrows arched up, apparently surprised by this. "Oh."

"So, this is my first... real... date."

"I'll try to make sure it's enjoyable," he promised. He leaned in and gave her a quick peck on the lips.

Ronnie felt herself blush. She smiled at him and wasn't sure how to respond. He kissed her once again, a little longer, his lips barely touching hers. Then he sat back and they continued to chat until the movie started.

Ronnie cuddled against his shoulder during the movie. He kissed the top of her head and they shared the popcorn, but they didn't make out.

CHAPTER

Twelve

AGE 17

(I)

Having Floyd over for Sunday dinner had become routine, so Ronnie wasn't sure why there was so much tension in the air. Maybe there was something going on with Dad at work, and he was worried about Floyd coming over or a conversation they had to have.

Mom kept looking at Ronnie, and when she caught Dad's gaze on her too, she went to the bathroom to check her hair, makeup, and anything else that might be askew. But nothing seemed to be out of place. She couldn't understand what their problem was.

Floyd arrived, freshly shaven and pink-cheeked, giving Mom a kiss on the cheek and Dad a firm handshake before hugging and kissing Ronnie. They visited in the living room for a few minutes, just polite small talk. Floyd started patting his pockets, and then he was down on the floor like he had dropped something. Ronnie looked at him, down on one knee in front of her, and was about to make a joke about it until she saw the jewelry box in his hand. Then any humor about the situation fled.

"Ronnie, these past months as I've gotten to know you, I couldn't be happier... I keep pinching myself, thinking it must be a dream... but I don't ever want it to end, so I want to know... if you'll marry me."

Ronnie looked down at the small solitaire ring in the jewelry box, stunned. Her heart pounded in her throat. She had enjoyed dating Floyd and was comfortable in his company. It was the first time she'd been allowed to have a relationship outside of the family, and it felt good. She had looked forward to dating others as she got older and was shocked by Floyd's proposal.

"I... I don't think I can," she stammered. She looked at Mom and Dad for their reaction. Surely they would think it was too fast. She wasn't even legally an adult.

"Floyd already asked for my permission," Dad said, smiling proudly. Ronnie wasn't sure whether he was proud of Floyd, Ronnie, or himself. "And I have given it."

"We both give our blessing," Mom gushed. "Oh, I'm so excited! A wedding in the family!"

Ronnie looked back at Floyd. He took the ring out of the jewelry box and took her hand. Ronnie sat staring at him, her hand limp, as he slid the ring onto her finger. It was a perfect fit.

Floyd's ears were bright red. "Thank you, Ronnie," he said fervently. "You've made me the happiest man in the world."

As the wedding date drew nearer, Ronnie felt a sense of panic. Everything seemed to be spinning out of her control. Of course, the wedding arrangements were carefully handled by Mom, who was a good organizer and had good tastes and knew just how everything should be done. Ronnie didn't really care about all of the fussy details. What kind of cake was under the fondant icing. How many tiers. Gifts for the bridesmaids. How long the toast should be. It all seemed unreal and far away and Ronnie was happy to have Mom dealing with it.

It was the hard facts of the marriage that frightened her. Everything that would happen after the wedding. All of a sudden, she would be an adult. She would be in charge of her household. Expected to cook and clean for Floyd. Expected to please him in other areas. The thought of intimacy worried her the most of all. How could she be expected to know what to do? She was just a teenager. Floyd was the only person she had ever dated and they had been very careful of the boundaries.

Save it until you are married, Mom had always said. Ronnie had done her best to stay away from any situations that might be dangerous. Even as the wedding day approached and she saw Floyd every day and spent every spare hour with him, they followed a strict protocol. They only met at Ronnie's home, never at Floyd's apartment. Only in the living room or kitchen, never the bedroom. When they went out on a date, they stayed in public areas. Where there were people around. They never went parking, or to racy parties, or anywhere else they might be tempted. The closest they ever got was at the movie theater, when the lights went down. Kissing and cuddling, but never anything more. Ronnie was terrified what was going to happen once they crossed the threshold. Her only intimate experience had been negative. It haunted her still, no matter how hard she had worked at forgetting those dark days.

What if being with Floyd brought flashbacks? What if it caused pain from the old scars? There were so many landmines, she was terrified about taking another step.

Floyd held the door for Ronnie and she got into the car. She sat down and waited in the silent bubble of the car for the few seconds that it took Floyd to circle to his own door and then get in beside her. He started the engine. When he grasped the gearshift, she put her hand over his, preventing him from going anywhere. Floyd looked at her with a curious, good-humored smile.

"What's up?"

"I want to talk to you."

"Okay... isn't that what we were just doing?"

"No... I mean really talk. About getting married."

"Didn't we already decide to get married?"

"Yes. I know. But when you asked me... you didn't know every-thing about me."

"I expect to be learning more about you for at least twenty years. That's what marriage is all about. Learning to love each other the more you find out about them. We can take our time."

"Not... you don't know some important things about me. And I think you need to."

Floyd sat back. "Okay. Shoot."

Ronnie tried to figure out what to say. How to go right from standing still to going sixty. How was she supposed to tactfully introduce the subject?

"You know that I'm adopted by the Dares, right?"

"Sure. I knew that before I even met you."

She thought about that for a minute. Pictured Dad talking about his family with his coworkers. What had he heard about her? Cute things? Brags? The things she did that drove him crazy?

"Did you know I was only adopted a couple of years ago? Before that I was in foster care."

"But with the Dares, right?"

Ronnie nodded. "They're the only foster family I ever had. I went right there from my bio family."

Floyd nodded. He raised his eyebrows. "You never talk about your bio family. Did you want to invite them to the wedding? No one ever said, and I didn't think..."

"No. It's not that. I wouldn't even know how to get ahold of them. Maybe Clive knows how to get in touch with some of my siblings, I don't know. He's never said."

"Who is Clive?"

"Mr. Clive. He was my social worker. Most of the time that I was with the Dares."

"Ah. Did you want to invite *him* to the wedding?"

Ronnie considered it. "No. We didn't have that kind of rela-tionship."

"So...?"

She swallowed. "I think you should know about me... when I was little... before I came to the Dares... my bio dad... he..." She could barely speak around the lump in her throat. She was back there again, his hands controlling her, the feelings of shame and revulsion.

Floyd touched her shoulder gently. "Ronnie... your Mom told me. It's okay."

Ronnie's face was hot and sweat broke out on her forehead. Mom had told Floyd? Told him her deepest, darkest secret without even asking Ronnie if it was okay? She felt betrayed. Humiliated.

"It's okay," Floyd repeated. "I still want to marry you. What happened to you when you were a little child, that wasn't your fault. You're not..." he searched for a word. "You're not damaged."

But that was how she felt. Damaged. Unclean. Guilty. She'd been trying to keep those feelings repressed, but they flooded up at his words. That wasn't why she had come to him. That wasn't why she had tried to tell him about her history. Ronnie covered her face with both hands, trying to regain her composure. Floyd reached down again to shift gears and this time Ronnie didn't stop him, too caught in the morass of her own emotions.

"So, are we okay now?" Floyd asked lightly, resting his hand momentarily on Ronnie's knee.

"You don't understand," Ronnie told him. "That's not... you don't understand."

"Then explain to me," he said reasonably.

"I don't know if I can... do that. I don't know if I can be your wife."

He smiled tolerantly. "It won't be a problem," he soothed. "There's chemistry between us. You've felt it. You can't deny that."

Ronnie admitted that when they kissed or embraced, she did feel impulses. She did, at those times, want more. Want to complete their union.

"I know I want to," she said. "I just don't know if I can."

"We'll take our time. You don't need to feel rushed or pressured." He rubbed her knee. "We've got our whole lives to get to know each other."

Ronnie fell silent, watching out the window. She knew that she should feel reassured by his words. He was older, more experienced. He was willing to let her take her time to explore their relationship. That was all good. It was all right. She should be relieved.

But she wasn't.

She was frustrated that he had just brushed off her concerns. What did he know about the way she felt or the damage she carried with her? How could he know what she needed or how to help her if he wasn't even listening?

Ronnie tried to focus on the TV, flipping channels restlessly for something that might be interesting. Nothing she found satisfied her. Normally, it was a treat to get control of the remote and to decide for herself what she wanted to watch. Usually, Dad had it and he was stubborn about what shows he wanted to watch. But he was in his study, working on some project.

"Is something wrong, Ronnie?"

Ronnie glanced over at Mom, working on a crossword puzzle on the couch. She didn't look up at Ronnie, but waited for an answer to her question.

"I'm just... out of sorts."

"Worried about the wedding?"

"No. Well, maybe. Sort of."

"All of the arrangements are under control. You don't need to worry."

"I know all that. That's not what I'm worried about."

"What, then?"

"It's just... after we're married... I don't know if I can... *be* married."

Mom frowned, looking up at her and squinting at her. "Of course you can be married. You're used to living in a family, being considerate and respectful of others. you and Floyd love each other. You'll work things out just fine."

"No... not that. I don't know if I can physically... you know... be with him."

Mom's face smoothed, her eyes suddenly understanding. "You just have cold feet, Ronnie. Everybody worries about the physical side of a new relationship. It will be fine."

"But what happened to me... I don't know if I can."

"You're completely healed. Physically and mentally. I don't have any concerns about it, and neither should you."

Ronnie went back to flipping channels on the TV, blocking Mom out. She tried to put the worries out of her mind. But she knew better. She knew that the wounds were not healed. They still festered, even after so many years.

(II)

They didn't go back to Floyd's apartment, which Ronnie had not yet seen. It was supposed to be special, their honeymoon, so Floyd had made a reservation at a hotel. A nice hotel. Ronnie didn't know if it was officially a honeymoon suite, but it was nicer than anywhere she'd ever stayed. The Dares didn't travel much, but when they did, with so many kids, they were all crammed into one or two rooms, and even if it was a nice hotel, there was just no way for them all to have their own space and really enjoy it.

The suite felt bigger than the Dares' house. Maybe it wasn't really, but the sitting room and bedroom were certainly bigger than the living room and master bedroom at home. The bed was huge, a king or something even bigger.

"This is nice," she observed. She couldn't think of anything else to say.

"I'm glad you approve, Mrs. Plum," Floyd said, a mischievous smile on his face that showed how much he was enjoying calling her by her new name.

Ronnie smiled weakly back.

"Would you like some champagne, Mrs. Plum?" he offered, gesturing to the bottle chilling in an ice bucket on the counter.

"Uh, sure."

She watched him unwrap it and pop the cork. Carefully, so that he didn't spill a drop. He poured it carefully into the provided champagne flutes, and handed one to her.

"To our health and happiness," he toasted, "for many years to come."

Ronnie gave a little nod, and sipped it. She wasn't used to alcohol of any kind, so she knew she had to be careful. She didn't want to get tipsy, or worse.

"Come sit down," Floyd invited, sitting down on a satiny couch. A love seat, built for two. Ronnie folded herself into it and cuddled up to Floyd, her back against his chest, facing away from him. He sipped his champagne, and kissed her head and neck, and ran his fingers through her silky hair.

"The wedding was nice," he murmured.

"Yes. Mom did all the planning. Everything went great, didn't it?"

"And the reception. It was nice to see so many family and friends."

"I didn't spill anything on my dress," Ronnie pointed out. She had been so worried that she was going to stain it. But she had made it through the dinner without spilling a drop. She hadn't eaten much of anything. She hadn't been hungry. Floyd ran a finger down the smooth skin of her neck, making her shiver and break out into goosebumps.

"Let's go check out the bed."

"I already saw it," Ronnie dismissed. "I'm not tired."

"You look exhausted," he pointed out, not believing it. "It's been a long day. Besides, we don't have to go to sleep yet."

He was shifting behind her, restless to press forward. She knew what he wanted, but she wasn't ready. He said that he could wait. He had said that they could take their time. However much time Ronnie needed.

"Come on," Floyd urged, getting to his feet and pulling on her hands to get her to stand up.

"Can't we just unwind for a little while?"

"In the bedroom."

He was relentless. Ronnie gave a little tug, resisting. "Floyd... no."

"Come on, Ronnie," he told her firmly. He pulled her into the bedroom. He had grabbed the champagne bottle to take into the bedroom with him, and poured it, starting on another glass. He motioned to the bed, and Ronnie sat down on it, smoothing the blankets with both hands.

"It's so pretty. I don't feel like I should touch anything."

"You're pretty too. Just like a princess."

Mom had helped her to pick out an outfit for after the wedding reception, and she still had on her wedding makeup. She had let her hair down, out of the awkward arrangement that had made her feel like she was balancing a hedgehog on top of her head.

She didn't feel like a princess. She felt nauseated and tense. That wasn't how it was supposed to be. She wasn't supposed to feel anxious and sick. It was supposed to be the best day of her life. The beginning of a new life with Floyd. Her gate into adulthood.

Floyd set down the glass of champagne and sat down beside her, leaning over to kiss and embrace her.

Ronnie tried to let the moment carry her away. Let nature take its course. Just let her body follow its natural instincts. For the first few minutes, that worked. Floyd's kisses were familiar. They had embraced and cuddled before, always stopping before either of them got to the point of no return. Always stopping before things got too serious.

Floyd fumbled with the zippered closure on the back of her dress. Ronnie was all goosebumps again. They both undressed shyly. Then Ronnie started to hyperventilate when he touched her again. Flashbacks filled her brain, an explosion of sights, sounds, and sensations that she didn't want to feel. She couldn't get enough oxygen.

Floyd hesitated, sensing that she was not merely out of breath from excitement and anticipation.

"You're okay, Ronnie. Everything is fine," he told her.

Ronnie pushed his hands away when he got too close to her. He was trembling. His face flushed.

"I can't," Ronnie told him.

"You can. I'll show you."

When she tried to pull back from him, he caught hold of her arm, his grip too tight. "Stay," he insisted.

Ronnie resisted. "Floyd, no. Let me go."

"Just relax. I don't want to hurt you."

"Then don't!" Ronnie tried to push him away from her, but he just pressed himself closer. Ronnie struggled against him, but he refused to let her go, using his weight to pin her down.

It was all black. Ronnie was swimming in memories. Memories that she couldn't see. She didn't want to see or feel any of it. Her brain refused to process it. But the feelings flooded back. Anger, fear, guilt, and disgust. She lay paralyzed, powerless to fight back.

"Mmmm." Floyd had pulled the blankets up over them both and lay with his arms around Ronnie, warm and protective. His body was soft and loose, molded to hers, totally relaxed. "I told you it would be fine," he pointed out.

Tears dripped down Ronnie's face unheeded. Her body was also limp and heavy, but not with a satisfied, relaxed stillness. Her whole body hurt, inside and out. It had been terrifying and agonizing and she never wanted to be with him again.

Floyd did not sense anything amiss. He kissed the top of her head softly, oblivious to her tears.

"I love you, Ronnie," he whispered. "You make me complete."

Ronnie couldn't pull away from him. There was no energy left in her body. She couldn't move a muscle without terrible pain. She remembered being in the hospital, how it had felt like something had been ripped out of her insides. They had given her painkillers. IV narcotics to dull the pain. Now she felt it all again, without the benefit of painkillers. She felt every movement.

Floyd cuddled with her for a while. Then, apparently deciding that she had fallen asleep, he left her there alone in the big bed, shutting off the light and closing the door softly behind him. Ronnie heard the TV go on in the next room.

CHAPTER
Thirteen

AGE 22

(1)

Ronnie picked up her sandwich and the paper, determined to cram in at least five minutes of time to herself before the children started to make noise again. It seemed like she could never get them both to settle down for quiet activities at the same time. It was always one or the other. And Kent constantly woke Carrie up from her naps. She sat down at the kitchen table and started flipping rapidly through the pages as she ate the sandwich. Five minutes without an interruption. It was like a miracle.

She glanced over the first page of the obituaries. No pictures of anyone that she knew. But her eyes stuttered to a stop on a name.

Adam 'Bubby' Taub.

She stopped and stared at it for a minute, trying to think of why it sounded so familiar. She had never known anyone by that name. She looked at the brief text of the obituary, scanning for anyone she did know. That's when she saw *Ibri Taub, brother.*

Ibri.

She hadn't thought about him for a long time. They had never kept in touch after Ronnie had pushed him away on Mom's orders. In the final years of school, she sometimes saw him in classes. Passed him in the hallway occasionally. But they never spoke again, and she had lost track of him. She didn't know if he had gone on to find a job or go to school. With his absentee parents, he probably had to find a job and stay home with his brother. Bubs. Now something terrible had happened and Bubs was dead.

There were details of the memorial service in the obituary. Ronnie tapped her finger, thinking. The children were still quiet, so she had a few minutes to think about what she wanted to do. She wanted to go. She wanted to support Ibri. To offer some kind of apology for the way that she had treated him, abandoning their friendship and not ever talking to him again. She was her own woman now, an adult who didn't have to answer to her parents or to keep them happy to remain a part of the family. She could renew their friendship. Make up for her faithlessness.

She entered the details of the funeral into her calendar.

There was a crash from the direction of the bedroom, and Ronnie hurried to see what Kent had gotten into.

She had made her plans to attend Bubby's funeral covertly, as if it were something she had to hide. She was sure that if she just told everybody that she had a funeral to attend, it would be easy. No one would object. But she felt the need to keep it a secret, something between her and Ibri. Not because it was something she was ashamed of. Just because she wanted it to be special, between the two of them. She knew how much Ibri would appreciate her being there.

She got Mom to babysit, saying that she was visiting an old friend. She didn't say anything to Floyd. It was during the day, so he wouldn't even know the difference. She didn't need to fill him in on the details. She was a grown-up, and there was nothing wrong with attending a memorial service. That was just something friends did.

She hadn't been to a funeral for a long time. She remembered her father's funeral clearly. She might have gone to a couple of funerals for extended family after that, but it was never anyone she really knew, and she wasn't the center of attention. Not like at her daddy's funeral when everyone had stared at her and whispered behind their hands.

Bubs's funeral was very different from the others she had been to. There were no flowers and the casket was a simple wooden box. She watched the people around her and copied their actions to ensure she did not embarrass herself. When the mourners came in, it took her a few minutes to identify which one was Ibri. He looked different from what she remembered. He was Ronnie's age, but he looked forty. Of course, he was tired and in mourning; no one looked their best at such a time. His facial lines were deeply creased, as if his mourning had started years earlier. When she had known him, he had been cheerful and philosophical, upbeat in spite of the rough life that he was leading. He was more likely than Ronnie was to buoy up the people around him.

She didn't think that she should go to the graveside ceremony. She wasn't part of the family and didn't even know Bubby. She tried to approach Ibri after the church service to talk and give him her condolences. One of the extended family or friends moved to intercept Ronnie.

"The mourners do not take visitors now," he told her in a quiet voice. "You can go by the house in the coming days to visit and offer your condolences."

Ronnie was stuck. She hadn't arranged for the children to be babysat later in the week and she didn't want to take them with her. Not for a solemn visit like that. She had fully expected to be able to see Ibri, to give him a hug and to tell him how sorry she was about the loss of his brother.

She still didn't know what had happened to Bubby. No one had given any details about his death. They talked a little about the boy that he had been. They chanted scriptures and prayers that Ronnie couldn't understand.

"I... I need to see Ibri... I can't see him later," she tried to explain. "This is... the only time I can see him."

The friend glanced in Ibri's direction, hesitating. "It's not usually done," he stalled.

"Please... I'll be quick. I know he still has to go to the graveside. I just thought... I thought I'd be able to talk to him."

The soft-spoken man finally gave in, motioning for Ronnie to stay put and then going over to Ibri to talk softly to him, gesturing and looking in Ronnie's direction.

Ibri gave his head a shake. The man continued to talk to him, and finally Ibri headed toward Ronnie. His brows were drawn down and his mouth was a thin, straight line. His eyes went over Ronnie as he approached her. He shook his head.

"Do I know you?"

"It's Ronnie. Ronnie Simpson? From high school?"

He frowned more deeply.

"Ronnie," he repeated.

"From high school," Ronnie repeated lamely. "It's Ronnie Plum now. I know we didn't keep in touch, but when I saw Bubby's name in the paper, I had to come and give you my condolences..." Ronnie reached to take his hand.

Ibri shook his head. "We're not friends, Ronnie. I don't know why you came here. I need to be with the people who are my friends, and Bubby's."

Ronnie stood there with her mouth open as he walked away from her and rejoined the other mourners. She didn't know how to respond, but the moment for reacting was gone.

Ibri didn't want to rekindle their friendship. He didn't want anything to do with Ronnie.

She didn't remember going back to Mom's to pick up the kids, or anything about the children's chatter in the car on the way home. She didn't remember driving at all. She sat at home, going through the motions of getting the kids their snacks and settling them in front of the TV when they wouldn't unwind for a nap. Nanna had gotten them too excited and their daytime routine was broken. They weren't going down for a nap after their exciting morning.

Then she sat on the couch, watching them, but her mind far away. She tried to remember all she could from the days when she and Ibri had been friends.

CHAPTER
Fourteen

AGE 15

(I)

Ronnie held the cigarette between two fingers like adults did, casually, as if this were something that she did all the time. Ibri was watching her with an amused expression and she was pretty sure that he knew it was an affectation.

"You don't have to," he said, nodding to the cigarette. "No one is forcing you to smoke."

"No," Ronnie protested. "It's okay. I can smoke." She put the cigarette to her mouth, but she didn't really inhale it. Just puffed a little smoke out.

Ibri grinned at her. "Your parents won't smell the smoke and get after you?"

Ronnie hadn't even thought about the smell of the smoke in her clothes. She would have to hand-wash the clothes when she got home. She'd have to think up some excuse. She'd spilled on them at lunch time. Sweated through them running home. Tripped and gotten mud or grass stains on them. It all sounded fake inside her head and she didn't know what excuse she would give.

"I get in trouble all the time," she said with a shrug. "It won't matter."

Oh, wasn't she the bad girl now. Hiding how scared she really was about getting in trouble over anything. How she agonized every day over every little thing that she did wrong or that her parents might judge her for. How any day they could declare that they had had enough of her nonsense and send her away.

"How are you doing?" she asked Ibri, turning the subject back to him.

He took a long drag in his cigarette and held the smoke in his lungs as if to fortify himself. He let it back out in a long, thin stream.

"Not so good," he admitted.

Ronnie nodded, not probing further. If he wanted to tell her, he would.

"I haven't seen my mom in three days," he revealed. "I don't know... if something happened to her... or if she just left... or maybe she just got distracted, and she'll be back when I get home from school."

Ronnie's mouth dropped open. She tried to fathom what that would be like. What would she feel like if Mom just wasn't there one day when she got home from school? Ronnie would be frantic. They'd call the police, even if they weren't allowed to report missing persons right away. They would call anyway. It would be the end of the world for them. But Ibri said it calmly, meditatively, as if this had happened before and he wasn't sure whether to be concerned or not.

"Did you... call the police?" she asked tentatively.

"No," Ibri shook his head, making a growling noise in the back of his throat. "I think she'll be back... and if I call the cops, that would get Social Services involved and they'd want to put us somewhere else. They'd split us up. No one wants teenagers."

Ronnie felt a knot in her own stomach at the assertion. What if her parents didn't want her anymore? What if they decided they'd had enough of teenagers and they didn't need the aggravation?

Maybe they'd pick up some younger kids, see if they had better luck that way.

"I can take care of Bubs. We pretty much look after ourselves anyway." Ibri took another draw on his cigarette.

"I can't imagine," Ronnie said. "That would be really hard." She could remember vaguely, back when she lived with her bio family, that the children had often been on their own in the morning and after school. But someone was always home when it was time for supper, certainly by bedtime. They hadn't ever been left alone overnight. "What about your dad?"

Ibri snorted. "The sperm donor? We're lucky to get a check a couple times a year and a phone call at Christmas. He's not suddenly going to take on two kids."

Ronnie knew that his parents weren't together. She should have had more sense than to ask him that. Just the two of them, Ibri and his brother, all on their own.

"What do you think happened to her?"

Ibri shrugged. "Probably just went out on a bender and forgot to come home," he said. "It wouldn't be the first time. But usually that just lasts a day or two. Three days with no sign of her... I worry she could be dead in an alley somewhere."

"Yeah. I'd be really freaked out. Are you guys okay? Do you need anything?"

"Nah. Nice of you to ask, but we're pretty self-sufficient. I can cash her check when it comes in, and I'm working after school so we've still got money to live when she clears out the bank account. Food stamps, free lunch program; we won't starve."

"Do you want to come over for dinner?" Ronnie asked, "I could ask Mom if you can both come over to eat."

Ibri puffed on his cigarette and shook his head. "Too dangerous. Can't have them asking questions, wondering if there's something wrong."

"You wouldn't have to say anything... it would just be me inviting a friend for dinner."

"Have you ever brought a boy home for dinner before?"

"Well... no."

"Exactly. So, they're gonna pay attention. Especially if I bring Bubs too. Besides, I've got to work after school."

"Okay…"

He gave her a warm smile that was like the sunshine breaking out of the clouds. "Thanks, though. You're a real friend."

Neither of them had been aware of the approach of the vice principal. By the time they spotted him, it was too late to drop the cigarettes and run.

"Mr. Taub and Miss Simpson. You're out of bounds."

Ronnie surreptitiously stepped on the cigarette she had dropped to make sure that it was thoroughly ground out. The look that Mr. Hackman gave her assured her that he wasn't missing a thing.

"Sorry, Mr. Hackman. I'll get back to class…" Ronnie took a step away from him, hoping that her apology and compliance would placate him. But he put a hand on her arm to stop her from leaving.

"No, I don't think so. You're going to come pay me a visit."

"I'm already late," Ronnie pointed out. "I should go…"

"Maybe you should have thought about that ten minutes ago. Come on, both of you. To my office."

Ronnie looked over at Ibri, who was still smoking his cigarette. He took a few more puffs and then looked reluctantly at the butt and flicked it away. Mr. Hackman stepped on it and ground it out.

"You know that smoking is not permitted anywhere on school grounds. You kids are not supposed to be back here."

Ibri shrugged, unconcerned. Ronnie was finding it difficult to breathe. She had been nervous going behind the school with Ibri, which she knew was forbidden, but she had never really thought that she might get caught. She went to great lengths not to do anything that might get her in Mom's and Dad's bad books, and now this, when she had been doing so well.

Ibri gave her a little smile as they followed Hackman to his office. It was fine for him to be smiling about it. He wouldn't get in trouble at home. He looked out for himself.

CHAPTER
Fifteen

AGE 22

(1)

Y ou're a real friend. Had Ibri really said that to her? What kind of a friend had she shown herself to be? The very next day, she had dumped him like a hot potato. Because her Mom told her to. Told her that she couldn't go behind the school or get involved with boys, or even talk to Ibri again.

She tried to imagine what that betrayal had felt like to him. She had been there, had acted like a concerned friend, pretended to care for him, and then she was gone. Wouldn't even talk to him again. He must have been hurt and angry, and if he had remembered that hurt all those years later, it was no wonder that he didn't want to be consoled by her or to talk to her. Give her a taste of her own medicine. See what it feels like to be abandoned?

How had he and Bubby gotten along in all the intervening years? Ibri supporting them with his job, unable to continue his education. Bubs had been what, five years younger? So, he was just seventeen when he died. Of what? The obituary hadn't given any kind of indication. Not 'died suddenly,' a euphemism for suicide.

Nothing about giving money in lieu of flowers to some cancer society. There hadn't been any flowers. But where had the money gone instead? Had he suffered through long years of disease? Had he been in a car accident? What was Ibri going through, now on his own? Ronnie didn't even know if his mother had ever returned after that three-day absence. She hadn't seen anyone who looked like a mourning mother at the funeral. No one pasted to Ibri's side. No one who looked like an estranged but concerned father. There had been a few people Ibri's age. A few people who were older, but who stood too far from him to be close family. Ronnie, standing outside the room, not even part of his world anymore.

Ronnie heard the sound of the garage door opening and blinked, looking around. Where had the time gone? The children had been parked in front of the TV for hours, and she had just sat there, lost in her own mind. She got up, glanced in at Carrie and Kent to make sure they didn't look neglected, and hurried into the kitchen. What could she get on the table quickly?

Floyd entered through the back door, through the mud room and into the kitchen.

"Hi, sweetie, how was your day?" he inquired, eyes distant. He leaned down to kiss her on the cheek. He walked through the kitchen like a sleepwalker, then turned around, looking around the kitchen sharply. "You haven't started dinner? Hard day?"

"Uh—yeah, sort of," she agreed. She didn't want to explain to him about the funeral and Ibri. Hopefully, if she were vague, he would just think it was something to do with the children fighting or fussing and wouldn't inquire any further.

"Do you want help?"

Floyd could be handy in the kitchen in a pinch. But the kitchen was small and she didn't want to be bumping into him as she cobbled together a dinner and she didn't want to have to fight him over who was making what and who needed the microwave first.

"No. I'm fine. I'll just be a few minutes." Ronnie opened the fridge and gazed inside. "We have a few leftovers that should be cleaned out. Add some salad and veggies… it won't take long."

He nodded, not looking excited about the line-up.

If he wanted something else, he could pick up the phone and order in. But she knew he wouldn't. He was too frugal and too conscious of his waistline, getting gradually thicker the longer they were married. In the first couple of years of marriage, when she was constantly pregnant, there had been lots of take out. Pizza, fried chicken, Chinese, tacos, the whole gamut. Ronnie had managed to lose the weight post-pregnancy, in the months that she nursed. She had the willpower. Restricting calories wasn't a new game for her, and it was harder to make herself eat when she needed to than it was to lose weight.

For Floyd, it was harder. Sitting in front of a computer all day, lunches with clients, tired when he got home, he hadn't been able to lose the weight like Ronnie. So, no more takeout. He would force himself to eat the leftovers and salad. Or he would have a coffee and pick at the food, and go most of the evening without, getting gradually grumpier all night and waking up ravenous in the morning.

Floyd greeted the kids in the living room, getting only lukewarm answers as they stared at the TV screen. She heard the bedroom door shut as he went to change into his grubbies, a t-shirt and sweatpants, in order to be comfortable for the evening. Even in the kitchen, Ronnie could hear him on the phone, his voice loud enough through the closed door to tell that he was talking, but not what he was saying.

She microwaved the leftover chili and shepherd's pie and cut up a few tomatoes to add to the limp salad greens. It wasn't exciting, but what was salad dressing for? As the microwave whirred, she put out plates and cutlery, a jug of milk, glasses, the salt and pepper. And the salad dressing. Three kinds. Like at a fancy buffet. Carrie was squealing in the living room, and Ronnie glanced that way as she hurried back and forth to the table. It probably really wasn't Kent's fault. They were getting hungry, blood sugar low. "The arsenic hour," Mom had called the hour before supper. Kids always fought before supper.

"Kent, leave her alone," Ronnie ordered. He pulled away from Carrie guiltily, looking over his shoulder at Ronnie. "You know better," Ronnie said, even though she wasn't sure what it was that he had done. It was obvious from his guilty look that he did, in fact, know better, and that was all she needed to know.

"Mommy, I'm hungry," Carrie fussed. She looked toward Ronnie for a moment, but her attention was quickly swallowed up again by the program on TV. Ronnie didn't bother to answer. The answer was the same every night, so why mouth it again? Dinner will be ready in a few minutes. Just be patient.

Ronnie put frozen Brussels sprouts in the microwave, setting the rest of the hot serving dishes on the table and pushing spoons into them.

"Dinner," she called. "Go wash your hands. It's time to eat."

In spite of complaining about her hunger, Carrie didn't move immediately toward the bathroom to wash up. Ronnie went into the living room and shut off the TV, to a chorus of groans and complaints.

"You guys have been watching TV all afternoon. Go get washed up for supper." Ronnie ordered.

They got up, slack-faced and stumbling. Much too long sitting inactive. She should have shut off the TV hours ago and made them do something active. Go outside or make a craft. Something to get off of their butts.

Ronnie headed down the hall to get Floyd, but he had apparently already heard her call, and the door to the master bedroom opened as she strode toward it.

"Oh. You're coming." Ronnie turned around and went back to the kitchen.

The children were in the kitchen much too quickly to have cleaned up properly, but Ronnie didn't have the energy to care about it, not even to tell them to go back and wash again. She ignored them fighting as they got settled into their seats. She dished up a bit of each item onto their plates, ignoring Carrie's complaint about the chili and Kent's complaint about the salad. But both of them dug in with gusto once she added a generous portion of ranch dressing to the offending items.

She sat down and looked at her empty plate. She really didn't want to eat anything. With a sigh, she added a small scoop of each dish to her own plate. Less than she had given the children. Floyd watched her as he tucked a napkin into his crew collar.

"You had your mom babysit today?" he asked.

Ronnie's stomach tied itself into a knot. How had he figured that out so quickly? Usually he had no idea how they had spent the day, even when Ronnie told him. He just tuned it all out.

"Yes," she agreed, with no further explanation.

Floyd dashed hot sauce onto his chili and started shoveling it into his mouth. "Why? Where were you?"

Ronnie didn't answer.

"Your Mom said that you were visiting a friend. So, who were you visiting?"

Ronnie shifted uncomfortably. He'd already talked to Mom? What was going on? He was monitoring her every move?

"It was a funeral," she said. "A boy I went to school with,"

She didn't say that the boy she went to school with had died, but she left him with that impression. That was best.

"A boy you went to school with? What was his name? You never told me about it."

"Ibri. I told you. Last night before bed."

Floyd frowned, thinking back.

"You were watching the game. I guess you weren't paying attention," Ronnie bluffed. He never heard what she told him while he was watching TV.

Floyd took a few more bites. "How well did you know this guy?"

"Not very well. We were just… acquaintances. Lost track of each other over the years. I wanted to support the family."

"Where was it? I don't remember hearing about any funeral. Have I met him?"

"No. Like I said, we lost touch. I haven't seen him either."

"Then why did you go?" Floyd challenged.

"I told you. To support the family."

"Mommy! Mommy, I'm full. I don't want the leaves," Carrie fussed.

"Eat them anyway. Or no dessert."

Ronnie hadn't planned any dessert, but she could whip something up, if Carrie did manage to finish what was on her plate. Probably she wouldn't and Ronnie wouldn't have to worry about it.

"I don't want mine either," Kent complained.

"Same for you. Eat it or no dessert."

"What did he die of?" Floyd demanded.

Ronnie looked at him blankly. "What?"

"This guy whose funeral you went to. What did he die of?"

"I don't know. Nobody said, and I think it would be rude to ask. They're in mourning."

"They usually say something. Even if it's a lie. So, what did they say?"

"They didn't say. Or maybe they did, but it wasn't in English. Most of the service wasn't in English."

Floyd scowled at this and continued to scoop food into his mouth. Ronnie looked away, not wanting to watch him chew. It got on her nerves. Why couldn't he chew more quietly? He looked and sounded like a pig.

"Come on Carrie, Kent. Eat up, or be excused from the table," she told them.

Carrie got down from the table.

"Carrie…"

"May I be excused?"

"You may. Go wash your hands."

"Me too?" Kent asked.

"If you can't eat any more."

He shook his head and slid down from his chair. Ronnie got up and grabbed their plates. She scraped the remainders into the garbage. As she put them into the sink, she realized that there was still something in the microwave. The Brussels sprouts. She'd forgotten all about them. Though why she had made them in the first place, she wasn't sure. She hated the little green cabbages.

"Do you want Brussels sprouts?" she asked Floyd, displaying them.

He shook his head. "I already took too much. Gonna have to work it off."

He never went to the gym or exercised, so she wasn't sure how he was expecting to work it off. She dumped the whole bowl straight into the garbage. Floyd choked.

"What are you doing?" He flew out of his seat, but was too late to stop her. The sprouts were already in the garbage.

"Throwing them out. No one wants them. I don't even know why I bought them. We never eat them. I hate them."

"You can't waste food like that!"

He had become more and more concerned with her spending over the last few months. She wasn't sure why. He had gotten a raise each year they'd been married. He surely had enough resources to tolerate a little waste.

Floyd's face got red and for one illogical second, Ronnie thought that he was going to hit her. But Floyd had never hit her and he never would. He stalked out of the room without a word, leaving the remains of his dinner on his plate for her to clean off, scraping them off on top of the sprouts in the garbage and leaving her to clear and wash all of the other dishes.

After all of the work she had done all day, she didn't think it was fair that she had to do all of the cleanup too. The person who made the dinner shouldn't have to clean up. Even after five years, she still felt resentful that she was the only one who ever washed the dishes, unless she harangued Floyd to help her. At the Dares', with all of the kids, she hadn't had to wash every day. She got to rest when it was one of the other kids' turn. And Mom never had to do dishes.

When Ronnie finished the clean up and went into the living room, Floyd was sitting on the couch with the paper open in front of him. He hadn't turned the TV on.

"I don't see an obituary for this person."

Ronnie took a deep breath. She walked over to him and scanned the obituaries, then pointed out Bubby's entry.

"There. That one."

"You said Ibri."

She put her fingernail under Ibri's name. "There. He's the brother."

"You said he was the one who had died."

"No, I didn't."

He opened his mouth to argue, but apparently couldn't remember her words well enough to contend the point.

"I don't like this," he said instead. "You go off to this funeral, abandoning the kids, not telling me what you are up to. It sounds like you are sneaking around behind my back. Is that what's going on?"

Ronnie felt her face flush. "No! I didn't abandon the kids, I left them with my mom. I wasn't sneaking around. I just went to a funeral. What's going to happen at a funeral? I was just there to support Ibri and his family. I didn't even get a chance to talk to him."

"What does that mean?"

"They do funerals differently than we do. There isn't any time to visit. You're supposed to go to their house in the week after the funeral to visit. I didn't know that."

"You're not going to this man's house!" Floyd growled.

Ronnie hadn't been planning to, but her anger flared at his edict. "I can go if I want to! You don't control me."

"Obviously not. You can go around doing whatever you want, with whomever you want. Do you think I want people talking behind my back about what my wife is doing? How she's making a fool of me?"

"I'm not doing anything! Even if I go to visit him, what am I going to do? There will be people all over the place. You think I'm going to sleep with him or something?"

Floyd's face was red and furious. Ronnie could hear Carrie starting to cry, calling for her mommy.

"Well, I know you're not sleeping with me!" Floyd snarled.

Ronnie gasped, the pain as sharp as if he'd slapped her.

She tried to swallow the lump in her throat. She knew that she hadn't been a good wife. She acquiesced to Floyd's demands when she felt like she really had to, trying to keep the peace between them. Hoping it would bridge the gap between them and bring them some kind of harmony. But he had eventually come to understand that for her, physical intimacy was an unpleasant chore. An ordeal she dreaded. So, to Ronnie's relief, he asked less and less, and she couldn't remember for sure when the last time had been.

She just stared at Floyd, unable to think of something to say. She cleared her throat and pressed the pads of her fingers over her eyes.

"I'm sorry," she said. "If you want to..."

"Why haven't you asked for a divorce?"

Ronnie had always assumed that Floyd would be the one to demand a divorce. Alienation of affection. Incompatibility. No fault. Then he'd be free to find a real woman. One who was more compatible with him and better equipped to fulfill his needs. Ronnie sat down on the couch beside him, her quivering legs too weak to support her.

"I don't want a divorce," she whispered.

"You're not happy being married to me."

Ronnie couldn't meet his eyes. She looked away from him, out the window. "I wouldn't be any happier with anyone else. You're a good provider and you don't hit me."

"Are those your only qualifications for a good husband? That's a pretty low bar."

Ronnie shrugged helplessly. "You love the kids. You're a good daddy to them." The lump in her throat was hot and painful. She gulped. "I'm sorry. I can't help the way I feel about... other things."

"You're not seeing this Ibri." His voice was calm, no longer jealous.

"No. He didn't even want me there. We haven't seen each other since high school. We weren't ever anything but friends, then. His mom... ran away, and he was taking care of his brother." She gestured at the paper and sniffled. "Bubby. I felt sorry for him. But Mom... decided I wasn't allowed to talk to him. So... I didn't. Never again. Until today. Then he just wanted me to leave."

"You're not seeing anyone else." Not accusatory. Just a statement of fact. Acceptance.

Ronnie shook her head. "I wouldn't want to have a relationship with anyone else. I... I just can't."

He touched her back tentatively. His attempt at comfort just made the lump in her throat bigger, made it harder for Ronnie to breathe. "You ought to see someone. A doctor. A psychiatrist. Didn't Chris and Cynthia ever take you to anyone?"

"No... not for that. I saw psychiatrists about my eating disorder. Or sleepwalking. Just a few times. They never really did anything to help."

"Did you talk to them... about... what your dad did?"

"No..." Ronnie pushed her hair back over her ears, shaking her head. "I didn't talk about it to anyone."

"Maybe you should. Maybe they could fix it."

Ronnie knew that she was damaged. Broken. But she didn't think that she could ever be fixed. She wasn't just a toy with a loose wheel. Irreparable damage had been done, physically and mentally. She couldn't ever be whole again.

"If you want me to, I will," she told him. If it would make him happy for her to see someone, she would. Though she wasn't sure how they would afford it with money being so tight.

Floyd reached out for her hand. She let him take it and he brought it up to his lips and kissed the soft, smooth skin on the back. He wouldn't initiate anything after an argument, Ronnie knew. He put his arm around her shoulders and gave her a little squeeze. Ronnie leaned her head on his shoulder and closed her eyes. She didn't want the tears to come. She just wanted peace between them.

They stayed cuddled there for a long time, neither one speaking.

CHAPTER
Sixteen

[1]

Ronnie had to find Chloe. She had to know that her sister was okay, to bring the family back together. She couldn't heal herself or change what she had done in the past, but she could try to heal the family and make it whole again.

A user in an adoption reunion forum online suggested that she search court records for a name change or marriage record for Chloe. Maybe after all that she had gone through, she didn't want to go by the name Simpson anymore. Maybe she didn't want people to be able to find her that easily.

Ronnie wasn't sure why she hadn't thought of that. She, who had gone by half a dozen different names, and still didn't know which one she wanted to go by. She didn't want to go by Plum, she wasn't comfortable going by Floyd's name when she had left him so many years ago and had no desire to go back and live with him or be a part of his life. She didn't want to go by Dare, even though she had worked so hard all of those years to be adopted and become one of them. She certainly didn't want to go by Simpson after all that she had learned about Mim and their family history. She didn't want to share a name with those monsters.

And of course, the names that she had assumed after her last amnesia episode were not hers. They never had been. Then there was Coleman. She hadn't been able to remember much about Dusty.

A few more courthouse searches, and she found the record of Chloe Simpson's marriage to Jozef Gould.

"Found you!" she breathed. She tried to glean all that she could from the few words of the marriage record. Jozef was older than Chloe. They had married at the courthouse, not a church. Chloe had been twenty. Her address and Jozef's were both the same, so Ronnie assumed they had been living together before getting married.

There was no divorce record since then, so perhaps they were still together. Unless they had separated and never got a divorce. Or either of them had died. Ronnie lived in fear that she would track down Chloe, only to find out that she had died before they had a chance to reunite. She searched for obituaries in Chloe's and Jozef's names before going any further, just to head off disappointment. Then she started directory searches for Chloe Gould, looking for a current phone number or address. There was nothing. She tried a broader search, looking for any records on Chloe. She couldn't find a business, blog, or any newspaper articles or club listings. Not that appeared to be for her Chloe. None of the images looked familiar. None of the social media hits seemed to be the right age or location. Of course, she could have moved halfway around the world. But if Chloe were still around, she was living a quiet life, outside the public eye. Ronnie switched to searches of Jozef Gould, and that turned up more local results.

A college professor seemed about the right age, and there were local numbers. Ronnie examined his online bios for any hint that he was married.

There was one picture, a photograph of a college fundraiser, where he had his arm around a blond woman who was turned away from the camera. Ronnie studied the lines of the woman's body.

Was it Chloe?

Could the slim figure really be her?

Ronnie took a deep breath and called the number listed for Jozef Gould. She braced for a man's voice, preparing herself to ask for Chloe. But it was answered by a woman who sounded like June.

"Hello?"

Ronnie took a shallow breath, unable to suck in enough oxygen. "Is this Chloe Simpson?"

There was a moment of silence. Ronnie waited, anxious. "Chloe Gould," the woman corrected. "I don't go by Simpson."

"But... did you used to be Chloe Simpson?" Ronnie asked tentatively.

"Who is this?"

"It's... Ronnie."

There was no response. Ronnie tapped the table in front of her. "Your sister," Ronnie said, in case Chloe hadn't understood.

"Ronnie? Where are you? Are you okay?"

After all that Chloe had been through, her first concern was that Ronnie was all right. After the way that they had all abandoned her to Mim Simpson, shutting her out of their lives, thinking that she was some kind of traitor. "I'm... I'm fine. I just wondered... I wanted to talk to you. To try to reconnect."

"Wow. Is it really you? It's been so long!"

"I know. I should have kept in touch..." Ronnie tried to think of a way to explain all the intervening years, "...but it was really hard."

"Yeah... you probably wouldn't have been able to keep in touch with me even if you'd tried. I was... unreachable for a lot of years."

"I read the court file and newspaper articles about what happened to you..." Ronnie confessed. "I'm sorry..."

"That was a long time ago. I try not to think about it too much."

"Yeah." Ronnie laughed bitterly. "Been there!"

There were a few minutes of silence.

"So... how are you?" Chloe asked. "I suppose you're married with ten kids."

She had no idea how close to home the statement hit. Ronnie's gut clenched. "Well... not exactly. It's complicated."

"Oh, boy." Chloe's voice was apologetic. "I'm sorry."

"It's okay. I've... had to work through some things."

"Sure. I guess we've all had a lot to work through."

"I think yours was the worst," Ronnie said. "We all just always thought you were the best off. The one who escaped the abuse. Then... reading about what happened to you..."

"All of us?" Chloe repeated, her voice going up a few notes. "Have you talked to the others?"

"Yeah. You were really hard to track down. Everyone else kept their names. Well, other than you and me, I mean."

"How... is everyone...?"

Ronnie found it difficult to admit that she hadn't met them face-to-face. That she had only talked to Ruby over the phone.

"Well... okay, I guess. None of them had kept in touch until about two years ago, when they reconnected. They want to meet with me. And you."

There was no response from Chloe. Ronnie let her think about it, but grew uncomfortable with the silence.

"Would you be okay to meet with us?" she asked tentatively.

"I dunno," Chloe said cautiously. "Could I just... meet with you, to start with?"

"Sure," Ronnie agreed. "I'd love that."

CHAPTER
Seventeen

AGE 24

(1)

R onnie Stern watch Dusty Coleman enter the lobby, where he stood around talking to some of the other workers for a few minutes, and then they all went into the conference room for a department meeting. She'd seen him a few times before, and thought that she had caught him eyeing her once or twice. Was he interested in her? It seemed unlikely; Ronnie was nothing special. Medium brown hair, medium length. Brown eyes. Tending to the thin side. There really wasn't anything about her to set her apart from other women. She was the right age for him. But other than that, what would make him take a second look? She wasn't particularly pretty, didn't dress stylishly. A blue collar receptionist didn't wear anything stunning. Pants and a blouse. She had a couple of understated necklaces, but that was about as fancy as she got.

Ronnie's attention was drawn back to her ringing phone, and she occupied herself with directing calls and taking messages, forcing all thoughts of Dusty out of her mind.

Until the door opened and he came out again. Not just Dusty. The meeting had obviously concluded and everyone was going their separate directions. Dusty drifted casually toward Ronnie's receptionist desk, and he gave her a warm smile.

"Ronnie, right?" he greeted.

"Yes. Good afternoon, Mr. Coleman."

He snorted. "Mister? I think you can drop the mister. It's just Dusty."

"Dusty," Ronnie repeated, smiling shyly.

"Yeah. Are you here permanently now? I've seen you around a few times."

"No, still just temping. But... indefinitely. I don't know what they're doing to find a permanent receptionist, but I'm here until they do."

"Well, I hope they don't hurry, then."

She answered a call, and he didn't drift away from her while she was dealing with it. She looked up at him as she hung up.

"What's Ronnie short for, then?" Dusty asked.

"Just Ronnie," Ronnie said automatically, and then she shook her head and corrected herself. "Veronica, actually. But I've never gone by that. I've only ever gone by Ronnie."

"I like Ronnie."

"Yeah... me too." A few beats passed. "I like Dusty too."

"Makes me sound like a cowboy. Which I definitely am not. But it's a name that grows on you. I can't imagine going by anything else."

"No," Ronnie gave a little laugh. It could almost be a giggle. "Me neither."

His eyes shut slightly while he was looking at her. Was he flirting with her? Ronnie wasn't sure. She felt awkward, not sure how to react. One of the other men Dusty worked with called to him, but he didn't turn around to look or answer.

"I wonder... if you'd like to meet for coffee sometime?" he suggested.

Ronnie's face got warm. "Uh... sure. That sounds really nice."

"Maybe… Thursday, after work? What time do you get off?"

"Not until six."

"Long day. But I can make that work. Should I pick you up here, or at your house?"

"You could just pick me up here." She wasn't sure she wanted to give him her address yet. He didn't need to know where she lived. She didn't want him showing up uninvited. He could be the stalker type. She didn't know anything about him yet. Although, she did have access to the human resources directory, since that was the department that the receptionist was in, and she had access to his personal information, like his address and birthdate. She didn't even feel guilty about having looked them up.

"Okay," Dusty gave her a broad smile. "Here, Thursday, at six, then."

"Yeah. See you then."

He turned around and walked back to the friend who had been trying to get his attention, a bit of a swagger in his step. She couldn't hear the comments that they exchanged, but both of them stole covert glances in Ronnie's direction, which she pretended not to see.

She didn't know what it was that he saw in her, but she was happy to have the attention. She didn't have many people in her life. Just casual acquaintances. The people at work, the neighbors to her apartment, the cashier at the grocery store. Just casual acquaintances who would never really notice if she were gone.

"I'm glad you said yes," Dusty said, smiling at Ronnie across his coffee cup.

He had done more than take her to coffee as he had promised. He took her to a little diner, and they ordered supper as well as coffee. It wasn't anything fancy; Ronnie didn't feel pressured. It was just a nice little place, with good food and friendly staff. She felt at ease there.

"Me too. This is nice. I haven't been here before."

"It's one of those gems that only the locals know about. You'd never know what good food they have, looking at it from outside."

"Yeah."

Dusty had ordered the meatloaf, and Ronnie the spaghetti. It was very good, the sauce spicy and tangy, and real meatballs not just on top, but hidden throughout the dish. The meals had included salad or fries. Dusty ordered the fries, and ate half of Ronnie's salad too. By the looks of it, he was going to have to finish off her spaghetti and meatballs too, if he still had any room. Ronnie didn't think she was going to make much of a dent in it.

"You like it, right?" Dusty checked. "You haven't eaten very much..."

"I don't have a big appetite. It is really good."

"You can tell me if you don't like it, I won't be offended. People are allowed to have different tastes. Maybe you like something a little more upscale?"

"No, no. Nothing fancy. Just the basics."

"Okay. Just making sure."

The waitress bustled over to refill their mugs, looking over their plates. "Can I getcha anything else? More fries, Dusty?"

"No, I'm good." He laughed as she walked away again. "I think I've been coming here too often. They know me too well."

"It's nice to go somewhere they know your name."

"Yeah."

They ate and sipped their coffees for a while in silence.

"So..." Dusty lifted his eyebrows at Ronnie. "I barely know anything about you. Where do you come from? Do you have any family around here? Or anywhere? What did you do before you started temping at StarCan?"

"Not much to tell," Ronnie said with a shrug. "I don't have any family. Been living here for a couple of years. I've been with the temp agency since I got here... so I've worked at a few other businesses around town."

"Where were you born?"

"Out west," Ronnie said vaguely, making a motion. "What about you? With a name like Dusty Coleman, did you come from Texas?"

"No. North of here, actually. No family. I was an only child, and my parents were older. Lost Mom to cancer five years ago, and my dad just last year." There was pain in his eyes, the wound still fresh. "So, now it's just me, Dusty Coleman, party of one."

"Same here," Ronnie agreed.

"What happened to your folks?"

Ronnie shook her head. "They're not around anymore," she said, not answering the question directly.

"That's too bad. I guess we're just two orphan kids, huh? Most of my friends still have both parents, so we're pretty unusual. Funny that we just happened to run into each other."

Ronnie nodded. She had run into the same thing with people she talked to. No one understood what it was like to be alone, with no family. Everyone had someone. Spouse and children, parents, siblings, aunts and uncles, grandparents. Their lives seemed to be saturated with relatives.

Ronnie looked affectionately around the diner. So many times, she and Dusty had ended up there on a date. Sometimes it had been the launchpad and sometimes it had been the nightcap. They were always open, the staff always friendly, and the food and the coffee always good.

"Two lost people," Dusty said, gazing at Ronnie. She smiled at him. "Two people, all alone, who found each other."

He didn't often wax poetic. Ronnie tentatively extended her hand on the table, and he took her hand in his.

"I love being with you, Ronnie. I really enjoy our time together, and when we're apart... I'm just counting the minutes until I see you again."

Ronnie nodded, not sure what to say to this. She thought she should profess her love to him, but she always had trouble with that kind of thing. Her shyness kept her from saying something that might sound stupid or be taken the wrong way. But Dusty didn't seem bothered by this. He always just laughed when she apologized for how awkward she was. For not knowing the right thing to say.

She had never explained her lack of memories to him. How she didn't have all of those past experiences that everyone else had to judge by. For her, it was all new. She could try to judge by what she had seen on TV, but that wasn't the same, because TV was always skewed. So, she just smiled encouragingly, letting him fill in the words.

"I want us to be together," Dusty said.

"You want to move in together?" Ronnie guessed. She had thought that it was coming. The goodbyes were getting more difficult, the last kiss and touch taking longer, reluctant to make the final separation and go their separate ways.

"You know I'm an old-fashioned kind of guy," Dusty said. It was the reason he always gave for holding back on their physical relationship. He was an old-fashioned guy. He didn't believe in having an intimate relationship with every girl he dated. That was something special, to be saved for later.

"Yeah."

"I want a real commitment between us. Not just moving in together because it's a convenient next step."

"Uh-huh." Ronnie nodded her understanding. Though she still wasn't sure where he was headed.

Dusty cradled her hand in both of his for a minute, before letting go with one hand and reaching into his pocket. He brought it back out, holding a small velvety jewelry box. Ronnie held her breath. Was he really...?

"Veronica Stern," Dusty said slowly and clearly. "Will you marry me?"

He used both hands to open the jewelry box and show her the small diamond solitaire.

"Oh!" Ronnie released her breath. "It's lovely," she said.

He waited, smiling at her. His eyes dropped down to the ring and he shifted it in the light, throwing off sparkles.

There was a squeal and Ronnie looked up, startled, to see

Sharon, one of the evening waitresses, looking at the box from across the diner.

"Is that what I think it is?" Sharon demanded, striding toward them, her smile huge.

Ronnie and Dusty exchanged a look, and both grinned. The staff at the diner were family. Neither of them was offended by the invasion of their privacy.

Dusty let Sharon see the ring and she squealed again. "Congratulations! Oh, I'm so excited for you guys!" she gushed. She wasn't over-acting, she really was the kind who took pleasure in other people's good fortune. Not like the women on TV movies, who were always fake-nice when they were actually jealous.

"Congratulations are a bit premature," Dusty said. "Since she hasn't actually said yes yet."

"Oh! I'm sorry. I'm intruding. How gauche of me."

"Yes," Ronnie said, before Sharon could go on any further, or leave them in embarrassment.

Dusty laughed. "Whew. You had me worried for a minute there."

"I didn't take long to answer," Ronnie protested.

"Not unless you're the one waiting for the answer. Then it took an eternity!" Dusty fumbled the ring box, pulling out the ring and holding it tentatively toward her. "I have no idea if it will fit, I couldn't exactly measure you without you noticing."

Ronnie gave him her ring finger and he slid the ring on. It was a perfect fit. Was that a good omen? Ronnie hoped it was. Dusty leaned across the table and kissed her gently on the lips. "You won't regret it, Ronnie. I promise."

Ronnie nodded. "Thank you."

Was that the right answer? Thank you? She thought she should have something more articulate than that, but at that moment, couldn't come up with anything better.

"Now I can say congratulations!" Sharon said. She bent down and gave Ronnie a little hug. "I'm so happy for you, Ronnie. Dusty is a catch; you know he'll treat you good. If he doesn't..." She glared over at Dusty as if he had already done something mean. "You just let me know, and I'll take care of him!"

They all laughed. Ronnie looked fondly at Dusty. He wouldn't hurt her. He was the nicest guy that she knew.

The engagement wasn't long, and the wedding wasn't big. Since neither of them had family, they attended at City Hall for a simple ceremony performed by a justice of the peace, and then went out for dinner with a few friends from work. After that, they went back to Dusty's apartment. Ronnie had one suitcase, and the rest of her possessions, meager though they were, would be moved in on Sunday. They cuddled a little in front of the TV, unwinding with a glass of wine after the full day, before retiring to the bedroom, both feeling a little nervous and shy.

"Ronnie?"

Two strong arms went around Ronnie from behind, and she cuddled back against Dusty's body, trying to wipe away all evidence of her tears.

"What is it?" Dusty questioned. "Are you okay?" He wiped away a further trail of tears, looking at her face in concern. "You're crying! Did I hurt you?"

"No." Ronnie sobbed and tried to stop the tears. "I don't know what's wrong with me. I guess... I guess I'm just emotional. About everything."

"Are you sure?" His arms and body radiated heat. She snuggled in his hold, trying to find comfort in the warm cocoon. Dusty stroked her hair. "I'd never want to hurt you. If I did something wrong... please tell me. I'd rather know."

"No. It just... came from nowhere." The emotions that washed over Ronnie were inexplicable. Pain, fear, anger and shame. They came out of the blackness of the past. She didn't have anything to attach them to. It was nothing that Dusty had done and everything that he had done. The tears had just started coming and Ronnie couldn't control them.

Dusty rocked her gently, kissing the back of her neck and below her ear.

"Just cuddle up with me," he told her. "I'll keep you safe. I promise."

CHAPTER
Eighteen

AGE 33

[I]

Ronnie awoke, and lay there staring at the wall, the images from her dream swirling around her. It was the first time that she had remembered Dusty.

When Adah Cruz had first told Ronnie about Dusty, she had pictured him as a clone of Floyd. In her mind, he had just been a shadow, one of Floyd's size and shape. A man who had grown just as angry and bitter as Floyd had. Both before she left and after.

The bitterness toward her for their incompatibility had rankled Floyd, had warped him into a frustrated, suspicious man, more a stranger than her partner in life. He was careful around the children. He loved and coddled them. But his anger was quick, even with them, and he would go long periods without even talking to Ronnie.

The Floyd that she had returned to was different. Angry and bitter, but tired and resigned. Distant. The years had smoothed the sharp edges of the schism between them. He'd transferred his anger and bitterness to the police who had unjustly imprisoned him for two years and left his life in tatters. All that was left was a hollow shell, a husk of who he had once been.

But Dusty... the man in her dream had been different. Ronnie's amnesia had been a kindness in their relationship. She didn't know where the unsettling emotions came from and she was able to distance herself from them. She was able to build up a relationship with Dusty, even though she didn't know where the tears and the pain came from. She could separate them in her mind, her love for Dusty and the pain that came from her past. She and Dusty worked together on reducing her baffling emotional reaction as much as possible, instead of just abandoning their relationship. Finding ways to express their love that didn't hurt her so much.

Tears filled Ronnie's eyes, her heart aching for the gentle man that she had left behind. Why had she left him? What had made her forget again, and snap, leaving him behind and returning home, where her parents and Floyd were? It had been more than a year since she had left him and her young children. They must all have felt so confused and abandoned.

And yet, he had made no attempt to reach out to her and contact her again. Unlike Floyd and Mom and Dad. They accepted that she was gone and that she had another family, another past, and they didn't chase after her or demand explanations.

"Oh, Dusty..."

She couldn't remember the children yet. When she tried to picture Dane and Mandi, she saw Kent's and Carrie's faces. She couldn't bring Dane and Mandi to mind. Would they be just as bitter as Kent and Carrie? Poor, motherless children? Were they teased and bullied at school? Hurt every time the other mothers helped in the lunch room or supervise on a field trip? Did they cry themselves to sleep at night?

Ronnie took a deep breath and forced herself to sit up and to get out of bed. Lying there feeling sorry for herself wasn't going to do her any good.

[II]

Ruby's house was a neat little bungalow tucked between similar houses on a quiet cul-de-sac. Away from the hustle and bustle, but close enough to the amenities that she didn't have to go far to get downtown or to shopping or professional buildings. There was nothing startling or unique about it, but Ronnie gave a little shiver of anticipation as she looked at it.

She had arrived early, a habit well-trained into her by the Dares. Her guts were tied in knots as she sat there in her car, looking at the house as she waited for the agreed-upon arrival time to appear on the clock. A couple of other cars arrived and Ronnie watched the strangers get out and go into the house. They knocked and walked in without waiting for an answer. A man and a woman with dark hair like Ronnie's. She couldn't see their faces clearly. A young lady with blond spiky hair accompanied by two taller boys with muscular builds.

Ronnie took a deep breath to fortify herself and headed toward the house. The door was opened before she had a chance to knock or ring the doorbell. The woman who answered the door was blond, with touches of gray, her hair pulled back in a loose ponytail. Her face was lined, a reminder of the rough life she had lived, but she smiled broadly.

"Ronnie?"

"Yeah. Uh—Ruby?"

"Yes." Ruby threw her arms around Ronnie and gave her a big hug. "It's so nice to see you! It's been such a long time."

Ronnie nodded. She gave Ruby a return squeeze. How long had it been since Ruby had given her that last hug, at the Dares' home, before getting arrested? Ronnie still felt guilty about it. Why hadn't she been able to convince the police that Ruby hadn't done anything wrong? Ruby had just been expressing affection and trying to comfort Ronnie. But Ronnie had been so confused about everything.

Ruby released her and held her at arm's length for a moment, examining her face.

"I can hardly see that little girl in braids anymore."

Ronnie touched her hair self-consciously. "Uh... no. I don't wear it long anymore."

"It's cute. I like it." Ruby stepped back, motioning Ronnie to enter the living room. "Come on in! Meet everybody else! Next time just come straight in, you don't have to sit out there in your car."

Ronnie's face flamed. "Oh... you saw me..."

"Sure." Ruby laughed. "Don't worry about it. Come on."

She led Ronnie into the living room to meet the rest of the family. Ronnie glanced around at them nervously.

"June and Justin, the twins," Ruby motioned. "Can you believe these are our chubby-cheeked babies?"

Both were slim. Justin's face was quite angular. He had earrings in both ears and slightly long hair. He was tanned from spending a lot of time in the sun. June's smile was tentative, like she was worried about what Ronnie would think of her. Ronnie gave each of them a cursory hug.

"Hi... it's been a long time," she murmured.

"And here are Michelle and Kenny, June's kids; and Michelle's friend, Dan."

Michelle was the spiky blond, who Ronnie saw closer up had a dyed pink streak as well, and numerous tattoos and piercings. She stood back looking reserved, not opening herself up for a hug or even a handshake. Ronnie nodded at her. Kenny was the slimmer of the two boys, and he didn't focus on Ronnie or meet her eyes, his gaze wandering out the window, to the kitchen, and to the blank TV screen.

Dan gave Ronnie a warm, welcoming smile. "Nice to meet you!"

"You too," Ronnie nodded.

"Have a seat," Ruby invited everyone. "I'll bring in some coffee. Tell us all about yourself, Ronnie. I don't think any of us have heard from you since you were adopted."

June and Justin sat beside each other on the couch. Ronnie sat in a chair. Michelle, Kenny, and Dan stayed on their feet, Dan behind Michelle.

"Before Kenny was born," June agreed with a nod.

"I tried to stay in touch," Ronnie said, feeling awkward. Talking to June had always been a problem. Mom and Dad didn't like her having anything to do with her biological family. After the adoption, the pressure to cut off their communications had been that much stronger. She was part of the Dare family, not part of the Simpsons anymore. "But the last couple times I tried to get you..."

June nodded. "We took off before Kenny was born. Didn't want any trouble."

"Oh. Yeah." Ronnie tried to imagine June having a baby when Ronnie was only fifteen. June would have been thirteen! Way too young for a baby.

The room went quiet, and Ronnie remembered she was supposed to be telling them about herself. What was she supposed to say?

"Well... the adoption was when I was fifteen. Then I guess... I got married when I was seventeen."

"Seventeen! That's so young!" June exclaimed.

Ronnie laughed. "Not younger than thirteen!"

"Oh... yeah." June got red in the face, just like Ronnie always did when she was embarrassed.

Ronnie shrugged. "I guess we just like to get a head start."

Ruby was back with a tray of mugs and coffee service, which she set down on the coffee table in front of the couch.

"Everybody just help yourself. What did your adoptive parents think about you getting married so early, Ronnie? I bet they were pretty steamed."

"No. It was a guy that my dad worked with. They were really pushing it. Kind of set us up."

Ruby looked at her for a moment, and shook her head. She grabbed a mug of coffee before sitting down on the arm of the couch.

"Why would they do that? That's really kind of weird."

"I don't know." Ronnie sighed, thinking back about it. "I guess... they thought I didn't have a lot of prospects in life, but they figured I'd make a good wife and mother." Ronnie looked out the window, shaking her own head at the fragmented memories she had of her time with Floyd. "They were wrong."

"I'm sure you were just fine as a mom," Justin said.

Everyone's eyes turned toward him for a minute. He took a sip of coffee.

"Well, she couldn't be much worse than the rest of us," he offered.

Ruby snorted. "I guess none of us had a very good example to follow," she said. "Leaving home at eight, bouncing around between foster homes and the street. You try to throw parenthood into that mix…" She made a grimace. "I had two babies and an abortion," she told Ronnie. "One of my babies died and I gave the other one to a guy who turned out to be… not a good guy to trust. Charlie and I got her back after a while, but he's a lot better at being a father than I ever was at being a mom."

Ronnie nodded. "I remember June telling me about Sheree." She looked at June, then looked away, remembering what Ruby had said on the phone. June's kids had run away and ended up in a gang. So, June's parenting had not been the best either. They still didn't all look comfortable being in the same room together. Ronnie looked at Justin.

"What about you? Do you have kids?"

He nodded, changing from a scowl to a bright smile. "I do. I have Marcie, she's just a year younger than Michelle and she has cerebral palsy. Then I have three younger ones with my wife, Sondra."

"Four kids. Like me."

There were looks exchanged around the room. Ronnie was aware that of an undercurrent. There was something she had missed. Or something they were keeping from her. But no one offered what it was, so Ronnie was left to shift uncomfortably and to try to fill the silence.

"I, uh… I don't have any of them now. But there's Kent, he's fourteen. Carrie is twelve. And Dane and Mandi, they're six and four."

"You don't have them?" Ruby said. "Are they in foster care?"

"No. With their dads. Kent and Carrie are with Floyd, and Dane and Mandi are with Dusty."

"You married twice? Or just…"

"I married twice," Ronnie admitted. She picked at a snag in her pants. "I kind of… it's a long story. You might have seen it in the news. I was with Floyd, and I had some kind of amnesia, and disappeared. I didn't remember that I was married, so I got married again, to Dusty. So, the second marriage wasn't really… legal."

Justin laughed. June turned and looked at him scowling. "Don't laugh at that!"

Ruby was scratching the back of her head. "If I'm remembering the story right… you disappeared a second time."

"Yeah. I did. Left Dusty and came back here, not knowing that I had any family here. Then Kent recognized me, and the police got involved… It's been pretty… stressful."

"No kidding!" Ruby agreed. "That would be crazy. So… do you remember now? Did it all come back when you saw them?"

"Not exactly… it's been slowly coming back. Not everything, but most of the important points…"

"You've met everybody again, gotten reacquainted? How do your kids feel about the whole thing?"

"I've met Floyd and Kent and Carrie. But not Dusty… I don't know what to do about Dusty and the little ones. Dusty never… he never contacted me or asked me to come back, when we all realized what had happened."

"Well, you've got to go back and see them," Justin said. "You can't just abandon them and pretend it never happened."

Michelle glared at Justin. "Like you?" she demanded.

"Yeah, like me," Justin agreed. "What I did was wrong. It was cowardly and stupid. I know that."

Michelle didn't look appeased by this. Ronnie tried to look as though she hadn't heard the exchange.

"You're right… I should go back and visit… say I'm sorry. But I don't know what to do about the kids. They're too young to understand what happened, and why I can't be their mom anymore."

"Why can't you?" It was Ruby who jumped in. "You could get

visitation, at least. Fight for custody if you want to. What happened wasn't your fault and it doesn't make you a bad mother. Just... someone with amnesia."

"I don't know if Dusty would let me..."

"It wouldn't be up to him. If he didn't agree, you go to court. Just like any couple that broke up for a normal reason. I'm sure he wants his kids to have some kind of relationship with their mom, doesn't he?"

"I don't know," Ronnie said softly. She shrugged and swirled her coffee.

"You should call him," Dan suggested. "You're just guessing at what he's going to say. If I'd had a second chance to be with my folks... I would have taken it. I would have been happy to find out that there was a good reason that they had left. Instead of just... walking away."

"But I *did* just walk away."

"Not on purpose," June pointed out.

Ronnie shrugged. She looked for a way to change the subject. They had talked about kids. They had talked about marriage. She didn't want to keep talking about what had happened to her. It was embarrassing and made her feel so ashamed and inadequate. Not just as a mother, but as a person.

"So... what happened to everyone else after I got adopted?"

"I've been here," Ruby offered. "With Charlie still. You'll meet him later, but I didn't figure you needed any extra people here today, so we kept it to the minimum number of introductions. I've had a pretty quiet life, after all the crap I did as a teenager. Just raising Sheree and being a cop's wife and trying to make up for all of the bad stuff..."

Ronnie nodded. She looked at June.

"I had my babies. But I was pretty messed up. I lost the kids." June glanced sideways at Michelle and Kenny. "I got them back again, but I wasn't ready, and just screwed things up worse. Did some time. Came back here to see Ruby and get some help."

"The kids migrated this way themselves," Ruby said. "Didn't know this was where June and Justin were originally from. They ended up with my old gang, and that's when Charlie met up with them." That was what Ruby had mentioned on the phone, but it made more sense to Ronnie now.

"I work at a hair salon," June said. "I'm not a stylist, just general help. But at least it's an honest living."

"Justin's a trucker," Ruby contributed.

"Still?" Ronnie asked, "I remember that's what you were doing before."

Justin nodded. "Still. It's good work." He looked at June. "Like June says, honest."

"I have to figure out what to do. Been temping and haven't really settled into anything," Ronnie said. She wondered, after the discussion about Dusty, if she had refused to settle into something permanent because what she really wanted to do was to go back to see Dusty and the children, to try to make amends. But she still couldn't tell him *why* she had left and she knew that question would always be between them.

"Dan talks to schools," Michelle spoke up suddenly. Her voice held challenge, like she expected someone to disagree with what she was saying. "About addiction. He's really good."

Ronnie nodded. "That's cool. Good for you," she told Dan. "And you guys, are you still with the gang?"

Michelle looked at Kenny. "No. Just trying to... figure out what to do with my life."

"I live with Michelle," Kenny contributed, his first words to Ronnie and the first indication that he followed anything that was being said around him.

Michelle and Dan nodded in agreement. "Kenny helps look after us," Dan said with a smile.

Kenny nodded seriously. "I'm older," he pointed out. "Older than Michelle."

Ronnie smiled at him too. "That's good. Sometimes I wish I had someone to look after me too."

He considered her. "You could come and live with us too."

Ronnie laughed and shook her head. "That would be a full house," she said ruefully. "I don't think you'd want me around."

"You could come," he said stubbornly. But Ronnie noticed that Dan and Michelle didn't second the invitation. Kenny didn't understand all of the implications; how difficult it would be to have Ronnie living with them.

"How about Chloe?" Ronnie asked. "Do you want to meet with her?"

"Chloe stayed with Mom after the trial," Ruby said, shaking her head. "She's never contacted any of us. Why would she want to?"

"Nobody tried to get ahold of her?"

"Why would *we* want to?" June demanded. "Chloe was stuck up and bossy. Always ordering us around."

"Chloe was thirteen," Ronnie pointed out. How else would a thirteen-year-old responsible for twin eight-year-olds behave?

June shrugged and looked down.

"We haven't heard anything from her," Justin repeated. "Don't know where she is now."

Ronnie considered how much of what she knew to tell them. Was she breaching Chloe's right to privacy by sharing with them?

"Mom was arrested when Chloe was seventeen," she told them. There were wide, surprised eyes around the room. "She's in prison now, for the rest of her life."

"How do you know that?" Justin demanded. "I never heard anything about that!"

"They kept their names out of the paper because Chloe was still a minor and didn't deserve to have her life ruined."

Ruby's eyes were distant. She stared out the window, then abruptly stood up and went into the kitchen.

"Arrested for what?" June asked in a low voice, glancing over her shoulder at the kitchen.

"For neglecting and abusing Chloe. For all the stuff she let her boyfriends do to her."

"Just like with us," June breathed. "Helping him instead of stopping him."

Ronnie nodded. "It was worse, though," she said. "They locked her up and starved her. Beat her. And Mom killed her babies."

"Chloe's babies?"

"Mom's."

June and Justin shook their heads. June made a motion like she wanted to take Justin's hand and then pulled back, clasping her hands together in her lap and wringing them. Michelle's eyes were wide. Dan hugged her from behind, pulling her close against him protectively. Kenny wandered over to the kitchen to see what Ruby was doing.

"That's... just awful," June said. "Poor Chloe..."

"We always figured she just got what she wanted." Justin said. "The perfect daughter. She got Mom all to herself."

"Yeah," Ronnie said with heavy irony. "Lucky her."

June and Justin were both silent, with no answer to that.

"Why would anyone do that?" Michelle demanded. "I mean... it's one thing to hit someone because you're mad or overwhelmed. But... torturing her? Letting men use her? Why?"

There was a period of silence. No one knew how to answer that. Ronnie looked toward the kitchen, where Ruby had retreated. "Is Ruby okay?"

June and Justin shrugged, mirror images of each other. Ronnie got up and went into the kitchen.

"Ruby...?"

Ruby handed Kenny a plate of cookies. Balancing them carefully, he made his way back into the living room, leaving Ruby and Ronnie alone together.

"I guess it's sort of like your amnesia," Ruby said, without Ronnie actually asking her any questions. "I don't remember much about what happened before I left home. I just have... feelings. When I hear about Mom... I feel trapped. Like I'm suffocating."

Ronnie nodded. "I've blocked a lot of it out, I can't remember now even when I want to. But then something will happen that will send me back..."

Ruby picked up her coffee mug and took a sip. "I've had a bit of therapy, the last few years. When I finally decided that it wasn't going to go away by itself. But I don't like talking about it, even with a psychiatrist. So, I don't go as much as I should."

"Yeah."

"June has a lot of flashbacks. She remembers... too much. She did a lot of therapy, but I don't know that it has helped her. It's hard to know what's best."

"There are things I don't want to remember, but I can't seem to choose between the things that I do and the things that I don't."

Ruby ran her fingers through her ponytail. "I feel bad about what happened to you," she said. "If I had talked about what was happening to me, instead of running away... maybe you would have been safe. You got hurt so badly. I left, and June had Justin looking after her, but you... I should have protected all of you younger girls."

Ronnie shook her head. "What could you have done? If they put him away, we would all still have been with Mim. The next one... could have been worse. Like it was for Chloe."

Ruby touched Ronnie's arm. "Yeah... you're right. We lived the lives we lived, and made the choices we did. We don't know what would have happened if we'd made other choices."

They wandered back into the living room. Ronnie thought about her choices. What if she had decided to stand up for herself and not marry Floyd? What if she had continued with her drawing, gone on to the arts college? Or just worked in retail and earned a living for herself instead of being forced into an unmatched marriage? Would she have still have suffered from amnesia? Was the amnesia caused by the stresses in her marriages, or was it organic and it would have happened anyway, no matter what she chose to do?

[III]

The charges against Ronnie had been dropped, but she still called Adah Cruz before leaving town to make sure that she wouldn't be breaking any laws requiring her to stay there. The last thing she wanted was another arrest and stay in jail.

Adah chuckled. "You're a free citizen. You're allowed to come and go as you like, and there will be no one following you," she assured Ronnie. "Where are you off to, if you don't mind me asking? You're not pulling another disappearing act, are you?"

"No, no," Ronnie protested. "I'll be back. I've let them know at work and everything. I'm just going... I'm going to see Dusty Coleman."

"Oh!" Adah's voice was surprised. "I didn't know you were considering it. You have his information?"

"Yes, I found it online."

"Have you talked to him yet? Does he know you're coming?"

"No. I didn't know if he'd want to talk to me, or if he would tell me not to come. This way... if he doesn't know I'm coming, he can't tell me not to. I'll see him face to face... and apologize for what happened."

"Well, I wish you luck. I hope he has a better attitude than Floyd."

Ronnie cleared her throat. "Floyd isn't wrong to feel the way he does."

"No. We didn't treat him too well after your disappearance. He suffered for something that wasn't his fault, so I suppose he has a right to be bitter about it."

"Yeah. And being abandoned with two young children in the first place. Even if I never meant to... it wouldn't have been easy for him even if he hadn't been arrested."

"Well, anyway, good luck with Dusty."

And then she was off. She listened to the radio and tried not to think about what she was going to face when she got there. Would he be like Floyd, bitter over the abandonment? Even Floyd had offered her a place with them. Not as a wife, but as a guest, maybe as a mother if she and the children could accept the old roles. He hadn't been mean to her, but she hadn't felt any connection to him, and felt guilty for what she had inadvertently done to him and his family.

It was a nice little town. Ronnie felt comfortable as soon as she got there. It felt warm and friendly, even without many specific memories to go with it. For a while, she just drove around, getting a feel for the layout of the town, letting it all seep back into her brain. From what she could remember, she had been happy there. How long would it take before all of the memories came back and she could remember the details of their life together and why she had left so abruptly?

She had a strong feeling of *déjà vu* as she drove down one street. She slowed, looking around at the little shops and businesses, trying to attach memories to them. Nothing clicked until she saw the diner.

Ronnie was sure that it was the diner she used to go to with Dusty. That was where they had ended up on so many dates. That was where she had gotten engaged, back in the fog of memories. Ronnie circled the block to drive by it again. Two times, then three. Finally she pulled into a parking space on the street a couple of buildings down and walked to the diner. Maybe she would get a cup of coffee there. Fortify herself before dropping in on Dusty. Looking at her watch, she saw it was late afternoon. He wouldn't be home from work for a couple more hours.

She walked in the door and a bell announced her entrance. Ronnie glanced around the interior, waiting for her eyes to adjust from the bright sunshine outside. There was a murmur of conversation. It wasn't full, but it wasn't empty either. A few individual diners. A couple. A man with his two children. One of the waitresses walked up to Ronnie to seat her.

"Can I—" the waitress began, and then she stopped, cutting herself off and staring at Ronnie. "Excuse me, but... is it... Ronnie?"

Ronnie looked at the woman, trying to remember her. She looked at the woman's name tag. Brenda. It didn't ring any bells or bring anything to the surface.

"Uh... Brenda. Yes, actually. But... I don't remember..."

Brenda had her by the arm and turned toward the man sitting with his two children. The little girl was giggling over something and the boy was blowing bubbles in his chocolate milk. They looked up at Ronnie's approach. The man's face turned toward them and Ronnie saw that it was Dusty.

She was glad for Brenda's grip on her, because her knees bent and she just about went right to the floor. Brenda held her up, shifting her grip to the other hand to put her arm around Ronnie's body.

"Whoa, there... Dusty, you'd better help me..."

Dusty sprang out of his chair and helped Brenda slide Ronnie into an empty seat.

"Ronnie? Ronnie, is it really you?" he was staring at her as if he couldn't believe it. Ronnie supposed that the short hair probably threw him off. "Sweetheart..."

"Mommy?" the little boy piped up. "Did Mommy come back, Dad? Daddy, I want to see her!" The little boy climbed down from his seat and pushed his way in between Dusty and Ronnie, his round face inches in front of Ronnie's. "That's my Mommy," he said, delighted, and he grasped Ronnie's shoulders and neck and pulled himself into her lap. "Mandi, it's Mommy. Come see Mommy," he told her.

Ronnie put her arms around Dane to keep him from sliding off of her lap again as he bounced around and called for Mandi to join them. In a moment, she was holding both of them in her lap, their small, soft hands patting her face and going around her in hugs. All Ronnie could do was to stare at Dusty, who stared back at her.

"It's a family reunion," Brenda laughed. "I'll get you a coffee. On the house. It's all on the house today," she said in delight.

Ronnie barely acknowledged her. "Thank you," she said faintly. She poured sugar into the coffee that Brenda brought her and barely stirred it before gulping it down, trying to bring herself back to reality.

She didn't remember the children, but as they lavished attention on her, love for them grew in her heart. Not like with Floyd's children, so remote and angry after all of the years. Dane and Mandi were young enough to accept her back without any reservations. It was only natural to them that she should come back again eventually. She had been away for a long time, but now she was back.

"Ronnie," Dusty whispered.

She gave him her hand, and for a while they just sat there, side by side, holding hands.

"You didn't ask me to come back," Ronnie said finally.

"You had another family. You're married to your first husband. I didn't have any right to ask you to abandon them and come back to me."

She squeezed his hand gently. "I still... don't remember very much," she said apologetically. "But I had to come back... to tell you I was sorry."

"You're not staying."

"I... I don't know what I'm doing."

He nodded, looking as understanding as he probably could. How could anyone understand what it was like for Ronnie with her half-memories and the litter of ruined families behind her?

"How did you know I was here?" Dusty asked.

"I didn't. I was going to go to the house when I figured you'd be off work. I just saw the diner here and I remembered we used to come here, so I thought I'd have a cup while I was waiting for you to get off."

"I took today off. It's a school holiday and I don't like having to use babysitters."

Ronnie smoothed hair back from Mandi's face, studying her sweet baby face. "I can't remember them."

"Will you remember more? Or... is this it?"

"I don't know if I'll remember everything. But... I'm still remembering more, a little at a time. Usually when I dream or when I'm just waking up."

"Do you remember us? You and me?"

Ronnie cast her eyes around the diner. "I remember us here... and Sharon. When we got engaged."

He smiled broadly at that. His eyes danced. "Yes! One of my best memories. I'm glad you remember that."

Ronnie sipped her sugary coffee and put it down on the table.

"Mommy? Mommy?" Ronnie looked down at Dane. "I like dinosaurs. Do you remember I like dinosaurs?"

She hadn't expected him to understand what she and Dusty

343

were discussing and was surprised by his question. She looked at Dusty for a moment, trying to read in his face how to respond to Dane. Finally, she looked down at Dane, giving him a tentative smile.

"I'm glad you told me that, Dane. That's important to you, isn't it?"

He nodded solemnly. Mandi reached up and touched Ronnie's face. "I like di'saurs too," she told Ronnie.

"Do you? What's your favorite dinosaur?"

Mandi looked at Dane.

"Tyrannosaurus," he told her.

"Tyra'sauce," Mandi tried, and smiled again.

"She can't say it right," Dane pointed out. He patted Mandi on the head. "She's just little. I couldn't say it right when I was little either."

"No, it's a hard word," Ronnie agreed. She kissed the top of Mandi's head. Her hair smelled like banana and coconut. "What else do you like, sweetie?"

"I like pie and ice cweam." Mandi looked at Dusty when she said it, and then looked significantly at the wait staff at the front of the diner.

Dusty laughed. "You didn't finish your dinner yet."

Mandi looked over at her plate. A little frown line appeared above her snub nose. "I won't have room for pie. I saving room!"

"Oh, I see." Dusty held his hands out for her, and Mandi crawled from Ronnie's lap to Dusty's. He cuddled her close. "You think I should get them pie and ice cream?" he asked Ronnie.

"It is a special occasion," Ronnie pointed out.

"Yes, it is," he agreed. "Very special."

Dane reached up and patted Ronnie's face without looking at her. "That's because you came back, Mommy," he informed her.

"Yes, that's right. But just for a visit for now, I need to go back to my other house after."

He looked at her then, his lip in a pout. "But then you're coming back, right?"

"I don't know yet, Dane. I'll come back to see you."

"And stay."

"I don't know. I have to figure that out. I'm still... I'm still sort of sick, you know."

"Oh." Dane nodded, seeming to accept this explanation. "I was sick when my class went to the zoo. I really wanted to go, but I threw up three times, and I couldn't."

"Uh-huh?"

"I don't like being sick."

"No... me neither."

Dusty ordered three slices of pie with ice cream. One for him, one for the children to split, and one for Ronnie.

CHAPTER
Nineteen

AGE 32 (ONE YEAR EARLIER)

(1)

The children were eating their breakfast and Ronnie's cramps were getting worse. She knew that she was leaking, and the pad wasn't adequate. She shuffled to the bathroom and sat down on the john. She wasn't just spotting. There was a lot of blood. Ronnie's heart sank. She couldn't be bleeding that much and still be pregnant. Her doctor always said not to worry about a little spotting. She had bled a little with both Dane and Mandi. But the heavy flow was different. She had surely lost the pregnancy.

Ronnie held her palms over her eyes, trying not to cry. She had only taken the pregnancy test two days before. She wasn't fully invested in the pregnancy. It wasn't like she had felt the baby move yet or heard its heartbeat on the ultrasound. It was barely as big as a speck.

She hadn't even found the right time and way to tell Dusty yet. That was a good thing. She could just pretend that her period had come and gone as usual, and never tell him that she'd lost a pregnancy. No point in mourning over something that had never been. The pregnancy test might even have been wrong and she was just having her cycle a couple of days late. She hadn't been regular since Mandi was born. Those tests warned that they weren't one hundred percent accurate. She was supposed to go to her doctor afterward to confirm the results. Good thing she hadn't. Better that she hadn't gotten her hopes up.

She cleaned up and went back to the kitchen to join the children before they got into mischief after being unsupervised for too long. They were both still eating, but starting to get silly, which before long would lead to a food fight and sugary pink milk on the floor.

"All done, guys. Put your bowls in the sink for me. Mommy needs to sit down for a minute, so you help clean up."

They were both eager little helpers and got their bowls into the sink without more than a few drops on the floor along the way.

"Mommy okay?" Mandi asked, her sweet little pixie face in front of Ronnie's.

"Mommy will be okay. How would you like to go to the park today?"

"Yes, please!" they both chorused.

Mandi leaned in and kissed Ronnie wetly on the cheek. "Kissies for Mommy."

"Kissies for Mandi," Ronnie returned, holding Mandi's head still and blowing a raspberry on her cheek. Mandi squealed with delight and ran away. Dane joined in running around for no reason, blowing off some steam.

They definitely needed a day at the park, lots of time to get rid of the sillies and wear themselves out. Then they'd go down for bed early and Ronnie could share a glass of wine with Dusty, being lazy and watching a movie on TV, ignoring the growing pile of laundry and just pampering herself for one night. That would be nice.

"Mommy, where is the park?" Dane demanded peevishly.

Ronnie jolted. She looked around, disoriented. It was like she had dozed off, only she hadn't been asleep. Her mind had been wandering... where? She had continued to drive the car on autopilot, keeping them from crashing into a light post in her fugue, but now she didn't know where they were.

"It's close by," Ronnie promised. There was bound to be a playground somewhere nearby. There was always a school or little urban park within a few blocks. The town was good about having lots of green spaces and monkey bars for the neighborhood children.

It wasn't the big city. Ronnie knew her way around. But she had managed to drive into a new development where she didn't know anyone and didn't know her way.

"There, Mommy! I see it!" Mandi crowed, gesturing wildly to the right. Ronnie caught a glimpse of a playground between the buildings, a little park with a fountain and a playground.

"There it is," she confirmed to the children. "Let me just find a place to park and then you can play."

She parked on a side street and helped the children out of their seats. They ran like wild animals released from their cages, joyfully joining the throng of young children already in the playground. Ronnie walked slowly behind them, cramps in her back and legs, feeling overwhelmingly tired. Eventually, she reached a bench and sat down, resting her body and watching the children. She let out a long sigh. The children would play for a long time without any effort from her. They mixed well with other kids and weren't whining and demanding like some of the other children she knew. She could just sit and rest and give her body a chance to get some energy back.

It was an hour later that Mandi came to Ronnie squealing that she got sand in her eye. Ronnie took a look, determined that Mandi's tears had already washed it out, and sent her back to the playground. She looked at her watch, thinking that they were going to want a snack or small lunch soon and Ronnie had left everything in the car. As a mother, she knew she couldn't go without her emergency bag. Snacks, clothes, wipes, water bottles, sun screen, bug spray, and any other comfort items that they might need on a day trip were in that bag, and she'd left it all in the car. Ronnie motioned for Dane to come and see her the next time that he looked in her direction. He left what he was doing reluctantly and walked toward her, a tear already glistening in his eye.

"Do we have to go already?" he whined. "I was just having fun..."

"You can still play," Ronnie assured him. "I'm just going to the car. I'll be right back."

"Oh!" He smiled brightly. "Okay!"

He ran back to the playground and resumed his interrupted game. Ronnie unfolded herself from the hard bench. She arched and rubbed her back and rolled her shoulders. The cramps were around front again, centered in her lower pelvis, a hard, pressing pain. She hoped that walking to the car and back might ease it a bit.

She unlocked the car and tossed her keys into the driver's seat. She leaned on the frame of the car, the pain expanding to fill her whole body for a few pulsing seconds. She rubbed her forehead in small circles, trying to separate from the pain.

Ronnie opened her eyes and focused on a spot in the distance. If she just walked there, and back again, she was sure the pain would ease. She stared at the point on the horizon. Once she reached it, the pain would be gone. It would all be behind her. And she could start her day over, a fresh slate.

CHAPTER
Twenty

AGE 33

(I)

Ronnie waited, looking up and down the street for Chloe. She didn't know whether Chloe would be walking, bussing, or driving to the restaurant. She hadn't given any indication on the phone, and Ronnie wasn't sure where she lived.

Chloe was almost right in front of her before Ronnie realized who she was. She had discounted the woman walking a dog automatically, not even realizing she had done so.

"Oh... Chloe?"

The blond woman nodded. Her features were similar to Ruby's, or maybe it was the blond hair that made her look more like Ruby than like June or Ronnie. Or Mim. The Chloe Ronnie remembered had been overweight, slovenly. This Chloe was thin and neatly dressed in pants and a blouse that complemented her slight figure.

"I didn't even realize it was you!"

Ronnie leaned forward, offering a hug, and the two of them met tentatively, awkward. Ronnie gave Chloe an extra pat on the back before they separated again.

"How are you?" she asked.

Chloe gave a little shrug. "A lot more nervous about this than I should be. Let's go in."

When Chloe gestured to the door, Ronnie could see that she was shaking. She didn't know whether to take Chloe by the arm to steady her, or to back off and give her space. They went into the restaurant together and were approached by a waiter to be seated. His eyes dropped to the dog at Chloe's side.

"There are no animals allowed in the restaurant," he advised, mouth turning down.

"He's a service animal." Chloe pointed at the dog's orange vest. "You can't deny him entrance."

The waiter looked down at the dog again. "It's not a seeing eye dog. You're not blind."

"He's a registered service animal."

"What for?" The waiter's tone was belligerent.

"Get your manager, please." Chloe's voice was firm and even. The waiter opened his mouth to argue, then left to find the manager.

"How do you stay so calm?" Ronnie asked. "I'd be really upset if someone treated me like that."

"I'm used to it. People have to be trained."

Ronnie giggled at this. It wasn't the dog that had to be trained to be allowed into the restaurant, it was the humans. It hit her funny bone.

In a couple of minutes, a woman approached them. Her uniform was as crisp as if it had been starched. She glanced down at the dog.

"I'm Joanne, the manager. Please forgive the staff and the delay. Would you like a booth? For two?"

"Three, including the dog," Chloe said dryly.

Joanne smiled. "Three, including the dog," she agreed. "I'm going to put you in the corner here, so you don't have as much traffic getting in your way. Okay?"

"That's great," Chloe agreed, giving her a smile this time. Joanne saw to them efficiently, and Ronnie and Chloe looked at each other across the table. The dog was out of the way, under the table at Chloe's feet.

"So, can I ask...?" Ronnie was curious. "What does the dog do?"

Chloe considered Ronnie for a moment before deciding to answer. "He's an emotional support animal. Helps to keep me calm and... coherent." She took a sip of her water while Ronnie looked down at the sad-faced Basset Hound. "I train them," Chloe explained. "I rescue and train service dogs. Not all rescues can be service animals, of course, so a lot of them I just find good homes for. The ones that have the aptitude, I train and place with the people who need them."

Ronnie nodded. "That's really cool. What a neat job. So, do you need this one? Or are you just training him?"

"Most of the time now, I'm okay. But sometimes I still need him."

Ronnie didn't want to push too hard for private information. She already knew what had happened to Chloe. It was no great surprise that she had some emotional issues.

"I wonder if a service dog would help me," she mused.

Chloe pushed a lock of hair behind her ear. "They can be very reassuring," she said. "Sometimes it's almost like magic, the way a dog will ground me. The first one that I had, Triumph... he knew me so well. All I had to do was touch him to stabilize myself."

Chloe didn't ask Ronnie why she might need a service dog, but instead waited for her to provide any further information herself.

"I sort of... forget things sometimes," Ronnie provided. "I wake up in the morning, and can't remember anything, or I get stressed out, and sort of... lose my place."

"What would you want the dog to do?" Chloe asked. "Go for help?"

"No... it wouldn't be good if he left me alone. I guess... keep me from walking away again..."

The conversation paused while they ordered lunches and picked back up when the waitress left.

"Walking away from what?"

Ronnie took a breath. With some difficulty she explained about walking away from her life, her husband, and her children. And the smaller breaks, where she was disoriented for a time, or had forgotten while still living with Mom and Dad. Chloe was nodding as Ronnie outlined it.

"Yeah. Yeah, we might be able to work something out. Where the dog would stay with you, maybe raise the alarm if you left your purse or keys behind... maybe lead you by the hand to get help..."

Ronnie nodded. She could picture that. Her own little Lassie to keep her from wandering off.

"The dog could carry papers that would explain your problem," Chloe said, showing Ronnie the zippered pocket on her dog's orange vest. "So that whoever helped you would know who you were and what to do about it."

"Yeah, that could work. I really... don't want to keep doing that. Losing myself. Trying to remember everything has shown me how much I lost, even before the amnesia. My biological family. All of those connections."

Chloe said nothing, swirling the ice in her glass. Her eyes were blank, not focused on anything around her. The dog sat up, whining. He nosed at Chloe's knee and pawed her shoe. Chloe put down her glass and held her hand out to the dog. It thrust its head under her hand and she stroked it. She looked down at it and massaged its neck with both hands. When she looked back over at Ronnie, her eyes were alert, but also showed pain.

"I haven't had any family for so long. I mean, Jozef and his family, but no one of my own. I go to his family reunions or celebrations, and there are all of these people, aunts and uncles and cousins and nieces and nephews, such a big family. But no one with a connection to me. It's been... twenty-five years since you were taken away. And twenty since Mom..."

Ronnie reached for Chloe's hand, but Chloe pulled back.

"I don't know how you could ever forgive me for my part in it... for not protecting you."

"Chloe!" Ronnie was shocked. "I don't blame you! You were eleven when I got hurt. You couldn't have done anything."

"I could have," Chloe insisted. "It was my job to take care of you and the twins. I should have done something. Helped them get June and Justin away after you got hurt. But I just... I just did whatever Mom said to do."

The waitress interrupted again with their lunches, chirping cheerfully at them. Neither of them started eating.

"What else were you supposed to do?" Ronnie demanded. She too felt the sickening guilt that Chloe did. The knowledge that she had refused to face what had happened to her and to tell it all to the social workers so that June and Justin would be taken out of the home. Then June wouldn't have been a victim and Justin wouldn't have shot their father.

In spite of the guilt, Ronnie couldn't stop herself from rebelling against that thought. He had deserved to die. If Justin hadn't killed him, he would just have found more victims. If June had been taken away, he would have victimized someone else. Just like Mim had continued to prey on Chloe and had killed her own infants.

"You couldn't have stopped them," Ronnie said. "How could you? I went to the hospital, and that wasn't enough for Social Services to take the rest of you out of the home. What could you have said that would have made any difference?"

Chloe rubbed the dog's head, her eyes swimming with tears. "I didn't even understand what was going on. It wasn't until years later I realized what was happening whenever she gave me sleeping pills."

Ronnie clenched her teeth to keep from gaping at Chloe. They had always thought that Chloe was the one who had escaped abuse because of her allergy to alcohol. He couldn't get her drunk, so he left her alone. But he hadn't. The molestation had continued. He'd just changed his drug of choice. Sleeping pills had ensured that Chloe wouldn't have a coherent story to tell.

"That's horrible," Ronnie said. "I didn't know. I always thought you got off easy. Until later, anyway, after Dad died and... all the stuff *she* was convicted of."

"Easy?" Chloe laughed. "You don't remember how many whippings I took for you?"

How many whippings Chloe took for her.

Ronnie teetered on the edge of a precipice. The dark secret of her past was the sexual abuse. That was the family's secret, what everyone had covered up. Ronnie knew there had also been neglect. They hadn't had much money and the children were often left to their own devices. They had never had new clothes and sometimes no food. The house was a disaster zone. But physical abuse?

When she closed her eyes, she could hear Mim and Ruby screaming at each other. That was Ruby. Rebellious. Incorrigible. She probably got whipped regularly and deserved it. Sometimes Justin got spanked for fighting at school or some other infraction. He too had that rebellious streak. He couldn't take correction. Not without a fight.

But Chloe? Ronnie vaguely remembered Chloe's fawning, submissive behavior. Always sucking up. Always trying to get Mim's attention and approval.

Ronnie's heart throbbed and hurt. She *could* remember Chloe's screams too. Not angry and rebellious like Ruby's. Begging, pleading, cries of pain between the falling blows. Ronnie had cowered in her bed, listening to the beatings. Mim's voice rising in fury and frustration.

"... the school called me because they were late again!"

"It was my fault, Mommy... I was playing a game on the way to school and I forgot what time it was..."

Blows raining down in fury. "... third time this month..."

"I know, I'm sorry. I'll make sure they're on time..."

"... Ronnie not turning in her work!" A particularly hard strike that made Chloe howl in pain. Ronnie squeezed her eyes shut tight, as if that would prevent her from hearing it or visualizing the punishment.

"I lost it..." Breathless. "I'm sorry... I tried to tell the teacher..."

It wasn't true. Ronnie had refused to do her homework when Chloe had told her to and had nothing to turn in when the teacher had called for her assignment the next day. Chloe was covering for her.

"You're older! You're supposed to be keeping them in line."

"Yes, Mommy. I'm sorry..."

It went on and on, until Mim had apparently exhausted herself and vented all of her rage. Ronnie cowered in her bed, sure that she would be next. But when the door opened, ever so quietly, it wasn't Mim coming to haul Ronnie out of her bed. It was Chloe, moving slowly, her breathing ragged.

"Chloe...?"

"Sh. Didn't I tell you to go to sleep?" Chloe's voice came in a snap, irritated.

"Chloe, why is Mom so mad?"

"She's not mad at you. It's just me. Now shut up and go to sleep."

Ronnie hugged her lumpy teddy bear close, trying to see Chloe in the dark. "Why'd Mom whip you? Are you okay?"

"I'm tougher than that."

But it took a very long time for Chloe to change into her nightie for bed.

"Chloe, I'm scared," Ronnie whispered.

"Are you still yapping at me? Go to sleep!" But Chloe's voice was soft, not mean. She sat on the edge of Ronnie's bed. Her warm hand found Ronnie's back and rubbed it soothingly. "You'll be too tired to get up in the morning and you'll be late again. You gotta get up in time so you're not late for school."

"Mm-hmm," Ronnie agreed drowsily, Chloe's touch soothing her.

"No more talking, now. Zip it."

Ronnie squinted her eyes open again for a few seconds. The light from the street outside fell on Chloe's face. In the dimness, Ronnie could barely make out the darkening bruises. When Ronnie woke in the morning, Chloe would already have makeup on and the bruises would be only a vague memory.

"I didn't know that," Ronnie told Chloe, tearing her mind from the past. "Or... I didn't remember it. Why would you do that? Why would you take the beatings for all of us?"

"I was oldest. I was responsible for you," Chloe said with a shrug. "She was gonna whip me either way. I didn't want her to hurt you too."

Ronnie shook her head slowly. "You took care of us and protected us… it's not your fault that you couldn't stop him. None of us could."

"Except Justin," Chloe pointed out. "He did."

"But he didn't stop Mom."

Chloe's narrow shoulders rose in a little shrug like that didn't matter. As if what had happened to her afterward had been unimportant. "How is Justin?" Chloe asked. "He didn't have to stay in prison?"

"No. He's okay. He's a trucker. Has been since he was old enough to pass himself off as an adult."

"So, he only had to be in prison while he was waiting for the trial. That wasn't *too* long."

"I don't think he was ever in prison," Ronnie said, shaking her head. "June and Justin were just in a foster home after the shooting."

"Both of them?" Chloe's eyebrows rose in surprise. "Really? I thought they were in prison. Justin, anyway."

"Uh-uh. They didn't want everyone to know that he wasn't. But they were just in a foster home."

"Well, that's okay, then," Chloe said softly.

"Why did you ask about him?" Ronnie asked.

"Just… Mom always said that he wasn't her son anymore. That I didn't have any brother anymore. So, I… I thought I didn't have a brother for a long time. Now… I guess I do again. It's weird. She hated him for what he did."

"I guess so. He *did* kill her husband." Ronnie thought about her biological parents. They had never really seemed like they liked each other. She couldn't remember any affection between them. No sparks or attraction. "Though… I don't think she really loved him…"

Chloe was poking at her sandwich. She ate a couple of fries. "She didn't love him," she confirmed. "It wasn't that… she had to have someone to take care of her. Provide for her."

"But she worked."

"Not enough to live on." Chloe finally took a bite of her sandwich. "She always knew she had to have someone to help out. It didn't really matter how he treated her. As long as he was there to take care of things."

Ronnie shook her head. "Well, I guess it's all good now. She's taken care of for the rest of her life."

Chloe looked up at her, eyes dark and bleak. "Do you know... I still miss her. I still resent them taking me away from her twenty years ago, even when I know she would have killed me, eventually." She shook her head. "How sick is that?"

"You could go see her."

"No. I could never do that."

"I did."

Chloe's jaw dropped. "What?"

"I went to the prison and saw her."

"Why?"

"I couldn't remember anything. Who I was and where I came from. So, when I found out my name before I was adopted was Simpson... I did some detecting. I found out about her trial. Went to see her to find out if she was my family. And you."

"And she told you?"

Ronnie nodded. "And she told me about the others. That's how I knew who to look for."

"Do you remember them all now?" Chloe asked, cocking her head slightly.

"Yes... not everything, but some stuff."

Chloe rubbed the dog's head. "And... how was she? Mom."

Ronnie thought back to the visit at the prison. "She seemed fine, I guess. Healthy. She didn't seem unhappy. Scared or depressed or anything. She's been there twenty years, so I guess she's had time to settle in and get used to it."

"Was she... mad at me?"

Ronnie was surprised. She thought back to her visit at the prison, trying to remember anything that Mim had said about Chloe. "No, she didn't say anything. Didn't act like it. I just asked her if you were my sister, and she told me yes, and that Ruby and June were too. She didn't mention Justin." Ronnie realized for the first time that Mim had neglected to say anything about Justin or his part in Ronnie's father's death.

"She said he wasn't her son anymore," Chloe repeated. "I just wondered… if she'd disowned me too."

Her face was pale and drawn, as if she were in pain. Ronnie put her hand over Chloe's and this time Chloe didn't pull back. "No. She didn't say anything like that. Chlo… you do have family. Not just *her*. Me and Ruby and June and Justin. All of us. Ruby has a daughter, and June has two kids, and Justin four. I have four too. You have lots of family, just like your husband. Maybe we could have a family reunion, with everyone there." Ronnie's chest tightened as she thought of inviting Floyd and the children to anything, especially if Dusty and his children were also invited. "You're not different from the rest of us. We don't hate you."

"You don't know what the others think," Chloe said. "You're the only one who ever tried to find me. The others… I testified against them. I sided with Mom and said they were liars. All of you."

"You were thirteen!"

Chloe rocked back and forth, anguish on her face. "I should have known. I shouldn't have listened to her. I knew *you'd* been hurt. You went to the hospital. But she said it wasn't Dad. *You* said it wasn't Dad right up until you testified!"

"I don't hate you."

Chloe gripped Ronnie's hand. "After all I did, you *must!*"

"No." Ronnie squeezed Chloe's hand tighter. "I love you. You're my sister."

The tears overflowed Chloe's eyes and she sobbed aloud. Pulling away from Ronnie and the dog, she buried her face in her arms on the table, crying. Her plate went spinning away. Chloe's hurt whimpers worried the dog, who got to his feet and nosed at her, pawed her knees, and eventually jumped up onto the seat beside her and tried to push his way into her lap. Chloe lifted her face and wrapped her arms around the dog, pressing her face into his fur. Her sobs started to slow.

The waitress walked by, gawking at Chloe and making a little motion to Ronnie, as if to ask what she should do. Ronnie just shook her head and waved the woman away.

"It's okay, Chloe," she soothed. Like Chloe was a little child. Like Ronnie would soothe Mandi if she were upset. "We're your family and we love you. You don't have to isolate yourself and make it on your own. We love you."

Chloe gradually managed to quiet her tears and blew her nose on tissues retrieved from her carryall.

"I'm so stupid," she said. "What a baby." She brushed at her shirt, wet around the neck from her tears. "Look at that. Ugh. Who'd ever want to be with me?" She wiped her nose. She didn't manage to avoid the hound's abnormally large tongue as he decided to lick the remainder of the tears away. Chloe yelped and tried to push him away. Ronnie laughed, and in a few seconds, they had both dissolved into near-hysterical giggles.

Chloe managed to get the dog settled at her feet again and wiped her whole face with a tissue.

"Well. Still sure you want to be my sister?"

"Yes."

Chloe pulled her plate back toward her. Ronnie's toasted sandwich was now cold and Chloe didn't look too eager to eat any more of hers. Ronnie studied Chloe's thin, bony hands.

"Can I ask something totally off-topic?"

Chloe nodded, sniffling. "Sure."

"Do you have an eating disorder?" Chloe opened her mouth to answer, but Ronnie kept going, talking over her. "Because that's something I've had trouble with and there's a genetic predisposition."

Chloe closed her mouth and reconsidered her answer. Her shoulders went up slightly in a shrug. "It's something my doctors keep an eye on. They say it borders on disordered... but I've been able to keep my weight in the healthy range. Low healthy. It took me a long time to get up to healthy after... you know... just about starving to death... It's hard for me to separate my body image from my self-worth."

That sounded like something straight out of a therapist's mouth. Ronnie nodded her understanding.

"It will make them happy that I've discovered a family connection," Chloe said. "Give them something new to talk about."

"Glad I could help."

They both stared at the remains of their picked-over lunches.

"So..." Chloe said. "What's next?"

"Do you want to meet the others?"

She expected Chloe to be eager to meet them, but Chloe frowned, shaking her head.

"Not yet... I'm too scared about what they'll think... How about... would you like to meet Jozef, and see my kennels?" Chloe looked down at the dog. "Meet my family next?"

Ronnie warmed at the suggestion. She nodded, smiling. "Sure. I'd love to meet your family too."

(II)

Ronnie wasn't as anxious making the trip to see Dusty the second time. They had agreed on a time, so she didn't drive around randomly and end up at the diner again. She drove straight to the house. Forcing herself to get out of the car immediately, rather than sitting and looking at it and trying to force her brain to remember everything, she walked up to the door. Dusty opened it before she had the chance to knock or ring the doorbell. He'd obviously been watching for her. Ronnie remembered sitting outside Ruby's house with them waiting for her to come in. She was glad that she hadn't stayed in the car for too long; she didn't want to hurt their feelings.

"Mommy!" Mandi launched herself at Ronnie, nearly bowling her over. Ronnie laughed and picked her up. Dane was more sedate. He didn't run into her, but grabbed her legs and held on tightly.

"You took a long time," he complained.

"Did I?" Ronnie looked at her watch to make sure that her arrival had not been late, and shrugged at Dusty. She was right on time.

"I want you to live here," Dane insisted. Dusty tried to speak, but Dane wagged his finger at his father, his face stern. "I know you said not to, but I want Mommy to come back and live here!"

Dusty raised his eyebrows and shrugged at Ronnie. "Sorry. I did my best to explain."

"It's okay. They're too little to understand." She sighed. "I think I'm too little to understand too. I just..." Ronnie shook her head hopelessly. "I just don't know how to handle this whole thing. Nobody gave me a manual for this brain."

"We'll try to figure it out together," he promised. "Come in and sit down. Dane, let Mommy's legs go so she can walk."

Dane reluctantly let Ronnie's legs go, but kept one hand on her and walked with her into the living room, where she cleared a couple of toys off of the couch to make room and sat down. Both children climbed into her lap and she hugged them close. Dusty sat in the easy chair perpendicular to the couch, giving her space.

"I remembered something about when I left," she told Dusty softly. "I want to tell you about it, but not in front of the kids. Remind me later, okay?"

Dusty's brows drew down. "Sure."

"Don't let me forget." Ronnie laughed once. "Like anyone could stop me from forgetting..."

"Give yourself a break, Ronnie."

Ronnie was going to make another self-deprecating remark, and then remembered her lunch with Chloe, how Chloe had repeatedly condemned herself for crying. *Give yourself a break.* Like Chloe, Ronnie was a human being with frailties, not someone who deserved to be beaten up for her failings. She pressed her lips together, thinking it through.

"Is it something I did?" Dusty asked. "This thing you want to tell me?"

"No! No, you didn't do anything wrong. It wasn't like that. And not like Floyd, where... we never were compatible. Don't think that. It's just something that happened."

"Okay."

She could see that he was still worried about it, but there was nothing else she could say to make him feel better.

"Are you going to show me your dinosaurs?" she asked Dane.

"Yes! You stay here." He jumped to the floor, and looked at her warily, as if she might get up and leave while he was getting his toys. When she didn't move, he ran down the hall to his bedroom.

"What do I show Mommy?" Mandi asked Dusty.

Dusty thought about it seriously. "How about your bracelets?" he suggested.

"Yes!" Mandi agreed. She gave Ronnie a hug and a kiss before climbing down. She passed Dane in the hall as he raced back with his toys to make sure that Ronnie hadn't left.

"She got a loom," Dusty told Ronnie. "It's a toy, but she can make bracelets and little things like that on it. It's really for older kids, but she has quite a knack for it."

Dane started to set up his dinosaurs to show Ronnie, occasionally poking one in her face and growling fiercely to make sure she understood which ones were carnivores. Mandi returned with a handful of bracelets and started to lay them out on the couch cushion next to Ronnie. Ronnie looked at them.

"Mandi! These are beautiful!"

"I told you." Dusty smiled.

Ronnie picked up a couple of the bracelets and examined them closely. "Who picked the colors?" she asked. "Did you get the patterns out of a book?"

Mandi shook her head placidly. "No. I just made them out of my head."

"They're really fantastic, sweetie. I'm proud of you."

"She must get her artistic nature from her mama," Dusty said. "I certainly don't have it."

"Did you know that I can draw?" Ronnie asked him.

He shook his head. "I've seen you doodle a little, that's all."

"I can!"

"Amazing." Dusty smiled and shook his head. "I'm still learning new things about you."

"Me too. There's lots to tell you."

"I can't wait."

But they both knew that it was the children's turn. They needed to show Ronnie everything and to spend time with her. They all had to get to know each other all over again.

Ronnie had helped put the children to bed, accepting sweet kisses and reading a storybook before turning out their lights. It was all very peaceful and domestic. Then she sat on the couch with Dusty, daring to cuddle up a bit, putting her head on his shoulder.

"It's been very nice having you here," Dusty murmured. "After so long, I never dared to imagine having you back. I held out hope for a few days after you disappeared, but then... reality set in."

Ronnie held his hand. "I feel awful about what I put you and the children through."

"I don't think that it was your fault."

"It wasn't intentional," Ronnie said, "but it was still... I was the cause. I can't help thinking that maybe... if I'd been better about seeing doctors and getting my brain straightened out... it wouldn't have happened."

He kissed the top of her head and said nothing. Ronnie thought about what she had to tell him and her heart felt as if it were being squeezed.

"I remembered... a little bit about before I disappeared," she said.

"Mmm-hm?"

Ronnie sighed and closed her eyes, letting the grief wash over her. She had pushed it away before, refused to feel the loss and sorrow. And now it was back again. This time she had to honor it and accept her feelings. She couldn't keep running.

"I was pregnant."

Dusty's quick intake of breath whistled in her ear. "Pregnant? Then...?"

"I miscarried that day." She hurried on to get it all out, tell him all of the details before he could ask. "I was only a few weeks along. I had just taken a pregnancy test and then I started bleeding. I knew I'd lost it. I figured I was fine physically and that I'd just push through it. The kids were rambunctious, so I took them to the park to blow off steam." Ronnie licked her lips, but her mouth was so dry it only made them more chapped. "I was still cramping and bleeding while they were playing. I went to the car to get snacks or something... and I thought if I just walked for a bit, the cramps would ease..."

"And then...?"

"I don't know. I was so upset and it really hurt... I guess, I just kept walking. I don't know where I went after that or how I got there."

His arm was around her, holding her close, mourning the loss of that unborn baby and the lost time with her.

"Oh, sweetie..."

"I'm so sorry." Ronnie's face was wet with tears. "I wish I could take it back."

"It's not your fault. You can't control what your brain decided to do."

Ronnie nodded. For a few minutes, they just cuddled and neither said anything.

"I remember things... that I didn't know when we were married," Ronnie offered.

"Mmm..." Dusty's voice was noncommittal. Not sure he wanted to hear anything else that she had remembered. It would hurt him if she talked about Floyd. But that hadn't been what Ronnie had intended. "You never talked about your past," Dusty said, "I thought... your parents had died. Maybe you'd had a rotten childhood and just didn't want to talk about what had happened. You never said anything about it, not even a slip."

"No. That was easy. I didn't remember anything."

"Why didn't you ever tell me that? It was quite the secret to keep."

Ronnie's eyebrows drew down as she thought about it, trying to put it into words. "I was trying so hard to just be like everyone else. Not to look or act any different. It was sort of a masquerade... don't let anyone see that there isn't even a face behind the mask."

"That must have been very hard."

"It got easier... when I'd lived here for a few years, I had the memories we shared."

"And now you remember that you used to draw?" he suggested.

Ronnie smiled, happy to be distracted by a good memory. "Yeah. I even got an award in school and got entered into a national contest. I really like drawing."

"That must be where Mandi gets it, because I'm about as artistic as a stick."

Ronnie giggled.

"You want to watch something on TV?" Dusty suggested.

"No... just wanted to talk."

"I haven't talked you out yet?"

"I have a family," Ronnie said.

"I know." Ronnie knew by Dusty's tone that he was thinking of Floyd and her older children.

"I didn't mean him... I meant... my sisters and brother."

"Oh... I never knew you had siblings."

"Me neither." Ronnie outlined meeting her adoptive family, and then finding out about her biological family. She glanced at Dusty's face a couple of times while she explained what she could. His face was somber and thoughtful.

"You have a big family," he observed. "That's a lot of people."

"Chloe wants me to meet her husband. And her dogs. She doesn't have any kids, so I think the dogs are kind of her children."

"How many?"

"I don't know. She rescues and trains them... so probably a lot."

"Is she a crazy dog lady?"

"I don't know. I'll have to tell you after I meet them. Unless you want to come..."

He bit his lip. "I don't know. It sounds like she's a little shy. Maybe it should just be you the first time."

"Yeah. And I don't know if the kids would be allowed in the kennels."

"Another time, maybe."

"I want you to meet the others too."

"In time," he agreed.

She knew he was thinking about Floyd. They couldn't keep avoiding the issue. "I don't want to go back to Floyd," she told him.

Dusty was still.

"We weren't compatible," Ronnie explained. "We never were. We fought a lot. And when I disappeared, they arrested him for murder."

"I read that."

"He was civil to me... he even said I could move back in with him and get to know the kids again. Kent and Carrie. But... I couldn't do that. I could never live with him again, even just as a houseguest." She remembered the dream of Floyd burying her and shuddered.

"So... are you getting a divorce?"

"They have to sort out what needs to be done. I was declared dead, so that dissolves the marriage. Except I wasn't, so no one knows what the next step is." Ronnie looked at him, forcing herself to meet his eyes. "But there is no marriage to Floyd. There hasn't been for a long time."

Dusty nodded slowly. "Good to know."

"I'm sorry I didn't come back right away, when they first told me about you. I couldn't remember, and I already had Floyd and my parents to deal with."

"I'm just glad you came back now and that you can be a part of the kids' lives, so they'll remember you."

Neither of them had suggested just what that relationship might be. They were still talking around it. Ronnie closed her eyes and sat there, cuddled in Dusty's warm, strong arms.

[III]

Jozef, Chloe's husband, greeted Ronnie warmly. He was a friendly-faced, dark-haired man, similar to Ronnie in height, and had a trim mustache and beard. He showed no awkwardness at meeting one of Chloe's sisters after so many years of silence. He took her hand in both of his and greeted her without reservation.

"It's so good to meet you, Ronnie!" He studied her face, and turned to look at Chloe. "I can see the resemblance. Something around the eyes and nose. And you have the same build."

Both skinny, just managing to stay within what their doctors dictated was healthy. Ronnie felt herself flush.

"It's nice to meet you, Jozef," she said with a nod.

He let go of her hand. He put his other arm around Chloe; gently, not pulling her tightly against himself. "Well, I'm not the important one. You're really here to meet the children."

Ronnie flashed a look at Chloe. She had said that they didn't have any kids.

Chloe rolled her eyes. "You can't call them that, you make me look like some crazy old lady," she admonished. And to Ronnie, "He means the dogs."

"Sure. I'm looking forward to meeting them," Ronnie said.

"Kennels are out here." Chloe led the way from the house to a building in the back. They had a big yard, and Ronnie could see that the back sidewalk led directly onto the walking path of a green park. An ideal location for someone with dogs.

"Wow, this is really nice."

Chloe opened the door to the outbuilding and ushered Ronnie inside. It was about the size of a large double garage, with pens or cages on either side of an aisle and a workspace on the other side of the inside aisle. The lights were already on, and when Chloe entered there was some initial barking, some of the dogs coming to the fronts of their cages for a better look at the visitors.

"Sh, there," Chloe murmured. "Calm. Just me and my sister."

Ronnie noticed belatedly that Jozef hadn't followed them out to the kennels. The dogs quieted at Chloe's voice and snuffled at her through the links of the cages. Chloe put her fingers through the links of the nearest one to scratch the ears of a dog that might have been partly husky, but mostly mutt.

"This is Jorge," she introduced. "He's a rescue. Been here a couple of months." Chloe looked him over with a professional eye. "He's filled out nicely. Was pretty skinny and ragged when I first got him."

"He seems very friendly. I wouldn't have guessed that he was neglected."

Chloe nodded. "He has a very nice disposition. I can't understand how anyone could ever hit him. He's happy here. He'll make a good service dog for someone."

"I guess not all rescues make good service dogs."

"No. It takes a special personality. They have to be able to stay calm around a lot of people. Not get upset or distracted."

"That makes sense. Do you train seeing eye dogs? Or just ones like you had the other day?"

"I do initial training for seeing eye dogs. Then they go for some specialized training after that. Hearing dogs, dogs for epileptics or diabetics. Emotional support dogs. They can do all sorts of jobs."

They walked down the aisle together, Chloe telling Ronnie about each dog in turn. At the end of the aisle, a dark, mottled dog that seemed to have a lot of pit bull in the shape of his head and jaw launched into a volley of vicious barking and snarling, throwing himself against the fence in an attempt to reach them. Ronnie jumped back, startled. She gasped for breath, clutching at Chloe's arm. Chloe patted her hand placidly, not turning a hair at the dog's threats.

"Calm, Lightning," she soothed. "Shhh. Just me. It's okay."

His threats gradually subsided to soft growls and he snuffled through the links, trying to get their scents. Ronnie released Chloe's arm.

"Sheesh, he scared me," she said, letting out her breath. She tried to calm the wild thudding of her heart. "Whew. What's his story?"

Chloe stepped up to the cage, offering her fingers to the dog to smell, and in a moment he was licking them through the links and whining at her. Whenever Ronnie moved a muscle, however, he looked back in her direction and growled. Just a little.

After letting the dog lick her fingers for a moment, Chloe poked her fingers through the links and scratched his head and foam-flecked muzzle. Ronnie winced, half-expecting the dog to snap at Chloe, but Lightning remained calm and as friendly as a family pet toward Chloe.

"He was a fighting dog," Chloe explained. "You know, people bet on dog fighting. They fight until one of them is dead or downed." She stroked the dog's tattered ears. "They beat them and shock them with cattle prods or tasers to make them more vicious."

"Poor thing. I'm surprised… that he wasn't put down. A dog that acts so vicious and was treated that way… especially a pit bull."

Chloe shook her head. "That's why I've got him. If he'd gone to the Humane Society, they would have put him down for sure. But I think he's trainable. He acts threatening, but he's never actually tried to bite anyone."

"What about other dogs? You couldn't take him to the park without worrying that he would attack the smaller dogs, could you? After he's been trained for ring fighting?"

"Muzzle him," Chloe said simply. "That usually keeps people from walking up to him, too. If looking like he does isn't a deterrent enough. It will take someone special to take him in, though. He might just stay here or with another rescue society. I'd never put him in a family with kids and there's always a risk of selling him to someone who wants to put him back into fighting."

"You're brave to take him on."

Chloe opened the latch on the cage and Ronnie took a couple of big steps back, panicking. Rather than letting the dog out, Chloe pushed her way into the pen. She took a muzzle and lead down from the wall. Lightning put his nose right into the muzzle when she showed it to him and she strapped it on and encircled his neck with a chain. Ronnie was still nervous when Chloe led him out of the cage. He was still a big, strong dog that could easily knock her down, even if he couldn't bite her.

Chloe led him closer to Ronnie, but stopped just out of reach.

"Sit."

The dog's haunches went down.

"Stay."

He made no move. Chloe moved around him.

"He had lots of injuries, but he's healing up." Ronnie had already noticed his ears. Chloe pointed out a long scar along his shoulder and side. Lots of healed scars on his legs. "Down," Chloe ordered, with a hand motion. The dog bellied down, and with another gesture, rolled over onto his back. Chloe pointed to a long gash down his belly, still pink and inflamed. "This was the worst. Just about disemboweled."

Ronnie felt nauseated at this. "That's horrible."

Chloe gave another hand signal and Lightning rolled back over and looked curiously at Ronnie, panting.

"You want to meet him?" Chloe invited.

"I don't know. He won't be threatened?"

"Not if you're slow and gentle. He can't bite with the muzzle on."

Ronnie inched forward a little at a time, watching the dog carefully for his response. He whined slightly, but didn't demonstrate any more threatening behavior.

"Just show him your hand," Chloe prompted.

Ronnie held out her hand. Lightning snuffled it through muzzle. His tongue flicked out briefly to lick her. Then putting his snout under her hand, he nudged her upward to scratch his ears and head.

Ronnie laughed and let out her breath. "Oh, he's just a big baby, isn't he?" she crooned, rubbing Lightning's head. He whined and squirmed under her touch.

Chloe smiled. "Yeah, he is. I hate the people who beat him and made him fight. He had a lot of broken bones that were never properly set. He'll have arthritis and maybe not have a very long life. All for 'sport.'" She snorted. "I'd like to see *them* in the ring."

Lightning, enjoying the head scratching, rolled over on his back again for a belly rub. Chloe stopped Ronnie from touching his stomach.

"No. He's too sensitive. Up, Lightning. Stand up, now."

Lightning wasn't in a great hurry to obey and needed a few nudges before he got to his feet, making a grumbling noise that was remarkably human.

"How long have you had him?"

"Just a few weeks."

Chloe took the dog back into the pen and took off the muzzle and lead. She kissed him on the snout and gave him a biscuit before locking him back in again. Without a word, they headed back into the house. Jozef was in the kitchen, just pouring coffee into three mugs.

"What do you think of our nursery?" he asked Ronnie. "Were all the babies okay?"

Ronnie smiled. "Yes. What you're doing here is really amazing."

"It's all Chloe. I help muck out and walk, that's it. She's the one who talks to the animals."

Chloe took two mugs and handed one to Ronnie. "You drink coffee, don't you? Let's go sit down."

She led the way and they all settled into comfy couches and chairs in the cozy living room. Chloe pulled a blanket throw over herself. "I know it's warm, but I still get cold easily. Help yourself."

There were plenty of other pillows and blankets within reach. Ronnie was soon settled comfortably. "I can't believe you've only had Lightning for a few weeks," she said, shaking her head. "He seems very well-trained, and has a really nice disposition once he settles down."

"He's my special project right now." Chloe took a sip of her coffee. "I spend a lot of hours with him."

"You have any pets?" Jozef asked Ronnie.

"No. I've actually never had a pet. Not even a fish."

"I could match you with a dog," Chloe said. "Not Lightning, one that was good with kids."

"You have kids?" Jozef asked Ronnie.

Ronnie nodded reluctantly. She glanced at Chloe, trying to discern what Chloe had already told Jozef about Ronnie's circumstances. "Yes... four. I'm not living with any of them right now. But... I might be having more to do with the younger ones. They're five and seven."

"Are you moving in with them?" Chloe probed.

"Maybe. We're taking it pretty slow."

"Ronnie might want a service dog," Chloe told Jozef. "In case she..." Chloe looked at Ronnie, choosing her words carefully. "... gets disoriented."

Jozef's eyebrows went up. "Really? That would be great. Chloe's very good at making matches and training the dogs to do what they need to. It would be a great way for you guys to get to know each other."

"Yeah, it would."

(IV)

When Ronnie had explained to Ruby about what she wanted to do, Ruby had given her wholehearted support.

"I think it would be great to get the whole family together. I don't think all of us have ever been in one place since I went into foster care." Her eyes got unfocused. Ronnie couldn't help but wonder what happened to Ruby when she thought back about the past. Did she forget, like Ronnie? Dissociate like Chloe? Or was she like June, her brain forcing her to relive it over and over again?

"Well, there was the funeral," Ronnie reminded her. "And the trial."

"Oh..." Ruby focused back on Ronnie and the conversation again. "I guess I meant... when we could all just be ourselves, and talk to each other. Not just being in the same room." She swore and shook her head. "The trial... how messed up was that? I was so mad at them for making me go and testify."

"I remember," Ronnie agreed, sorting through the shadowy memories. "You didn't even want to take the oath."

"Do you want tea?" Ruby asked abruptly, standing up. "I need something to do with my hands."

"Uh... okay."

"Just come into the kitchen. It's easier for me to talk in there."

Ronnie followed her into the kitchen and sat down at the table. "You were on crutches at the trial. You'd hurt yourself."

"I had a stroke," Ruby said. "Got in a fight at rehab, and got a clot in my brain."

"Oh, yeah. A stroke." Ronnie watched Ruby moving confidently around the kitchen. "You recovered completely?"

"Well, not one hundred percent. Maybe... ninety five. I start to slur when I'm too tired or have had a bit to drink. I don't have quite the same strength on my left side as I used to, and my hand-writing is crap. But..." She shrugged. "Recovering from a stroke isn't nearly as hard as..." She trailed off while she got down a basket with a variety of tea bags in it, and sorted through them. She eventually just put it down on the table, no tidier than it had been to start out with. "It's the mental and emotional stuff that's hard," Ruby said. She checked the kettle. "I've done lots of ther-apy. *Lots* of therapy." She drew the word out. "There's some stuff that I just can't access. But then... I'm not sure that I want to anyway."

Ronnie nodded. "But you think it's a good idea? Getting every-body together?"

"I think it's long overdue," Ruby agreed "Celebrate the fact that we all survived. I'll tell you, I never thought I'd live to see twenty. Forget thirty. Next year... can you believe I'll be forty? Do you know how many times I had cops or doctors tell me if I didn't clean up my act I'd be dead within a year? How many times I woke up in hospital after doing something stupid?"

"We can invite everyone? Kids and spouses and... everyone?"

Ruby gave Ronnie a long look. "Everyone," she agreed. "All of our families."

Ronnie nodded. Her stomach tightened and anxiety lightninged through her. But she needed to do it. She needed to heal herself and heal her family. As much as she could. No more compartmentalizing and trying to keep the various parts of her life separate. No more forgetting.

"If I gave you Chloe's number, would you call her?" she asked Ruby.

Ruby didn't answer immediately.

"You were the closest one to her," Ronnie reminded her. "The two big girls. She's afraid that everyone hates her, for staying with... our mom. And for testifying against Justin at his trial."

"Well... I did that too," Ruby said.

"That's why I thought, maybe she'd talk to you. You could reassure her that no one has hard feelings..."

"We were all just *so* messed up."

Ruby set teacups out on the table and poured the boiling water from the kettle to the teapot. She put it on the table with fake creamer and sugar, and sat down. She selected a tea bag and poured the hot water over it in her mug.

"You really think I should call her? I didn't treat her very well the last few times I saw her. You already saw her and she didn't want to meet the rest of us..."

"It isn't that she doesn't want to see anyone else. She's just scared. I'm the one who called her, so she said yes. But she doesn't think the rest of you want to see her."

Ruby stirred and smushed the tea bag with her spoon. "Okay. I'll call her. Tell her... we were all just kids. Damaged, immature kids."

Ruby would look after inviting all of the siblings and getting their families lined up. She would book the hall where they would meet and organize the refreshments.

Ronnie dreaded calling Floyd. He was the next on her list. If he refused, she would at least have done all that she could. She couldn't control his decision. She hoped that he would just flat-out refuse.

Floyd answered the phone on the fourth ring. Just long enough that she was starting to hope she could just leave him a message. He would delete the message, and they would never have to discuss it.

"Hello?"

"Uh… it's Ronnie."

"I know. I can see your caller ID. What is it?" His voice was neutral, but Ronnie couldn't help but feel like there was irritation or accusation behind it. What kind of a person forgot her family and just walked away from her life?

"Uh… this is sort of hard… I'm having a thing… sort of like a family reunion… getting everyone together. My birth family, the Dares, you guys… Dusty…" She finished so softly he could easily have missed Dusty's name. It would be better if he missed it. Unless he was really thinking of going, then it would be best if he knew that Dusty and the children were going to be there too.

"Why?" Floyd demanded. "Is this a media thing?"

"No. No media. Nothing like that. I just want… I want all of my family to get to know each other. Instead of being… fractured, with each family unit being separate like the others don't exist."

"You want me and the kids at this thing?"

"Yes. If you'd consider it…"

"It's asking a lot, Ronnie. Kent and Carrie have been through a lot already. It's not fair to ask them to go through this circus as well."

"It's not going to be like that… no one is going to be on display. And no media. It's just going to be my families… trying to integrate everything."

"Is this your therapist's idea?"

It would be an easy out. Easy for her to just lie and say yes, it was a psychiatrist's idea of how to consolidate all of her memories.

"It was my idea."

There was silence, and then a long sigh from Floyd. "Give me the information," he said finally, "and I'll think about it."

Ronnie let out a slow breath and gave him the information about the get-together.

~

Ronnie brought up the reunion at the next Dare family Sunday dinner. Everyone was there. Ronnie waited until they had eaten and were relaxed and contented before bringing it up.

Mom looked at Ronnie, then looked at Dad and frowned. They exchanged a look that sent a wave of cold and nausea over Ronnie. She had never anticipated that they wouldn't approve of the idea. Weren't they the ones who were always saying how important family was? Hadn't they encouraged her to marry Floyd in the first place? How could they disapprove of a family reunion?

"Are you a Simpson or are you a Dare?" Mom asked at length.

Ronnie shifted and considered her answer. "I'm both," she said finally. "I can't be just one or the other. I grew up in both families. And then with Floyd... and Dusty. I never really stayed more than ten years in one place. So, you all..." She shrugged, not sure what else to say. "You're all my family. I want to honor that."

"Your *biological* family has nothing to do with the woman you have grown up into," Dad disagreed. "That is behind you. We raised you. We molded you into what you have become. Or did our best to. Your *biological* family... they never did anything but harm."

"No..." Ronnie fought against the tide of images that crested in her mind. "That's not true. It's not. My sisters and Justin... we took care of each other. Helped each other. You can't say that they aren't anything to me."

"I don't think you're remembering clearly, dear," Mom said slowly, her words soft and concise. Like a nurse who was afraid that if she said something the wrong way, Ronnie would explode. "I know you don't want to think about how it was that you came to us, and we don't want you to dwell on that either, but those people... they did nothing but hurt you. You worked really hard to become a part of this family. Part of the deal was putting your former life behind you. Renouncing it."

The way that Mom said it, she made it sound like Ronnie had been a hooker redeemed from a life of shame by the hardworking Dares. But that wasn't how it had been.

"That was my parents. Not my brother and sisters. I want them to be a part of my life."

"Really?" Dad said, his tone barbed. "Are you really thinking about just who you're talking about? I remember Ruby. The fact that she was abusive toward you too. All of those girls, they're just as likely to turn out to be abusers. And Justin... you really think that starting out life by killing his father makes him a person you want to be part of your life? Are you forgetting that part? Not only did he kill a man, but he dragged you and all of the others into court, made a spectacle out of you. Do you remember how traumatized you were by having to testify?"

Ronnie swallowed. She scratched at a spot of something spilled on her pants. "I know," she agreed. The memories the trial had forced to the surface had been too traumatic for her to deal with, triggering that first episode of amnesia. She had sleepwalked, she had withdrawn from the family, and her marks had suffered. But she'd gotten through it. It wasn't Justin's fault that their father had hurt Ronnie. He had done what he had to protect June, so that their father could never hurt her as badly as he had hurt Ronnie. To stop him from ever hurting anyone again. "But that was to protect June..."

"And running with a street gang, was that to protect her too? How many people did he hurt or kill while he was running with them?"

"When he was ten!"

"Does that make it okay? Do you think he's changed from the person he was when he was eight or ten? Someone who starts killing that young, they don't just stop. They don't just mellow out and go on to live a quiet life. You don't want to get involved with someone like that."

"Justin is just a truck driver. He's not involved in any gangs or violence. That was just... self-protection, when he was little. He didn't have a good foster family like I did. He had to find other ways to protect himself."

Mom gave a little smile and put her hand on her husband's arm.

"How would you know what he's into now?" Dad challenged.

"Long distance truckers are away for days or weeks at a time. What do you think he's doing while he's away? These are the kind of men who victimize young hitchhikers and runaways. He could be following in your birth father's footsteps; how would you know?"

Ronnie thought of Justin's tanned, sun-lined face. His self-deprecating humor and how he had lit up when she asked him about his children. Sure, it could all be an act, but she felt a connection with her brother. He wasn't like that. He had spent all of his growing-up years protecting June, staying by her side. Someone like that didn't go on to become a predator.

"Justin isn't that kind of person," she insisted. "Neither are my sisters. Neither is Ruby."

Dad glared at her. He didn't believe it for a minute. Ronnie could see that it wasn't just an act, just an argument. He truly believed that Ruby would hurt her, even now, almost thirty years later.

"Ruby didn't hurt me," Ronnie insisted.

"That wasn't what you said when it happened."

"Because she didn't hurt me. She didn't. Everybody had me confused and I didn't know what to say. She never did anything to me."

"You don't remember," Mom contributed in her soft, reasonable voice. Ronnie had forgotten how much she hated that tone. The voice she used to talk Ronnie out of doing whatever she wanted to do and to make her do what the family wanted her to do. So measured and logical and reasonable. So loving and caring. Saying that they only wanted what was best for Ronnie. The voice that was designed to make her feel guilty for having an opinion of her own, especially one that differed from Mom's and Dad's.

"I *do* remember," Ronnie choked out. "She never meant any harm. She slept in the same bed as me. She hugged me. That wasn't wrong of her. She didn't mean to confuse me or stir anything up." She shook her head. "That was decades ago. Can't you forgive a confused teenager for making a mistake? If there really anything wrong with it?"

379

"Of course we forgive her," Dad said. "But that doesn't mean we put you in harm's way again."

"I'm a grown woman! I'm too old for you to protect me or for you to make decisions for me!" Ronnie took a deep breath and tried to lower her voice. "I didn't come here to get your permission or ask what your views were on me getting together with everybody. I came to invite you and ask you to come to this little... reunion. I want you to meet my family. Really meet them, instead of just making judgments without knowing anything. I just want you to come."

Her plea hung in the air for a long time. Mom and Dad looked at each other. Eventually Dad shook his head.

"No, Ronnie. We don't think this is a good idea and we're not going to do anything to encourage it. If you're going to go ahead with this... it will be without us."

Ronnie bit the inside of her lip. She nodded, and stood up. "Okay. That's your choice."

Mom stood up as well, but Dad didn't. He looked up at Ronnie from where he sat, like a king in his throne.

"You need to think about whether you want to be part of the Simpson family, or part of ours."

Ronnie caught her breath. She looked at Mom for her reaction, but didn't see any regret or embarrassment there. "You're telling me that if I visit with my siblings, I'm not a part of this family anymore?"

"I don't see how you can be a part of both. It's a slap in our faces, after all that I and your mother have done, for you to go back to the Simpsons again."

"But they're my family."

He looked away from her, toward the TV, which was silent, for once not playing during Ronnie's visit. "Then we wish you the best."

(V)

As promised, Ruby had rented the hall and organized all of the arrangements. It was to be a pot-luck meal, with an ice cream sundae bar for dessert. Everyone was invited. All of the siblings, their partners, and their children. In the case of Michelle and Sheree, partners of the children were, of course, invited as well.

There had been a lot of talk about how to keep everyone comfortable, without any of the cross-currents. Ronnie gathered that there was friction between June and Sondra, Justin's wife. She supposed it made sense that with June and Justin being twins, it would be difficult for June to let Justin start a new life with someone else without some jealousy and perhaps disapproval about his match. And Ronnie could see the rift between June and her children. They were working on it, she knew, but Ronnie could still see a lot of anger and bitterness between them.

Ronnie, in turn, had her own family relationships to deal with. If Floyd showed up, it would be the first time that he and Dusty would see each other, or that her older children and younger children would meet.

Ronnie arrived early. She knew that Ruby would be there to open the building up, but none of the others were there yet.

"You must be Ronnie," greeted the man who opened the door for her. He was tall, with light brown hair and eyes. Older than Ruby. He had to be her husband.

"Yes. Hi. Charlie?"

"That's right. Come on in."

Ronnie motioned behind her. "I brought reinforcements. This is Janessa and Alex. My adoptive siblings."

Janessa and Alex, thankfully, did not feel the same way about Ronnie having more than one family as Mom and Dad did. They had been quick to agree to coming to support Ronnie and to meet the rest of her family. Provided that word of it did not get back to Mom and Dad.

"They just need time to get used to the idea," Janessa said.

"They'll come around eventually. They're not going to totally disown you."

Alex had listened to this reassurance, but he did not nod or express agreement.

Charlie smiled at the two newcomers. "Welcome. Come in, come in. I'll show you where to put your dishes."

Ronnie followed his lead, and soon she and Janessa were put to work by Ruby, while Charlie and Alex talked sports and watched for the other arrivals.

"Name tags," Ruby said, pointing out the check-in table in the hall as it got to be time for everyone else to show up. "Fill out a name tag for each person in your family, with their relationship to you."

Ronnie went to the table and made out tags for herself and for Janessa and Alex. Then for Dusty and his children. And with her stomach a tight knot, for Floyd and his children. She wondered whether they were going to come. She was okay with it if they didn't. At least she had made the effort to invite him and be part of the reunion.

June arrived, followed by Michelle and Kenny. Then Chloe arrived with Jozef and a couple of the dogs. Not Lightning, Ronnie noted. Ronnie greeted everyone cheerfully, pretending she wasn't feeling any anxiety. As another group arrived, Chloe pulled Ronnie to the side.

"Would you hang onto Fernand for a minute?" She held a leash toward Ronnie.

Ronnie looked down at the dog. A collie or sheltie mix. "Fernand?" she repeated.

Chloe nodded, continuing to hold the leash out to her. Ronnie took it slowly. The dog came to her eagerly and pressed against her leg. He was wearing a service dog vest, with one of the name tags stuck to it. 'Fernand Gould, Chloe's dog.'

Ronnie looked to see who else had arrived. Justin, his face looking freshly-shaven this time; the woman and children behind him had to be Sondra and their brood. Ronnie was surprised to see Michelle make a beeline for the girl in the wheelchair to give her a hug and warm greeting. Michelle avoided anything more than a cursory greeting for Justin and Sondra, but took the girl in the wheelchair over to the name tag table to get her a stick-on label.

The next person to come in the door was Floyd. Ronnie's mouth went dry. She really hadn't expected him to come.

Fernand pressed against Ronnie's leg and thrust his nose into her hand, whining and licking her. Ronnie rubbed his head, a bit of the anxiety receding. There was only one way to deal with Floyd's arrival, and that was to face it head-on rather than running away. Ronnie took a step toward him, but a wave of dizziness came over her, making her stumble and stop.

The vertigo turning to nausea, she looked around for the restrooms. She had already identified them when she had come in, but she was disoriented and couldn't remember which direction they were. Ronnie turned around, trying to find the right doorway. Black spots were filling her vision.

Fernand was nudging Ronnie's leg, but he couldn't have known where she wanted to go, and she resisted. She felt his pull on the leash, and then his mouth over her wrist, so gentle that his teeth did not go through the weave of her sweater. Thoroughly disoriented, Ronnie allowed the dog to pull her by the hand, until her knees met with the edge of a metal chair. Ronnie turned and sat down, her head spinning and breath coming in short gasps.

Fernand barked. Ronnie tried to quiet him. "Sh, Fernand. Calm."

He barked again. Chloe came over. "Ron? You okay?" Ronnie could hear Chloe's voice, but not see or respond to her query. "Oh... Ruby, can you come here and help?"

There was a hand on Ronnie's wrist, big fingers resting lightly over her pulse point. "How are you doing, Ronnie? Can you talk to me?" It was a man's voice, but not Floyd's. Charlie? The voice went on in a calm, quiet tone. "Heart rate's really fast. She's sweaty. Maybe a panic attack?"

A thin hand rubbed Ronnie's back. "It's okay, Ron. You're going to be okay. How about a drink of water?"

There was a glass pressed to Ronnie's lips a few seconds later, and she sipped the cold water. She steadied herself and found her voice.

"I'm sorry... I'm fine..."

"She has psychiatric issues." This time it was Floyd's voice. "Maybe we should call somebody."

"No," Ronnie said. "It's passing." She took a deeper breath. She blinked and looked around at them. "It's okay. Just give me a little space. I'll be fine."

They all stood around her, reluctant to leave her alone.

"Floyd, why don't you sit with me?" Ronnie suggested, even though it was the last thing that she wanted. "Are the kids here?"

He dragged out a chair. It scraped noisily on the floor.

"They're right here."

Ronnie blinked again and looked around, separating out Kent and Carrie from the rest of the group. "There's name tags for you at that table. Why don't you guys get them and bring Floyd his?"

People started to move around more normally.

"Thanks for coming," Ronnie told Floyd. "I'll introduce you to everyone... in a minute."

"I can do that," Janessa offered.

"Sure... I just need a minute," Ronnie said. Floyd already knew Janessa. She and Alex could take charge of him and head off any problems. They wouldn't tiptoe around him like her bio family might. He wouldn't be able to bully his way around.

Floyd got back up with an exasperated sigh and Janessa led him away to make introductions. Ronnie rubbed the bones above her eyes, trying to relax and get her heart rate back to normal again. The dog kept snuffling and whining at her. Patting him was helping her to calm down.

Ronnie saw Michelle hovering nearby, watching her worriedly.

"It's okay," Ronnie told her.

"Do you... want to meet my sister?"

Ronnie looked at the girl in the wheelchair, frowning. Justin's daughter would be Michelle's cousin, not her sister. Michelle pushed the wheelchair forward, close enough that Ronnie could read both of their name tags. "This is Marcie."

Michelle's name tag, which June had initially filled out as 'Michelle Simpson, June's daughter,' had been amended to read 'Justin and June's daughter.' Likewise Marcie's name tag, which had read 'Marcie Simpson, Justin's daughter,' had been amended to 'June and Justin's daughter.' Ronnie raised her eyes to Michelle's face. The girl stared back at her challengingly.

"That's right," she said. "Their dirty little secret. *That's* why they ran away. And why Justin abandoned us."

Ronnie had no idea what to do with this. Michelle obviously intended to shock her. She wanted a reaction. Ronnie decided to avoid the issue and smiled weakly at Marcie instead. "Hi, Marcie. It's nice to meet you."

Marcie's head wobbled and she opened her mouth in a wide, drooly grin, saying something that Ronnie couldn't understand.

"She wants to pat your dog," Michelle said.

Marcie reached a spastic, contorted hand toward the dog.

"Oh." Ronnie looked down at the dog's name tag, trying to collect her thoughts. "This is Fernand. He's actually your aunt Chloe's dog."

Ronnie used Fernand's collar to steer him closer to Marcie. Once the dog got the idea, he eagerly obliged, putting his paws on Marcie's lap and getting right in close to her face. Marcie patted at Fernand with ill-controlled motions, chortling with delighted laughter. He licked her hands and her face, making her squeal.

Justin approached, hearing Marcie's happy noises. He stood next to her, bending down to scratch Fernand's ears.

"Marcie loves animals," he said. "She doesn't get to see them up close very often. She used to have a guinea pig that would sit in her lap for hours at a time."

Marcie grabbed at Justin's hand, giggling.

"Yes, he's very nice," Justin acknowledged. "Yours?" he said to Ronnie. Then he saw the dog's name tag. "Oh... Chloe's..." He looked around for Chloe, biting his lip.

"She's really nice," Ronnie told him. "She feels really bad about testifying against you at the trial. She asked me specifically about you. If you were all right."

"Oh." Justin nodded awkwardly. "Okay."

"You should talk to her about dogs. She trains service dogs. Maybe she could match one with Marcie."

"We've thought about service dogs before, but they're so hard to get and there's not a lot that a dog could do for Marcie. She's not independent."

"They could pick things up for her," Michelle suggested. "Or bark if she woke up in the night or needed help."

Just like Fernand had barked to call Chloe's attention to Ronnie's panic attack. If she hadn't had the dog with her, would it have been another situation that was just too overwhelming for Ronnie? Would she have just phased out and walked off in a fugue? When Chloe had talked before about how a dog might be able to help her, Ronnie hadn't really seriously considered the possibility.

Justin and Michelle wheeled Marcie away after saying good-bye to Fernand, and headed toward Chloe. Ronnie patted Fernand and looked toward the door. Another girl came in. Older than Michelle, college-age perhaps, accompanied by a good-looking, preppy sort of boy. Sheree, Ronnie suspected. She resembled Ruby a little, but was dark-haired. She was a pleasant, cheerful-looking girl. No hint of the way she had started out her life, abandoned by her mother in the care of some less-than-desirable man.

Then at last, the door opened to admit Dusty and the younger children. Mandi spotted her mother and a dog and was off and running, Dusty too slow to grab her. Ronnie caught Mandi up in her arms before she could land on top of Fernand.

"Whoa! Hey, sweetie. Did you want to see the puppy?"

"Yes!"

"Okay, you need to put your hand out for him to smell. That's like saying hello. You can't just run at him, you could scare him."

Ronnie was helping Mandi to make friends with Fernand when Dusty made it over to where she was seated.

"Hi, Ronnie."

He didn't bend down to give her a kiss, glancing around the hall to survey and identify who else was there.

"Floyd is already here," Ronnie murmured. "I really didn't think he would come, but he did." She pointed him out and identified the children.

"I can't believe how much Carrie looks like Mandi!" Dusty said.

"Yeah. I guess they do look a bit alike."

Floyd had finished all of the introductions and headed back toward Ronnie, his stride purposeful and gaze fixed.

"Oh, no... don't let him make a scene..."

Floyd stopped a few feet away. He looked at Mandi, still in Ronnie's lap and patting the dog, and at Dane standing beside her. Then at Dusty.

For a while, they both just looked at each other. Floyd's face was red. Ronnie could feel Dusty's tension as he rested his hand on her shoulder. Ronnie swallowed and cleared her throat.

"Umm... Floyd, this is Dusty. My, umm... other..." she trailed off. How did a person introduce one husband to the other? It would be one thing if she were at least divorced from one of them. But as it was, neither was an 'ex.'

"So, she left you too, did she?" Floyd blustered, and reached out to shake hands.

Dusty gave a weak laugh. "Yeah. It's... nice... to meet you."

Floyd snorted. They released the handshake and Ronnie wondered which of them had won the contest of grips. Were they adversaries? Or were they, as Floyd had indicated, fellow sufferers, joined by their shared experience? She tried to interpret the looks that passed between them.

Floyd motioned for Kent and Carrie to join them. The teens were both reluctant, approaching slowly, faces blank. They nodded at the introductions to Dusty and his children. Mandi looked up at Carrie and put out her arms to be picked up, smiling widely. Carrie hesitated for a moment, glancing at Floyd uncertainly, then she bent down and picked Mandi up.

"Hi, there."

"I'm Mandi."

"Yeah. I'm Carrie."

Mandi put her finger on Carrie's chest. "You are my sister?"

Carrie opened her mouth and looked at Floyd, Dusty, and Ronnie. "I... I guess so," she agreed.

"What's that say?" Mandi tapped Carrie's name tag. "That says Carrie?"

"Yes."

Mandi touched the words under Carrie's name. "Sister of Mandi," she pretended to read.

Carrie considered for a moment. She looked again at her father and then at Ronnie. Her expression softened for the first time since Ronnie had come back. She gave Mandi a little squeeze. "Yeah," she agreed. She swallowed and nodded her head, meeting Ronnie's eyes. "Sister of Mandi."

Having everyone turn their attention to the meal was a relief. It took some of the pressure off and let Ronnie relax just a little. She didn't have to introduce anyone else, didn't have to meet their eyes while she was eating.

After getting her plate, Ronnie sat down beside Chloe. She was still feeling protective of Chloe and wanted to make sure that she had someone at her table she felt comfortable with. The dogs were happy to lie down together. Jozef smiled his welcome and nodded at Ronnie.

Before Ronnie had a chance to motion anyone else over to the table, Floyd made his way over. Ronnie looked for a way to deflect him. But she couldn't think of a way to get him to go to another table without being rude. He could have gone over to sit with Alex and Janessa. He knew them.

Floyd sat himself down, and the teens, still somewhat sullen and reserved, sat down as well, completing the table of six. Ronnie would have to visit more with Dusty and the children later.

Jozef was a good conversationalist and he soon had Floyd engaged so that Ronnie didn't have to worry about entertaining him all by herself. She contributed where she could. Chloe made a comment or two, usually waiting until Jozef dangled a conversation opener in front of her and waited for her to take it. Floyd said little directly to Ronnie. Carrie and Kent texted and busied themselves with their phones, staying aloof.

Ronnie couldn't really get much down, her insides knotted inside her like they were, but she played with the food with her fork, putting on the appearance of eating. No one was fooled by it, she was sure.

The men and children appeared to enjoy the ice cream bar for dessert. Ronnie noticed that Chloe had a bare spoonful of ice cream, with just a little fruit, the same as Ronnie. Floyd and the teens had heaping bowls with all kinds of sauces and sprinkles. Ronnie had no idea that putting gummy bears on ice cream was a thing. Was it something she had forgotten, or just a fad she had never had occasion to notice?

When Floyd finished his ice cream, his pushed his bowl away from him, and neglected to cover his mouth before belching. He leaned back, giving his gorged belly a little more space. He looked at Ronnie. She looked down at her little puddle of ice cream, pretending to give it her attention.

"I know that you're not going to be coming back to me," he said in a flat, unemotional tone.

Ronnie ventured a glance at him. "I'm sorry."

"I've been without you for eleven years, so it's not exactly a shock. And the kids..." He looked at Kent and Carrie, who were studiously ignoring her. "They're not looking for a mother, old or new."

Kent looked up at this and Ronnie wondered whether he was going to object. Kent was the one who had seen her. Who had stopped her in the middle of the street and been persistent enough to get the police involved. He might not want a mother in his day-to-day life anymore; that opportunity might be lost, but did he really want nothing to do with her?

Kent looked over at Carrie for her reaction, but she didn't look up, and eventually he looked back down at his phone again, his mouth set in a pout that hadn't been there before.

"I can still visit," Ronnie promised. "Or talk on the phone... or whatever. Whatever you guys want."

"Yeah," Floyd was impatient. "We know all that. That's not what I mean. You're not tied down to us. You can go back to Dusty. Raise Dane and Mandi. We can get a divorce or annulment. Whatever is required to make it legal."

Ronnie raised her eyes to look him fully in the face. She saw no deception in his features. No anger or hate. "Thank you."

"I'm glad that you're not dead. For you and for the kids' sakes. But I don't have any reason to hold you back. Our marriage ended a long time ago."

He didn't say whether it had ended before or after she had disappeared. Ronnie supposed it didn't make any difference. He was willing to free her. She wouldn't have to fight for it or persuade him that it was the right thing to do.

Ronnie looked across the hall to Dusty's table. He was sitting with Ruby and Charlie, with an empty seat at the table. He looked up and met her gaze.

"I'll be back," Ronnie murmured to her table and went over to take the empty chair.

Epilogue

I don't know if it will work," Ronnie said. "You're supposed to do it first thing in the morning. If it's early on, anyway."

Dusty smiled and nodded agreeably.

But Ronnie didn't go directly to the bathroom. Her stomach was tight in anticipation, but she was afraid of getting an actual answer.

Instead, she went into Dane's room to make sure that he was asleep, and just to look at his angelic face for a few minutes. A boy at his age was always in motion, and his friends and games were far more important than sitting still and reading a book with Mommy. Even at the dinner table, he couldn't seem to sit still, always in a whirl of excitement. Ronnie had thought that he would settle down once she had been back for a while, that it was just the novelty of her being home, but in the weeks since she had moved back in with Dusty and the children, he had remained in perpetual motion.

He was asleep, one fist resting against his smooth, round cheek. So reminiscent of when he had been a newborn, all swaddled up.

She picked up a few toy dinosaurs littering his bed. She didn't want him to roll over in his sleep onto one of the hard, sharp points. She lined them up on the edge of his dresser so he'd see them as soon as he woke up in the morning.

Ronnie smoothed the blanket and left the room. Dane played hard, and he would sleep through the night. It was Mandi who was more likely to waken in the night and wander out looking for Mommy or Daddy. If Ronnie were too tired to deal with her, she would awaken in the morning to Mandi nestled on the bed between them.

Ronnie pushed open Mandi's door slowly, hoping that it wouldn't squeak and wake her up. She had asked Dusty to oil the hinges, but she didn't know if he had gotten around to it. She breathed a sigh of relief as it opened silently and smoothly. Ronnie tiptoed up to Mandi's bed.

Mandi stared up at her, eyes wide open.

"What are you doing awake, little monkey?"

Mandi smiled. "I can't sleep, Mommy."

"You need to close your eyes."

"I did... I try..."

"Close your eyes now..." Ronnie sat on the edge of the bed beside Mandi and straightened and smoothed the blankets over her.

Mandi obediently closed her big blue eyes.

Ronnie stroked her hair. "Just relax and go to sleep, sweetie."

Mandi mumbled something indistinguishable.

"You were a good girl to stay in bed," Ronnie said, brushing her cheek. "You can't sleep if you're up wandering around, can you?"

Mandi rolled over onto her stomach and hugged her pillow to her. Ronnie rubbed her back in long, soothing circles.

"I knew you'd come in," Mandi murmured.

Ronnie was glad that she had not disappointed Mandi. More than that, she was glad that she was home and that Mandi trusted she wasn't going to leave again, but would be there for her. Remembering Kent's and Carrie's bitterness and distrust, she was amazed at how trusting her younger children were. She had expected them to be traumatized, to be damaged by her disappearance and sudden reappearance in their lives. But they seemed remarkably unaffected by her abandonment of them. But they hadn't had to grow up without her like Kent and Carrie had. It had

been a year. They had been with Dusty. They hadn't been abandoned by their mother and then had their father imprisoned and
been forced to live with the Dares for four years. Which part was it
that had traumatized them the most?

Mandi's breathing was long and even. Ronnie waited, counting
out the seconds, until she was sure Mandi had fallen asleep. She got
up carefully, ever so slowly, knowing that if Mandi felt Ronnie's
weight leave the mattress, she would wake up again and it would be
twice as hard to get her back to sleep again.

Then she finally made it to the bathroom. Dusty was surely
wondering what was taking her so long. Or maybe he wasn't. He
knew how important it was for her to look in on the children and
make sure that they were all right, in spite of everything that had
happened.

Ronnie sat and waited. She pulled out her phone and checked her
social networks, afraid to look at the test results. She didn't want to
keep looking at it, wondering if it was going to change, or if the
little window was just going to stay blank and unchanged.

She was afraid that Dusty was going to start knocking on the
door, asking her if she knew anything yet, before enough time had
passed. She should have gone back out to sit with him on the
couch, visiting until enough time had passed and they could look at
the test together, sharing the moment of discovery.

But she couldn't do that. She needed the time and space to
process the results herself before he found out.

She read all of her updates. She glanced at the time. It was
getting late. She knew enough time had passed. Eventually, Ronnie
forced herself to turn her head and pick up the test stick. She
looked at the results window, unable to breathe.

Dusty was reading a book, music turned down low, when Ronnie
returned to the living room. Fernand slept at his feet. Dusty closed

the book and put it to the side immediately. He patted the cushioned seat next to him, inviting her to sit and cuddle.

"It's positive," Ronnie said, all in a rush. "We're pregnant!"

Dusty's expression changed. A big, broad smile replaced careful composure. He held both arms out to Ronnie. She leaned in to hug him and let herself be pulled into his lap.

"Sweetie," Dusty breathed. He brushed her cheek with a kiss. "I'm so happy. Are you okay?"

"Yes, of course. I haven't been sick or anything."

"I know that. But I mean... mentally...? You're happy with this?"

"Yes. We both wanted it."

"I just want to make sure... it's not too stressful on you. You'll tell me if you feel like things are getting to be too much...?"

"I'm good. I'm feeling good. And I've got Fernand to keep an eye on me."

At the mention of his name, the dog lifted his head and looked at her.

"You'll look after me, won't you, Fernand?"

He continued to stare at her, head cocked slightly to the side as if puzzled by her words. His tail thumped the floor.

Dusty cuddled Ronnie to him. "I want you to tell me about everything," he insisted. "Good or bad. I want to know what's going on. And if... *something* happens..." He didn't use the word miscarriage for fear of jinxing the pregnancy. "If anything goes wrong... I want to know about it."

Ronnie nodded. "Yes. Of course."

"Right away. No waiting until it's a good time."

She supposed it was natural for him to be afraid that if she miscarried again, she might have another psychotic break and wander off. It gave them some peace of mind that she had Fernand now, always at her side and on duty unless Dusty was home. But that still wasn't a guarantee that she wouldn't forget again. The dog couldn't force her to go home. He couldn't make her read the papers he carried for her and believe them, and seek the help she needed.

"It's going to be okay," Ronnie said.

And she truly believed it.

She would be okay. Dusty and the children were her family, and she wasn't ever going to lose them—or herself—again.

Did you enjoy this book? Reviews and recommendations are vital to making a book successful.

Please leave a review at your favorite book store or review site and share it with your friends.

Don't miss the following bonus material:
Sign up for mailing list to get a free ebook
Read a sneak preview chapter
Other books by P.D. Workman
Learn more about the author

DON'T MISS A THING! GET THE LATEST NEWS AND A FREE EBOOK

Your First Taste

PDWORKMAN.COM/SIGNUP

Preview of June, Into the Light

CHAPTER
One

J une focused on trying to keep her gun hand from shaking, supporting it with her other hand. She stared at the clerk of the convenience store, doing her best to exude confidence and danger, to show him that he needed to do what she said if he didn't want to get shot. Gone were the days when she could lift cash or keys from right under the owner's nose. The man looked frightened. He was there by himself; he was always by himself that time of day, she had been in the neighborhood long enough to know that.

"Just do what I tell you to!" June ordered. Her mouth was dry. She should have had something to drink before she started. She should have had more to drink. If she'd had more, maybe then she wouldn't have been so wound up. "Put everything in the till into the bag."

He was moving too slowly. She didn't like it. He hadn't argued with her and hadn't tried to talk her out of the hold-up, but he was moving way too slowly. She wanted to reach across the counter and start grabbing hands full of cash herself, but she had seen enough blooper videos on TV to know how that would go. She wouldn't be able to keep control of the gun and grab the money, her arm stretched out over the counter. The cashier would be able to catch her gun arm and maybe get her under his control.

"Hurry up!" she screamed, tearing her throat raw. Why wouldn't he hurry up? Was he moving that slowly, or was it just her perception because she was so hyped up?

He didn't say a word to her. That wasn't right. He should have been answering her. Either arguing or trying to assure her that he was going to do everything she said to. But he wasn't. Pale as a ghost, he just kept pinching bills between his fingers and putting them into the gym bag, his own hands shaking so that he kept fumbling with them, dropping them, not scooping the money efficiently like she would if she were in his position. How hard was it to grab the stack of cash from each slot?

It was taking too long. There had to be a few hundred in the bag, and that was all she needed. She could get some more cash from another store, maybe one farther away from her home, once she was feeling better.

She reached across the counter and grabbed the bag. The cashier held on to it for a moment, startled, but then he let go and put his hands up, letting her know he wasn't going to fight her for it. June waved the gun at him one more time and hurried out of the store. All she had to do was get her hands on the drugs she needed, and then she'd be fine. Then she could stop and think over her next step.

June hadn't been able to find Jason, so she had ended up having to pay top dollar to a dealer that she didn't usually buy from. Her money had disappeared into his pockets, and the heroin he had provided had been cut. It was barely enough to calm her shakes and, within a few hours, they were back again, worse than ever.

Jason would have the good stuff. She couldn't trust anyone else. She needed to find him and get some good product. Enough for a few days. It had been a while since she had seen Michelle. The girl was bound to come home soon, and she would have money for June to get groceries and to pay Jason what she owed. She just needed to convince him to extend her a little more credit. Only June wasn't sure how she was going to do that.

The gun was heavy, weighing on her like a sack of rocks instead of the sleek little handgun it was. She took it out of her hoodie pocket and again checked to make sure it was fully loaded.

The volume of a child's voice in the hallway made her turn her head and realize that she had left the apartment door open. She was going to walk over and close it, but then realized she still had the gun in her hand and someone could see it and report her. Or worse yet, feel threatened and blow her away.

She turned her back to the door to shield the gun from view and checked it one more time.

She wondered what would happen if she held Jason up for his product. How much did he carry on him? How long would it last? If she did something like that, he would never sell to her again, and he'd see to it she was blacklisted by all of the local dealers.

Not a good idea.

June let out her breath. She would talk to Jason. She would explain to him that she was going to be getting money soon. He would give her enough to tide her over until she could get her hands on some more cash. Everything would be fine.

"Freeze, police!"

June startled and whirled around, the gun finding its place in her hand and her finger sliding onto the trigger by the time she faced the door, drawing a bead on the cops before the words even registered.

Her heart pounded so hard she thought it was going to explode. She pointed the gun at one black-uniformed cop and then the other, trying to figure out an escape route. She had faced danger before. She had faced arrest before. But it had been a long time since she had been in a gang and trouble like that had been expected.

Why were they there? Because someone had seen her gun? Because they knew about the robbery? Had the dealer she'd bought from been a narc?

If she went down for armed robbery, it was bad, but if she shot up the cops, it would be much worse. She would never get out. That was if she even made it to jail. If she shot one of them, or if they thought she was going to shoot one of them, they were going to open fire. It was two against one, and even if she managed to kill one of them, and maybe wing the other one, she wasn't going to get out of there. If she managed to get both of them—and her skills with a firearm were not that great—she wouldn't get far. The whole police force would be out looking for her in seconds, and she had nowhere to run. People in the neighborhood knew her. If the cashier had been able to describe her to a sketch artist, people would recognize her and know where she lived. That was why they always said never to pull a job in your own back yard. Don't piss in your own drinking water.

"Drop the weapon and put up your hands!" one of the cops shouted.

June tried to decide. Her body had seized up, and the shaking was worse than ever. She could drop the gun, or she could end everything there. If she fired, even if she intentionally missed, they would take her out. They would put an end to her miserable existence there and then.

But was that really what she wanted? She had lost everything but her children, Michelle and Kenny. Did she want to lose them too? They didn't have a good relationship, but at least Michelle still came by to check on June now and then. If June committed suicide by cop, what would that do to them?

She remembered a blaze of gunfire. She was thrown way back into the past—eight years old, sitting in her father's lap when Justin filled him full of bullet holes—the end of life as they had known it. The smell of gun smoke and blood. The thunder of the gunshots filling her ears, along with her mother's screams. Justin's face, calm, pale, and pinched, as he lowered the gun, put it down, and calmly took the phone from their mother to dial in the three digits she couldn't seem to manage with her shaking fingers.

June couldn't shoot anyone. She remembered later when they were part of the Fourteenth Street Gang, and Justin had acquired his own gun for the first time, how devastating it had been for him. A tough hood, and he couldn't look at or touch a gun without remembering how he had fired those shots way back when they were both eight, changing the courses of their lives forever. What kind of a hood was traumatized by holding a gun? She had assured him that it was okay; she didn't care whether he could carry and fire a gun. Neither of them had to carry just because they were with the gang. They could use other things. They could use knives, fists, feet.

The shots echoed in her ears, so sharp and distinct that she looked from one cop to the other, sure that one of them had shot at her. Her body was clenched, waiting for the pain. But it didn't come. The only pain she felt was the withdrawals that had been racking her body all day. The craving of her body that couldn't be satisfied with anything else.

"Please help me!" she begged.

The cops looked surprised, exchanging looks with each other. "Help you? How can we help you, ma'am?"

When had she gone from being a kid to being *ma'am*? She had three children, but she didn't feel any older than she had when she was fourteen. She was still waiting for that strong, confident, grown-up feeling that all adults had. She kept bluffing her way through it, pretending that she could be a good mother. Pretending that she could take care of herself and knew what she was doing, all the while so lost and alone, the same eight-year-old girl she had been when they put her in an ambulance and took her away from her family, from her brother, from everything she knew. She had thought that she would never see Justin again. She had cried and screamed when they were separated, sure that he was going to prison and that she would never be able to see him again. Maybe it would have been better for him if that had happened.

"Just tell us what we can do to help," one of the cops said. "Why don't you put the gun down, and we'll see what we can do?"

"I gotta have a fix," June said, admitting the ugly truth. As much as she wanted Justy back, as much as she wanted her children to

P.D. WORKMAN

live with her and love her again, as much as she wanted everything to be idyllic, her immediate need was for nothing more than the drugs her body craved.

"We can help you to detox," the darker of the two cops said. "If you just surrender, we'll take you into custody, and we'll help you out."

"I don't want to detox." She hated the way that it felt when they cleaned her up. She hated the empty feeling, the anxiety, the feeling of being lost in the universe. That wasn't the feeling that she wanted. She wanted the drugs to numb the pain. To quiet the anxieties and help her to forget how miserable her life had become. She didn't want to be clean. She just wanted the chemicals flowing through her veins, helping her to forget, for just a few minutes.

"Of course not. But you can't keep going on like this. Can you lower the gun? You're looking pretty shaky there, and no one wants to be shot by accident."

June saw her father, the blood that had spattered over everything, the holes in his chest and blankness in his eyes. He'd looked so startled, so surprised at being dead. She allowed the weight of the gun to pull her arm down slowly so that it went from the cop's center mass down to his legs, and finally down at the floor. She knew her finger was still through the trigger guard, and that they now had the drop on her. It would take little effort if she really wanted to die.

But the gun had become so heavy in her hand that she was no longer sure she would be able to raise it again. The aching in her chest grew. Maybe she'd have a heart attack right there, and they wouldn't have to kill her. She would die right there, her heart unable to take the pressure anymore. She knew that some of the prescriptions she had taken over the years had side effects that could damage the heart. So could the street drugs. Maybe they had, and these were her last few seconds of life. Alone, no family, just the cops.

"That's right," the cop said reassuringly. "You're making the right choice. We want to keep everyone safe here, don't we? You don't want to hurt anyone. You're just jonesing. But everything is going to be alright."

She couldn't see how. She couldn't see any possible positive outcome. They were going to put her away. Not just detox this time, not just the hospital, but in prison for armed robbery. She had blown it. She had been given one more chance to be a mother to her children, to get them back and show everyone that she could do it, and she had blown that all to hell. No matter what, she would never be getting her children back again. Not only that, but she had lost them long ago.

They hadn't wanted to come back to her after being in foster care. Neither one of them had wanted anything to do with her. Instead of showing them she could be a good mom, she had just reinforced how inept at the role she was. How was she supposed to be a good mother when all she'd ever known was abuse and temporary foster care? How had that trained her to be the kind of parent that she'd always wished she had?

"It's not going to be alright," she objected.

"I know that's how you feel," he agreed. "I know you can't see your way through to things being better now, but they can be. This is the best thing that could happen to you."

"What?" June was baffled. How could he think that anything good could happen to her? She was going to prison. She was never going to see her children again. She was never going to see Justin again. Her whole life, all the things she had ever valued, were gone forever.

"It is," the cop told her earnestly. "This is your opportunity to get cleaned up, to get your life turned around. You can get clear of the drugs, finish your education, maybe even learn a trade. You can get all of that crap straightened out and live the kind of life that you want to live."

He was crazy. He had no idea what he was talking about. There was no way that her life was ever going to get any better. She had been spiraling down into the blackness for so long that she no longer remembered what it was like to walk in the light. There was no way out of the hole she had dug herself into.

"I've seen people a lot worse off than you turn their lives around."

"No, you haven't," June challenged. Her whole body was shaking with fatigue, with her need for more drugs, with the loss of the adrenaline that had sustained her through the hold-up. "You don't know what it's like."

"I've seen convicted murderers turn their lives around and become contributing members of society. People with purpose. Giving back to their communities. Helping other people who are in the same position to get a step up and avoid having to go through the same thing. I've seen complete turnarounds."

June had a brief glimpse of what that would be like. How it would feel to be clear of drugs and addictions and be contributing something to society. To be able to help others who were on the street and in trouble. She could help the kids who were lost like she had been before they went so far that they thought they could never return.

"Really?"

"Really. Trust me. Now I want you to listen to me, and I'll tell you what to do. We can get you out of here without anybody getting hurt, and we can help you out. We can put you onto that path."

June swallowed hard. Her mouth was still as dry as cotton. She wished for a bottle. She didn't care what kind of nasty rotgut it was; she just wanted to numb herself. She nodded, not trusting her voice.

"Good," the cop approved. They were still holding their guns on her. She knew that outside, they were marshaling their forces, bringing in more and more cops, surrounding the building, bringing in a helicopter and a special response unit and starting to work through their strategies of how they would capture her—an armed gunman.

They didn't know how harmless she was. That she was no longer the hardened street kid, but just a mom who had never figured out how to make it work, soft and beaten-down.

"I want you to put down the gun. Just let it go."

She worked at loosening her grip and pulling her finger back out of the trigger guard. She opened her hand and let gravity pull the gun out. It finally hit the floor with a clatter. Both cops visibly relaxed. She waited for them to rush in and jump on her, throw her to the floor, and crank her arms back behind her back to cuff them. That was the way she had seen it done.

"Okay, hands on top of your head. Interlace your fingers."

June wasn't sure she could raise her arms again. They hung so heavy at her side. But she focused all of her flagging energy on them, and managed to bring them up over her head, and then to settle on the crown of her head, over the mouse-brown hair, settling there. She was so tired. She just wanted to drop.

"Good. Kick the gun toward me."

It took a couple of tries, but she managed to send it skidding across the dirty tiles in his direction.

"Good. You're doing fine. You're doing the right thing. Turn around so that your back is to me."

That was easier, in spite of her exhaustion. She didn't have to look at him. She didn't have to see their guns and face the reality of what was happening to her.

"I want you to kneel down, and then lay flat on your face. Can you do that for me?"

June obeyed numbly.

When she was lying down, she could hear their heavy shoes on the floor approaching her cautiously. But what was she going to do, unarmed, lying flat on the floor, her hands laced behind her head?

She remembered how they had tackled Justin that one day on the playground, beating him down and kneeling on his back, when he was still not fully recovered from his car accident, breaking bones kneeling on him. She could still hear her own yells and remember how she had tackled the cops, furious that they would hurt her twin, her other half.

But these cops didn't do that to her. Their approach was slow, and though they went through the same motions of patting her down and cuffing her hands behind her back, they didn't hurt her.

When she was back on her feet, the cop who had talked to her went methodically through her pockets. There was nothing to find. She didn't have any drugs on her. Nothing that she could take to calm the demons. No more weapons. Not even a penny to her name. She was destitute, wrung out, and empty. She knew that her life was over.

CHAPTER

Two

The cop murmured soothing words to her as he walked her down the stairs toward the street. She could feel the eyes of everyone in the building on her. All of them judging her and seeing how low she had fallen. Whispering to each other that they had always known she was no good and would end up like this. She didn't care. The pain was worse than ever.

"It's going to be okay. You did the right thing," the arresting officer told her.

How had she done the right thing? When she decided to rob the store to get the money she needed to buy more drugs? Had that been the right thing? When she had hidden from her social worker that she was drinking and doping? When she had failed to tell Marsden that she had lost her job. The job that had only lasted a few days? Had she done the right thing when she had been so hard on her children? Her flesh and blood? Hers and Justin's?

She'd never had the patience that she should have as a mom. She'd always been the first to break, to get frustrated with their demands and to snap, whether it was just a sharp word or whether it was a slap, or whether, in the later years after Marcie was born, it had been much worse than a slap. She was eaten up with guilt.

When was the last time she had done the right thing? When had she ever made the right choice, given the opportunity?

Out on the street, there was another police car and another car she recognized. Marsden's. She immediately tensed, looking for some escape. The cop tightened his grip and kept pushing her toward the car they had parked askew on the street, lights flashing, when they had entered the building to find June.

"Take it easy," he warned.

"I don't want to talk to her."

He looked at Marsden, not understanding. He wouldn't let June pull away, but looked at the professional in her skirt-suit, waiting for her to introduce herself.

"Roberta Marsden," she introduced herself, reaching her hand out to shake automatically, but then realizing that the cop had his hands full already. "I'm the caseworker for June and her children."

The cop nodded. "What can we do for you?"

"What is June under arrest for? What's going on?"

"Armed robbery," he advised in a dry, clinical voice.

Marsden's mouth dropped open. "Armed robbery? What's going on, June? What happened?"

June looked down, not wanting to talk to her. "I needed the money," she said lamely.

"Needed the money? For what? You have a job; what do you need to be committing armed robbery for?"

June wished that the cop would take her away and put her in the car. But he didn't. They stood there, waiting for her answer.

"I don't have a job," Michelle muttered.

"Since when? You have a job."

June shook her head. "Haven't for a long time."

"Why didn't you tell me? You're supposed to be keeping me informed on these things. You said that everything was going fine. That's not fine."

"If I told you, you would have taken the kids away."

"I would not necessarily have taken the kids. I could have helped you to find another job."

"They were always calling me names and feeling me up. I'm not going to work somewhere like that."

"I wouldn't expect you to stay somewhere you were being harassed. But there are other jobs. I could have helped you find something else. That's why I'm here, June."

June shook her head, staring down at the pavement. She made a movement with her hips like she was going to walk over to the car. The cop didn't take the hint. Marsden squared off in front of her to make sure she couldn't get by.

"Where are Michelle and Kenny?" Marsden asked, looking at her watch. "Do they have after-school clubs?"

Clubs? The idea was laughable. Kenny would never be smart enough to be in any clubs, and Michelle was so mouthy and so averse to going to school that there was no way she would last in any of them. If school was out, then who knew where Michelle and Kenny were? They could be anywhere.

"They're not at school."

"Where are they, then? Library? Friend's house?"

June shook her head. "I haven't seen them for a few days. I don't know where they would be."

Marsden's face was as pale as wax. She looked like a statue. "What do you mean you haven't seen them for a few days?"

"They don't come back here. I don't know where they are. Michelle comes by sometimes, but she doesn't stay."

Marsden stared at her. "Where are they sleeping, if they're not coming back here? Where are they eating? Who is supervising them?"

June gave a hopeless shrug. Her insides were quaking, and she wished she could melt into the sidewalk. Where did Marsden think the kids were? They were on their own. They took care of themselves. Just like June and Justin had taken care of themselves when they were that age.

"You told me everything was fine," Marsden said, her voice rising. "You told me that everything was okay, that you were all getting along, that school and work were going fine..."

June didn't feel it was necessary to confirm the obvious. Those had all been lies. She had been lying to Marsden the entire time. Nothing had ever been fine. Nothing could have been further from the truth.

"We need to take her in for processing," the cop told Marsden. "We'll do our best to find out what's going on here and give you any leads we can on the kids."

Marsden handed him one of her cards so he would know how to reach her. She looked at June, shaking her head in disbelief.

The cop finally walked June over to the car and helped her into it, making sure she didn't bang her head. He got into the passenger seat, and the other one got into the driver's. They pulled out, leaving June's old life behind.

June, Into the Light, Book #6 of the *Between the Cracks* series by P.D. Workman
can be purchased at pdworkman.com

About the Author

P.D. Workman is a USA Today Bestselling author, winner of several awards from Library Services for Youth in Custody and the InD'tale Magazine's Crowned Heart award, and has published over 100 mystery/suspense/thriller and young adult books, including stand alones and these series: Auntie Clem's Bakery cozy mysteries, Reg Rawlins Psychic Investigator paranormal mysteries, Zachary Goldman Mysteries (PI), Kenzie Kirsch Medical Thrillers, Parks Pat Mysteries (police procedural), and YA series: Tamara's Teardrops, Between the Cracks, and Breaking the Pattern.

Workman loves writing about the underdog, who the reader may love or hate. She has been praised for her realistic details, deep characterization, and sensitive handling of the serious social issues that appear in all of her stories, from light cozy mysteries through to darker, grittier young adult and mystery/suspense books.

> P. D. Workman, does not shy from probing the deep psychological scars of childhood trauma, mental illness, and addiction. Also characteristic of this author, these extremely sensitive issues are explored with extensive empathy, described with incredible clarity, and portrayed with profound insight.
>
> —KIM, GOODREADS REVIEWER

Some of Workman's titles have been translated into Spanish, French, Portuguese, German, and Italian.

Workman began writing at an early age and is a prolific reader as well as writer. She is also passionate about teaching and learning, expresses her creativity through art and cooking, and loves exploring the Calgary parks and green spaces where the Parks Pat Mysteries are set. She was a legal assistant for many years and has done extensive charitable work.

Workman was born and raised in Alberta, Canada, and is married with one adult son.

Please visit P.D. Workman at pdworkman.com to see what else she is working on, to join her mailing list, and to link to her social networks.

If you enjoyed this book, please take the time to recommend it to other purchasers with a review or star rating and share it with your friends!

tiktok.com/@pdworkmanauthor
facebook.com/pdworkmanauthor
x.com/pdworkmanauthor
instagram.com/pdworkmanauthor
amazon.com/author/pdworkman
bookbub.com/authors/p-d-workman
goodreads.com/pdworkman
linkedin.com/in/pdworkman
pinterest.com/pdworkmanauthor
youtube.com/pdworkman
patreon.com/pdworkmanauthor
reamstories.com/pdworkmanauthor

Find P.D. Workman's books at

PDWORKMAN.COM

Scan the QR code below